Legon
Awakening

Legon Awakening

Book One in the Legon Series

By Nicholas Taylor

ISBN-10: 1453740279
ISBN-13: 9781453740279

Editing: Tom Peterson
Interior Design: Jenni Gasparrini
Cover Design: Mick Brooker
Photography: Nate Isaksen www.Nateographer.com

www.LegonBook.com

Acknowledgments

First of all I have to thank my family for all their
support through this whole process.
My cousin Ryan for being one of the biggest
supporters.
My wonderful editor Tom Peterson.
Chris Snelgrove and his constant help.
Collin Earl and all of his encouragement.
My good friend Denise Garrett for always being
willing give me her input.
And most of all I would like to thank the
Legionaries.
You guys are amazing.

Table of Contents

Prologue
A New Star

"Those at the serpent's head first swallow the tail of defeat."
-Articles of the Mahann

The Senashow walked down a passage taking in his surroundings, trying to remember how to get to the Queen's study. His eyes scanned the dim torch-lit hall. Flickering light played on the granite, giving it the appearance of shifting in and out of existence. The smell was earthy with the recent rain; he could still taste the last bit of moisture in it. The scent was not unpleasant; it reminded him of home, as did stone. Most men would have had a hard time walking these dark halls without tripping on the uneven stone floor or occasional rug, but this was not a problem for the Senashow, for he wasn't a man. He was not even human, for that matter.

It was a cool spring night and the castle seemed drafty and cold, no doubt from the feeble craftsmanship of the dull human hands that made it. The Senashow hated these old human dwellings; they were so poorly made that they didn't even keep out the cold. It was cold at home too, but at least you didn't feel the wind. He honestly didn't know how these creatures had made it out of the Stone Age.

A particularly uneven stone on the floor caught his attention. *Pathetic beasts,* thought the Senashow as he walked, *they aren't fit to clean our boot straps, and here our queen…their queen for that matter… is living among them. Disgusting!* That was beside the point now; there were more pressing matters on the Senashow's mind. *What if the prophecy is true? What if the new star in the sky this night is a sign that it is coming true?* It was not in his nature to believe in what he would call "mindless mysticism," but while he might not believe in such nonsense, he did know that the resistance and the crusade twigs did. If there was anything worse than people believing in prophecies, it was that people usually found ways to make them come true. It was for that reason that he was in this horrid place tonight; one of the signs of the prophecy had come to pass not more than one day ago.

As he passed another corridor he saw a door at the end open, flooding the hallway with light. *Bah,* thought the Senashow, *the animals can't even see unless it's as bright as the noonday sun.* He was by the kitchens that, when revealed, were full of light that enabled the servants, or rather the slaves, to see what they were doing. As the warm air from the cook fires flowed into the hall, the smell of the food made him have to admit that at least the animals could be taught to cook. Whenever the Senashow passed too close to people he would catch little glimpses into their minds, if you could even call them that. Most showed the fear and panic that the servants felt upon seeing him. *Good; fear your masters, filthy apes,* he thought with derision.

Now that he was getting closer to the Queen's study, he could see the door at the end of the hall. There was a man coming out, another Iumenta like himself. He knew this person; it was Parkas, the Queen's chief warlord. He was a tall, slender man, with a firm jaw line and an almost wolf-like appearance. His light grey skin shone in contrast to the dark hall, accented with thin lips and pale yellow eyes. At first glance he might look almost weak and frail, but he was an Iumenta like the Senashow. Iumentes, like elves, had deceiving appearances. They were at least fifteen times stronger and faster than any human, with sight rivaling that of any bird of prey, and such sensitive hearing that they can hear a heartbeat across a room. They also were as close to immortal as was possible; they did not age, and would live forever unless physically killed.

None of the Elves or Iumenta looked to be over twenty-five years old. Parkas had been the queen's chief warlord for over one hundred years. His long silver hair came down past his shoulders, and he was wearing a black belt with a sword attached to it. The sword was in a grey sheath with a polished steel handle. A sapphire embedded in the hilt glinted in the near non existent light, so fine was its quality.

The Senashow could see that Parkas was looking flustered and displeased; he obviously did not have a good conversation with the queen. *Fantastic,* thought the Senashow. The queen was temperamental in the best of times, but to have her already upset before he even delivered the news of the prophecy.... The Senashow knew that the news of the prophecy would enrage the queen if she took it seriously, and she should; it was always an uncomfortable subject.

He walked up to the door and knocked three times. A cold voice came from within.

"Enter."

The Senashow opened the door and entered the room. The Queen was standing in front of an archway that led outside to a terrace and the castle gardens. The candle light mingled with moonlight, bathing the room's many books and paintings in warmth. The light from the fireplace against the far wall added an almost peaceful glow. The fireplace itself was square and framed in white marble. His eye moved up the large mantle piece above which was a tapestry.

It was this tapestry that held his attention. It was about half as tall as the room and was made of black silk. In the center of the tapestry sat a silver six pointed star with a solid pale green circle in the center. Around the star was a half circle in the same color green, and on the other side of the star were four smaller six pointed stars, dark gold in color. He walked across the study to place a roll of parchment on the marble inlayed desk, unrolled it and took a quill from the gleaming bronze set to sign his name. Out of the corner of his eye he watched the still silent queen as she gazed at the fireplace, where on either side sat two polished bronze dragons. Their tails wound toward the fire and reflected the light back across the dragon's bodies, giving them the appearance of almost dancing in the shifting light.

The Senashow moved to stand in the center of the room. A fine white and black rug with a depiction of two dragons battling was at his feet. Like the bronze set by the fire, the queen would often look at these dragons for hours as she thought. Tonight was no different than most; she stood on the rug looking at the fire. She was wearing a floor-length dress of crushed black velvet, her long sable hair flowing like a waterfall down her back. He caught the aroma of her perfume; it was a light sweet scent that reminded him of the sap of scrub brushes from their homeland. The fragrance was deceiving; it made her seem playful and gentle, just another silly noblewoman, something she was not.

She turned to look at him. Her yellow eyes bored into him. Irritation was etched onto her strong face, her thin maroon lips pursed in a way that he knew all to well. She was wearing a black pearl necklace high on her neck; from it hung a large pale green stone the shape of a tear. The stone was not a gemstone, but it still shone brilliantly, and was surrounded with gold. A small grimace crossed her face. She knew that he did not bring good news.

"Good evening, my queen," the Senashow said, vainly hoping her mood would soften with some pleasantries.

"Is it?" asked the queen in a cold voice. "My dinner is late and I just spent over an hour with Parkas listening to excuses about why the resistance is still standing. Now I suppose I get to listen to more good news from you?"

It was obvious that she was indeed in a bad mood tonight, and that there would be no swaying it. The Senashow paused for a moment to contemplate how to deliver his news to the queen.

She stood there looking at him with those yellow eyes. Her lips were pressed together again and her grey skin seemed to glow with a hot anger. Despite the heat of the fury flowing off her, the Senashow felt ice cold. Her rage would break soon, and he wasn't sure he could stand the force of it. He didn't know and, thankfully for him, he would not have to find out.

At that very moment there was another knock at the door.

"ENTER!" said the queen with a growl; she was starting to lose control.

A small servant wearing a cream colored tunic entered the room carrying a gilded silver tray of food in one hand and a glass of wine in the other. As he entered the room, the Senashow stole into the boy's mind. It was full of fear; he knew that he was late bringing the queen's food. The chefs in the kitchen were running behind because the queen had changed her mind at the last second, and the boy was terrified that she would hurt him, or worse, his older brother who worked in the stables. His thoughts were plain on his countenance; the boy looked as though a breath of wind could destroy him. He was trembling slightly and froze in the doorway. The boy could see that the queen was angry.

"DON'T JUST STAND THERE DOG! BRING ME MY FOOD!" roared the queen. Her anger was palpable in the room now. A wicked sneer began to tug at the Senashow's lips.

He knew that the queen's rage would soon and be taken out on the servant; he might be able to salvage the night after all.

As the boy crossed the room, his foot caught on the fine rug. He tried to catch himself, but to no avail. The contents of the tray went flying at the queen as the boy toppled over towards her. With inhuman speed the queen sidestepped the oncoming food and grabbed the tray out of the air. She swung it at the boy, catching him in the mouth. There was a crunching sound and a stifled scream. Blood sprayed out of the servant's mouth and arced across the room, covering the wall with crimson droplets. The Senashow felt a slight plop on his chest. He looked down to see a small white pebble on the floor covered in blood. It was one of the boy's teeth. The boy was on the ground with a hand clamped over his mouth, his tunic now scarlet and copious amounts of blood pouring from his ruined face onto the fine rug. The air became saturated with the salty metallic tang of blood. Oddly, the Senashow thought that this new smell somehow added to that of the food. He thought he might go by the kitchens after he left the queen's study and grab something to eat.

"Get out," said the queen in an icy deadly voice.

The servant grabbed the food as fast as he could and backed out of the room holding his mouth. The queen and the Senashow, now with a sneer plain on his face, watched him go without a word. Yes, he would definitely stop by the kitchens.

The Senashow looked at the queen and started to talk as if nothing had happened. She appeared calm, and the look on her face was now impassive.

"I am sure that you have noticed the new star in the eastern sky." The queen nodded indicating that she had.

"It is one of the signs of the rebel prophecy. It says that when the hero approaches manhood and the time when he will cleanse the land, a star will appear in the eastern sky. The star will be brighter than all other stars, and will never dim or change its position in the sky."

At this point the queen interrupted. "We do not know that this is the star that is spoken of; it may just be a star." There was an almost bored tone in her voice.

"Possible, my queen, but that does not change the fact that the resistance could take it as a sign that the prophecy is coming to pass. I agree with you that a star is just that, a star, but these animals and twigs are superstitious creatures. They will believe anything that might even look like a sign." His voice was patient. He knew that the queen had been getting scattered reports for years of signs coming to pass, but nothing ever came of it. But the Senashow knew that this time was different; never before had a new and bright star been seen in the sky, let alone one that fit a prophecy.

The queen took her time in replying. The Senashow knew that she was thinking hard of what to do.

Finally, and with a careful voice, the queen said, "I do not think that the prophecy is coming to pass, as there is no way for anyone to see accurately into the future. I agree with you that the resistance will be moving now that the sky has a new light in it. Send out men to look for one that fits the prophecy's description. Tell them that if they find one who does, bring him here so I may examine him."

At this point the Senashow stifled a small cough. "Your Highness, if he is the chosen one and you bring him before you, he could… could… oh forgive me for saying it, he could kill you, my queen!" There was worry in his voice as he said this. The possibilities rushed through his head. *If the queen is killed all these years of work will be lost.*

The queen laughed. "My dear Senashow, it pleases me that you worry about my well being, even if only for your own safety. It also worries me that you would entertain this mindless mysticism, as you like to call it." Her voice was becoming cruel

Chapter One
A New Dawn Rising

"Love and empathy are a matter of perspective and time. As time passes and perspectives change, we grow together like the tree and the vine, our destinies and lives intertwining in such a way that, if separated from each other, both will certainly perish."
-Tales of the Traveler

Legon was drowning in an icy abyss.

He tried to hurl himself upward and pain exploded in his head. He opened his eyes to find himself sitting up in bed with his head against the rafter of the slanted roof next to him. Groggily, he rubbed his head and looked around his room. There was an open window in the wall behind him with a hint of pre-dawn light shining through, a blank wooden wall in front of him, and to his left was a door that opened to the stairway that led down to the rest of the house.

His view of the door was obscured by a girl with a mischievous smile on her face. Her dark brown curly hair came down past her shoulders, framing a soft face with bright blue eyes, long dark eyelashes, a petite nose, and full red lips. She was wearing a light brown dress with a white lace collar. Over the dress was her signature pale blue apron. She wore no jewelry or makeup. She was standing next to the bed holding an empty bucket in her hands, and the smile on her face was now growing into a grin.

"SASHA! WHAT DID YOU DO THAT FOR!" he barked.

"What?" asked Sasha, who was clearly trying not to laugh, "You told me to wake you by whatever means necessary." She tried to look put out, as if he was the one who had just done something wrong.

Rubbing his throbbing head again he looked up into the twinkling eyes that looked down on him, he growled, "And you thought that a bucket of cold water was necessary?"

A mock look of deep contemplation came over Sasha's face. "You see, I couldn't find a bucket of warm water and well … I suppose I could have been a bit less… oh what's the word I'm looking for… rude. But then I supposed I would not have been so apt to rudeness if someone hadn't put a beetle in my soup two nights ago."

Legon's anger subsided a bit. He had put a beetle in her soup two nights ago and she did owe him for it. He took a moment to think about that night, reminiscing about bean soup flying across the dining room, Sasha screaming… *Ah, it's the little things in life,* he thought. He'd worried about what she would do for revenge ever since.

Now that he was drenched and boasted a spectacular pain growing in his head, he didn't have to worry anymore. He should have known better, though, when she had invited him on a breakfast picnic. Legon and Sasha would often go on picnics together, and despite the fact that they liked to play jokes on one another, they were closer than twins. Sasha had brought the idea up to him last night, egging him on by questioning if he could get up in time. *And like the idiot I am I gave her an opportunity.*

Sasha smiled, glanced over her handiwork, gave a small giggle and left the room with a slight skip in her step. Legon took a moment to get out of bed, then went to the dresser in the corner of the room and got out some dry clothes. He pulled on a pair of grey woolen pants, an off-white button up shirt, and a pair of dingy socks. Lastly he put on a pair of brown leather boots and went into the hall connecting his room with the rest of the house.

To his right was a railing and open space that looked down on the lower floor. To his left were closed doors that lead to different rooms in the house. The first he passed was Sasha's and then his parents. The hallway was lit by the light coming from the kitchen below. He came to the staircase and made his way down the creaky wooden stairs into the kitchen. As he went down the stairs he smelled food cooking. He picked up his pace at once. Getting up would normally be a lengthy project this early in the morning, but one benefit of Sasha's little prank was that he felt like he had already been awake for a few hours.

He walked into the large open room that was their kitchen, dining and family room. A heavy wood table stood in the center of the room, and in the corner opposite the front door was a counter and cast iron stove that Sasha was standing at. To the left of the stove and counter was the back door and next to it on the wall was a small mirror with a copper frame. Legon stepped up to the mirror to make sure that he didn't look too beastly. Staring back at him was a teenage boy with short brown hair, dark green eyes and a firm jaw line. His skin was unusually smooth. He inspected his face with a look of disappointment, hoping to find the small pricks of a beard. *I'm like a girl! I couldn't grow a proper beard if my whole family's life depended on it!* he thought ruefully.

Sasha noticed him inspecting his face and chimed in, "I like it that way, Legon. Your face reminds me of a little baby."

He could see her smirking in the mirror. "You're on a roll this morning aren't you?" She shrugged and went on packing for the picnic. Legon went to a cabinet under the staircase and got some blankets and two long buckskin tubes containing their hunting bows, along with some arrows. Sasha was no hunter, but she was a fine shot and they enjoyed practicing archery, shooting into the hillsides of the mountains.

She wrapped four pocket pies that she had made into a red and white checked cloth, put the cloth into a wicker basket lined with a wool towel blanket and wrapped the towel around the cloth. She then procured a dark green bottle of cedar from a cabinet that was built into the lower part of the counter and turned to Legon.

Legon looked down at the package wrapped tight in the towel. "Why did you wrap them in the towel and the cloth?"

"It's chilly this morning. I don't want the pies to be cold by the time we get up to the top of the hill," she replied conversationally.

"Oh, good thinking Sash. Let me grab your cloak and we can be off."

Legon went to the wall next to the front door where four black traveling cloaks rested on hooks. He put on his own, then walked up to Sasha and wrapped hers around her. Prepared for their outing, they stepped out of the back door of the house and began to walk to the woods. The back of their house faced directly into the woods at the edge of town. As they walked out they could see to their right the fenced in paddock where an assortment of sheep, pigs, cattle and the family's horses were. Other than the horses, the animals were mostly livestock that townsfolk had brought to be slaughtered in the family butcher shop. In the corner of the paddock was the shed where Legon and his father slaughtered and cleaned the animals. In most butcher shops the shed would be attached to the main building, but Legon's mother had complained about the smell. One of the benefits of building a separate shed was that they were able to turn the old space where they used to slaughter the animals into a smoker and a large ice box. This gave them the ability to cure meat for people and keep their stock of meat fresh for longer periods of time.

The morning air was crisp and sweet, perfect for a hike. They were able to walk straight into the woods, since the town of Salmont had no town wall. Instead, the city was surrounded by a beautiful view of the woods and mountains.

They walked together into the woods and soon they were completely surrounded by trees as they ascended a steep hill with tree roots jutting up here and there. The pines were small on this hill, but still far above their heads. Sticky sap ran from some of them, giving the forest a pungent smell that they could taste on their tongues. This hike would be difficult for most people in the predawn darkness, but Legon and Sasha had spent their whole lives playing in these woods, so the faint moonlight was more than enough for them to walk in. After about a half hour they reached the top of a hill that overlooked the valley where they lived. The sun was just beginning to make itself known to the world as they rolled out a grey blanket on the soft turf and sat down. They took off their cloaks and put them across their laps, and Legon took a blue blanket and placed it around their shoulders. He uncorked the bottle of cedar as Sasha began unwrapping the pocket pies.

"Sash, did you remember to bring glasses?" Legon asked, looking around for them.

"Oh..." she said, looking perplexed, "I suppose those would be handy wouldn't they?"

He chuckled. "Yeah, they would. Oh well. We can just drink out of the bottle, mom doesn't need to know."

"That she doesn't."

Sasha had been right to wrap the pocket pies. It was chilly this morning and the cloth and towel had kept the pies hot. Legon looked down at the four pies. Three of them were made with eggs, bacon, onion, and cheese, and he knew the fourth would be fruit-filled.

"Sash, did you make enough? There's only three breakfast ones here."

She looked down at the food. "Yes, I think so… there are two for you, one for me, and a strawberry one that we can split."

"You're just going to have one? I can split the third with you, I don't mind," he said sincerely.

"No, that's fine. I only need one."

"Oh come on, you'll be hungry by ten if you just have one," he said as if he were pointing out the obvious, which he was. One pie was nowhere near enough.

Sasha laughed. "I'm not a bottomless pit like you, brother. I can eat one and be full, whereas I don't think I could make enough to ever sate your appetite."

A smile crossed his face. When he thought about it, he had to admit that he did eat a lot. He was big to be sure, but not fat. He was all muscle, but even for his size he ate a ton. He remembered once going over to Kovos's house for dinner. Kovos's older brother was supposed to be visiting with his wife, but had been unable to make it. By the time the family found out that their oldest son was not going to be there, Kovos's mom had already made a huge dinner. Legon remembered with some satisfaction the looks on their faces as he went for a fourth helping.

Now sitting on the top of the hill with his sister he thought that maybe he did eat too much. Or perhaps the rest of the world didn't eat enough. That sounded right.

Sasha and Legon sat enjoying the pies and cedar together as they watched the sun rise. The pies were incredible. It seemed that everything Sasha touched tasted good. Legon had finished both of his by the time Sasha was done with her pie. They drank from the bottle of cold cedar, which was sweet and good with the pies. Sasha leaned over the basket and uncovered the last one.

She had saved the best for last. It was filled with sliced strawberries in sticky syrup, which covered their fingers with sugary goodness. Legon wished there was another when he finished his half of the pie. He was sure to tell Sasha what an amazing cook she was, and that it was possible that no one in Airmelia could compare to her, which made her smile.

They talked about how much they liked the early spring and how beautiful all the new life was in the reddish orange sunlight. There were thin clouds in the sky that were turning from dark blues and purples to pink and orange. They looked out over the small town they lived in. It looked peaceful and serene, bathed in soft colors. The town sat in a valley with tall mountains on all sides of it. There was no town wall, which was strange for a town in Airmelia; most towns had large stone walls and keeps in the center of town. This was done for many reasons, the most important of which was to discourage bands of robbers from trying to loot the town, and to give the people a general feeling of safety. There hadn't been a full-on war since the queen took control, and that was almost fifty years ago, but many towns still kept the walls intact. Most towns could not withstand an attack from a large force, but even small villages would have stockade fences surrounding the village proper. However, this was not the case for Salmont.

The town's people were not amazing fighters, but Salmont was remote, and the people lazy. Salmont was in the middle of the Empire and was surrounded by mountains; most people didn't even know that it existed. The town had no exports and was not a center of trade. This meant that robbers were not apt to come because the pickings were to slim and the mountain passes restricted the routes they could take.

Legon once thought that he lived in the most boring and uneventful town in all of Airmelia. "Even the name of our town is boring," he told Sasha one day. "We live in the Salez territory so we get 'Sal', and in a mountain valley so we get 'mont'… Salmont," he said with a shrug.

Now they could see the town from above. It was disorganized, and from on high the streets looked like a big maze. In the center were the old remains of a stockade fence where the town had started. The only strong building was the keep.

The keep was two stories high and made of dingy grey stone. It was a large building and looked almost like a warehouse. Above it flew a black banner with a silver crescent moon curling around a many pointed star, beside which were three long waving lines. The moon and star were the symbol of the Iumenta Lord Sodomis who was over Salez; the three lines represented Regent Kooth, who was the human in charge of this part of Lord Sodmis's territory. Kooth was over five towns and ten villages. The town hadn't been visited in years by either Kooth or Sodomis, but their tax collectors were sure to visit every year, along with the occasional soldier patrol that kept the passes and roads safe from robbers, so the townspeople flew the banner.

They were enjoying the warm sunlight on their faces, when all of a sudden Legon noticed that there was something wrong with Sasha. Her eyes rolled up into the back of her head, her face contorted and her whole body became ridged. *SHE'S HAVING AN EPISODE!* he thought, panicked. One moment Sasha was lying on the blanket thrashing and twitching, then the next she was off the blanket on the bare turf convulsing. He ran around behind her and wrapped his arms around her so she would not roll away and get hurt in the bushes or brambles. He was used to these episodes, but that did not make them any less scary. Fear was tearing through him as he struggled to hold on to Sasha.

"Come on, you're okay, you're okay Sash, come back to me, you're okay," he said again and again to her, trying to keep his voice soft and reassuring.

She was making a horrible gargling noise and he was worried that she was going to throw up as sometimes happened. After a few minutes that seemed like hours, Sasha began to calm. Her breathing became steady and her body relaxed, and she soon fell asleep. Legon was still lying behind her with his arms wrapped tight around her; they both were covered in sweat and trembling. There was a slight metallic taste in his mouth and he realized that he had bitten his tongue.

He had done this many times before; some of his first memories were of Sasha's episodes. He could remember as a boy sitting next to her bed holding her hand as she slept after having a particularly bad one. This was one of the things that made them so close; Legon never left her side, and caring for her made him love her more.

He held her, willing her to wake. Her hair tickled his noise. He sniffed back a sneeze and breathed in the scent of her hair, which calmed him. The trivial problem of a wanting to sneeze and noticing what her hair smelled like was welcome; it meant that the episode was over. He wasn't sure how, but he knew when they were over, knew when no more tremors would rock her body. He always noticed something mundane like the scent of her hair or that one of his socks had a hole in it. After a bit Sasha's eyes opened.

"Where… where am I?" she asked. It was common for her to have a hard time remembering what she had just been doing after an episode.

When he spoke he tried to speak softly, tried not to show the overwhelming relief that he felt. "On top of the hill having a picnic."

She was silent for a bit, almost like her mind was catching itself up to the present.

"Oh now I remember. What am I doing on the ground covered in dirt, and why are you holding…" she trailed off as she realized what just happened.

"I had another episode didn't I?" her voice was full of fear and sadness; he knew if he could see her face there would be a look of worry on it.

"Yes."

They sat up and Sasha looked at him. He could see her eyes filling with tears that began to roll down her cheeks.

"Why?" she sobbed. "Why does this happen to me?"

She buried her head in the crook of his neck and he felt her hot tears soak his shirt. He did not answer her questions; they were not meant to be answered. Legon kissed the top of her head and now felt his own tears welling up in his eyes. Why did she suffer like this? Was there some purpose to it? He didn't know, and he didn't share these feelings with her. She needed him to be strong, to be a protector. They both needed him to be that.

"I wish I could take this from you… I would do anything to make it stop… I would take it on my self if I could." His voice sounded choked.

"I know you would." Her tone turned bitter. "But then you would be a freak like me."

Legon gently moved her back so he could look into her eyes. "Don't you say that. You're not a freak. I love you, sister, more than anything in this world. You know that don't you?" There was warmth and firmness in his voice.

He would take it from her if he could, he would take it and so much more, anything to keep from seeing the pain in those eyes. He wanted her to know that she wasn't alone; he wanted her to understand that as she suffered so did he, though not in the same way. He tried to convey this to her in his gaze.

* * * * * * *

Sasha turned her head. She couldn't bring herself to look at him.

"I know you do… and I you." She smiled a bit; she could almost feel the love and concern radiating from him. *How does he do that?* she thought to herself. *It's like he can make me feel his emotions.* That was one of the wonderful things about Legon: he had an ability to comfort people and convey love in a way that was unimaginable.

They sat on the hill holding each other, both sad, both scared, and both more thankful for each other than the other could ever know.

It was for this reason that Sasha was not liked in town. Sure, people were polite to her most of the time, but the only person other than family members that was truly kind to her was the town carpenter, Arkin. Sasha had once had a friend that was good to her, but that girl was gone now. She had been taken by the queen's tax collectors when her family could not pay. People in the town said that Sasha was a good girl, but that daemons possessed her and caused these episodes.

"You'll see one day, Legon. She'll slit you throat when they take over," a lady named Moleth said once. Sasha was two years older than Legon and should be married, but was not because none of the men in town were willing to risk it. "Yeah she's a nice girl now," they would say, or "Have a daemon like that lying next to me? No thanks!" Her brother had gotten into many fights defending her from these attacks; his friends Kovos and Barnin would back Legon in fights and would defend her honor when Legon was not around. Both boys were a little uncomfortable around her, however; they weren't sure about her themselves, but they were loyal friends and so they backed Legon. Still, the violence disgusted her; she was thankful for the protection, but she was sad that it was done because of her, even though to a large extent it was necessary.

Barnin had left seeking adventure a year or so ago. He was headstrong and had always wanted to find the resistance and join them. He wasn't anything amazing on a physical level but he made up for it in determination and confidence.

All three boys were tough. In truth, one of the only reasons certain townsfolk hadn't done anything violent to Sasha yet was that Legon's dad was the town butcher and they were worried he would do something to their food if they hurt her, which was true. The other reason was that they were truly afraid of what Legon would do; no one in town had won a fight with him in years, and he helped his dad as a butcher, so he had all sorts of knives and cleavers to use if he saw fit.

* * * * * * * *

Legon felt Sasha's crying ebb away. She looked up at him. Her eyes looked like glass and her face was red and tear-stained.

"Are you ready to go home? I know you have a lot to do," she said.

"Are you strong enough?"

He didn't want to rush her; in truth, if it would help he would hold her here all day. That's what he wanted to do, keep his arms wrapped tight around her fragile body, keep her safe from herself or anything that could hurt her. But he knew that no matter how hard he tried, he couldn't protect her from everything, not from her own body. He could protect her from unkind townsfolk, and he did, but what would happen when the tax collectors came? He didn't want to think about it and returned his attention to his sister.

"Yes, I think so," she replied. "Hold my hand on the way back in case I fall."

"Ok, let me pack up... no, you stay here and rest. I'll do it," he said to her softly.

He rolled up all the blankets and packed everything in the empty basket. He hoisted it on his shoulder and helped up Sasha with his other arm. They began the descent to their house. It was slow compared to the climb up, since Legon didn't want her to fall. As they entered the trees they saw shafts of morning light penetrating the canopy. There were flower buds on the ground; over to there right some pretty red ones had already blossomed, their sweet scent mixing with the musk of the moist earth. Thick green moss grew on the trunks and roots of the trees, and vines with little orange flowers were crawling up them. The air was thick in the woods, and when you entered it felt as if the rest of the world had been shut out. Mist was forming in the low-lying areas, and dew collected on the leaves. As they passed one tree, they noticed that between one of its branches and its trunk was a large spider web covered in dew. Legon marveled at the little structure. *How can a bug build something like that?* he wondered.

Both of them loved the woods; they would live right in the heart of them if they could. They both cheered up as they saw some rabbits running on the forest floor and squirrels high in the trees, chattering their disapproval of the visitors. Birds were singing and life was bursting all over the forest. They didn't stop to practice archery as they didn't have the time, and Legon didn't want Sasha to over exert herself. Soon they came to the foot of the hill and were crossing the field to their house. The field was green with wildflowers growing all over. Everywhere there were splashes of color, red and white here, purple and yellow there. The dew covered plants shimmered in the morning light, reflecting tiny rainbows. It was beautiful. As they passed a clump of tall yellow flowers, Legon picked one and gave it to Sasha. She shortened the stem and placed the flower in her hair above her right ear.

"Thank you," she said with a slight smile. She was apparently still feeling weak. Soon they could see the back of their house. He could see his mother outside beating a rug. The resemblance between mother and daughter was uncanny; their mother looked just like Sasha but a bit older. As soon as they were close enough to see her face they saw a worried expression cross it.

"Sasha, you've had an episode," she gasped. She dropped the beater she was holding and rushed over to them.

"Yes mother," Legon said.

"Get her in, get her in!" Her voice sounded panicked as she reached over and swung Sasha's arm over her shoulders and began to pull them in the house. "I want to have a look at her."

They got Sasha inside and to the kitchen table. At that moment their father, an average sized man with brown hair and thick burlap clothes, walked down the stairs and into the room. He saw what was happening instantly.

"Is she ok, Laura?" he asked in a deep concerned voice.

"Oh, Edis, I think so," she replied. "Legon, what happened?"

"It happened on the hill after we ate," he explained, giving the details of their morning picnic up until Sasha's episode.

"Thank the gods your brother was with you!" their father exclaimed.

Sasha nodded and sipped a hot cup of something that her mother shoved in her hands. Sasha winced. "Mother, what on earth...?" she started.

"It's herbs," interrupted Laura. She was the town healer, which had its benefits if you felt ill but also had its downside, as she was always giving them new concoctions to cure various ailments that none of them knew they had. This was especially true in Sasha's case, since their mother was unable to figure out what caused her episodes. Sasha had been subjected to cure after cure for years, none of which seemed to help, but a few did cause her to get quite sick in other ways. Once after drinking one of their mother's brews she couldn't eat for two days without throwing it back up. Their mother said that this was her body's way of cleansing her from her illness. These remedies of course didn't make a difference. Sasha still had episodes, and their mother kept coming up with new ways of fixing them. Legon didn't know what the remedy was today, but he could smell it and it was horrid.

"Will you be ok, Sash?" he asked giving the drink a look.

"Yes, I think so" she said, but her voice wasn't confident. She gave the glass a glance and shivered a bit.

"Ok, I'm going to go change my clothes and help dad, I'll see you before lunch okay?"

"Ok, don't worry about me. I'm fine now." She gave the glass another look and placed in on the table.

Legon smiled at her, leaned over and kissed her on her head. He walked to the stairs and started for his room. On his way up his father stopped him and placed his hand on his arm to bring him in close. He said in a soft voice, so Laura and Sasha couldn't hear, "I want you to stay close today incase Sasha has another one, you're the best with her."

"I was planning on getting a new cleaver from Kovos today, but I think you're right. I can get it tomorrow and Sash can come with me. It will be good for her to get out and about," he said, looking at his sister.

"I think she'll like that. Now go get ready, I want to hit it hard today so we're not working late." His voice was business-like as he patted Legon's shoulder.

Legon chuckled. "I hit it hard every day old man, you're the slow one."

His father laughed, shook his head and walked over to the table.

Chapter Two
A Hard Day's Work

"To many, the Everser Vald was at one time no more than a commoner, struggling with the everyday woes of the world. Only the trained eye could see the servant and master, laboring by day and by night for those that mattered most."
-Excerpts from the Diary of the Adopted Sister

Legon hustled up the stairs to his room and began to undress. He went to the dresser and pulled out a pair of rough brown pants made of thick cloth and an off-white shirt made of the same material. His room was flooded with light coming in from the window, and outside he could hear signs of the town coming to life.

At the sound of soft footsteps in the hall, Legon poked his head out of the door to see Sasha being led to her room by Laura. Sasha was starting to look better, and he thought that a good nap would probably help. He got his clothes on and rushed downstairs, stepping out of the front door onto the dirt street. The street was lined with buildings of varying sizes, all made of the same dark brown wood. Many of the structures were starting to gray with age the constant bombardment of snow, rain, and sleet. Most people in town built their home next door to their place of business, and in some cases the buildings served both purposes. The town did have a central

He grimaced and resigned himself to an unpleasant encounter, "Yes Moleth, we're here, how are you today?"

"O-oh there you are," she said with a nervous chuckle. "I was supposed to pick up some…. hmmm…. some meat." As she spoke she looked around the shop noticing the knives and other sharp objects on the walls and shook her head disapprovingly.

Well how else are we supposed to cut the meat you idiot? he thought. Moleth was very odd and probably mad; he was already getting annoyed with her. She walked to the counter now and was clasping onto it like Legon was going to pull it away from her. She started to speak but he cut her off.

"I'm just finishing up now, Moleth. The meat will be ready in just a moment."

"Ah, oh well ok… ok I-I guess that that works." Her voice sounded confused and tired as if she was worried that Legon would do something to her; in truth she wasn't worried at all. She was always like this. She fidgeted with her hands in a way that reminded him of a chipmunk. A fake smile played across her face.

"Why… why is it so late getting done? I am a paying customer after all, I know," she started with a shaky but surprisingly accusatory voice.

Legon tried to cut her off. She continued to talk but he just spoke over her.

"Sorry Moleth, it will be done in a sec and you can be on your way."

She can't hear you, you know? said a voice inside his head. *She's in her own world right now; she'll be with you in a moment, not the other way around.* This was true. Moleth was prattling on about something completely unrelated to meat and seemed not to take notice that he'd spoken. After what seemed to be hours to Legon, Moleth registered what he'd said.

"Ah, so I take it you got off to a late start this morning?" She said this as if she had figured out the solution to some challenging riddle that he hadn't solved yet. "Yes, I can see it in Edis's eyes. He looks worried," she said, growing more and more confident.

It was true. Edis did look worried. He was thinking about his daughter, and he seemed not to have noticed that Moleth was even in the shop. *Why does he always do this? He pretends that's she's not even here and I have to deal with her the whole time!* thought Legon bitterly. In the last few years Edis hadn't said much of anything to her, and when Legon thought about it he wasn't sure if his father had ever said anything to her at all. Legon knew that Edis did not approve of the way Moleth talked about his family, and would have understood if his father had banned her from the shop or even gotten into fights with her, but he didn't. Instead it seemed that she just didn't exist to him.

His attention was jerked back to Moleth. "It was that demon half-sister of yours, wasn't it?" Moleth said knowingly.

She had apparently been born without the ability to figure out that you don't say things like this about somebody's sister. It was true that Sasha and Legon were not related by birth. Legon was by all accounts adopted, but they were still brother and sister. He felt his face flush.

"My sister is fine, Moleth," he said through gritted teeth. His anger was rising fast.

She tittered. "Na, na she's not, I've always said there's something wrong with her, just you wait… not that it's going to matter anyhow. The queen will be taking care of her soon, so don't you worry." She said this like she was telling a sick person that they were going to get better.

Her statement pushed any kind or nice feelings from his mind. If any man had just made the statement that Moleth had, Legon would be all over him. He attempted to hold back his fury and counted to ten slowly in his mind. He tried to keep his voice calm but the attempt didn't work.

"Sasha is not going anywhere, Moleth so get used to it!" He felt his hand tighten around the handle of the cleaver.

There was a warning tone in his voice that a person with any sense would heed unless they were ready for a fight. Moleth did not have this sense and she pushed on, oblivious to the now quivering man in front of her.

"Oh come on now, you people can't keep paying the taxes that she costs you. In the spring they will take her away and be gone with her. I dare say the queen's men will have a lot of fun with her, don't you think? She is a pretty girl after all, and the queen's men do deserve it, they work so hard to keep us safe." Her voice was warm and a smile came over her face as she winked at him.

Legon's face contorted and rage filled his body, tearing through him like a wild animal. All rational thought left his mind, replace with an overwhelming bloodlust. The arm that was holding the cleaver jerked up of its own accord. Edis seized Legon's arm hard, all the man's strength holding him back. With his other hand Edis threw the packages at Moleth, who stepped back with the sudden weight of the packages, and barked "GET OUT!"

Moleth looked perplexed and angry. Her voice was rough and irritated as she spoke.

"What, what's the matter with you?" She was oblivious to how rude and dangerous her comments had been.

"I think its time you leave, Moleth. Legon and I have a lot of work to do." This time Edis's voice was calm and controlled, but he still had a look of murder on his face. Moleth looked at them both reproachfully and left the shop muttering about rude people under her breath.

After that the morning went by quickly. Legon was still fuming, and the hard work was good for him. For once in his life he was happy about the prospect of a long and difficult day. He and Edis brought in a cow carcass and hung it from the ceiling. He felt the rage in is heart dissipate as he heaved the cow. Work had a way of clearing his mind. He looked back on the morning and felt a twinge of shame. If Sasha had known that he was planning on hurting, if not killing, Moleth, she would have been very disappointed with him.

Sasha knew what people said about her, and Legon knew that it hurt and bothered her, but that didn't mean that she would be ok with him attacking a woman in cold blood. Sasha was a kind person and couldn't stomach violence or cruelty in any form. She had always been a compass for him; she made him a good person. Sasha was sweet and innocent, kind to everyone and would do anything to help. It tore at him watching her do kind things for people in town who, as soon as her back was turned, said things like, "Don't think that will buy you any grace with me freak." *How could people think so poorly of someone so good?* he thought. Legon turned his attention back to the bloody carcass in front of him. He now understood his father's approach to Moleth - it was better not to acknowledge her rather than do something rash.

"Thanks dad, I'll split it and then I'll need your help again to put one half in the ice box until I'm ready for it."

"Sounds good. I'm going to get started on that deer that we got the other day."

Legon smiled at Edis and said with a playful taunting voice, "The deer *we* got?"

Edis looked confused for a moment and then said sarcastically, "Oh, forgive my mistake, o mighty hunter, the deer *you* got." As he said this he gave Legon a slight bow.

"Very good, peasant, you may go back to your work now." Legon tried to make his voice sound pompous and important.

Edis laughed and shook his head. "You should respect your elders."

Before Legon could retort, Edis walked to the ice box to get the deer. Legon walked back to the wall and grabbed a large cleaver. This one boasted a three foot handle and a blade that was about a foot and half long and six inches wide. They used this one for splitting carcasses. He walked to the cow hanging from the ceiling, raised the cleaver high above his head, and brought it down on the center of the cow's back. His aim was perfect; the cleaver cut right against the vertebrae about two feet down the back. Legon pulled the cleaver out and repeated the cut, and within a few minutes the cow was split in two. Legon and Edis took one half to the ice box and then placed the other half on a counter in the back of the shop. He spent the rest of the morning cutting up the piece of meet.

They didn't break for lunch until two. When Legon walked into the house he saw Sasha sitting in the kitchen looking put out and talking to their Mother.

"Mom, I'm okay now. Everything is fine. Let me help you," she said.

"No no, dear, I can do it myself. I have been making meals without your assistance for some time now and I can do it today. Besides, you need to rest," protested Laura, waving her arms and hands in a dismissive manner.

"Hey Sash, how do you feel?" Legon asked sitting next to her at the table.

"I'm feeling fine. I can help mom, but you know how she is," she said, shooting a look at her mother and folding her arms.

He chuckled. Laura placed a plate of food in front of him. She'd made chicken and some flatbread for lunch. He began to eat his food with delight. He was very hungry from the day's work, and they ate fast since they didn't have much time.

"Ey ash ii," he began with food in his mouth.

"Swallow," Sasha said flatly, shaking her head and rolling her eyes. *Boys they can be such animals* she thought.

Legon swallowed and began, "Sorry Sash, but if you're feeling a bit useless you can always get me some water. You know, if it will make you feel better."

"Put the food back in your mouth. I liked it better that way," she said, giving him a stern look, but she got up and brought him some water. Legon nodded his thanks.

"Are you going to go over to Kovos's today?" she asked.

He began to talk with food in his mouth again but he realized what he was doing, swallowed, and began again. "Sorry, no. We have too much to do, you know how it is. Either we are bored to tears or there's not enough time in the day."

"I'm sorry I made you late this morning." She sounded mournful.

"Don't ever say that, it's not your fault." He was serious. He hated her thinking that things like this were her doing.

"Its not you, its dad, because he's such a slave driver!" Legon said in an elevated voice to Edis.

Edis gave him a wicked grin. "Ha! Wait until this afternoon!"

"I love you too, dad." At this, Edis nodded his head and took another bite.

It was a hard afternoon, but it wasn't the work that weighed on Legon. The work was nothing to him; he was in good shape and his dad had been training him to be a butcher from the time he could hold a knife. In fact, Legon would be setting off in a few months to start his own shop. He was turning eighteen this year, which meant that he would be a man. His family would keep him around for awhile since he was a help to them in the shop, but the problem was taxes.

In The Cona Empire, the queen had decreed that all should be taxed fairly. This meant that families who pooled their resources together were treated as though they were trying to put themselves above their fellow men, or at least this was the queen's public stance on the matter. Therefore, a house consisted of two adults and however many underage children they had. If a child grew to be eighteen still lived at home, you had to pay considerably more on your taxes, and if you could not pay that amount, the member of the family that was the cause of the increase went into the queen's care. The queen's care was slavery; people could rent you for a price from the empire, or you were sold to Iumenta for their own uses. This exact thing had happened just a few moths ago to Sasha's friend when her family couldn't afford her. When it was time to pay the annual taxes, the queen's tax collectors took her into the queen's care and she had not been seen since.

The problem now was not Legon; he made the family a good sum of money and his mother, who was the town healer, did decent enough. The problem was that Sasha was overage already and the family would have to pay a lot for her again this year. Because the townspeople didn't care for her, she had a hard time making any money, and her condition prevented her from becoming a certified healer. This coming January when the collectors came, the family would now have to pay for both Sasha and Legon, and they could not do it. In fact, Legon was going to be forced to leave solely due to the fact that the town was not big enough for two butchers. The family's best hope was for Legon to make as much as he could and bring it to his family to continue paying the taxes for Sasha, but he couldn't see how it could be done. *I will not allow them to take her*, he said to himself. He could feel his face flush with anger as he thought of Moleth's comment that morning.

Something of his thoughts must have shown on his face, because Edis said, "Son, we'll find a way. We won't let her go."

"I hope so."

As if in answer to their conversation the door tinkled again. Legon turned to look at the newcomers and he felt his heart drop just a bit. Because of the type of work their family did they were subject to quarterly tax appraisals and inspections. These were, in short, a chance for the government to come in and make sure Edis and Laura were fulfilling their requirements as a healer and a butcher. The inspections and appraisals weren't pleasant, but not that bad either.

The two men stood side by side, and Legon could tell who was who right away. The one on the right had greasy hair and a bent nose that looked to have been broken on several occasions. This man was the collector; it was his job to secure payment. His deep blue robes were slightly disheveled, showing the slightly physical part of his job. The other man's robes looked brand new. He was shorter than the first and had a round face. It looked like he took the time to part each hair on its own every morning. This man was the appraiser. The collector spoke first. His voice also sounded greasy and unclean.

"Edis I take it? We are here for your quarterly appraisal."

Edis spoke. "Oh, I wasn't expecting you for a week or so…"

The appraiser cut across him calmly. "Sorry, do forgive us, we are running a bit ahead of schedule. If you are not ready for us we could come by tomorrow." There could not be more of a difference in the two men, as Legon knew. He liked the appraisers for the most part; they had the personality of bricks, but they were a lot more polite.

The collector looked scandalized. "I have things to do, Harper. This is only a quarterly, anyhow. Do you really need to look at their books and all that stuff?"

Harper looked irritated. "Fine, but we have more to cover this time than normal." He pulled a piece of parchment from a shoulder bag. "This says here that you have a son coming of age this year?"

"Yes, my boy Legon here," he said as he patted Legon's arm.

Harper went on. "Very well. We have a bit of paperwork then. May we sit down somewhere?"

Edis took them into the house, and with the rest of the family sat at the table. Laura looked flustered at the unexpected visit.

"I have records of treatments, if you would like. It shouldn't take me long to get them."

The collector, who still hadn't introduced himself, spoke. "Won't be necessary. Harper here has agreed to the short version."

Harper took out a large stack of paper. "In years past there has been no denying your ability to pay for your daughter...," he paused, looking at the sheets, "...Sasha. This year it is unlikely that you will be able to pay for her and your son, so I have some paperwork to do with her."

A very unnatural silence filled the room and the appraiser looked up at Sasha. "May I ask you a few questions?"

"What for?" she asked

"Because you are going into the queen's care girl, that's why," said the collector, taking Sasha in with hungry eyes.

"But I ... I thought we had until...."

Harper interrupted. "You are not going now, and your family may have enough for you this year. This paperwork is just a precaution so that when you go into the care, or I should say if you do, it saves time."

Without another word Harper started in on the paperwork, asking Sasha everything from how tall she was to what she could do. During the entire interview Laura and Edis sat in stunned silence. Finally the interview was done.

"Thank you, miss."

"So what does this mean?" Sasha asked.

The collector spoke. "What do you mean? You say here that you have been turned down for an apprentice healer's license because of your affliction, and being a good cook isn't much of a skill now is it? You will most likely go into a service field."

"Service?" asked Edis for the first time.

"Maid, cook, farmhand, escort, things of that nature," said the collector coldly.

Sasha blanched at the last one on the list. Edis's face glowed with sweat.

"Well, we have taken up a lot of your time today. Thank you for the help, and we will see you in January," Harper spoke, and he got up.

The collector followed him but turned back to face Sasha at the door. "Dear, I would not think to leave if I were you. We will find you if you try, and I can promise you, you will not like that. I will be the one to collect in January, and I look forward..." he paused as his eyes looked Sasha over again, "... look forward to getting better acquainted at that time." The door clicked shut.

There wasn't much talking after that, and Sasha went up to her room. Legon followed, wanting to see if she was ok. He poked his head in the doorway. Sasha was sitting on the bed with her arms around her knees, a solemn look on her face. Legon knew that she hated not doing anything all day and that she felt like she was a burden on the family, and today's visit must have only confirmed those feelings. He walked into the room and sat at the foot on her bed.

"How was your day?" he asked as he leaned back on the wall. He knew that neither of them would want to talk about the appraisal, but he didn't want her to be alone.

"It was fine. I just watched mom all day. She wouldn't let me do anything. I know she means well, but it's still annoying."

"Yeah, I can see that. Hey, I'm going to pick up that cleaver from Kovos tomorrow. Do you want to come?" He hoped she would say yes. It would be good for her to get out of the house.

Sasha's face brightened a bit. "Are you sure?"

"Yeah, of course I am. I'm going to head over in the morning. Don't worry about waking me up, I'll be fine." He said this last part with a smile.

She laughed. "Are you sure? I don't mind helping."

Legon's face darkened a bit he reached up and felt the lump that was still on his head. "I know you don't."

They sat quietly for a while. Legon closed his eyes, thinking that he may have been a little overzealous at work today. He reached around his neck and rubbed the top of his shoulders a bit.

"Had a long day?" she asked.

"I think I may have strained something today, but it shouldn't matter. I got ahead, so I'll have most of the day tomorrow." His neck and shoulder were really starting to hurt now that he was thinking about it. *The perfect end to the perfect day,* he thought. Sasha scooted around behind him and started rubbing and pushing at his neck and shoulders.

"Sash, you know you don't have to…"

"I know, but I haven't done anything today and the muscle does feel tight. Let me fix it now so you're not hurting for the rest of the week."

"You're the best, you know that?" he said, turning his neck to her.

"You're just lucky I haven't done anything today. Don't expect this to become a regular thing. Besides, I owe you from this morning on the hill."

He reached up, stopping her hand, "You don't owe me for that."

She didn't answer, but he heard her sniff and knew what she was thinking.

* * * * * * *

Sasha was surprised at how knotted his back was. *He must have had a hard day,* she thought. She moved her hands along his shirt along the top of his shoulders to try and get a better fix on a knot. In truth this was as much for her as him. She needed to be doing something. She just wanted a semi-normal evening. She paused and looked down at his slightly exposed back, at the tattoo that had been on him from before Edis found him in the woods. Normally it was a dark green that was almost black, but tonight it was a deep purple.

It wasn't like any other tattoo that she'd seen. Most tattoos were of names and pictures, all the lines coming together, but not on this one. None of the lines touched, and if they overlapped the image would end right before the other and continue again just past the other side. In the center of the tattoo was a circle that was filled in. Three curving branches came from it, spaced out and symmetrical and covered in little leaves that were amazingly detailed. The circle and branches overlapped what appeared to be a triangle that was filled in except where the circle and branches went over it. There was another circle surrounding everything, with only the tips of each branch breaking out from it. In whole the tattoo was about three inches wide and three inches tall.

Nobody had been able to figure out why someone would do this to a baby, but now Sasha knew the question was not why but how. Tattoos didn't change color and they distorted with growth. This one had not, and that meant one thing: *magic.*

She continued working on the knot, Legon blissfully unaware of her momentary pause. She should say something to him, but what would she say? He, like everyone else in the family, was at the breaking point today. She would wait until tomorrow, wait and collect her thoughts. After a bit she stopped rubbing his shoulders and sat back down. She was still thinking about the tattoo. If it had been made by magic, then why? And did that mean that there was more to it than just decoration? She never worried that much about her brother. He was tough and could take care of himself, but if he had been marked with magic....

"Thanks Sash," said Legon with a yawn. "It's getting late I think I'm going to go to bed."

Sasha smiled at him and nodded her head. "If you must. I will see you in the morning."

* * * * * * * *

Legon got up and stretched his arms above his head, then leaned over and gave her a huge hug. He walked out of the room, shut the door, and walked into his own. The bed was bathed in soft moonlight and looked wonderful. There was a slight breeze outside that made the room feel cool and nice. He undressed down to his under shorts and slipped under the covers. His mind drifted from thought to thought in a haze as oftentimes happens when one is falling asleep. Legon drifted to sleep in what felt like moments, never knowing that next door his sister lay awake, thinking and worrying.

Chapter Three
The Arrow's Flight

"Gray is sometimes seen as a mix of light and dark. This, however, is incorrect. To the trained mind and soul there is no gray, simply light and dark, good and evil, joy and sorrow. Gray is only misconception, and it is in this misconception where failure occurs. Yet dark is not always evil, nor is light always good; you may move to one and find the other."
-Lectures of Logic, House Paldin

Legon was walking in a misty field of soft heather. He couldn't see the sky through the mist, but there was enough light to tell that the sun was up. He could barely see five feet in front of him. He could feel the mist fill his lungs with each breath and feel the weight of it. The mist was cool and felt good. Legon knew that he was not anywhere he'd ever been before. The weight and moisture in the air made his skin feel moist, like after a heavy rain storm. He was in the lowlands somewhere. *I'm probably by the sea. Arkin told me they get... what did he call it? Fog. Fog down by the sea, that's what this mist must be,* he thought.

There was sound coming from ahead of him. Something heavy was dragging, accompanied by thumps of something large hitting the ground. He heard a deep rumble that reverberated in his chest. The sound was moving towards him. He could feel his heart race. A branch snapped in the far distance and the dragging sound stopped. He could tell now that whatever was making the sound was right in front of him through the fog, but the snapping branch had made it stop. Which meant that there was more than one of whatever was here.

Silence. A sound from overhead and a bit forward. *What is it?* Legon's ears strained trying to place the sound. It was like breathing, but it couldn't be. The breaths were long and deep, he couldn't think of anything big enough to breathe like that. Then a thought came to his mind: *Only a dragon would breathe that deeply.* His body became rigid. *IT'S A DRAGON!*

Up to this point his heart had been pounding with a sense of adventure, but now his blood ran cold and his heart seemed to stop beating altogether. The only dragons in the land were Iumenta dragons, and they were cruel and clever. The deep breathing caught for a moment. Legon stood stalk-still, hoping beyond hope that it couldn't hear, smell or see him. Then a new dread tore through him. *Dragons can read thoughts! It doesn't need to smell me!* He had to run. He turned on his heels and bolted away from the sound, his legs and lungs burning as he sprinted. There was a snort and a grumble from behind him and from above there came a resounding THUD… THUD…. THUD. The other dragon.

Legon felt the air in his chest catch with every thud. The sound was at first far away, then over him… and now in front of him. The ground shook and he heard the sound of claws scraping against rocks in the field. He was trapped. One dragon was behind him and the other in front. He wondered if dying was going to hurt. Then the fog parted and Legon saw a flash of bright blue.

He sat bolt upright in his bed, covered in cold sweat from head to foot. He could almost hear his heart trying to beat its way out of his chest. He was trembling almost uncontrollably and his breathing was heavy and labored. The dream was slipping through his memory like sand. Soon he remembered none of it and began to calm down. "It was just a dream, nothing more," he said in a whisper. "You're fine. Go back to sleep".

He lay back down, more tired then he had been when he went to bed. His legs ached as if he'd been running. The room was dark. He felt himself drifting again. He soon fell asleep, and by morning would not remember even waking up in the night.

* * * * * * *

Legon woke to the warmth of the sun's rays on his face. He slowly sat up in bed, rubbed his eyes and stretched his arms above his head. *Hmm, I feel tired still. I must not have slept well,* he thought with a yawn. He lay back down and considered going to sleep again, but an image of Sasha and a bucket popped in his head. "Maybe I should get up," he said aloud to himself.

He got out of bed, walked over to the dresser, and pulled out a blue shirt and brown pants. He pulled on some socks and boots and walked out of his room into the hall. Sasha's door was open and he could hear her downstairs. When he got downstairs he could see her flitting around the kitchen, making breakfast and humming to herself. Her red dress spun as she turned to smile up at him. He could tell that she hadn't slept well last night either, though it didn't seem to slow her down. *Maybe I was snoring really loud last night and kept us both from a good sleep,* he thought.

He walked in front of the mirror for his normal pre-day inspection. There was a dark spot on his chin, and for a moment his insides squirmed with excitement. He reached up to feel the stubble… and his fingers slid across his smooth face and smudged a spot of dirt. Feeling stupid, he looked at Sasha in the mirror to make sure she hadn't seen his mistake. She was to busy scooping eggs onto plates. He breathed a sigh of relief.

"You look tired this morning. I didn't keep you up snoring, did I?"

She looked up at him, her eyebrows furrowed in thought, and said as if she was having a hard time remembering, "No, I just had a hard time falling asleep. You weren't snoring... although I kept hearing you say something like 'Sasha is the most beautiful girl in Airmelia and so smart and funny and...' oh, I can't remember the rest."

Legon shook his head. "No wonder I'm so tired - I was delirious last night."

Sasha laughed and said curtly to him, "Rude!"

They sat down and Legon ate his eggs. They were good, but not as good as Sasha's pies were. After they ate Sasha took the dishes and took off her apron, then went upstairs to get her money pouch. Legon walked to the space under the stairs to get their bows. Kovos was always up for shooting, and they hadn't gotten the chance yesterday. Legon grabbed Sasha's hunting bow and his combat bow.

Legon, like most of the men in town, had two bows, one that was for hunting and the other for combat. A hunting bow usually had a fifty to sixty pound draw weight on them, perfect for bringing down all but the largest animals but underpowered against armored targets. Chain mail was expensive, so very few people had it, but bandits and soldiers that didn't have chain mail wore a thick doublet that was made of layered cloth and leather. The doublet would not be able to stop and arrow cold at close range, but it could from a distance. For a hunting bow to penetrate the armor at close range the shooter had to be about ten feet away. It was for this reason that combat bows were significantly stronger.

The average man had a bow with a draw weight of one hundred and sixty to one hundred and eighty pounds, which gave it an effective rage of about two hundred yards and the power to go through leather armor and punch through chain male from about eighty yards away. Combat bows were way over-powered for hunting but were a necessary precaution. Most men got to the point to where they could fire between ten and twenty arrows a minute using a combat bow.

Legon, however, was unusually strong, and his bow had a two hundred pound draw weight. A beautiful weapon, it was made of yew and as was as tall as him. He could hit a head-size target nine times out of ten from one hundred and eighty yards away and could fire eighteen arrows a minute. Only two other men in town, Brack and Arkin, could fire such a bow, but neither could claim Legon's accuracy.

Legon walked over to the door and waited for Sasha. She came down the steps and they walked outside. The town was alive at this time in the morning, and people were moving in all directions in the streets. They began to walk in the direction of Kovos's house. They waved and said hello to townspeople as they passed, and soon they were walking by the town carpenter's house and shop. As they passed, Sasha touched Legon's arm. "Let's go say hello to Arkin. I haven't seen him in awhile." Sasha liked Arkin. He was the only one in the town that was truly kind to her, and Legon liked him too. He had always been a good family friend.

"Ok, that sounds good." They walked up to the door of the shop and walked in.

As Legon opened the door their noses were filled with the sent of oak, cherry, pine and other kinds of wood. They skirted around the counter and headed into the open work area. Sasha walked to the center of the room and ran her hand over a large table.

"He's inlayed a checkered pattern on this. What do you think - cherry and oak?" she asked, inspecting the unfinished wood.

Legon glanced at it. "Yup, looks like it, and big too. I'd say for a family of eight. Looks like he's got the chairs in that corner. It doesn't look like he's here, though. His tools are on the wall." *Way too many tools,* he thought.

"You're right. The back door is closed, and there isn't even any dust in the air. Odd. I don't think I've ever seen this place like this. Do you think he's in today?"

She was right. Normally dust motes filled the air, swirling up to the skylight high above them. Lighting a place like this was difficult. Fire was an obvious liability with everything being made of wood, and more importantly the air usually being filled with sawdust. It was rare but not unheard of for a carpenter's shop to burn down from a fire stated by stray sawdust. Arkin's shop was well lit with the two skylights and large windows on either side of the door.

A smooth warm voice greeted them. "Sasha, Legon, how good to see you. To what do I owe the pleasure?" Arkin said, stepping into the room.

He was tall and of a medium build, with long blond hair and hazel eyes, a thin jaw line and a small nose. He was wearing a white shirt and brown pants, over which he had on a leather apron with three pockets built into the waist. He walked with a smooth gait and perfect posture. He was not what you would envision a carpenter to be; he was refined and confident, qualities that shined through not only his countenance but his work. He was not an arrogant man, however. He was kind and fair, slow to anger and had a balance of sternness and patience. Legon and Sasha had always liked him and had gotten along with him well. There was a smile on his face that revealed straight white teeth.

"We were on our way to see Kovos when I realized that it has been far too long since I've seen you," Sasha said brightly.

"Yes it has, and unfortunately you have caught me at a bad time. I've been out hunting for the last few days and am behind on work."

"Did you get anything?" Legon asked.

"Ah … no, I didn't but it was nice to get out," Arkin said. Legon detected a hint of apprehension in his voice.

Arkin said abruptly, "Will you come by later this week and have tea with me? Then we could catch up."

"We would love to," said Sasha, and Legon piped in, "Yeah we'll catch you in a few days… see ya, Arkin".

They walked out of the shop with a wave and continued to Kovos's. After they had walked a bit Legon leaned over to Sasha. "Did something seem off to you with Arkin?"

She tilted her head slightly to the side. "I don't know. He did seem a bit preoccupied, and he was a little vague about his hunting trip."

"Yeah, and I've never known him not to bring a kill in for us to butcher. That must mean he didn't get anything, which is odd for him." As Legon spoke he looked at the ground and his voice was soft, almost like he was talking to himself.

"Oh well. There's Kovos'," Sasha pointed out.

They had arrived at their friend's house. To the right of it was a stone shop with smoke belching from a flu. They both walked up to the door of the shop and walked in. They were met with a wall of heat. The one-room shop was large. Brack was by the wall on the right side of the building, standing in front of a large furnace that curved up from the ground like a teardrop. There was a long pipe that rose from the furnace to the ceiling. The furnace was made of some sort of clay, but it was impossible to distinguish from the black soot that covered it. Brack was working a billow with one hand and holding a metal rod in the other. The rod was deep in the fire; red was creeping up the rod towards Brack's glove. He was also wearing soot-black pants and what had once been a white shirt with sleeves rolled up past his elbows. As he worked the billows, sparks and flame roared out from the opening of the furnace like some monster from a children's story.

Benches and anvils were scattered throughout the room. It was lit only by the furnace's glow which cast the room in a sharp contrast of dark and bloody hues of red and orange. In the center of the room was Kovos. Both he and his father were wearing thick aprons made in the fashion of leather armor. They were scorched and cut in places, signs of the hot iron's angry touch. Kovos was wearing a thick pair of gloves and pounding on a piece of red-hot iron. Each time the hammer hit, sparks flew from it in protest. Kovos and his father were amazing to watch. They brought their hammers high in the air and then down with incredible force and precision.

* * * * * * *

Sasha was having a hard time hearing over the roar of the furnace. Legon had to shout over it. "Kovos! Kovos, pay attention to me you great buffoon!"

At this Kovos looked up, made a rude hand gesture at Legon, and continued to work. Legon and Sasha laughed. "Good to see you too."

Kovos nodded to them, telling them to wait a minute. He raised the hammer high and brought it down with force on the rod, showering the floor with sparks. Sasha noticed the muscles on his bare arms ripple when the hammer reached its target. His stocky build was made for this work. Kovos was wearing the same black pants and blackened shirt as his father. He put down the hammer and walked over to them with the rod still in his hands. "Let me give this back to dad and we can go out back." They nodded and walked to the back of the shop.

It felt good to get out of the heat and into the alleyway behind the shop. The spring air was cool and inviting. A moment later Kovos came walking out with a large cleaver of the type Legon had used the previous day to split a cow. He wasn't wearing the apron any more and looked happy to be out of the shop. He handed the cleaver to Legon, who began to inspect it. "Looks good, Kovos. Thanks."

Kovos and his father were amazing smiths, or at least they were in Legon's opinion. He hadn't seen much of the work of other blacksmith's since Salmont only needed one. Kovos was not as good as his dad, but despite his insistence that he was not very good, everyone in the town trusted him with any project. Kovos was a hard worker and a perfectionist. He was also incredibly loyal. Legon knew that Kovos would stand next to him no matter what. He also knew that Kovos feared Sasha but would still defend her with his life just because she was Legon's sister. This was not a fact lost on Sasha, and though she knew that Kovos, like most of the town, feared her, she was grateful for him. He was nice to her, and if she was on her own and saw Kovos, he would talk to her and escort her wherever she was going. Barnin had been that way too. Both Kovos and Barnin, while flawed men, had incredible character.

"No problem. Thanks for killing and butchering that deer for me, it was great." He looked at Sasha. "Hey Sash, how are you feeling today?"

"How... how did you know I had an episode?" she asked, amazed.

"Easy. Legon didn't come by yesterday, and he would only miss out on a new cleaver if you weren't well."

"Oh. Thank you, Kovos. I'm feeling fine now." As she said this she looked at Legon and smiled inwardly. She was so grateful to have him in her life, and she was sad to think about him leaving.

Kovos looked at the buckskin tubes that Legon was holding and frowned. "I don't think dad will let me go shooting today...," he paused, "Unless...."

Kovos shot back into the shop and came out a minute later. "Great, I'll get my bow. You talked me into it."

* * * * * * * *

Legon laughed. There was no talking Kovos into it, but rather talking his dad into letting him leave for a few hours. Legon wondered how he did it, but when Kovos rejoined them he knew how, and his heart sank a bit. Kovos brought with him a large boy with the same black hair, though matted, who was wearing a pair of blue pants and a stained green shirt. Keither.

Keither also had on a look of annoyance. The two brothers couldn't have been more different. Kovos was short and stocky and Keither tall and rather large. Kovos was leading, or more like pulling, Keither from the house. It looked like someone trying to pull a dog away from chasing a deer or a small child from his favorite toy. When they came out Kovos had two bows; one was his combat bow and the other Keither's hunting bow. Keither didn't have a combat bow. His family wouldn't let him get one until he could shoot his hunting bow with some degree of accuracy, which Keither had yet to do. The boy hated going outside and didn't like to shoot, but it was important to learn, so whenever Kovos was having a hard time leaving the house he would tell his father or mother that he would bring Keither and try and work with him. Keither never wanted to go, but Kovos was much stronger so Keither didn't have much of a choice in the matter. Sasha attempted to greet Keither by waving at him, but the boy only returned her wave with a glare.

They walked down the alley and got back on the street they were on before. They continued on the street until they got to a large field at the edge of town. On one end of the field was a line of padded targets with little flags that marked distance.

Red was for fifty yards, yellow for one hundred, green for one hundred and twenty five, purple for one hundred and fifty, and beyond that were black ones for two hundred yards. On the other side was a line of white flags that marked where to stand while shooting. They walked to the line of white flags. At the moment the four of them were the only ones there. Everyone except Keither strung their bow and prepared to begin. Kovos hit Keither in the arm and the boy began to string his bow.

"Lets just fire a warm up volley and then we can move two of the targets further back," said Kovos to the others. They nodded their agreement and all knocked an arrow, pulled back, took aim, and fired.

The air hissed with the sound of the flying arrows and stings twanged. The arrows flew down the field and hit the targets with a thump, all but Keither's.

Sasha looked around. "Why didn't you fire?"

"I did," said Keither with a bit of irritation.

"You... oh I'm sor... sorry about that, Keither." Sasha's face turned red. She looked away from him and began to fidget with her bow.

Kovos broke in. "Well, where did it go, then?" he asked, looking hard down the field.

"How am I supposed to know?" said Keither.

"Um, I don't know, maybe because you shot it?" Kovos said sarcastically, holding his arms out in front of him with his palms up.

"Well, we've got lots of arrows, and I'm sure we can find that one. It couldn't have gotten far." Said Sasha, trying to redeem herself. Then in a hurry she continued, "Not that I'm saying you can't shoot far. I mean... um, well you know that you probably only missed by an inch or so..." she spluttered.

Legon and Kovos laughed. "If were lucky we may find it later. Come on, Legon, let's move the targets," Kovos said. They walked to the targets and began to move them down the field. As soon as they were out of earshot, Kovos said, "Sasha is going to make a good wife, buddy. I'm happy for you, but it's a little sick you went for your sister...."

He was cut off by Legon. "What are you talking about?" Then Kovos's comment clicked in Legon's mind. He reached out and punched Kovos in the arm. "Shut up, that's sick."

"What, you mean you're not? Oh, I'm sorry man, I just thought with you two being so close and you being adopted..." Kovos was smiling. Legon hit him again.

"Ow! What? Stop hitting me! I mean, she's a good looking girl, and hey, beggars can't be choosers. Ow!"

"You're sick. I don't know how your family is, but I'm not into my sister. You're right though, she is good looking, but she would look better by your side."

Kovos laughed. "Hey, I would, but I don't want to be looking over my shoulder for you my whole life."

"Shut up and move the target."

They made it to the targets and began to move them across the field. Kovos loved to give Legon a hard time about his relationship with Sasha. He knew that they were close, brother and sister, but that was it. Legon had to admit that they were unusually close; he suspected that it had to do with their situation growing up. They had supported each other, and at times they were almost like one person instead of two. Emotionally, there were no real boundaries between them. He knew that there was something odd about the relationship though; he didn't know of anyone in town who needed to be with one particular person the way that he felt he needed to be with Sasha. Or anyone who had a strange sixth sense as they seemed to have with each other. Sometimes it almost seemed like he could predict what she would say or do. But never once had he had an inappropriate thought or emotion about her, and he knew it was the same for her.

His attention came back to Kovos, who was walking next to him hefting his own target. He was still smiling but his voice was serious now. "Honestly, I think you're going to need to take her with you, there's no way you'll be able to make the money for the taxes and get it here in time." Legon began to open his mouth but Kovos cut him off. "It can't be done, and don't tell me otherwise. Take her with you. You can live in the same house and fall under the two adults rule for taxes, there's a lot of people that do it." His face darkened. "And I also don't think she will be safe here when you're gone. People worry about Edis but there terrified of you, and…"

Legon interrupted. "I know. I have a lot to think about, but not today. Let's just shoot, ok?"

Kovos nodded.

* * * * * * *

Standing next to Keither, Sasha watched them go. She looked over at the boy who, was slouching and didn't at all look like he wanted to be here.

"So Keither… how are you doing?" she asked tentatively.

"Meh," said Keither in a grunt.

Sasha was having a hard time thinking of what to say. She always had problems with Keither. He was a quiet boy and a bit socially awkward, or extremely socially awkward if she was being honest. He sighed hard and looked down the field at his brother and Legon, who were carrying their targets to the purple flags. He obviously hated being dragged along like this.

"So have you decided on a trade to pursue yet, or are you still thinking about it?" asked Sasha.

"Ahh I don't know, I haven't thought much about it. I think I'm going to go find my arrow before they get back." And with that Keither walked off to find his arrow.

Sasha stood alone and looking a bit irritated. *He has no manners! What will become of that boy?* she thought to herself. Legon and Kovos had finished moving the targets and were walking back to her now. She could see Kovos throwing his arms in the air at Keither, and she could also see that he was yelling something at him but couldn't hear it. Soon they were all back together and Kovos was scolding Keither.

"I don't care if you were looking for your arrow, you can't just wander around the field like that," Kovos said angrily.

"There's no one else out here. What's the big deal?" Keither said in a defiant voice.

"Are you sure there's no one here? Did you look around before you walked across the field? No, I don't think so. Legon and I walked straight to our targets and moved them. You were walking along the row of targets. What if you got hit?"

"Bleh bleh bleh. You worry too much. Nothing could have happened." Keither waved his arms lazily.

It was true. The field was still empty, but Kovos's anger was warranted because Keither never took the time to think about what he was doing. Once he had walked onto the field while others were shooting and a stray arrow had only been missed him by a hairs breadth.

"Well, look before you do that again, ok?" Kovos said imploringly.

Keither didn't answer him but gave a harrumph.

* * * * * * *

Legon shook his head and took his place next to Sasha. They all pulled back there strings and shot another volley. The arrows hissed down the field again and this time they only heard Sasha's hit the target. Both Legon's and Kovos's arrows hit their mark, but they were too far away to hear. Legon spoke to Kovos as he knocked his next arrow.

"So do you still think you want to leave town with me?" After saying this he fired again, hitting the target in the center.

"I'm not sure. It's a big decision, and I know I'll have to leave Salmont, but I'm not sure if I know enough yet, you know?" said Kovos after a shot.

"Yeah, I know what you mean, but you're pretty good. You know enough to make a go on your own."

"Yeah I'm sure I'll end up going, but I don't much feel like leaving and striking out on my own. I wish there was enough in Salmont to support two blacksmiths."

"And two butchers," said Legon flatly.

"Why can't you both stay here?" asked Keither, puzzled. Kovos lowered his bow and stared incredulously at him.

Legon responded in a patient voice, "Because we have to pay taxes and feed ourselves."

"Yeah well, why don't you just say you can afford the taxes?"

Legon shook his head. "Because they make you a slave then, Keither. Have you not been living here your whole life?" asked Legon.

Kovos turned towards Keither and said, knocking an arrow, "I'm going to shoot him. It's better we put him out of his misery now."

"KOVOS!" Sasha said loudly.

"No Sash, it's better this way, trust me," Kovos said, giving Sasha a sideward glance.

"Ha ha, very funny. Can we go home now?" asked Keither.

"Go home?" Legon said, surprised. "We've shot three arrows! No, we can't go home. Come on, Kovos."

They continued shooting the targets for awhile, and after an hour or so they decided to go home. They would have stayed a bit longer, but Keither had managed to lose most of the arrows they brought, and Legon and Kovos were forced to walk down the field to get their arrows every five or six shots. The arrows Keither shot were gone forever. They were on the field somewhere, but the field was large and people were starting to show up to practice, and Legon and Kovos were not excited about becoming a human quiver while trying to find the arrows.

They made it back to Kovos's house in time for lunch and they spent much of the afternoon there talking and having a good time. After a few hours Legon and Sasha decided to start for home. They walked out of the house and headed towards the edge of town. They would often skirt around the town to take more time getting home and to give them more time to talk. It felt good to walk after sitting on a wood bench all afternoon. The sun was starting to set and the sky was beginning to turn a variety of colors, the grey clouds taking on hues of pink and lavender. The valley was soon covered in shadows and they could hear crickets starting to chirp. Legon noticed that Sasha wasn't talking much.

"Why so quiet, sis?"

"I don't know. I guess there's a lot on my mind," she said softly.

"Well, like what?"

"Like what's going to happen when you leave, I've spent my whole life with you and I'm not sure what it will be like when you're gone."

"I'll visit, you know. I'm going to try to go to a town within a few weeks of here. But I suppose it won't be like it is now. I'm going to miss you, too."

That was a lie. In truth he wasn't entirely sure how he was going to live without her. It was like they were linked.

"That can't be all that's on your mind Sash. What else is bothering you?"

She took her time answering him. "It's your tattoo. I noticed yesterday that it's changed from that dark green to purple. Why would it do that?" There was a hint of concern in her voice, and even a bit of fear.

"It's what? Sash, tattoos don't change color," he said confidently.

"I know they don't, but yours has… I saw it just last night." Now the concern was evident in her voice and face. "If it has changed colors then that mean that it must be…"

"Magic," Legon finished. He felt his blood turn to ice and his heart beat faster.

Magic was rare in humans, which scared Legon, because magic was treated with great fear and respect. Iumenta and Elves could use it, but there weren't any Elves in their area that he knew of.

"Do you think it was put there by an Iumenta?" he asked Sasha quietly.

"I don't know. I hope not, but it may not be much better if it was put there by and Elf. The queen hates them. And if it was a human then who knows what it means."

They walked silently, neither wanting to talk about Legon's tattoo. They opened the distance between them and the town and soon they couldn't hear the town at all. The only sound was that of two sets of feet stepping on the soft ground. The town was surrounded by farms and fields, all green with spring's life. The sun was almost bellow the mountain's high peaks, and sat above them like a crown of gold and fire. They both felt themselves relaxing as the air started to grow cool. Legon looked over at Sasha. Her face seemed to glow in the orange light and the last shafts of the sun's rays danced in her hair. She still looked a bit worried; he could see it in her eyes. He could tell that there was more she wasn't telling him.

Sasha broke the silence. Her voice was conversational. "So, have you given any thought to where you are going to go when you leave?"

He took his time answering. "Yeah, I'm thinking Salkay. It's just a bit south of here. The town is growing and they don't have a butcher. Also, they're still under Regent Kooth's control, so it should make it simpler."

"Hmmm. Salkay, huh? That's only about four days from here, isn't it?"

"Yep, that's the idea. I want to be close, and Salkay is about as good as I'm going to get."

Sasha looked like she was thinking. "But it's still a small town. You won't make a huge amount of money, or at least not enough to start a family with. Speaking of which, do you think you will be able to find a wife there? Wouldn't Salez be better?"

Legon stumbled over his words a bit. "Well, Salez is a big city, and as far as Salkay goes, I will make a decent amount of money. I'm not worried about it."

Sasha didn't pursue the subject any more. They got home just after dark. When they got in Edis greeted them. "Your mother had to go. Arkin cut him self or something like that." he saw worry instantly cross Legon and Sasha's faces. "Oh, it's nothing bad, he's fine. I think he got a small cut today. He didn't even want her to come over, but you know your mother."

Sasha gave a deep sigh and said, "We know her." She looked around the kitchen. Something was off. *There's no smell of food cooking. She must not have made dinner,* she thought. Edis was smiling politely at her, that kind of smile you give to your daughter to tell her she's the most wonderful thing in the world or…

"Sash, dinner!" Legon said in a commanding voice and snapped his fingers.

She turned and scowled at both of them. Legon winced, but Edis, having gotten many of these looks from his wife over the years, kept smiling as if this act would somehow make her feel better. "What, you two aren't capable of making dinner?" she spat.

"Puddin', its not tha…," began Edis, whose smile was beginning to fade.

"Don't you give me that! Why do I have to cook?"

Legon spoke, "Dad, Sasha is right. Why should she do it?"

"Thank you," she said.

"We can make dinner. Come on, we do it all the time when we go hunting," Legon said to Edis.

At this something clicked in Sasha's head.

"Oh… well… that's ok, I really don't mind," she said in a much calmer and placating voice.

"No Sash, Legon's right. We'll cook I'm sorry, that was pig headed of me." Edis gestured for her to sit down.

"No, no I insist. I can do it. You two set the table and sit down, I don't mind." She swept over to the counter and began putting on her blue apron.

"Are you sure?" asked Legon one last time.

"Yes, I'm sure," she said and as she began to get out pots and pans. As Legon sat down, Edis mouthed to him, "Good one, son," and gave him a thumbs up. The fact of the matter was that both Legon and Edis could cook. They were not as good as Sasha or Laura, but they weren't bad. Sasha didn't know this, of course, since she had never let them cook on the two occasions when she had gone hunting with them. Legon had thought the for sure that she wouldn't fall for his trick, but she had, and this bothered him. It meant that there was a lot on Sasha's mind that she was not telling him.

Chapter Four
Coming of Age

"Life is a series of decisions, each moving us along the ropes of fate. How to make the right decision? This is a question that all ask yet few understand. As options are weighed and consequences revealed we see bondage, but in reality we are free. Look up the rope of fate and choose your place, then go to it. Let that guide your decisions today."
-Diary of the Perfectos Compatioa

The day after Legon and Sasha had gone over to see Kovos, Legon found himself walking into his house after an uneventful morning. There was almost nothing to do in the shop; it was one of the famine days as far as work went. The only thing that Edis could find to keep himself busy was making sausage, and for that he liked to have Sasha's help. Legon didn't mind; he hated to make sausage and it was a great opportunity for Legon and Sasha to switch roles. He would help his mother if she needed it, and Sasha got some time with Edis.

When he got inside, his mother was sitting at the table sorting herbs, or at least he thought that was what she was doing. There were a lot of dried plants on the table and she was sifting through them. She was wearing a brown dress and a white apron. She was sitting on a chair hunched over, her hands moving quickly over the herbs. He was amazed that the little plants didn't crumble as she picked them up. She looked up at him, smiled and gestured with her head for him to sit down.

She was deep in concentration and he knew that she would get to him eventually, so he contented himself with sitting and pulling his shoulders back, feeling the muscles across his broad chest stretch and relax.

"How are you today dear?" she said, not looking up from her work.

"I'm doing good mom. What are you doing?"

"I'm trying to get these sorted out. They fell off the wall and got all jumbled up."

On either side of the fireplace were herbs drying on the walls, and sure enough there was a spot that was missing a patch.

"Do you want me to fix it? I don't think it would take long," Legon said, gesturing to the wall.

Laura didn't see him point as she was still hunched over the herbs. "What dear? What would you fix?" she looked up, confused.

"The wall," he said flatly. She looked over and shook her head as if she was ridding herself of day dream.

"Sorry. You know I can be a flake when I'm concentrating. Let me finish this and we can have some tea."

An image of the look on Sasha's face from two days ago when she had "some tea" rushed through his mind like a herd of stampeding cows.

"Oh... I feel great mom... I don't need anything. Not thirsty, really. You have stuff to do, so I'll just..." his mind reached into what seemed to be nothingness, coming up with a reason to avoid tea. "I'll fix the wall, that's what needs to be done." He instantly knew this hadn't worked. As soon as he said it she looked up at him, and he could see she was trying not to laugh.

"We're not going to have that kind of tea, just good old mint will do today," she said with a chuckle in her voice.

Legon sat back and sighed with relief. Soon she was done, and before he knew it she seemed to make mint tea appear out of thin air. As he sipped it he felt the hot liquid flow down his throat to warm his belly. They sat quietly for a bit. His mother broke the silence.

"You'll be eighteen in a month. How do you feel about that?" Her voice was soft and carried with it all the sincerity in the world. This subject had been playing over and over again in his head for the last few weeks.

"I don't know how I feel about it. There's a part of me that is excited about coming of age but… there's a bigger part that is terrified, you know what I mean?" He looked at her and she nodded a bit. He continued on.

"I just feel… I feel like I'm racing towards something I can't control and something…" he seemed to have a hard time thinking of the words.

She tried to help him. "Scary?"

"Yeah, but not like the scary you would think, it's not the excited scary."

Her face looked concerned. "Legon, what's wrong?"

He paused, wondering if he should tell her about his tattoo. *It's better to tell her now than later,* he thought.

"Come and look," he said.

As he said this he gestured to his back and pulled the back of his shirt down. His mother looked a little frightened now and came around back of him to look. He heard a sharp intake of breath and then he felt her fingers inside the back of his shirt and then he heard the fabric rip. It caught him off guard. His mother would never damage good clothes. She held his shoulders in place when he tried to turn. Her hands were moving across his back, over the tattoo. The movement felt frantic and scared. It felt like she was trying to remove dirt or a smudge off his back. They stopped moving and she walked slowly over to the chair. She sat and held her face in her hands. Her whole body was shuttering, and he could hear her say between sobs, "Not my son… not my son…"

Fear crawled up the back of his neck and he was surprised by a crack in his voice. "Mom what's wrong? What's going on?" She looked up at him. There was a pleading look in her tear-stained face, a look that said, 'Don't make me, please don't make me.'

Her voice was rough. "I think its time I told you how you came to us."

His forehead scrunched. "Mom, I know how I got here. Dad found me while he was hunting. They came across a camp site that had been raided; they figured that I was left behind by mistake when people fled from the robbers." But as he said this, like so many other times when he thought about it, he somehow knew that it wasn't right, nobody would leave a baby in a campsite. Even the robbers would at least kill or try and sell it. He had never given too much credence to the story of how he came to be with Laura and Edis. They were his parents now, and that's what mattered.

"No, Legon that's not how we came to have you in our family," she said softly. Her face was still tear soaked, but he could see resolve cross it as well. After pausing for a moment she continued.

"Your father was hunting, that part is true. He found you and brought you home, but that's where the truth ends."

Trepidation began seeping into him, as she went on.

"He was in the woods when he heard a baby crying. He was with Brack and Arkin. They moved to the sound and found a cottage, or at least that's what your father thought it was. He said it seemed more like a tree, but I'm not sure about all of that, he was upset when he got home and I don't think that he was in his right mind. When they came to the cottage they could see that it was horribly damaged…"

At this she paused and he could see fresh tears filling her blue eyes again.

"When they entered the house they found a woman. She was dead. Your father has never said much about her. I think that what he saw frightened him. Apparently the inside had been ransacked, but it appeared that nothing had been taken. They found you in the house in a hidden space under the hearth."

Legon interrupted. "They found me in the fire!" It was a statement, not a question.

"No, dear, there wasn't a fire burning and I don't think there had been in a long time. I think that your mother put you in a very safe hiding place."

My mother, he though. His birth mother hadn't forgotten him or left in a hurry, running away from robbers. She had been murdered and had most likely spent her last few moments alive hiding him, in a place apparently prepared for just that. This also meant that she had at least planned for the possible day that she would have to hide her son from people who wanted to hurt them. The fact that the house had been searched was disturbing as well, because nothing was taken, or at least nothing obvious had been taken. That probably meant that whoever had attacked was there for reasons other than financial gain. Before Legon had time to fully comprehend what he just been told, his adopted mother pushed on, almost as if by saying this she was free of some burden.

"After they found you they took you home. You know the rest. We adopted you and now you are our son, and we love you like you are our own." She placed her hand on his at this last statement.

Legon felt every emotion coursing through him. On the one hand he was mad that he hadn't been told this, but on the other he knew his parents were just trying to protect him. He understood the desire to protect the ones you love; when he thought about it he didn't know if could have handled this news when he was younger. Still, something didn't seem right. Where had his birth father been in this whole affair? He had to know about the hiding place and had to know that his son was missing... unless he was killed too, and Edis, Brack and Arkin hadn't found the body.

And what had they been looking for in the first place? A thought came to him then that bothered him: if Edis hadn't been willing to share all the details of what he saw with his wife, then what he had seen must have been pretty bad. Also, the house had been secluded, and so his mother must have been hiding from something. She may have had or at least known something that whoever did this wanted, and it was possible that they had interrogated her before killing her. That made sense; it also explained why Edis had been unwilling to talk to his wife about it. If his birth mother was interrogated, that meant that they had probably tortured her, and Legon could understand why Edis didn't want to relive the sight in his head. A thought bubbled up.

"Mom, it's going to take some time for what you just said to... well, sink in, but I still don't understand why you got so upset about my tattoo. Isn't it possible that my birth mother did magic and that's why it's there?"

She paused. He could tell she was trying to figure out what to say.

"Your tattoo was put there by magic. I'm sure of that now, but the thing that has me so upset is that your tattoo is, well... I'm not sure how to explain this. Arkin knows more about this kind of thing than me. The tattoo is Elven." She sighed deeply after saying this.

"'Elven'? What do you mean, 'Elven'? Does that mean that an Elf put it there? Why would they do that?" he stammered. He didn't like the thought of magic, but to think that an Elf of all things had put the tattoo there was almost too much. The queen hated the Elves and would stop at nothing to kill any in her territory or anyone connected to them.

"It's a crest, Legon. An Elven crest, the kind they mark all of their children with. Like I said, I don't know much about it, but Arkin somehow does. Before I thought that maybe the tattoo was just done in the same style as the Elvin ones, but now…" Her face was blank and pallid; the color in her eyes seemed to leak out, leaving them weak and frail.

As this last statement hit home Legon felt his jaw begin to fall open. All brain function came to a screeching halt. Now fear came in, then terror, then denial. Arkin was wrong, or his mother had misunderstood him. His first parents probably knew magic and liked the Elven tradition like she said. He knew that if it was an Elven mark then the people who killed his parents, or at least his mother - *maybe my dad is still alive* he thought - worked for the queen and may have even been Iumenta. This placed him in danger. If the tattoo was from an Elf then he could be seen as a spy and killed, or if the mark was from a human he could be seen as an Elven sympathizer and killed. Two possibilities with only one outcome.

For the first time Legon began to appreciate the sacrifice his adopted parents had made on his behalf. They had placed themselves in danger by harboring a possible enemy to the state. At the same time he was angry with them, not because they had done anything wrong, but because they were there and he needed someone to be upset with. His mother was looking intently at him. Her face was dry, and it hit him that he had been quiet for a few minutes.

"Sorry mom… I blanked out," he began.

"It should be me who is sorry. We should have told you sooner than this, and it's a horrible thing to drop on someone."

For some reason this made Legon even angrier. They knew they should have told him but they hadn't. Was it because they didn't care about him? He had been of use, taking care of

Sasha so they didn't have to, and working in that shop… was he nothing more than labor? No, that wasn't right. His parents loved him and they just wanted him to be happy. What was wrong with that?

He stood suddenly. "I need to get outside and get some air. There's so much going through my mind. I'm sorry mom. Thank you for the tea."

She nodded at him and seemed relieved. "Take your time dear."

He walked out the back door and toward the forest. A walk in the woods would be good for him. It was overcast today, which matched his new mood. The gray sky made all of the bright colors of the field become more vibrant, and made the ground soft under his feet. When he got in the woods the air was thick and misty; there wasn't a sound. The heavy air and the mist reminded him of something… a dream maybe. It felt as though his feet were carrying him of their own accord; he had no idea where he was going. He saw a deer go bounding by and snap a branch. That too seemed to remind him of something.

His mind flooded with thought; he knew that this news of his tattoo would change his life in ways he could not yet comprehend. He couldn't go to a big city. If he did his tattoo would be seen for sure. He might have to go south to the resistance, but he didn't like that idea. He would be too far away to help the family with their taxes. But that wasn't his problem - it was his family's. He had to protect himself or he wouldn't be able to do anything for them. It felt like his emotions had been taken over, controlled by something other than himself.

It's not my fault if something happens. There's no point in both Sasha and I getting hurt, or worse, he thought. He could just leave them to their own devices. His mind and emotions jumped wildly from fear of the unknown to anger. He thought maybe they had the hardship coming anyway. It would have come sooner if not for him. They were lucky he had been around.

He stopped and looked around, trying to see if he recognized his surroundings. He thought he was on top of a hill. He couldn't see any landmarks through the mist, but the ground in front of him looked disturbed, like there had been a struggle there not more than a few days ago. There was something else that was in a bush, something small, brown and square. Puzzled, he went to the bush and bent over. It was a book. He picked it up and thumbed through the pages. It was handwritten and looked to be a diary. He knew he shouldn't look at it, but he couldn't return it to the person if he didn't know whose it was. He stopped at and entry that was dated three weeks ago and began to read.

Today was a bad day. I had another one. It was horrible. I threw up all over the place, and I hit the back of my head on my brother's mouth.

It was Sasha's! He knew he should stop reading, but couldn't seem to bring himself to. He remembered that episode, Sasha writhing on the ground while he'd tried to hold her. He felt his lips where the back of her head had hit. He didn't know he was bleeding at first; his mother was the one to see. By the end of the episode his face and chest were covered with his own blood and he'd cut his face on the ground. He read on:

I can't remember what happened. I almost never do, but he was covered in blood when I came to. Oh I hate this! I'm a monster! He's so big and I still hurt him. I feel so bad. If it wasn't for my brother I don't know what I would do. The people in town are right, I'm cursed, I'm a demon, and when Legon leaves the queen will take me. I'm so scared. A lady in town told me that they will make me a whore and give me to the queen's men for their pleasure. Maybe I deserve it for being a freak. I mean look at me, I can't make a living, I'm a burden on my family… at least when I'm gone my family can have their lives back again and…

He stopped reading. The string holding his emotions broke. Now his problems seemed not to matter. He thought back on what just crossed his mind, how selfish he'd been, how… he felt an odd flash of heat and without warning his stomach turned. He tossed the book aside and began to throw up on the grass. He felt more heat, saw blue spots, and then nothing.

Legon's eyes opened and he felt his head pounding. He raised himself up on his hands and saw a pool of semi-dry vomit in front of him. He must have been out for a few hours.

He wondered what time it was. He got up and walked to the book and picked it up, but something was off… what was it? He took an inventory and it hit him - he didn't have a torch, candle or anything else to make light. The sky was still covered in clouds, so he shouldn't be able to see the ground at his feet, but he could.

Legon swept his gaze out to where the town was. He gasped. It was there right in front of him. Just a hazy outline, but it was there. He began to feel uneasy. Maybe there was something wrong with him. He began back towards his house through the woods that were dark to all but him.

He got home in near record time. When he walked in his family was sitting at the table talking to one another. They started when he came in and his mother stood up a bit.

He walked into the now silent room and handed the book to Sasha.

"I was on top of the hill and this was in a bush. When I saw it was hand written I closed it… it's probably a diary or something. Maybe you know whose it is?"

She took it and opened the cover. Her eyes widened a bit and then relaxed. She got up and hugged him. "Thank you. I was worried sick looking for this thing. Thank you, Legon!" She kissed his cheek and dashed up to her room.

He thought about what he was thinking earlier and a voice came unbidden into his head: *You don't deserve that, you bastard; you don't deserve her in your life at all.*

He began to walk to the stairs when Edis's voice called him back. "Come and sit down son." Legon turned and sat.

"Your mother told me about today, and I just wanted to say I'm sorry for not being honest with you and… if you want to talk about it, we're here."

There you go giving aid and concern to someone you should have left in the broken house, someone who doesn't deserve it.

"I know you are, and I know you just wanted me to be happy and have a normal life. I'm fine, but I have a headache and I need to go to bed."

He stood and walked up the stairs straight to his room. He could see that Sasha's door was closed and he was thankful. He didn't care to talk to her right now; he was still feeling guilty about his desire to leave the family to their own devices and save his own neck.

He peeled off his clothes as he entered his room and flopped onto his bed. He felt so tired and his head was pounding. He laid his head on his pillow and felt himself begin to drift off to sleep. He hadn't even take the time to close his bedroom door.

He wanted to sleep but he was cold and his bed felt hard. He rolled over and opened his eyes. To his surprise he realized he was on the ground, on the ground outside. He stood up and looked around. The ground that he was on was just dirt and rocks. He was in mist and couldn't see more than a few feet in front of him. This felt familiar but somehow unfamiliar at the same time. He must be dreaming; this place had that feel about it. He began to walk and realized that he had a dream like this not too long ago. *Odd. How come I couldn't remember it before?* he thought.

The last time he was in a field when… *there was a dragon* he thought. Legon went rigid. This may have been a dream, but he still didn't want to deal with a dragon.

He heard the sound of moving rocks, which didn't help his feeling of foreboding. He began to pick up his pace a bit, looking for a place to hide until the mist cleared. He felt his lungs burn and he moved faster. Before he knew it he was in the field by the sea from the last dream.

But in this dream the air was thin. He knew that he must be up high, perhaps on a mountain top, and that this mist was probably a cloud. So was he by the sea or wasn't he? It seemed like he was in both places, high on a mountain and by the sea. Suddenly from behind him there came a resounding THUD. He moved faster, feeling his legs begin to burn. THUD. This time it was above his head. THUD. Right in front of him. The sound of claws sinking into earth and breaking rock filled the air. He skidded to a halt as he saw a huge shadow rise in the mist ahead of him.

The mist parted and he tried to scream, but his voice wouldn't respond. In front of him was a hulking black dragon with scales the color of coal, seeming to absorb light. Its giant claws looked to be made of solid gold. Long flat plates crossed its chest at the bottom of its long, snake-like neck. At the top of the neck and more than forty feet off the ground was its head. It was triangular with two golden horns that swept back, and when the dragon breathed out, orange circlets appeared in the nostrils. Two long teeth that looked like they were made of pearl jutted from the top of the mouth.

A row of gold spikes ran down its back and tail. The thing that scared Legon the most were the eyes. They were as large as serving platters and were blood red. Everything on the dragon seemed to leech the light from the world, but not the eyes.

They glowed with a cruel intensity, and they were looking at him.

Not only could he not scream, but he felt like his feet were planted in the rocky ground. It was stupid not to run, but he couldn't. He was going to die and there was nothing he could do to stop it. As this realization came, his fear subsided and was replaced by remorse. He was sorry that he had wanted to leave his family, sorry he couldn't be there for Sasha and sorry he hadn't been a better brother and son.

The ground shook as a growl came from the black dragon and a deep growling voice filled his head. *"YOU ARE MINE!"* Then the dragon opened it huge jaws. Legon didn't even have time to register the gaping mouth flying towards him.

Pain erupted in his head as once again he snapped up, hitting the ceiling by his bed, but this time the pain was welcome. Welcome because only the living felt pain, not people who had just been eaten by a dragon. He still hadn't opened his eyes he didn't want to, just on the chance that it hadn't been a dream. He felt cold clammy hands on his neck and face.

"You're ok, Legon. It was just a dream, you're ok." The voice was Sasha's.

He opened his eyes to see her in her night gown, looking terrified. He must have been talking in his sleep or making some other noise. His heart was racing and he was covered in icy cold sweat. He started to shiver uncontrollably. Sasha sat behind him and wrapped her arm tight around him, the same way he would do to her when she was having an episode. Her hands began to warm as her fear subsided. The warmth was most welcome. He didn't feel worthy of the love and comfort, but he took it anyway. Warmth began to make its way through him as his ragged breath slowed and heart calmed.

His voice was slower to respond and he began to stammer, "I'm... I'm his... he's going to get me... I, I . . ."

"It's ok, it's ok, it was just a dream, you're fine. No one is going to get you." Her voice was calm and reassuring as she stoked his hair. He leaned back against her and forced his body to relax.

"I was on a mountain and…"

"Not tonight. You can tell me in the morning. Now relax."

After a bit his heart resumed its normal rhythm and he felt himself start to drift. He was so tired. He felt Sasha run her fingers through his hair one last time and he fell asleep.

* * * * * * *

Sasha did not fall asleep. She sat gently stroking his hair, wide awake and her mind so full it almost hurt. She was scared. Legon had been having some horrible dream and she knew it wasn't the first. She heard him talking in his sleep last night or the night before, she couldn't remember, and tonight when she heard him she had gotten up to go to his room. She knew that it was not uncommon for people to talk in their sleep, but it was what he was saying and doing that sent fear coursing through her.

When she entered the room he was whimpering almost like a little child who was hurt, but soon he was thrashing in his bed, his arms flying around and his legs pumping like he was running. He was covered in sweat and the look on his face was one of panic. As if this wasn't enough, he had all of a sudden stopped moving and just laid trembling in bed. Up to this point she'd planned on waking him up so he could relax and go to sleep, but it seemed to be over. She began to turn when Legon sat up in bed and looked right at her.

"You are mine."

He then laid back down.

The hoarse voice was not his, and she thought that it wasn't aimed at her, but rather at him. As soon as his head hit the pillow he jolted back up fully awake and terrified.

She wanted to know more but he needed to sleep. She could find out more later. Something inside her whispered that this had to do with his tattoo, but she didn't know how.

Her parents had explained to Sasha how Legon had actually been found early in the evening while Legon was still out walking. She was horrified to hear what had taken place, and her fears only seemed to get worse when he walked in, covered in dirt with vomit on his chin. No one had said anything, but they all were worried. He had also found her diary, which she assumed he had found at their picnic site. She had a hunch that he read part of it, but she wasn't sure how much or what. She didn't mind if he saw the entries on her normal days, but on the days she had an episode .... She didn't plan on asking him about it because she believed that he had read it only to figure out whose it was.

Her mind came back to his former parents and more importantly his tattoo. It couldn't be covered up forever, and she knew that at some point in time someone would see it and know that there was something off. The tattoo had always elicited comments and questions before, but no one suspected that it had been put there by magic. But now if anyone saw the purple crest they would know instantly. When her father told her how he found Legon, he had shuddered when he said they found a body. He refused to talk about it more. She really didn't care to think of what he had found there.

The more Sasha thought about it, the more sure she was that they were looking for Legon and that his mother was hiding in the woods to keep her son safe and out of notice. No matter what the past had been, Legon was in trouble now. He would not be able to go anywhere near a large city and it was probably not a good idea for him to be in the empire at all. He would probably be fine in most small towns; people there seemed to keep to themselves more and there were less government officials at any rate. He could always go to the resistance and find sanctuary with them. The resistance was to the south, and if he started that way he would find either them or the Elves in a few months.

But Sasha knew that Legon would not be willing to go that far from Salmont, if for no other reason than for her sake. She knew that he was planning on going to Salkay because he could still help their family with taxes.

She felt his head turn a bit. She looked down at her sleeping brother. She was going to miss him a lot. Tears started to form in her eyes. It was hard for her to think of Legon in trouble, and it was worse because she couldn't do anything about it. She hoped vainly to herself that perhaps he wasn't in that much trouble after all, that he had been living in Salmont for seventeen years and nothing had happened thus far. Still, there was a sense of foreboding in her. She felt that something bad was coming, and coming fast. As she thought this a slight breeze from the open window played on the back of her neck as if to enforce the point. The life she had always known was over, and she wasn't sure what lay ahead. Sasha felt her eyelids getting heavy and felt her mind become fuzzy. She tried to fight the feeling. She had to stay up. She needed to figure this out.

No matter what she tried, sleep was coming for her and there was nothing to do about it. Her head tilted to the side, resting on the top of Legon's, and she fell asleep.

Chapter Five
Truths Revealed

"Perspective is one of the strongest dictators of self. How we perceive ourselves is paramount; though this is considered a trite argument to make, it is nevertheless true. Does that mean that we cannot combat our current state, or in some way lessen or increase our standing in the world by merely changing our perspective of ourselves? Perhaps."
- The Wondering Way (Author Unknown)

Legon awoke leaning against a sleeping Sasha, her head against his. He could feel her breath against the top of his head. *I hope she didn't drool in her sleep,* he though. As he started to move his head she woke, and they both sat up. He tilted his head to the side and heard the satisfying sound of his neck pop.

He turned to look at Sasha. "That was a bad one last night. I don't think I've ever had a dream like that."

"I figured as much. You were thrashing in your bed and making all sorts of noise when I came in. What was the dream about?"

He relayed what he remembered of the dream to her. She listened and spoke when he got to the part about the dragon speaking to him. "I remember that you sat up and looked right through me and said 'You are mine' in this growling voice."

"I did? That was the worst part, and then right after that it ate me, or at least I think it did. I woke up."

He left out what he was feeling right before the dragon spoke. It ran through his head and he felt a twinge of shame. Sasha had stayed with him all night with only the wall for a pillow, and just a few hours ago he had been thinking about leaving her to save his own neck.

She paused "We were talking last night about what your tattoo may mean."

Of course they were. It wasn't a new topic of conversation, but changing colors would have added a new wrinkle.

"And?"

"Well I guess Arkin told our parents a few years back that Elves only marked their own. So he thinks you're part Elf."

He tensed. "And why didn't mom tell me this yesterday?"

She looked at him. "Well, we don't know for sure, and do you think you could have handled it? Was it worth adding more stress to your day over a theory from the town carpenter?"

If he was being honest, the answer was no. He couldn't have handled it. But how was Arkin an expert on this?

"Do you agree with Arkin?"

She shrugged. "Maybe. I don't know. Think about it: what do we know about Elves? They are like Iumenta."

"Yeah, but I don't see how that connects."

"You are stronger and faster then anyone your size, Legon. You seem to have an edge at everything. Maybe that has to do with your parents."

He was about to protest, then thought about walking home in the dark last night. "Maybe you're right. It just doesn't seem real to me, you know?"

She laughed. "No, I don't know, but it's something to consider. Don't be mad. We didn't say anything horrible about you last night. It's just a theory, and one I don't think our parents think is possible."

He shook his head. "I'm going to get ready and help dad for a bit, but after lunch I want to go see Arkin. I need answers and I think he can give them to me."

She nodded her agreement, got up and walked out of his room, shutting the door behind her. He could tell there was something on her mind. She was normally talkative in the mornings, and he thought that she would want to talk about the news of his adoption and his dream, but she didn't. She seemed distant.

He knew that his parents had told Sasha about how he came to their family last night; he could see it in her eyes. She knew and it scared her. He wondered what that fear was. He wouldn't blame her if she was scared of him; after all, if he was marked by an Elf it would be understandable.

He was on his feet and putting on his work clothes. He tried to push everything out of his mind. He could feel another headache coming on and he didn't want it to get worse. He was getting so many headaches lately; he made a mental note to talk to his mother about it and walked out of his room and down the hall.

It was early, and only Sasha and he were up. Sasha's door was shut and Legon figured she was getting ready for her day. He walked down to the lower level of the house, went out the door and turned to the shop. *Work will be good for me. It will take my mind off things for now,* he thought. There wasn't much to do today, but Legon began to work as if he had a week's worth to do. After an hour or so his father came in.

"How are you today, son? Sasha told me that she mentioned the Elf thing to you, and you should know that I don't buy into it." He looked tired and Legon figured no one in the family had slept well last night.

"I'm fine, I guess. I don't know, maybe I'm not fine. It just seems like…" He struggled, not sure what to say. It was hard to fathom the news that he had received yesterday and this morning, and he was feeling like his life up to this point had been a lie, but he didn't want to say this to his father; he knew this would cause unnecessary pain.

"I guess I just don't know what or who I am now. I mean, before, I was a butcher in Salmont, and in a few months I was going to be a butcher somewhere else, but now…"

"You're my son, like you have always been and always will be. It's not your blood that matters; it's what you make of yourself." His father spoke with just the right blend of warmth and sternness. Legon began to talk but was cut off. "You are not a trade. You are a person. You are a person, and a good one at that. You cannot look at your life as just the work you do. If you do you will lose your mind. This life is about the relationships you have and lives you touch. So what if you might be part Elf? That's nothing to be ashamed of. If anything you should be proud."

"Yeah, but the queen hates the Elves…"

His father gave a hoarse laugh. "What, and you think she likes humans? We're animals to the Iumenta, that's it. The Elves are kind and I wish it was them that we served, not the Iumenta. All they are is a drain on the land."

Edis walked over to Legon and placed his hands on his shoulders. "You are my son." His tone had finality in it, a tone that made it clear that there was no greater thing in the world than to be Edis's son.

Legon felt himself relax a bit. He hadn't noticed it but his whole body had become rigid.

"What is going to happen to me?" he asked.

"What do you mean?" asked Edis concernedly.

"My body - what's going to happen to it if I am part Elf? Something will happen, right?" He didn't say anything about last night, but after that, Arkin's theory seemed pretty likely to him.

"I don't know. Elves are much different than humans. Truth be told, I didn't even know we could have children with each other. Its Arkin's theory - he has lots of those. He may know, but I doubt it."

"Dad," Legon began, "how does Arkin know so much? You have to admit his theories tend to prove actuate." Edis's brow furrowed and Legon could almost see his mind working.

"Honestly, I don't know, and I don't want to. Some things are better left a mystery, in my mind."

After that they got on with their day. They didn't talk much. Legon got the impression that his father was somehow a little embarrassed by the boldness of his speech. Legon spent most of the morning away from the front counter as he wasn't in a mood to talk to people, but he was happy by the time they went in for lunch. He had gotten a lot done and wouldn't need to come back after lunch, which freed him to go to Arkin's. When they got in, Sasha was sitting at the table. She looked surprised to see them back so early. She got up quickly. "Is everything ok?"

"Yes, we just got a lot done today," their father said, taking a seat.

"Oh, well are you hungry? Do you want something?" she began to get up and move to the kitchen.

"No Sash, I'm not hungry yet," Legon said.

His father was looking around the room. "Neither am I. Where is your mother?"

"Shopping. She said she needed something, I didn't ask what." She paused and looked at Legon. "Are you still going to see Arkin today?"

"Yeah. Are you still up for going?"

"Yes, if you're ok with it."

"You're more than welcome. I think it would be nice to have you there. Let me change and we can go," he said as he got up and walked to the stairs.

Soon he was out of sight and Sasha looked at her father. "Is he ok?"

He took his time answering. "I don't know. I think so, but I think he just needs understanding and answers right now. I can give him the understanding, at least."

Legon came back downstairs in a pair of brown pants and an off-white shirt. He walked up to the table. "Are you ready?"

She got up and started to walk to the door. He joined her and waved to Edis. When they got outside the air was dank. The previous day's moisture still clung to the streets and shady part of buildings. There was activity everywhere. They saw Margaret walking, red hair bouncing in time with her strides, holding two large bundles under her arms. They waved at her as she moved along and she nodded her greeting. They made their way down the streets of the town until they reached Arkin's shop.

Up to this point they hadn't spoken. As they approached the shop Sasha tugged on his arm. He turned to look at her; she looked apprehensive. He noticed the dark blue dress she was wearing seemed to make her eyes look pale and somber, and she held his gaze for a moment before speaking. "I don't think you should tell Arkin about your dream."

He looked surprised. "Why not?"

"Because there is a lot that we and our parents haven't been told, and I know Arkin is a good person, but still, we don't really know who we can trust." As she spoke he could see fear in her eyes. It was obvious that she was planning on taking every precaution. The look also told him what had been on her mind for the last few days. He suspected that she had considered every possibility she could come up with.

"And how will we know if we can trust him?" For some reason he didn't question her unwillingness to trust others. Sasha was good at reading people and he trusted her judgment.

He also still had the conversation from the other day in his mind, the day when Arkin seemed unwilling to disclose information about his hunting trip. He also knew there had to be something up with the carpenter because of his mother going over to tend to him. Arkin didn't make mistakes. He never got hurt, not a scratch. There was something going on with him, that was for sure. It could be innocent or it could be bad, but either way it was wise to not divulge information that wasn't necessary.

"Good thinking Sash. I'll follow your lead."

She smiled a bit and walked to the door. Once again Legon was shocked by the lack of saw dust in the air. It was after noon! It should be hard to breathe in the place by now. He also noticed the table that was there from the day before hadn't been touched. The shop looked exactly the same as it had the last time they were there.

"Arkin? Arkin, are you here?" called Sasha, raising her voice.

"Oh, hello you two. How are you? I suppose you're here for the tea I promised," Arkin said, walking into the shop from the back alley.

He smiled tightly at them. He clearly wasn't happy they were there.

* * * * * * *

Sasha noted the lack of dust in his hair and face. His clothes and apron would always have dust in them from the previous day's work, but the lack of it on his face and hair showed that he hadn't been working at all today. She found this odd. Arkin was a hard worker and he had said the other day that he was busy and needed to get stuff done, but he didn't look like a carpenter that had been hard at work.

"Yes, we came for tea," she said. She figured that he would ask them to come back another day but she wanted to play this smoothly.

"Ah… you guys are going to be disappointed, but this is a bad time. Perhaps next week?"

She broke in. "We know about Legon's mother." She tried to keep her voice conversational.

"You know… Edis and Laura told you then?" he spluttered.

"We know you were there and we know that you are busy, but we need to talk to you Arkin. What's wrong? It's obvious that you haven't been working in the last few days. The air in the shop and your face are free of dust." As she spoke she gestured around the room.

Legon was surprised by the tone in her voice and how she went from being sweet and nice to formal without skipping a beat. He could see that she had taken Arkin off guard. He would have to give in to her requests or face interrogation about whatever he was up to.

"Ok, ok I'll talk about how we found you. Let me close the shop," Arkin said with resignation. He walked over the main door and clicked the lock and pulled some blinds down over the windows.

"Thank you Arkin. What kind of tea do you have?" asked Sasha sweetly.

Arkin chuckled. "The same as always: mint, or mint." He smiled.

"Ooo, I think I'll have the mint," said Legon.

"I'm going to change it up and go with the mint," chimed in Sasha.

"Ok you two, let's go in my house. I don't have anything for tea out here"

They walked out of the back door and turned right to walk in the back of Arkin's house. The inside was immaculate.

Everything had its place. The wood in the house was a light pine which was a change from the normal dark color on the inside of most houses. The air smelled of cinnamon despite the lack of candles or incense. The house had the same layout as Legon's, with a large table in the center of the main room and a kitchen towards the back. It was in the kitchen that you could see how tidy the house was. The counter was wiped clean, and all of the knives and other cooking articles were grouped together in a neat line. Everything was perfect, and it was obvious that Arkin would see if even one thing was moved. On either side of the fireplace were paintings of landscapes of the mountains. Above the mantelpiece there was nothing. The table at which they sat was made of redwood.

Sasha noticed that the table stuck out in the room. Everything in the house was light in color but the table. It was dark and red, drawing your eye when you entered. You couldn't help it. The more she thought about the house, the more she realized that it commanded respect and, moreover, action. The room led you through it, making you naturally go where the owner wanted. She had been in this house hundreds of times and never noticed the genius of it. She began to see that Arkin was much more than a carpenter.

"So Legon, you have been told how we found you," Arkin said, placing cups in front of both of them.

"Yes, and …"

"And you know what your tattoo is, don't you?" continued Arkin.

"Yes, and …," he began, but this time was stopped by the look on Arkin's face. It was somber.

"What color is it?" asked Arkin flatly.

Legon began to sputter, but Sasha silenced him by placing her hand on his. "What color is it supposed to be, Arkin? It's a tattoo." She knew that Legon's reaction had given away the fact that his tattoo had changed colors, but she wasn't planning on losing control of the conversation that easily.

"Legon, guard your reactions. I don't know what color it is, but I would venture to guess red, green or purple." Sasha could hear the change in Arkin's voice. It was obvious that he had taken control back.

Arkin was impressed with Sasha. She was smart and noticed more than she let on. She wasn't as good as him, however. Maybe in time and with some training, but not yet. *I have to figure out what they know,* he thought. "So what is it?" he said confidently.

She had lost. There was no way around it. Legon had given them away. Arkin had been waiting for today. "Purple," she said.

"I was hoping you were going to say green." She could hear the sadness in his voice.

"Why green? What's wrong with purple?" she asked in a calm but commanding tone.

"Green means that you're not part Elf. Any change in color means that you are."

"So what does that mean, Arkin?" asked Legon looking agitated but not unsurprised.

"It means that one day the Elf in you will die and you will be full blooded human. Or the day will come when the Human part will die and you will be full Elf. The change in color shows that the Elf side is winning."

She noted the resignation in his voice; he didn't want this to be true. He wanted Legon to be full human, but why? Elves were immortal. The thought came to her then: *But humans are unnoticed.* Legon was looking down at his drink. She knew the same thing was going through his mind. There was no need to ask Arkin about how or when it would happen; the day would come when he would change.

"Why does the queen hate the Elves? I need to know why she is going to hate me or why she already does," Legon said.

"I will tell you, but you need to save your interruptions to the end. I will have to give you some history and you will have to accept that what I tell you is true, and that I will not answer all of your questions. Does that work for you?"

"Yes," said Legon. Arkin turned to look at Sasha. "Yes," she said.

"There was a time when Elves were like humans. They died just like us and lived just like us. There was no magic. They were led by two Dragons, two brothers, one whose scales where white has pearl and glittered with brilliance, and the other whose scales were black as coal and pulled the light from the sky. One was good and the other evil. I don't know too much more about how they parted or what all happened, but the Elves say that when they did they used magic so strong that they can't take physical form anymore. I don't understand it, so don't ask." Arkin sipped his tea and continued.

"Up to this point only the two dragons could use magic, and after they disappeared, magic was available to all. The Elves split into the three races: the Elves, the Iumenta, and Humans. I don't know how this happened, but the Elves clam it did. The Elves were loyal to one of the brothers and the Iumenta to the other, and it was at this point that Dragons began to appear in the land. You see, if a magic user gets strong enough he will Ascend and become a dragon."

Legon always knew that Dragons were strong in magic, but now he began to appreciate just how strong. He couldn't imagine the power it would take to turn a person into what he'd seen in his dreams. He knew now that what he'd seen in his dream was one of the brothers. He didn't know how he knew this but he did, and the knowledge was frightening. Arkin was going on. Legon focused, trying to catch everything. He could think later.

"To put it simply, the Elves and Iumenta are blood enemies. The Iumenta went to the wastelands to make their home. They rebelled against anything that connected them to the Elves. There came a time, however, when they realized that humanity could be of use to them. Not only could humans be used for labor, but they could be a tool for destroying the Elves."

Sasha interrupted. "How can humans destroy the Elves? Humans are weak compared to Iumenta and Elves."

"Humans can do the dirty work," Legon answered. "They can fight and die, and that will save an Iumenta's life." The thought was disgusting to him, that one race would use another to kill its enemy. At the same time, the logical side of his mind said, *It's an effective plan if you view the fighting force as animals.*

"And humans breed faster than Elves and Iumenta so their stock will never run dry," Arkin added. "Humanity is the perfect resource. It is easy to control with magic and dragons; it will work hard, breed hard and kill your enemy. There is some extra pleasure in turning humans against Elves, as the Elves have always been advocates for our race."

Something Arkin said didn't seem to stick. "Arkin, how are we easy to control with Dragons and magic?" After Legon spoke he could see that Arkin was impressed by his perception.

"That is a good question for another time, but suffice it to say that Dragons influence the people in whatever area they are in, so the minds of those around can be turned to what the dragon desires. This is how the Iumenta took control. It was a slow process, taking over a hundred years. They won us by planning and stealth. They didn't make a military move against the Elves and free lands until they had the noose around our necks. Is there more you want to know?"

"Yes, what does Legon's tattoo mean?" asked Sasha politely. She was impressed how Arkin managed to give them a huge amount of information and not answer their question.

"Ah yes, the tattoo. I almost forgot. It's a crest, as I'm sure your parents told you. Every Elf child is given one at birth. It is put on by magic and does not cause the pain that our tattoos do when they are applied. Furthermore, it can be altered. That tattoo is unique to you and only you. The dot in the center represents your marital status. When an Elf gets married that dot is hollowed out and an exact replica of their partners tattoo is placed within. The only other thing that I have heard is that when an Elf comes of age the tattoo will change color, and that color will stay the same for the rest of their life. Now have I answered your questions?" he asked tentatively.

"Yes, thank you Arkin. We'd better go now," said Legon. When he spoke Sasha noticed him scratch above his left ear. This was a sign they made for each other to say "It's time to leave".

They had many such signs. They came up with them when they were little as a way of getting around their parents when they did something wrong. It came in handy later in life. Sasha could remember several situations that Legon told her to leave before a fight would break out, or times when she had warned him of impending danger. She didn't need the warning twice because like Legon, she could tell that Arkin was not only holding back information, but he may not have been the person they had always thought him to be. She wasn't sure if he was a threat, but she wasn't going to take the chance now.

They got up and gave their goodbyes to Arkin, who walked with them to the door. As they left he touched Sasha's arm. "I know what is going on in your head, but I'm not an enemy, and I'm not with the Iumenta. Think about it and you will see." She nodded and walked out the door.

The sun felt good as they walked out of the shop and headed towards the town's central market to get produce for dinner that night. They seemed to move with semi-awareness of the people around them, and didn't notice when people waved at them or greeted them in any way. There was so much to think about and all of it was way too big for both of them. Dinner was also a haze. None of the family seemed to want to talk. Legon originally planned on talking to Sasha that night about what they'd heard, but both agreed that they needed a good night's sleep before thinking about anything.

Sasha lay awake in bed long after Edis and Laura had fallen asleep. Her mind moved with the slow rhythm of her father's snores from the room next to hers. She was still thinking about what Arkin had said about one side of Legon dying and the other living. It sounded so... so *brutal,* she thought. She shuttered at the thought of part of herself dying. Or maybe it felt good, she wasn't sure. The concept boggled her mind.

She heard a sound to her right, coming from Legon's room. He was having another dream, and no wonder after the days news. The sound made the hair on the back of her neck stand up. There was something scary about it. She heard the whimpering and wondered which brother was coming for him tonight. She didn't know how she knew it was the two dragons, but somehow she did, and this was even more frightening to her.

She wondered if he would remember it. She thought about going and waking him up, but she stopped. *Maybe his dreams can help us figure this out,* she thought. It felt cruel to leave him, but at the same time something tugged at her mind, telling her to lay down and that all was well tonight. As this thought came to her she began to feel better about the situation and was having a hard time concentrating on the problems at hand. She was having a hard time thinking at all. It wasn't like an episode, but she felt herself losing control of her mind. *Is magic being used on me?* she thought. The feeling of emptiness tugged harder at this thought. *Well if it is, I don't think it's... it's....* She didn't finish the thought before she fell asleep. It was a deep sleep, a peaceful one, probably the most peaceful she'd had in a long time, and most certainly the most peaceful she would have in the near future.

Chapter Six
The Plan

"When I asked the master about life's movements, he told me that he likened life unto a river. When I asked what he meant he said, 'Picture yourself as a drop of water. Now see yourself on top of a great hill. Where would you like to go? What land would you like to bring life to with your moisture or, conversely, what land would you flood? Now step off the edge of the mountain and flow down; the rapids and twisting of the river is your life. Plan for the destination and the direction; after that, hang on tight.'"
-Conversations in the Garden

Sasha knelt down to pick a mushroom that was growing at the base of a tree. As she pulled it out bits of moss came with it. The moss was all over the tree's roots, which gave it the appearance of having a green rug wrapped around its base. It was still relatively early in the day. The morning dew still glistened on the plants and the air was sweet and clean. Her mother had sent to her to the woods to find certain rare mushrooms that she used for healing various ailments. Sasha placed the mushroom in a little basket that was on her shoulder and stood up. As she stood she noticed a little bean-sized black beetle crawling up the tree trunk. She smiled, not at the memory of having one of these creatures in her soup, but at the thought of getting back at Legon. More importantly, this was her last memory of a life that was innocent and seemly free of magic, Elves and Dragons.

Of course it had never really been free of these things. They had always been there and she just hadn't known about it. She wondered what else had affected her world that she was now blissfully unaware of. It had been three days since they had talked to Arkin; three days of going into each other's bedroom after their parents fell asleep to talk about what they thought was going on. Three days of Legon's nightmares. He didn't wake from them anymore, and he didn't remember details in the morning. She noticed that if she came in while it was happening and spoke to him as he slept he would calm down a bit. She felt a pit in her stomach as she thought of the years that Legon had been doing the same thing for her, the times he had needed to restrain her and spend hours comforting her. She stepped over a fallen tree and looked on the ground for more mushrooms. She found one and walked to it.

Her mother sent her mainly because she was so good at finding things in the forest. They just seemed to leap out to her. *I wonder why I'm so good at this,* she thought. *I guess it's like the games I used to play at Arkin's when I was a little girl.* Arkin had spent many days watching Sasha when her mother was busy with a patient. He had played all kinds of interesting games with her, some with memory and others with finding things. She marveled at how the games she'd played as a child now helped her as an adult. The teacher was also interesting, especially lately.

Legon and Sasha had decided that Arkin was not working for the empire and that he probably wasn't a major threat. They came to this conclusion after Legon made the observation that Arkin had taught him, Barnin, and Kovos everything they knew about fighting. It wouldn't make sense to train your enemy how to fight. He had also taught Legon everything he knew about hunting, from tracking to stalking. In truth it scared her to see that many of the skills that seemed so unique and important were taught by one person.

She continued to walk, looking for places that the mushrooms would be. They had also decided that just because Arkin wasn't an imminent threat didn't mean that he wasn't a threat. The fact was, they didn't know how Arkin knew as much as he claimed and why he had taught them so much. Their training, because they now saw it for what it was, was different for both of them. There were similarities, but no two lessons were the same. He'd used memory games with both, so they both could remember everything with crystal clarity, and he had taught Legon how to fight, and fight well.

Legon and Kovos went over to Arkin's a lot as youngsters to learn how to fight with swords. Arkin would let them fight with wooden staves from the shop and gave them pointers. Kovos came out on top with the blade, although Legon was also extremely good. Arkin also taught them hand to hand combat. They always assumed that he did this because of how often Kovos and Legon got into fights with people about Sasha, but the training was too good for brawlers. Nobody in town could hold a candle to either man. There was so much more going on that she couldn't wrap her head around.

She diverted her attention to some birds pulling worms out of the ground. She felt for the worm. It was how she felt, like she was being pulled out of her world and thrown into much larger and more dangerous one. She could only hope that, unlike the worm, she wouldn't be eaten.

* * * * * * *

Legon was tired. He hadn't gotten much sleep, and from what Sasha had told him, the sleep that he was getting was haunted by nightmares. They didn't wake him up anymore, and he didn't remember much of them in the morning, but he knew that they were still there but somehow a bit better.

He hefted a pork shoulder onto the counter, reached for a knife and began to cut the meat. He should be thinking about what was going on with him and his Elven side, but right now he didn't give a heap of dung about it. The only thing on his mind this morning was Sasha. He was going to come of age in one month, and that meant he was going to have to leave regardless of whether he became an Elf or not. He decided to go with the original plan of moving to another town and starting a life there, and if he became an Elf he would cross that bridge then. He would avoid large cities and probably move to a new territory to ensure that no one would know anything about his past.

The biggest problem was Sasha. Kovos was right; it would be impossible to get enough money to the family before next spring. She was going to have to come with him and Kovos. There was really no way around it.

He turned to his father. "I'm taking her with me." His father didn't need an explanation. He knew what Legon meant.

"Are you sure? It's a big sacrifice. You won't be able to get married or start a family of your own until she gets married or is able to live on her own, and neither seems likely," he said, turning to look at his son.

"I know, but it's the only way to give her a chance. I don't like the idea. I don't know what my life holds, and that may put her in danger, but we know what will happen if I don't take her," he said flatly.

His mind was made up. Sasha's situation was precarious from any angle. If she stayed here she would be made a slave; if she came with Legon there was a chance that she would get hurt.

There was a little comfort in the thought of Kovos coming along. He knew that if things got bad he could always send Sasha to Kovos and that would at least give her a shot. He explained this to his father, who gave a deep sigh after he was done explaining.

"You think it's a good idea, I take it?"

His father took his time answering. "No, I think it's a bad one, but it's also the only way. Your mother and I have always hoped that you would take Sasha with you when you left, but we didn't want to press you one way or the other. It had to be your call because you are the one who has to pay the price." His face was somber. Legon could tell that he hated the thought of either of his kids being dealt a bad hand in life.

"I understand. Don't worry dad, I'll take care of her. I'm going to try and tell her later this week. She'll fight me on it, but if you and mom back me then Sasha will cave in eventually."

"You have our support, but we hate to have this happen to you two."

"It's fine. Everything will work out."

In truth part of him was happy at the thought of Sasha coming with him, but the other part was sad, not because of the future that he was probably giving up, but because he knew there was a hard road ahead and he didn't want Sasha's life to be any harder than it already was.

He decided to tell her the next day. He would take her on a picnic so even if she got upset, she wouldn't be able to walk away and lock herself in her room. He knew that this was going to make her mad, not because she had little choice in the matter, but because she would see it as Legon throwing his life away. The biggest argument that he would have to make was that it was very unlikely that he would be getting married any time soon, if for no other reason than he didn't know if he was going to be Elf or human and so he would always be in just a bit of danger. He finished with the pork and began to clean up. They would go in for lunch soon.

When they entered the house Sasha was home, standing over a pot and stirring. She turned and smiled at them as they walked in. "I hope you guys are hungry. I found some great mushrooms in the forest that I made soup with.

"That sounds good, honey. Where is your mother?" asked Edis, taking a seat.

"She had to go over to see someone who fell off a horse and broke their arm or something. I don't know much about it," she said, carrying over the pot and placing it in the center of the table.

Now seemed as good a time as any. "It's been nice lately," Legon began. "Would you be up for another picnic, Sash?"

"Yeah, that sounds good. When were you thinking?"

"Oh I don't know, how about tomorrow? We can go for lunch. How does that sound?"

* * * * * * *

Sasha thought about Legon's proposal. There was more to this invite than just a pleasant outing, she could see it. Legon could mask his feelings well from most people, but not her. She wasn't sure who the cover was for. "Yeah that works great," she said, smiling.

"Good," he said with a slightly relieved smile. He spooned some soup into his mouth

"Wow, Sash, you really are something else! This is amazing!"

"You're welcome. I'm glad you like it." She could see that this reaction was the truth. He did like the soup, which was saying something - Legon hated mushrooms. After lunch Legon and her father went back to the shop. Sasha stayed in the house cleaning up.

She was trying to figure out what was on Legon's mind. He seemed tense when he had asked her to go on a picnic. She had tried to use one of their hand gestures to figure out what was wrong, but he had only told her to wait. She didn't like waiting, not when her brother was holding back from her. There could have been a thousand reasons why he was hesitant, but she couldn't think of one that made sense.

The rest of the day and night passed without incident. Sasha was having a harder time sleeping than before, and she could hear in the room next to her that Legon was too.

By eleven the next day she had lunch prepared and was wrapping two glasses into cloth so they wouldn't break. She heard the front door open.

"Hey Sash, are you ready?" came Legon's voice.

"Yep, I've got the food, the cedar and this time the glasses." she held up the cloth-covered glasses and smiled.

Their mother was sitting at the table scribbling something on paper and she looked up. "'This time'? You two haven't been drinking from the bottle have you?"

"What are you talking about mom? You know you can't work and listen at the same time," Legon said.

"Sorry dear, you're right. I shouldn't have been eavesdropping. I know you two wouldn't do that," she said, looking back down at her paper.

* * * * * * *

Legon saw Sasha give him a thumbs-up. It was good she wasn't paying full attention to them or they would be getting a lecture about drinking out of the bottle right now. It was a pet peeve of hers. Sasha nodded towards the back door and Legon walked over to her and out of the house. They were greeted by the smell of all the fields in full bloom. The sun was out and the sky was clear. She was wearing a bright white top with her hair pulled back. The white cloth seemed to make her cheeks glow. She was on his right and the basket with food was slung around her right shoulder.

"Do you want me to carry that?" he asked

"Yes, thank you," she said with a smile, passing him the basket. He placed it on his left shoulder.

They were entering the woods and he felt the air get cooler as the smell of the woods intensified. It was a nice smell, and he liked it better than the smell of town. It was funny that he only noticed that the town had a scent to it when he left it and was surrounded by a new smell. *There is so much around us we don't see until we leave it,* he thought. They were climbing the hill to their favorite spot. When they broke though the trees they saw the town in full swing. Little lines of wispy smoke rose from most of the buildings, as well as the thick greasy line that was Kovos' and Brack's smith. They sat down on the grass and began to pull out lunch. Sasha unwrapped the glasses and uncorked the cedar.

"Are you going to tell me what's going on now, or do I have to wait?" she asked not unpleasantly.

Legon sighed. He figured it was better to get over with now than later.

"Yeah, we can get to it. Listen, I can't be in this territory anymore. My best chance at not being noticed is going someplace where no one knows me or this town. That means that it will be rare that I can visit here. My life could get dangerous and I want to protect everyone, including you, from that."

Her eyes narrowed and a crease crossed the space in between. "Ok, that makes sense. So what's the part I'm going to have a hard time with?"

"I want you to come with me. Now wait, hear me out," he said as she pulled back from him. "Look, we both know what's going to happen next spring. I was originally going to try and get money here before taxes, but that isn't going to work. Furthermore, you aren't safe here. I have no choice but to leave, and unless you want to be a slave or killed by some idiot here you don't have a choice either," he said, trying to be calm and reassuring in his tone.

The look on her face was blank. He could see her body becoming more and more rigid. He knew she was upset with him.

"So what, I come with you and then what? What do we become? Legon, don't you get it? I will be seen as a freak everywhere I go. Nobody will ever want me as a wife and I will never be able to support myself. You'll be stuck with me. I won't let you throw your life away!" she said angrily, but by the end there was sadness in her voice. It tore at him knowing the pain she felt, but that's why she needed to come. That was why he needed to be with her, to protect and shield her from the sorrows of the world.

"Look, we would be going someplace new and people won't know anything about you, so you could be a seamstress or something. We can keep it quiet. Also, I'm not throwing my life away. I have to keep my head down until I find out what I'm going to end up being. Look, my way has more danger than I want you in, but staying here is worse. You are not going to be hurt by someone in town, nor are you going to become a slave. Do you get me?"

* * * * * * *

Sasha heard the resolve in his voice. She did 'get him'; the tone in his voice made it clear that if she stayed he would too, and when the day came that the collectors came for her, he would die fighting them off. She didn't have a choice, and in truth she did want to go with him. She knew that there was going to be a high chance of danger and she understood that he didn't want her in it, but he didn't have a choice.

"Ok, fine. You made your point. When do we leave?" She was surprised at how it made her feel better.

Legon leaned over and hugged her tightly, kissing her on the cheek. "Thank you, Sash."

She laughed. "Thank you for what? Why are you hugging me? You had to know I would give in."

"Yeah I knew, but I thought I was going to have to fight you for awhile and pull the 'mom and dad think it's a good idea' card on you. Now we can actually have a nice lunch."

"The mom and dad card, huh? So you talked to them about it, did you?" It was no surprise that they would gang up on her, she thought wryly.

He didn't respond, instead pouring the cedar into the glasses and handing her one.

* * * * * * *

Legon could feel the tension between them drop. It was nice to sit at the top of the hill looking out over the town, eating lunch. As he thought this a slight shiver ran up his spine. Not too long ago he had looked out over this town in pitch black and seen everything. He knew now that it must have been the Elven side of him that night. The thing that confused him was why he was having dreams with the black dragon. After all, he was part Elf, not Iumenta, and that meant that he should belong to the good brother, not the bad.

"I'm going to talk to Kovos today and tell him that I'm going to head away from the Salez territory and that you're coming with me."

"Ok. Do you still think that he will want to go with us?"

He took a sip of cedar. "I think he will, but I want his input on what part of the empire he wants to live in. I think he'll want to go to the south where it's warmer. That could be good for us too, in case we need to leave the empire."

Sasha paused for a moment as she thought. "That's good. If we get into trouble we will be closer to the Elves, and the people in that part of the empire aren't as loyal to the queen."

"Good. I'm glad we agree on that. Let's pack up. I want to find Kovos," Legon said as he stood up.

"You should tell him about your tattoo. He needs to know everything if he's coming with us. He's earned that right." Legon nodded and reached down to help her up.

They walked back down to the house. As soon as they could see it, Legon headed off towards Kovos's. He moved quickly and with a bounce in his step. The thought of having Sasha with him made the future seem a bit less doubtful.

It didn't take him long to get to the smithy. When he entered he found Kovos and Brack hard at work. He was surprised to see Kovos working on what looked like a sword.

"What are you working on?" Legon yelled over the persistent roar of the furnace.

"I'm making myself a sword… I don't want to put up with you anymore… sorry man." Kovos gave him a wicked smile.

Legon laughed. "Shouldn't you learn how to use it first?"

Kovos was a much better swordsman than him, and he knew that if they ever got into a real sword fight he would lose. Kovos didn't have a sword of his own; he always used his father's. The one Kovos was making looked to be a hand and half broadsword. He could see that the blade was almost done and that he was putting the finishing touches on the edge.

Legon had always had a hard time thinking of a broadsword as a 'blade', because they weren't incredibly sharp. They could cut through an arm or leg that wasn't protected by chainmail, but the blades could not be as sharp as a knife because they would chip in a fight, and even then it would take incredible strength to go through chainmail and plate armor. They could pierce leather armor, but it was the force behind the blow that did the work. The only truly sharp part of the blade was the tip, but other than that they were about as sharp as an axe.

Kovos was running the new blade across a grinding stone and seemed to be happy with it. He held it out for Legon to inspect. He was impressed right away. The sword's handle was wire wrapped, the hilt was cross shaped and the pommel was a large ball that could be used to hit your opponent. All in all it was a fine weapon. He turned it in his hands, feeling the balance of the blade. The weight was good and the blade was straight. Kovos had gone above and beyond by etching flames up the flat side of the blade.

"Flames? Are you serious?" Legon asked.

Kovos took the sword and inspected it. "Is there something wrong with them? Did I mess one up?" He almost held the sword against his face as he looked for the mistake.

"Yeah, you put flames on it. I mean, it was fun to put on wooden staves when we were kids, but flames on a real sword? You have got to be kidding me. Are you planning on your opponent laughing to death?" Legon was smiling at Kovos.

"I hate you. Now what do you want?"

"We need to talk."

"Whoa there buddy. I don't mean to sound rude, but I just see you as a friend. Sorry, I don't go that way. Sasha will be so heartbroken when she finds out . . ." Kovos began, trying to look like he was wary of Legon.

"Shut up! I don't mean like that!" Legon shook his head but gave a small laugh.

Kovos laughed. "Let me tell dad I'm stepping out."

Kovos walked over to Brack and said something Legon couldn't hear, and he doubted Brack heard either as the man pointed over to a set a clamps and nodded his head vigorously. For a moment it looked like Kovos was going to try and tell his dad that he was stepping out again, but then decided otherwise. He motioned for Legon to go out the back door. The new sword gleamed in the sunlight, and Legon had to admit that, flames or not, it did look good.

Inwardly he thought, *It's a good thing he has that. We may need it in the months to come.*

* * * * * * *

Kovos looked at his friend. "So what's up?" Now in the light it was obvious that there was something wrong. He could see that Legon was trying to figure out what to say and how to say it.

"Come on, what's up?" he asked again. Legon started to talk.

"You know that tattoo on my back?"

"Yeah, the strange looking thing?"

"Yeah… well, take a quick look at it."

Kovos frowned and motioned for Legon to turn around. He came and lifted up the back of his shirt. He looked where the dark green tattoo was supposed to be and felt his breath catch in his chest. He looked harder at the now purple mark, as if by doing this it would somehow change its appearance. For a fraction of a second he thought Legon was playing a joke on him, but the look on his face told him this was no joke.

"What did that? Please don't tell me magic."

Legon's answering silence told him more than he wanted to know. He felt a strange sensation in his stomach, the same he got every time he'd gotten in trouble as a little kid.

"Ok, lay it on me."

Legon relayed the story to him, a story that, if he hadn't just seen the purple tattoo, he wouldn't have believed. He heard about Legon being part Elf and his dead mother, what he might turn into, and way more than his mind could wrap itself around right then. At the end Legon appeared to be feeling better. Kovos rolled the new information around in his mind. He needed more time to think about this. He thought that paying Emma a visit might help.

The Plan

"Ok, so how does this affect me?" he asked, not unkindly.

"Sasha is going to come with me when I leave. You were right - anything that might happen to me and her on the road is better than what will happen if she stays here. How it effects you is this: I understand if you don't want to go with us, and if you do we would like to go somewhere south, but if that doesn't work for you then…" he said, tapering off.

He was surprised by the in the pleading look on his friend's face. Legon was tough, and if he was this upset he must be expecting the worst. Kovos knew Legon would go to any length to protect Sasha, and would go south regardless of what he had to say about it. He also felt worried at the look on Legon's face. If Legon was scared or worried about something then it had to be bad. A visit to Emma was definitely in order. Kovos only felt a moment's hesitation in his head.

"The story you just told me is one of the most messed up things I've ever heard, and a smart man would tell you to shove off, but . . ."

Legon interrupted, "But you're not a smart man."

"Lucky for you, I'm not. You're my best friend, and if it's a question of sticking with you, then you know the answer." Kovos smiled and stretched his arms. "I think I'm going to enjoy the warmer weather in the southlands. And I hear the women wear less clothes down there."

Legon laughed. "They do not, and even if they do, I doubt it's the ones you want."

Kovos chuckled. This was probably true. "I'm going to get back to work. We'll talk later about when were going to leave. I won't tell anyone about your freaky back, don't worry." As he said this he turned and walked back into the shop.

As Legon headed home he felt better. For the first time he felt a slight edge of excitement come over him at the thought of the adventure that Sasha, Kovos, and himself were soon to have.

Chapter Seven
The Hunt

"Our instincts keep us alive and out of trouble, but sometimes they are wrong. Sometimes they lead us away from trouble that is good for us and others. The question is this: When is it a good idea to trust those instincts? Certainly they aren't always wrong; if anything they are rarely wrong, but then again, that depends on your definition of right."
-Tales of the Traveler

Kovos' feet hit the ground hard. He looked up into the smiling face of Emma in the window. Her sable hair was playing around her face in the dawn breeze. He couldn't see her brown eyes but he knew they were looking right at his. Even at this time in the morning with almost no light, her smile made his heart leap a bit. He waved and got on his way. These little visits they had were nice. There was something about waking up next to her he loved, and there was the excitement of her parents being in the room next door. Emma's dad hated Kovos with every ounce of his being, and if he knew that once a week or so Kovos was spending the night with his daughter he would probably try to kill him.

That wasn't why Kovos went over, though. There was something about Emma; she was always in his head. He knew she was probably "the one", and that scared him just a bit. He was leaving soon and wasn't sure she would join him. He thought she would, but he had been too much of a coward to ask last night, and it would have been perfect. She had told him that she loved him right before they fell asleep. He should have asked then, but he couldn't change that now. It didn't help that her parents didn't like him, but Kovos' father had gotten over that hurdle back when he was courting. He had been shot in the arm with an arrow while running away from his now father in law. Kovos hoped that wouldn't happen with him.

No one was up yet, so he was a little surprised to hear the sound of horses in the street. As he turned the corner he saw five of the queen's soldiers on horseback, presumably looking for a place to rest.

One of the men called out to him. "Hey you, come over here."

He did as he was told. The man's face was a blur to Kovos. The sun was coming up right in front of him. "What can I do for you?" he asked sincerely. He didn't fear the queen's men. He was a good fighter; he also didn't think they had a reason to bother him.

"We're here looking for a man about your age," the soldier said menacingly.

There was a hint of hesitation in Kovos' voice when he spoke this time. "Ok, can you tell me his name or what he looks like?"

"We don't know his name or what he looks like, but we'll know him when we see him. Do you have any tattoos?"

"No," said Kovos, his mind racing to figure out what these men were up to.

"I don't believe you. Take off your shirt." As he said this, another one of the soldiers who'd circled behind him reached out and started to pull at his shirt. Kovos pulled away, taking the garment off on his own. He was mad now. *Who do they think they are?* he thought to himself.

"Whoa there, buddy. You keep this up and you're going to have to buy me dinner."

"Shut up," said the soldier with a sneer. "Is there anything there?" he asked the soldier behind Kovos. The other soldier shook his head.

"Well then, I guess you're not who we're looking for. Do you know anyone who has a tattoo on his back, someone around your age?" asked the soldier.

"What, am I not your type?" He was always more confident and stupid after seeing Emma. These were certainly not men to be toyed with, and he knew that he was walking a fine line. A few of the soldiers laughed at his comment, so he knew that he was all right for now.

"No, you're not. Sorry to disappoint you, but do you know anyone with a tattoo? I'm not in the mood for games."

"Not around my age. A few of the old guys have them…"

"Well, if you do see someone with one you'll tell us, won't you?"

Kovos just nodded his head. This seemed to satisfy them and they continued on their way. He needed to find Legon. It was clear that these men were looking for him. But the men were already heading toward Legon's house. Kovos thought he could go around the town, but he wanted the cover of people going about their daily business. The soldiers would probably go to the town center and start asking around. He headed home to get changed so the next time they saw him he would be harder to recognize. He would also drag Keither along so it would just look like he was out with his brother running errands. Legon would be safe for now. People in town would be slow to talk, and Legon didn't venture into the town center often.

* * * * * * *

Sasha came out of a restless sleep. She had been waking up every few hours with lists of things to do rushing through her head and an eerie feeling that not all was well. She decided to get up and on with her day. The sun was coming up now and she wasn't going to get any sleep anyway.

She rolled out of bed and began to get dressed. There was a lot that needed to get done. Late last night she came to the conclusion that her and Legon needed to be able to leave at the drop of a hat. After that the lists had started to run constantly in her mind. The thing was, they weren't just leaving to go camping for a few days, they were leaving for good, and if they were forced to leave quickly they would need to pack light. This was a problem because, when it came right down to it, they needed to take a lot or they would be unable to start a new life somewhere.

She paused for a moment to decide what she wanted to wear for the day. She settled on an earthy green skirt and white blouse. She inspected herself in the mirror. It wasn't good. There were huge bags under her eyes and her face was pale and looked a little odd to her. She leaned closer to the little mirror above the vanity. As she looked she noticed a slight twitch beneath her left eye. *That's odd, I wonder what it...* she began to think, but the thought stopped as she felt her body become rigid and her vision blur.

There was the sound of something hitting the ground and she felt incredible pain all over her body. She was faintly aware of herself on the ground thrashing about, but the pain was so bad she couldn't think any more. She had to be dying. And then she thought and felt nothing as the episode shut down her conscious mind.

She awoke to the usual scene: Legon was holding her, her parents were fussing about. A dull pain in her left hip told her were she had hit the ground. She didn't remember much about it and was still trying to get her bearings. It felt like her mind was disconnected until she heard Legon's calming voice. As his voice came, most of her mind came back with it, like somebody had uncovered a candle or removed a blindfold. This wasn't uncommon. She had never told anyone in the family, but she noticed that if Legon was around after an episode her mind seemed to start back up faster then if he wasn't. Stranger still, she knew that even though the episodes made her unconscious, she sometimes had flickers of thought or images, but they were just flickers, and only when Legon was there.

"Sash, Sash are you ok? Are you back?" he said concernedly.

"Ye… yeah I'm back. How long was I out?"

"Only for a moment, dear. We heard you hit the floor," said her mother. Sasha tried to raise herself from the floor.

"No honey, just wait a minute before you try and get up," came her father's voice.

Sasha raised her hand to block the now dazzling light that was starting to come in through the window. Everyone was still in their bedclothes. Legon was on the floor beside her. He placed his hand on her shoulder and this seemed to give her strength. Having an episode in the house was the worst. Every time it happened she got a huge bruise from hitting the hard floor. At least when it happened outside the ground was softer. A dull throb on the side of her head confirmed this.

"I'm fine now, really I am. I'll try to take it easy today. I just need to run an errand or two so it won't be bad."

"Don't worry about going out, Sash. I can pick up whatever you need when I go over to visit Kovos. I don't mind. I'm sure whatever you need is on my way." Legon squeezed her shoulder a bit in a loving way, but also one that made it clear that there was not going to be any debate. It was things like this that made her love him so much.

He had a lot on his plate, but still he was going out of his way for her.

* * * * * * *

Legon help raise Sasha from the ground and walked her to her bed. He could tell that she was a bit tender on her left side. As he steered her along he also noticed a slight tremble. The bags under her eyes made it clear to him that she hadn't gotten much sleep in the last few days, and for all he knew that may have been what had caused the episode. She lay down in bed and he got a list of the stuff she was planning on buying that day.

As he stood up he could see that there was a lot more that was on Sasha's to-do list than just getting a few odds and ends around town. He went to ask what was on her mind, but she used one of their hand gestures to tell him that they would discuss it later. This surprised him since there was no reason not to trust their parents with anything she may be planning on doing. The thought came to him that if she did say what she had planned for the day then their mother would make sure she stayed in bed to rest, but if Sasha appeared to not be fighting it then she would leave her alone and Sasha could do whatever she needed to.

"Ok, well I guess I'll go. I'll talk to you later Sash. I hope you feel better," he said as he walked to the door.

He went to his room and finished getting ready. When Sasha had started her episode Legon had put on only one sock and tossed the other aside. He reached under his bed to get the sock and put it on. Soon he was walking out into the warm morning. It felt good to be outside. He began to make his way to the town center. He would pick up the cloth Sasha needed on his way to see Kovos. As he was about half way to the town center he saw Kovos and Keither walking quickly to him. It was obvious that Kovos was flustered, but Legon wasn't sure if it was from having Keither with him or something else. He was almost dragging his brother along.

"You need to get out of here. There are soldiers looking for you," panted Kovos as he closed the last few steps to Legon.

"What do mean there are…" Legon began.

"Five soldiers stopped me this morning looking for a man around our age with a tattoo on his back. We need to get away from the town center, that's where they are." As Kovos spoke he looked over his shoulder, searching the crowded street for a threat.

Legon didn't need to be told twice. A week ago this news would have surprised him, but now…. They started to walk away from the town center when they heard a voice, one that was almost timid but full of glee. "That's the boy there, the one I told you about, the one with the demon sister." Moleth's voice rang over the sound of passing people and horses.

Legon turned to look at the woman. Standing next to her were three men in leather armor and all with the same symbol emblazoned on it, a silver many-pointed star with a green circle in the middle and a half circle in the same green around the star, and on the other side four five-pointed dark gold stars. These men were the queen's royal guard, not the half-whetted servants of Regent Kooth. These men were the real deal. The royal guard was the most highly trained human military unit in the empire. It was rumored that the royal guard was trained by Iumenta and that they had all swore undying loyalty to the queen. Failure was not in these guys' training, and Legon knew that three on two was not good odds - Kovos could fight, but Keither was more of a danger to himself than to others. As the soldiers got closer he could see from the way they were sizing them up that they too did not see Keither as a threat.

They all dressed alike. The one to the right of Moleth played with his long red beard, his blue eyes flashing everywhere. He looked to be around twenty-eight or thirty, but it was hard to tell. The one next to him walked like he was in charge, and Legon figured this man was the commander. He didn't have a full beard but he did have about four days worth of stubble. His face was scarred. The last man was young and didn't have a beard. He looked stupid, more like the trolls from stories than a man. In truth, at first glace Legon was a little surprised by how the men looked. They had more of the appearance of robbers than royal guard. Of course, Legon had never seen royal guard before, so this might be how all of them looked.

Moleth was bouncing around like an over-excited puppy. She was elated about helping the queen's men, but she was obviously wearing on them. The one standing next to her placed his hand on the hilt of his sword in a longing sort of way.

When they reached them, the man who appeared to be the commander looked at Kovos. "You don't know anyone, huh?" he said in a gruff voice.

The man turned his attention to Legon. "Take off your shirt and show us your back, boy."

This was how the whole thing was going to end. He was going to be killed or taken by the queen's men. There was no stopping it. Or was there? Moleth had decided to give her opinion on the matter one last time.

"Oh good, I have always disliked this one, he's…" she was stopped by a command from the man in front of Legon.

"Shut up, woman. You have brought to much attention to us already. If you don't be quiet on your own we will silence you," the man said, and for once Legon hoped that Moleth would use some sense and keep her mouth shut. This desire was not for his well-being, but hers. Sadly, she didn't have the sense.

"Now you wait just one moment - I helped you b…" she started.

"Shut her up!" barked the commander. Legon watched in horror as the man closest to Moleth moved behind her and in one fluid movement unsheathed his danger and brought it to her throat. Moleth became quiet in an instant and a very real fear crossed her face.

"This is what happens if you don't cooperate with us," said the commander. As if on cue, the man holding Moleth pressed the dagger hard and dragged the blade across her throat, slicing the arteries in her neck.

A gurgled scream of pain and terror rose from Moleth. Blood sprayed out of the wound, covering her front as she began to pass out from the loss of blood. Her face washed white as blood left her body, and she gave a slight twitch. The man let go of Moleth and she swayed for what seemed like an eternity before falling to the dirt.

Rage filled Legon. These men had slaughtered an innocent woman to make a point. This was an injustice that he would not stand for. He moved to his left towards the troll man. Kovos followed his lead and they both engaged their respective targets. His elbow came up to the man's temple before he got a chance to react, and Legon felt the satisfying feeling that comes with knowing that your opponent has just been knocked unconscious. Kovos went with a different tactic, kneeing the commander hard in the stomach, dropping him to the ground and then kicking him hard across the face. The last man, who up to this point had been wearing a wicked grin, came at them, but Legon and Kovos didn't get their shot at this one. To everyone's surprise, Keither screamed a horrible, insane man's scream. The three men turned to look at the boy, who no longer looked like a boy at all. There was rage in his eyes, hate pure and clear. Keither lunged for the man. He was no match for a member of the royal guard, but the soldier was taken by surprise, and Keither had a lot of weight behind him. The boy slammed into the man, sending them both to the ground, Keither on top and punching every inch he could find. Each blow did almost no damage and the soldier was getting his bearings again. As the scene progressed, a clear thought came to Legon: *Kovos said there were five men, not three.*

"We need to get out of here now!" yelled Legon, and together he and Kovos lifted Keither from the soldier. The man stumbled up, and seeing his two comrades down backed away and drew his sword. The man began to call out for help and the other two solders were getting to their feet. Legon, Kovos and Keither all turned and sprinted towards the edge of town. As they ran they could hear shouts from behind and the distant sound of hooves hitting the ground. They turned up a side street, running into people as they went. Keither tripped on a woman's skirt and fell, cutting his knee. The edge of town was right ahead, and just past that were the thick woods that surrounded Salmont.

Legon looked back as they passed the buildings that marked the end of the town. Panic took a firm hold of him as he saw five men on horses, three with swords drawn and two with bows. The two with the bows were pulling back their strings to fire.

"Arrows!" yelled Legon as he started to weave.

Kovos did likewise and the two of them pushed Keither back and forth, almost like they were trying to knock him down, but every time it looked like the boy would fall, Kovos or Legon corrected his balance. As they entered the woods Legon heard the hiss of two arrows fly past and saw them embed themselves deep in a tree. The soldiers were firing combat bows, so the arrows would be moving incredibly fast and could kill from long range. They needed to get higher into the cover of the trees. More arrows flew by, accompanied by the sound of five horses crashing through underbrush. Legon felt one of the arrows scratch his neck as it passed.

They ran, weaving through the trees, jumping over roots and logs, anything that might slow down or trip up the horses. There was yelling coming form the queen's men, but Legon couldn't tell what they were saying. All he heard was his own panting and the panting of the other two. His legs were on fire and his body stung from hitting branch after branch. He could see Kovos' white shirt getting speckled with blood from the many scratches.

Next to him Keither slipped and Legon caught his arm. He felt the weight on him for only a moment before the boy continued on. He was worried. He knew that Keither had to have some strength, if for no other reason than he was fat, but he knew the boy couldn't have too much in the way of endurance, and he had hit his knee pretty hard when he fell.

The sound of the hooves stopped. The forest in this part was too dense to ride in, so the men would be forced to go on foot. This was to Legon's advantage - this was his forest.

"Whoa, hold up guys, there's no point running. We'll just be easy to track. You can't hear in these woods and it's too dark in here to see very well. They will have to go slow, and if we are quiet and hide our tracks they won't find us," Legon said in a soft voice, placing his hand on Kovos' shoulder. All three of them were breathing hard and all were doing their best to calm down.

"You lead the way. I don't have a clue what to do up here," said Kovos. Keither nodded in agreement. Legon was impressed with the boy. He always thought that Keither would fall apart in a bad situation, and maybe he would, but up to this point he had more than exceeded Legon's expectations.

He took a look around to see what kind of cover they had. It wasn't too bad. There was lots of growth along the bottom of the trees and a thick wooly moss that they could pull over themselves. He went to work, first hiding Keither. He instructed him to rub dirt and mud on any exposed skin and then placed him at the base of a bush and covered him in debris from the ground. When Legon was done, Keither was just barely visible, and if he stayed still the soldiers might not find him. He did the same with Kovos and then hid himself in the wooly moss at the base of a tree. His was the most exposed area, but if he didn't move a muscle he would be fine. The sound of boots tromping on twigs gave his trembling body the willpower it needed to go still.

* * * * * * *

The dirt on Kovos' face made it sting, and for the first time he realized that his whole body was covered in little cuts and scrapes from the trees. Thoughts rushed through his mind as he tried to stay still and keep his body from shaking. This was unbelievable. He had seen a woman get killed. Her body gad hit the ground right in front of him; he had stepped over her to get away, stepped over the body of a person he knew.

As the scene played over and over again in his head he fought back the urge to vomit. He tasted bile in his mouth and swallowed hard. He would *not* be found covered in his own vomit, dead in the woods.

Whenever he had thought about someone getting killed it always seemed so different in his mind. He had never envisioned all the blood. Sure, there was some, but not like in real life. In real life there was a lot, more then he knew the body could hold. A chill ran down his back as he remembered Moleth's last attempt at a scream, and the look on her face.

He tasted the bile again and tried to stare forward. There was sound coming from up ahead.

* * * * * * *

This was bad, real bad. Sasha felt her stress levels rising out of control, and a bead of sweet rolled down her back.

Her palms were covered in sweat too, and her heart was someplace around her chin. A few hours ago, townspeople had started coming to the shop telling Edis that Legon, Kovos, and Keither had assaulted three members of the royal guard after they witnessed the men kill Moleth. They also said that the men were looking for Legon. It was just too much. She couldn't stand Moleth - the woman had been calling for her to be run out of town for as long as she could remember - but that didn't mean that she wanted her dead. Killed just to make a point, just because they could. After the fight Legon and the other two had run into the woods to hide, and for all she knew it had worked because nobody had seen anyone come out.

Sasha knew that Legon was good in the forest and he could probably evade them on his own, but with Kovos, and especially with Keither, she wasn't sure. She still wasn't sure she believed that Keither had tackled one of the soldiers. She felt so bad for Keither. She couldn't imagine what it must have been like watching someone get killed. She felt for Legon and Kovos too, but they had always been so tough and used to violence on a small level. But Keither.... He didn't leave the house, much less see fights, or even see an animal get killed. This must have been one of the boy's first tastes of the cruel world they lived in.

She needed to clear her head. She didn't have time for this right now. She needed to concentrate. Legon would be coming out of the mountains at some point, and when he did they needed to leave and leave fast. She had already packed two backpacks with clothes and other essentials. Her father had collected Legon's knives and cleavers and her mother had put together a package of medicine and food.

There was one road in and out of the valley. At the edge of the valley it split three ways. All they had to do was make it to the crossroads and then the queen's men would be hard-pressed to follow. From there she didn't know what to do; they could stay in the empire, or they could make a run for the Elves, but either way they would need to be careful. Sasha knew that Brack and Margaret were doing the same thing for Kovos and Keither. They all needed to leave the town for at least a few years, if not for the rest of their lives. She knew that all of the citizens of Salmont would be more than willing to help them leave; after all, one of their own had been killed. She also knew that if the men hadn't been royal guard they would have probably been killed by the townspeople, but they *were* royal guard. That meant you didn't do anything in the open because that was treason, and that meant a whole lot more people would be killed. Sasha spent the remainder of her day preparing to leave home for possibly the last time in her life, and hoping beyond hope that Legon was safe.

* * * * * * *

Safe was not how Legon saw himself at the moment. He found himself instead scared out of his mind and laying in mud. The men had been in the forest for hours looking for them. They had finally managed to track them to about ten feet from where Legon lay in the mud. He was right to think they were easy to track; even he hadn't thought about what he was doing when he was running, so he figured a blind man could see the tracks they'd left.

But the soldiers were having a bit of a hard time now. They knew that the three fugitives were someplace in these woods, but the tracks ended and so they'd been branching out looking for them, and then returning to this place to start over again. One man always stayed behind, giving the others a point of reference. Legon was fine. He had spent many hours stalking deer while out hunting, so his muscles wouldn't cramp for a long time yet. He knew how to move his weight without being seen.

However, he knew Kovos and Keither couldn't do this, so he had put them somewhere they could just lay and not have to move. Legon was curled up in the roots of a tree and with the moss he had on himself he just looked like another root. The only problem was that this moss was full of bugs, one in particular that was trying to burrow its way into his back. After a few hours of this he didn't know what was worse: the thought of being killed like Moleth, or having this bug spend another few hours burrowing into him. The more he thought about it and the more the irritation and pain in his back grew, the nicer the knife looked.

The bug bit into something sensitive. Pain shot through him and he gave an involuntary twitch… the soldier turned and looked right where he was but he didn't do anything. He could see that the man was looking for whatever had made the noise, but was confused at the lack of anything other than moss-covered roots. Legon heard the sound of a bird landing on a branch above him.

The man relaxed and shook his head. Legon heard him mutter something but couldn't make it out. He couldn't see much. He needed to keep his head down, but after listening to the men he figured out who everyone was. The man in their area now was the one who had killed Moleth, something that he had spent a lot of time laughing about. This made Legon want to stand and fight the man, but he couldn't. He needed to keep his head in this. He had to get Kovos and Keither out of here and then he had to make sure that his family was ok.

After a bit the man started over to the tree and Legon felt the fear of knowing that, while he may look like a root, if stepped on he wouldn't feel like a root. The man's feet stopped on either side of his head. Legon had his body contorted to look more random and sprawled out. He had most of his back against the tree. He wasn't in a good fighting position. He couldn't look up without giving away his location. He heard cloth being moved above him… the man was fumbling around with his cloak. He wasn't making much noise, as if he were slowly and carefully getting something. It had to be a dagger. Probably the same that killed Moleth.

He heard a soft chuckle. "There you are. You couldn't hide forever."

Chapter Eight
Into the Night

"Some say that when something ends, it's just the beginning. Does this mean that nothing ends? No. Sometimes the end is just that - the end."
-The River of Change

Arkin thought of the years of planning that had just gone out the window. They were early, way too early. It was probably the blasted star that had made them anxious. If only they had waited just two more months, everything would be going according to plan. At least one plan, anyway - he had three. He had always planned for this day but had hoped it would never come. Still, there was excitement coursing through him. The fact that they were here meant the prophecy had to be true, and they weren't going to stop him, not after this long. All was fine for now. He had time to pack and get ready, but first it was time to report in.

* * * * * * *

Legon's nose crinkled again at the pungent smell of urine. He had thought he was a goner. One of those bastards had been standing right above him fumbling around for something that Legon had thought was a knife. But it wasn't a knife, or anything like a knife. He was only able to lie there motionless as the soldier urinated on the tree he was hiding under. It was humiliating. Nothing got on him, he thought, but still…. In truth he would have laughed if it had happened to someone else, but not him. This wasn't funny.

He fought back his gag reflex and focused his mind back on the present. They were in a better position than before. The men were heading back down the mountain and would presumably set up camp on the outskirts of town or get a room at the tavern. The tavern was more likely. People in town would be looking to get revenge for Moleth's death, and a room at the tavern would be easier to defend.

The sound of the men walking through underbrush was getting faint, and Legon thought it would be safe to stand up soon. Kovos and Keither were still motionless, waiting for Legon to make the first move. As soon as the sound of tromping feet faded to silence he began to stand up. His muscles were reluctant to move after spending the past few hours cramped and motionless. The sun was all but gone, and the moon was starting to rise overhead, casting the forest floor in shifting light that made everything blend into one speckled image.

"Get up quietly," he said in a whisper.

There was the soft rustle of leaves and twigs as Kovos and Keither emerged from their hiding places. Kovos seemed to have developed a limp and was rubbing his leg.

"Leg fell asleep about a half hour in," he said.

Keither also had a slight limp from the knee he fell on. Legon motioned the boy over. "Come here, Keither. Let me take a look at that knee."

The boy came over and Legon bent to look. It was hard to see in the dark. He felt the area around the knee gingerly, telling Keither to lift his leg so Legon could move the joint. He rolled Keither's muddy pants up past the injured knee and began to feel around the joint. He moved it in all directions and was amazed at his knowledge of it. Having his mother as the town healer helped, and being a butcher gave him a working knowledge of philology, but the thing that seemed to tie it all together was Arkin's lessons on anatomy and physiology.

Everything felt like it was in order. There was only slight inflammation of the knee, which suggested that the ligaments were intact. As he ran his fingers over the kneecap Keither started a bit, but the bone felt fine. There was a small gash that would take a few days to heal, but other than some bruising that was the extent of the damage. "Everything seems to be fine, just try not to hurt it again in the next few days. That was a nasty fall, and you took it like a man. You did good today, Keither."

A look of pride and astonishment crossed Keither's face at the praise, and Legon realized that it was probably rare if ever that the boy was told that he did something good. Perhaps Keither was just in need of motivation.

"Do you have any other injuries?"

"No, no I'm fine I think… I don't know," said Keither timidly.

"I know what you mean. I don't know up from down right now," Legon said as he turned to Kovos, who held up his hand.

"I'm good, I didn't get hurt."

Keither broke in with a bit of a frantic voice, "So what the hell is going on? Why were those people after us?"

Kovos put his hands on his hips. "There's a lot you don't know about Keither, and we'll tell you all about it later, but for the sake of this conversation I'd say its fair to guess that the empire knows there's someone of Elven descent in Salmont, and the only way I can think that the empire would know that is if someone is trying to finish something they started eighteen years ago." He let the last bit hang in the air.

Kovos had hit it right on the head. Somebody was here finishing a clean up job, but what was even more frightening was that it was the queen who was cleaning up, not some no-name Iumenta. Legon didn't know much about the queen, but from what he did know, making mistakes was not in her nature. And if the queen of The Cona Empire did make a mistake, he assumed she would send in Iumenta to take care of it quietly, not the royal guard. They were not quiet in the least bit. If she had made a mistake then she wouldn't want anyone in the empire, or out of the empire for that matter, to know about it, so why send royal guard? She had to know that her quarry was part elf, and maybe full elf. It didn't make sense.

Legon started to pace. It didn't make sense unless she didn't know what part of the empire to look in. If that were the case, then she would need to send agents out to large parts of the empire. This helped explain part of the situation, but using humans still didn't seem to make much sense.

Kovos broke his concentration. "Talk to us! I hate it when you pace."

"Oh, sorry. Here's what I'm thinking: the queen is looking for someone who fits my description, someone who may be part or full Elf. But she doesn't know exactly where I am, because if she did…"

"… then she would send Iumenta for an Elf, not humans. I'm with you," Kovos continued.

"Right. Now, because she doesn't know where I am she has to send her men out all over the place to find me, and probably in small parties."

"And she has to be counting on you not being full Elf yet, or not having been trained in combat, if she sent out royal guard. That's perfect! The royal guard won't cause too much comment and would be able to handle an untrained human," Kovos said.

Both Kovos and Legon started when Keither broke in. They had almost forgotten he was there.

"I bet the men don't even know what they might be dealing with, because if they did they would have used a little caution when trying to bring you in."

"That's probably true, Keither. I bet they think I'm some sort of a fugitive or something." Legon said.

"Maybe. What about your back? I mean, do you think they would suspect magic?" asked Kovos.

"What's wrong with your back?" asked Keither

"I have an Elven tattoo that was put there by magic, and now it's turned from purple to green," said Legon. He was caught of guard by the casual tone in his voice. Apparently his mind had decided that magic tattoo's were old news compared to the current situation.

"A tattoo can be any color, and if the royal guard had suspected magic, don't you think they would bring magic users themselves?" Keither asked.

Legon did a double take at this. Keither knew a lot more than he let on, or maybe the pain and panic of the day had jolted him into thinking. It was probably the latter. There are two kinds of people: those who fold under pressure and those that focus. Keither had to be the latter because not only was he thinking, but the news of Legon's tattoo didn't faze him at all. Keither had taken the news as just another piece of information.

The question was, how much pressure could Keither stand before he caved in and lost control? Everyone had a limit, and when they hit it they hit it hard. Keither would need to keep his head for some time to come, because he was now in just as much trouble as Legon and Kovos. He had not only run from the royal guard, but he had also assaulted one, and that meant that he was going to have to come with Legon, Kovos and Sasha. Legon came to this realization when he was hiding like a coward from the queen's men, sometime between becoming a bug's new burrow and a rather large and foul smelling man almost urinating on him. The look on Kovos' face also said that he too knew that his younger brother was no longer able to call Salmont home.

"We need to get back to town if we're going to have a chance at getting out of this alive," said Kovos grimly, and he nodded for Legon to lead the way.

* * * * * * *

Arkin's senses were attuned to everything in his surroundings, from the cooling breeze that let him know he was almost to the top of the hill he was climbing, to the rustle of leaves in the distance. The air told him that he had about a half mile to go before he could find a way to get word out, and the leaves, well, that was just rabbits. They were young by the sound they made. If a predator didn't pick them off in a few months they would learn to make less noise. He, on the other hand, was silent as he moved. The only sound anyone would be able to hear would sound like nature, nothing out of its place. They wouldn't even know that an animal was there. A lifetime of training made sure that no one could track him. Soon he would be at the top and could report back in, and then hopefully he would get orders before someone messed things up.

* * * * * * *

Kovos felt his legs burn from staying crouched for so long. It had taken them twenty minutes to run to their hiding spot and three hours to get back down. They moved slowly now as Legon plotted a safe course. They wrapped around the town and were entering close to his house. They didn't have a huge amount of time. The moon told him it was about eleven at night and they needed to pack and get out long before daybreak.

As they closed in on the sleepy houses he felt a pang as his eyes crossed Emma's house. He wasn't going to have time to say goodbye, and even if he did, what could he say? He would come back for her in two or three months. He'd come back and they could start their life together. That's what was going to happen, if he didn't get killed first.

He didn't blame Legon for being forced to leave. He could have told the queen's men the truth. He could have hid like a coward, but he wasn't a coward. He had made his choice, and if he died it was his fault, not anyone else's. Keither had chosen as well when he had charged that soldier. Maybe leaving would be good for Keither, teach him how the world works and how to live in it.

They moved in the shadows of the buildings they passed, keeping close to the walls and doing everything not to make a sound. This wasn't new to Kovos. After all, he did it all the time when he was going to visit Emma. If he could just have spent one more night with her or maybe... *Get yourself together! Now's not the time to get sentimental!* he thought to himself.

There was still no sign of the soldiers. That was worrisome; they could be anywhere, maybe at their homes, maybe watching from somewhere out of sight. After all, it was royal guard they were dealing with here. Kovos could see his house. There was light coming from inside, but nothing to suggest that anything was amiss. They had made it home for probably the last time.

* * * * * * *

The hours after Legon got home were intense. His father had come home right before him, bringing the news that the soldiers had set up camp by the pond, putting them right next to the only road out of the valley. That wasn't the problem

Sasha was having right now. Right now she had to figure what to bring, what they were likely to need over the next few weeks. They only had two horses, and they just couldn't bring that much, not if they needed to move fast. She had packed all the essential things early in the evening, but now it was down to what she wanted to bring that was hers, things to remember her parents and her old life.

She picked up her diary. That was a given, but what else? She didn't have a lot of jewelry or fancy things, which depressed her because she didn't have that much after all, but still…. In the end she managed to get everything into a few bags and began her way downstairs to load up the two horses and go. The abruptness of the day had removed almost all emotion from everyone. Normally people would be sad and crying at the parting of a family, but not in these circumstances. There was no room for emotion; things just needed to get done.

Her mother was in the kitchen writing down a few last notes in a book, which she handed to Sasha. "Here. I know you don't have much room, but I've been making this for you over the last few years. In it is everything I know about healing. I'm not saying you need to follow in my footsteps, but on the road…."

The tears were coming now. Sasha knew what her mother was thinking, because it was the same thing that had just crossed her mind: This was it. This was going to be the last time they had together as a family. After tonight nothing was going to be the same.

She did want to follow in her mothers foot steps. She knew everything her mother did, and would be a healer herself if it wasn't for the episodes excluding her from getting a license. The book would be useful. Living on the run meant that she might need to get creative if someone got hurt.

She wrapped her arms around her mother and felt herself losing control, wanting to say that she wasn't going, but this farewell was better than the one that would happen in a few months. At least now she would be leaving willingly. They parted, and without speaking walked out the back door. The air outside was cold, with a bite that only came in the early hours of the morning. Legon and her father were finishing up with the horses. Both were already saddled and had most of their meager belongings attached to them. The family owned a horse for each person. Legon's black stallion was named Phantom and was a little on the older side, but still a great horse. Murray, Sasha's horse, was brown and about five. She loved him, although he tended to bite.

Legon walked up to his mother and hugged her, and his father went to Sasha. She loved getting bear hugs from her father. She felt safe and secure, and she got the feeling like nothing bad could ever happen. Then he let go and the feeling left. The goodbyes were short; they had to be. They needed to meet Kovos, needed to get out of town before they could be followed. She got on Murray and looked at her home and parents for what was probably the last time. As if Phantom and Murray knew what was going on, the two started to carry them away from the house, their home and everything they had ever known.

* * * * * * *

Kovos had known this was going to happen. He knew that as soon as they got home this new-found intellect was going to leave Keither. The boy had gone into panic mode about two seconds after the door closed. Thankfully, his parents hadn't lost their heads by the time they got home. Brack had the horses saddled and Margaret was finishing packing their belongings. Kovos wasted no time in making a bee line for his room and grabbing his sword. *I am such a moron for not having it with me*, he thought. He reached under a loose floorboard and pulled out the brass knuckles he had made about three years ago. Boy had they been useful.

If they got a good head start on the soldiers there was a good chance of getting away for now. There might be wanted signs on city bulletins eventually, but it was unlikely. Their encounter with the men had been short, and it was unlikely they would remember enough to make a good illustration. Even then it was improbable that the empire would do that much. Wanted posters meant attention, and even if posters went up, the empire was a large place to hide in and its agents corrupt. A small amount of coin could buy their way anywhere. Of course they would need money for that… at any rate, he didn't have time to figure that out now. Time was running out.

Keither needed to get his head on and get ready to go. There was a slam in the room next to him. Keither had probably tried to lock himself in his room. Kovos didn't have the patience for this, but convincing Keither was going to take some time. He started to the boy's room. As he left his room and turned, he saw his mother looking put out and pounding on Keither's door.

He gently moved her aside and placed his mouth close to the door, speaking in a soft voice. "Keither it's me. Are you there? I know you've had a hard day."

"Yeah, I'm here, and no, I won't open the door!" barked the voice inside.

"Ok. I'm not going to ask you to open the door, but I want to talk to you, ok? Where are you?"

"On my bed, and I don't want to tal…" Keither started but was stopped by the sound of splintering wood and his mother's yelp.

Kovos walked through the devastated door and looked down imperiously at the boy on the bed. He had been pampering the little snot his whole life, and he was done. It was time to be a man.

He felt the muscles in his face contorting and he knew that he looked terrifying. "Do you remember what happened to Moleth?" he roared.

He thought he saw Keither nod but wasn't sure. "Do you want your throat slit?" There was a definite shake this time. "Then get your stuff together. We're leaving. Now! If you don't have the will to live I can't make you, but so help me I will spare our parents the displeasure of having one of their own kids slaughtered before their eyes, you get me?"

Keither was starting to resemble a puppet with its head bobbling around. He was in line now and that was all that mattered. As for the door, well, no one would be needing the room anytime soon, and better to break down a door and have Keither alive than have the royal guard break down the door and have him dead.

He tried to push emotion out as he walked downstairs in to the overly pink living room. He noticed a lace cloth in the middle of the table. There were birds stitched on it. He paused. He had never noticed that before. *Why do you notice odd things like that when you're in a stressful situation?* he asked him self. *Because you never know when you may see it again* said a voice in his head.

He walked out the back door. It was time to go. There were two horses in the alleyway that Brack was finishing up with.

Emma. He needed to see her, needed to hold her.

No! he thought. Time was blurry now. He didn't seem to notice the farewells and the tears, didn't notice himself get on his horse. The only thing that floated though his mind was Emma and the knowledge that he would never see her again.

* * * * * * *

Arkin wondered why things took so long when he was in a hurry. He paused and repeated a calming script in his mind, controlled his breath, felt emotion ebb away. He closed his eyes and repeated the script again. As he calmed, clarity began to restore itself in his battered consciousness. Not too much longer. Just the climb back down and then they could proceed on with the mission.

* * * * * * *

Legon was vaguely aware that he was freezing cold, but his body and mind didn't seem to be talking with each other. Kovos and Keither were approaching. He could see them coming along the archery field. Phantom snorted and he patted his neck. Legon knew the horses could sense the panic in their riders, but he knew they would keep their cool. Well, at least Phantom would. He'd taken him hunting many times and nothing seemed to bother him. Murray, on the hand, wasn't used to any extreme riding and might be a problem.

Kovos and Keither were near to them now. "Are you ready?" Legon asked.

Kovos patted the sword on his belt. "Yeah."

Legon pointed to the trees. "Ok, we'll travel along the edge of the woods until we're out of sight and ear shot. Then we need to ride at least until tomorrow night to make sure we get as much space between us and those guards as possible."

"How will we know which path to take? It's dark as hell out here."

Sasha spoke. "Horses have better eyes than people. They can see fine, don't worry." She turned Murray and began riding towards the forest. The other three followed close behind.

As hoped, the horses were able to make it through the dark woods without incident, but it was slow going. They had to curve out away from the where the soldiers were camped out. By the time they made it back to the road there were rays of sun coming over the distant mountains.

They kept the horses going at a pretty good speed after that without tiring them out. They needed to open a gap between them and the town. As the sun got brighter Legon felt himself getting hungry, but he ignored the feeling. One day with out food wouldn't hurt him. They could only stop to let the horses drink, and even then it would have to be fast. There was a silence over them as they went. No one wanted to say anything. There was too much tension in the air, and with every word came the chance of emotional upheaval from the previous day and night.

Legon's face was starting to burn as the sun peaked around noon. Sweat rolled down his brow, causing the dust in the air to stick to him and covering his face in grit. As the sun started its descent it began to burn his neck. He lifted his shirt collar a bit.

The air was still and quiet except for the sound of hooves clopping on the ground. The rhythm was hypnotizing. His mind started to get fuzzy. His vision slipped in and out of focus. He started to become aware of all the sounds in the woods, sounds that he couldn't normally hear on horseback, the sound of the breeze in the tree tops, the sound of a bug crawling on a log. All the sounds must have been from yards away. *This is the Elven side*, he thought. The soft whoosh of a bird taking flight, the creak of wood …. Ah, he loved that sound, the creak only a bow could make, the creak it made as it was strung.

He snapped back to awareness in an instant, tightening his reins, bringing Phantom to an abrupt halt.

"Legon, what is it?" Sasha started, but was interrupted by a sound that all could hear, the sound of hooves that were very close. Sensing danger, everyone spurred their horses forward. Out of the trees about fifteen yards away came three men on horses, men with bows drawn, wearing leather armor emblazoned with the queen's crest, all unfamiliar faces, all with their bows pointed at Kovos and Legon. Legon was aware of two more horsemen with bows behind them. All had the satisfied smile of knowing they had surrounded their prey.

Chapter Nine
The Lesson

"What drives us to act? What is it that makes us capable of the great and the horrible? It is the events in our lives and how we choose to react to them. How we see the event, how we respond to it, these are the things that define us."
- Excerpts from the Diary of the Adopted Sister

The men wore a look of triumph tempered with wariness on their faces. It was clear that they weren't sure exactly who or what they were dealing with. They looked the four fugitives over, sizing them up, figuring out who would be the greatest threat. Sasha would instantly be ruled out. She would be easy to overpower. Keither was fat and young and looked terrified, so no problem there. Kovos and Legon were the problem. Both men were more confident and didn't back down from the glances they got. Both had been in so many fights that they could be beaten to a pulp and not be bothered. In truth, if the soldiers were to hurt someone to make a point it wouldn't be Legon or Kovos. Breaking the strongest of a group to intimidate the rest usually worked, but doing that didn't make a lick of difference to the next strongest guy. However, hurt one of the weak ones and the strong would comply just to spare the others pain.

The Lesson

"Why don't you join us in our camp?" one of the men said, pointing with his bow up the road just a bit.

They went without a word, Sasha and Keither intently staring at their hands. This was a good strategy for Sasha. If a woman appeared submissive and scared the men would be less likely to harass her. After all, that's how people like this thought women should be. But Keither needed to at least look like he had a back bone or the men would teach him a thing or two.

They entered a small clearing off to the right of the road. There were three tents set up and a smoldering fire in a pit. They maneuvered the horses to the left side of the camp, leaving plenty of room for more tents when the other guards arrived. Legon figured it would take about a day for a messenger to reach the town, so if they played their cards right they could escape before the other five showed up. Two on four didn't suit Legon, but it was better than two on ten.

"Get off your horses, throw down your weapons and stand in a line," a guard said. They dismounted and placed their stuff on the ground before them, Sasha trembling, Keither shaking. Legon knew the look Kovos was wearing, the "I'm going to do some damage" look that he always got before a big fight. Kovos was a nice guy, but cross the line with him and, well, Legon just hoped his friend would keep it under control until the right time. He didn't blame him. His own feeling of fear was slipping away and his body coursed with the energy that came with losing himself, letting go and letting his fists or maybe that big cleaver do the talking. But not now.

One of the men pointed at Sasha and threw her some ropes. "You tie them up, starting with those two. Tie them to that tree."

No surprise there; have the least threatening take care of the others so they only had to take care of her.

Sasha came up to Legon, who turned his back and allowed her to bind him. Her hands were damp with sweat and cold, her fingers barely able to form the knots. Legon knelt down next to the tree, never taking his eyes off the men. He wanted to aggravate them, wanted them to go for him. Soon Kovos was next to him and Keither's hands were bound, but not to the tree.

"Good work, pretty. Now turn around and place your hands behind you. Do anything dumb and we'll see if your insides are as nice as your outside, got it?" She nodded and turned. The man came up behind her and wrapped the rope tightly around her wrists. He leaned in and whispered something in her ear. She turned her head away and her breath caught when he grabbed her backside. She quickly walked to Legon and knelt down by him, almost like she was trying to hide behind him. He had expected them to grab Sasha. Soldiers were always grabbing women in town. It made him mad, but all in all it could have been worse.

"Our commander should be back before nightfall, so you four just sit tight," he said and started to turn, but then turned back around. "Oh, I almost forgot... gag."

At the command one of the men came up to them and placed a large wad of stained and dirty rag in each of their mouths and tied it in. The rags had probably been used to wipe sweat from the soldiers' faces and necks. There was a taste of salt, dirt, and several other things that Legon didn't want to think about. Keither gagged a bit. This was not good. If their commander was supposed to be back tonight then that meant they would have to try to escape from ten royal guards, not just four, and that this whole thing was a trap. A bead of sweat ran the length of his back, and he was feeling weak from the lack of sleep and food.

The sun was getting lower in the sky and the light coming thought the treetops was getting fainter. Soon they could hear the sound of hooves clopping in the distance and the soldiers arose, looking to see who the new visitors were. Five more soldiers came riding into camp, the same five from town. The commander looked very smug.

"Thought you could outsmart us, did you?" he jeered. They said nothing.

The men were off their horses and walking to them. The one that had killed Moleth looked down, surveying them. He stopped when he saw Keither. "Well looky here, if it isn't the tough one that tried to best me in town."

The commander looked at Keither, who was still hunched over and shaking. "I think they may need a lesson on how to treat authority."

Kovos attempted to say something through his gag. One of the men kicked him hard in the ribs.

The men chuckled and the leader said, "There's no teaching this one, at least not in the field. We can tutor him back in Bailaya." They were headed to the capital, then. This was not good at all.

The man continued, pointing at Legon. "You won't get this one either, but we may be able to teach the fat one," he said, reaching down and pulling off Keither's gag.

The one that killed Moleth laughed. "Permission to have some fun, sir," he said in a dark tone. The commander waved his hand and stepped back.

The man pulled Keither into the center of the camp by his shirt, the whole time the boy mumbling incoherently. The man turned and hit Keither across the mouth to cheers from the other men and a groan from the boy. Keither hit the ground and was pulled back up to be hit again, this time cutting his lip. Legon felt Sasha bury her head in the back of his shoulder. She hated violence. Two of the men walked out and held Keither up, allowing their friend to have an unmoving target. With every blow Keither tried to yell, but with the blood in his mouth it was getting harder. The other two men were starting to join in now, hitting him in the kidneys and on his sides. The beating seemed to take a long time, and in the end Keither lost consciousness. The men dropped him to the ground and gave him a few kicks that Legon suspected broke his ribs.

The sun seemed like it was taking forever to set. The commander walked forward to address them. "Now we have a long journey ahead of us, and I hope this shows you what happens if you don't do what you are told. We will leave bright and early in the morning, but don't worry. If you need anything, two men will always be awake to help you," he said with a gracious smile.

He started to turn and stopped at a look from one of his men. He turned back around, knelt down in front of Sasha, and said in low but carrying tone, "My men and I spend a lot of time on the road, and we don't get the luxuries that most do. That means that they're going to need something to do to keep them occupied. I hope you can sleep well in the saddle, because I can guarantee you won't be sleeping at night." Sasha's eyes jerked up.

He laughed and his men joined in, starting to make cat calls at Sasha. He reached forward, pulled off the gag, and grabbed Sasha's hair, pulling her up bodily from the ground. She tried to pull away. "Good. I like it when they have some fight. Don't worry, honey, you get me first. I'll be real gentle," he said, pulling her screaming along.

Legon lurched forward, yelling though his gag. The man turned and smiled. "Oh, do you like to watch? Ok, you can watch." He threw Sasha to the ground in front of him. The man placed his knee on her back and cut the cords holding her. More cheers came from the men. "Give it to her, sir!" He rolled her over and she tried to hit him. His hand came across her face hard, causing her lip to bleed. He was on top of her then, pulling up her skirt, trying to part her legs. He hit her again. Her eyes were full of tears. She looked up at Legon, pleading for him to stop this, but he couldn't. He felt the rope cutting deeper into his wrists. This wasn't happening. Where was the Elven side now when he needed it? He'd gotten her legs apart and pinned her wrists above her head with one hand, smiling wickedly as he felt up her shirt with the other. His hand went down to his pants that were now covered in Sasha's skirt. He was fumbling around, grunting, trying to hold her down. He pulled down his pants. There was a look of triumph

"Are you ready honey?"

She tried to beg. "No please, no please, please NO!" The commander laughed.

Legon heard a slight hiss and felt a breeze, saw a slight blur by his eyes and then heard a gurgled scream from the commander. An arrow shaft rose from where his neck met his body. Blood sprayed from the wound, peppering Sasha's face scarlet. Before the man could get his hands up to the arrow Legon felt a second breeze and saw a figure leaping from the trees, long hair flowing in the air, two long blades in his hands. The ropes binding him were swiftly cut.

The soldiers were running for their swords, but their ambusher was on them. The soldiers had left their captives' possessions nearby, and Kovos and Legon lunged for their weapons. Kovos's hands wrapped tight around the handle of his sword. The look on his face was that of an insane man. Legon's hand found the handle of the cleaver, the new one for splitting animals, the one he hadn't gotten a chance to use. There was no one to stop the rage this time, no one at all.

One of the men rushed at him with a sword in his left hand, arm outstretched. *That won't do,* he thought. Legon moved forward and stood, roaring as he swung the huge cleaver up. It made contact with the man's left armpit, passing through cloth and flesh with ease. He felt the blade jerk as it separated the joint, making a crunching, slurping sound. The rest of the tendons and ligaments cut with ease. The blade went in shiny and silver and came out red and with bits of bone and flesh stuck to it. The man screamed as his arm fell to the ground followed by its owner, bleeding everywhere, slicking the rocks and turning the dirt to mud. He only got flashes of the fight the others were in before two more men came at him. Maybe it was the surprise of the attack or perhaps the ferocity of it, but the royal guard seemed to be outclassed.

As the next guard approached him he lashed out, swinging at the man, who dodged and parried with his sword. The man aimed a stroke at his head but was deflected by the cleaver. This thing was not a battle ax, and even if it was Legon had no idea how to use it. He needed to end this fight fast. His opponent was gaining ground and his companion was soon to join. As the soldier brought his sword back, Legon slammed into him with his shoulder, making him slip in the bloody mud. As he fell his companion ran forward wildly. Legon side stepped and as the man passed him, swung the cleaver high above his head and brought it down on the passing man. During their fun the soldiers had removed their helmets, and the man's skull didn't do much to stop the blow. There was a thudding sound as the metal passed effortlessly thought the brain and neck, then along his spine, popping ribs from vertebra just like it would in every other animal. It stopped about a foot into the man's upper body. He turned on his heel, pulled out the blade with a squelching noise and brought it down on the man that had fallen. He tried to raise his arm to protect himself, but there was just a slight jolt as the cleaver cut through his forearm and a crunch as it buried itself deep in the man's chest.

* * * * * * *

He's going to rape me, Sasha thought.

There was no way it could be stopped, and all of the others were going to do it too. She tried to fight, but it just seemed to make him stronger. Her vision jarred as he slapped her. He was trying to part her legs and move up her skirt. He was so much bigger than she, and he was toying with her, enjoying the sport. Again he hit her and again this gained him ground. He was between her legs now and had her skirt up. His rough hand ran up her body, under her shirt, grabbing and feeling her. His hand went down to his pants. She could feel the rough fabric against the insides of her thighs as he tried to get them off. His breath stunk. Yellow teeth glinted back at her from his wicked grin.

She was talking but she wasn't sure what she was saying. This wasn't how it was supposed to be. Fear was ripping through her, along with humiliation. She looked over at Legon and Kovos. He was going to make them watch, they were all going to watch. Both men were a blur though the tears, but she saw the murder in their eyes, both so close and yet neither could save her. If only she could have an episode. Then at least she wouldn't have to be awake for this.

Something warm sprayed her face. She tasted metal. She looked up at the man. There was an arrow shaft growing out of his neck; blood came from it like a fountain. He was falling forward on her, but there was movement, something off to the side.

There was noise all around, but somehow she didn't hear it. She rolled the man off her and looked to see Legon running forward with a meat cleaver. She jumped as the cleaver severed a man's arm. She turned her head and saw Kovos with a sword. He was fighting two men. The look in his eyes scared her. Everything else was numb, but those eyes... there was savage hate in them, a look she'd never seen before. This wasn't how fights were supposed to be. In her head men had always gotten cut and just died. They didn't bleed to death, thrashing on the ground.

There was also far more blood than she'd previously thought. Every time someone got hit with a blade it looked as though the assailant had a wet cloth that they were waving around, but instead of covering the tents, trees and e horses with water, it was with blood.

There was another man there as well, the one that had started the fight. His back was to her, but his long hair was familiar. He was holding two swords that were curved along the forward edge and thicker about two-thirds of the way down. Then they came to sharp points. *Who is he?* she thought. *I wish he would turn around.*

* * * * * * *

Surprisingly enough the morons had managed to do something right, Arkin had to admit. Their ambush was good, not as good as one of his, but still good. He was up in a tree looking down on them. One of the big ones was beating Keither. This made him mad, but he needed to wait for the right moment before acting, and maybe this would be good for the boy.

Now the one in command was talking to Sasha. He knew where this was going, but he hoped he was wrong. He preferred that most of the men be asleep during his ambush, but there was a line he would not let the soldiers cross. Beating Keither was one thing. Rape was another.

Anger and annoyance built as the soldier threw Sasha down and start to get on top of her. That was it; it was time whether he liked it or not. Sasha was putting up a fight, which in a way made his job harder. He aimed, felt the weight of the bowstring pulling back. Now the idiot couldn't find his fly. This was good; he made a perfect target. He let go of the string, and as usual the arrow hit right were he intended.

He lunged from the tree, drawing his blades and landing next to Legon and Kovos. A quick flick of the wrists and the ropes were cut, and now it was time to do what he did best.

He crossed the camp in a few steps, swinging the two blades as he went. They were great for close-quarter fights. The Elves and Iumenta could deflect arrows with them, but he couldn't. Not that it mattered; none of the idiots went for a bow. In fact they were way under-armed. The undisciplined fools had put down weapons and armor after they had started in on Keither and Sasha.

Unlike the broadswords most of them were using, his weapons were nearly unbreakable and very sharp, so sharp that he barely felt one of them cut through the soldier's armor. They passed in between the man's ribs, slicing lungs and heart. They flashed around him as another man went down, missing his head. He saw Legon taking on two with that cleaver. It wasn't meant to be a weapon, but it seemed to be getting the job done. There was already a man thrashing on the ground missing an arm.

Arkin turned to look at Kovos. As one of the pathetic soldiers passed by, Kovos hit the man hard in between the shoulders with the pommel of his sword, dropping him to the ground. He looked paralyzed. The pommel had probably broken the man's back. He'd live for long enough to be interrogated.

Now Kovos was fighting the last man, the one that had beaten Keither, the one that had killed Moleth. Kovos brought the sword down, knocking the soldier's sword out of his hand, but instead of killing him Kovos threw down his own sword and shoved the man against a tree, holding him by his throat. There was a wild, hateful look in his eyes. He reached down to the soldier's belt, pulled out his dagger and raised it to his neck. He slashed down, cutting veins and arteries. Then he cut the other side of the neck. He continued to do this again and again until the man's gurgled scream stopped and he slipped from Kovos's blood soaked hands. Kovos turned, letting the lifeless body hit the ground. He looked at Arkin dead in the eyes. The surprise was instantaneous, but was quickly replaced with a wide smile, like nothing had happened.

"What took you?" he said.

Arkin weighed his options. Kovos may have snapped and become unstable, but it appeared as though the killing rage had run its course, at least for now. He was as close to normal as possible,

"Laundry."

Kovos nodded his head. Arkin spoke. "Are you ok?"

"Other than watching my brother get beaten to a pulp, Sasha almost getting raped, and killing three men, I'm doing great!" He smiled sarcastically at the end. Arkin could tell Kovos wasn't actually smiling, and the gallows humor was a good thing. Kovos was still with it.

"Ok. How did it feel?" he asked.

Kovos's face darkened as he thought. "Not good. But not bad either. They deserved it. I don't know how I should feel."

"That's a good sign, then. Go clean up Keither. He should be waking up soon."

He turned and saw Legon with Sasha. Her eyes looked blank and out of focus. She was probably in shock. Legon was next to her with his arms around her, talking into her ear. She was rocking back and forth slightly. Her clothes were still covered in blood, but it looked like Legon had wiped it from her face. She had been through a lot, and Arkin hoped that she could keep it together for just a few more days, and then she would be fine. He knelt down and wiped his blades off on one of the dead men's pants. He reached back and re-sheathed them as he walked back to the tree he'd been in to get his bow.

Legon looked up at him. "Thank you for coming when you did. I know it wasn't the most opportune time."

Arkin walked to Sasha and bent over, placing his hand on her cheek. "Are you ok?" he asked in a warm voice.

"I will be. I'm just shaken is all, I'll be fine."

"Good. You just sit here for awhile, ok?"

She looked up and wrapped her arms around her knees. There was a small groan and Arkin turned to look at the man Kovos had paralyzed. "Sasha dear, on second thought, Keither is getting up now. Will you take him to go get cleaned up? There's a small stream on the other side of the road."

She got up without question and walked to Keither, helping him out of the camp and out of ear shot. Arkin stood and beckoned Legon and Kovos over as he walked to the man on the ground. It appeared that he could still use his arms, which was good. He looked scared, which was also good. As Arkin walked up to him he pulled a small knife out of the sheath on his belt. He knelt down next to the man, Kovos and Legon on either side of him.

* * * * * * *

Sasha was helping Keither along, or was he helping her? He didn't know what was going on. He was covered in blood and there had been bodies in camp. Also, why was Arkin here? His head was pounding and fuzzy. The last thing he remembered was getting beaten.

They were crossing the road. There was the sound of water running. Sasha's lip was bleeding and she was shaking. He remembered what the man had done when he tied her and he knew what happened. All of a sudden the pain in his body didn't seem to matter, and he was suddenly thankful he was unconscious when they... when they.... He wasn't going to think it. He saw the stream, moving fast in the mountain pass, the light playing on it, illuminating the trees. He knelt down with her. She scooped up water, splashed it over her face and then started wiping his. He needed to say something to her, something supportive, but what? He had never been able to talk to people, never. But Sasha, she was different. She was nice to everyone, and everyone disliked her for something that he knew wasn't her fault.

Anger, sadness and hate coursed through him, but also love. Love for some that was kind to him, love for someone good. That someone could do that to her, could hurt her . . . . But maybe they hadn't. Maybe that's what the fight was.

He placed his hand on her wrist. "They didn't…?"

"No. Arkin came right before they were able to." She looked down. Shame and humiliation filled her expression and voice.

He breathed a sigh of relief. She was standing now, and he stood shaky on his feet. She steadied him. She was helping him, after what had just happened to her, after what she'd just seen, she was helping the guy who was out for the whole thing. Who would do that?

"Sasha." She paused. "You're a good person, the best person… I don't care what people say, you're not a daemon, you're an angel. You deserve better than how people treat you. I just thought you should know." That came out bad, and awkward. She probably thought he was crazy or something. Why had he talked?

He looked down at his feet. This was why he didn't talk to people. She placed both her soft hands under his chin, raising it. Tears were forming in her eyes and her voice shook. "Thank you." The tears started rolling down her cheeks and he knew she meant it. He wondered how many people had ever told her that.

* * * * * * * *

Arkin knelt down next to the paralyzed soldier and spoke in a soft voice. "We require information from you, information that we will get, and after that, we will kill you."

The man's eyes bulged and he stuttered, "Why . . . why should I talk then, if you're going to kill me either way?"

Arkin didn't like doing this, but the bastard had it coming.

"I'm glad you asked that. Because it is going to be up to you how long it takes me to kill you. One way is fast and relatively painless. The other is… hmmm, well, messy." The man looked at Arkin intently for a minute.

"What do you want to know?" the man asked.

He wasn't surprised to hear this. Of course he would crack. This pathetic animal didn't have any training, any back bone. He was a blunt instrument, nothing more.

"What was your mission? And what did you know about it?"

"That's all you want to know?" the soldier groaned. He was clearly in pain.

"That's it. Now talk," Arkin said, and gave the man a slight shake. These royal guards were the easiest to interrogate. No discipline, no honor.

Breathing hard from the pain of having his spine broken, the man began. "Ok. We're here looking for a man that's a smuggler. We didn't know where he lived, just that it was in the Salez territory and that he was around eighteen with a tattoo on his back. We were told that he would be armed and dangerous. After we caught him we were to take him back to the capital for interrogation."

"You needed ten armored men for a smuggler?"

"No. We went in two groups of five. This was just the last town on the way."

"So why did you set a trap?"

"We knew that whoever we were looking for must be here, and the commander said that it would be good training for us. Also, ten of us in a town would draw too much attention."

"Very well. I believe you." Arkin knew that these people just took orders, they didn't think. He reached down, and before the man could say anything, he broke the soldier's neck.

The sound of shuffling feet told him that Sasha and Keither were returning. It was a good thing the soldier had talked so quickly. He didn't want either of them to have to see more violence today.

As he got up Legon looked him in the eyes. "I appreciate what you have done, but we need answers, and…"

"You will get them, but first we need to move away from here. Go and cut all the men's purses. Take anything of value."

"You want us to rob them? We need to get out of here before more men come! We need to run! We need to get as far away as we can!" Sasha said, getting more and more frantic. Legon started to pace.

"We need to leave and go to Salez. I have to find out why I'm being hunted, how they found out about me. We can't just make it look like these men were robbed and hope for the best. We need to get answers," Legon said

"Salez? Are you out of your mind? We just killed a bunch of royal guard looking for you. If we go anywhere near that city, we're dead," said Kovos

"Yes. Salez is not a good idea. They'll know about you," Sasha started.

"No. I have to go there and try and get some answers."

"You're part Elf. Why not try and kill you? What more reason do they need?" interjected Kovos.

"How did they know what part of the empire I lived in?"

Arkin needed to get them moving. It was unlikely that anyone would come by, but that didn't mean it was smart to take the chance, and he did need to go to Salez. Besides, it was on the way. "I agree with Legon. We need to go to Salez, and I will come with you. If anyone comes by here they need to think these men were robbed and killed. Trash the place, but make sure to take anything of value. Don't argue now, just do it."

Kovos looked as though he was going to protest more, but stopped at a look from Arkin. He punched the air and began to tend to the men. Keither looked woozy.

"Sasha, take care of Keither. Don't worry about doing this, we can handle it." They also needed to get out of here for all of their sakes. Sasha was on the edge of losing it, and Kovos, well he had been downright scary. Sure, he had fought well, amazing for that matter, but it wasn't the total lack of caring that was the problem, but more the situation. Legon and Kovos had every reason in the world to fight and kill the way they did, which was good, because now they could do it again. But at the end Kovos hadn't just killed that man like the others. He had butchered him, and it was only then that he had calmed down, that his fear and anger had subsided. He would have to watch Kovos to make sure he didn't turn, make sure he stayed grounded.

* * * * * * *

Legon didn't really see these men as people anyway, and in truth they did need the money and supplies, so he didn't fight Arkin on it. The thing that had him going was that the carpenter was here at all. And what were those swords that he was using? They sliced the men without effort, even with the armor, and the commander, how did he make that shot? As he thought about the commander he approached his body. Something seemed off in some way. It was the arrow that was sticking out of him.

As Legon got closer he noticed something strange about the end where feathers should be. He reached out and felt a bristle-like fiber on the end of the arrow. The shaft was narrow and as it led down it was covered in blood. A lot of blood. Way more than should come from an arrow wound.

Sasha was over his shoulder staring at her dead assailant. "Legon, why did he bleed so much? Does that always happen?" she asked, curiosity apparently getting the best of her.

He pulled on the shaft. As it came out he noticed another oddity about the arrow. "Arkin, maybe we should get those answers now." Arkin looked up from the man he was robbing and a frown crossed his face.

"Please, Arkin," Sasha said.

Arkin reached over his shoulder and plucked an arrow out of his quiver and tossed it to Legon. It was odd looking too. The arrow was amazingly light. It had a three bladed head, but the blades weren't metal. "Wood," he said softly. There was more. He ran his fingers up the arrow that was covered in holes for about an inch and then more about seven inches up. Understanding took hold as Sasha spoke. "What are the holes for? Is that wood?"

"Why the holes, Legon?" Arkin asked as he stood over them. Kovos and Keither were now moving toward them.

"When something is shot with an arrow you start to bleed out, but the arrow plugs the wound. Once removed the wound bleeds a lot, so you have to wait until a healer is around to pull it. But not with this arrow. You see these holes at the front of it?" he said, placing it in Sasha's hand and pointing out the holes.

"Yes."

"And how light it is?"

"Yes."

"Well, my guess is that the shaft is hollow and the holes in the head vent blood to the holes up farther, basically holding the wound open so you bleed out fast, and I mean real fast. Arkin, what is this? There is no way a wood arrow is that strong."

"It is if it's made by an Elf," Arkin replied. Legon felt his stomach drop.

"I am an Elven agent, Legon. I have been the whole time I've been in Salmont. I knew your mother, and you have been my mission."

Chapter Ten
The Compass of Time

"I remember the first time my eyes were opened. From that point on I've had a hard time taking things at face value. Most people and things are so much more than what they seem. The question is, do you want to see what they are, and how do you know you're seeing the correct thing?"
- Conversations in the Garden

Legon couldn't believe what he was hearing. There was no way that this was happening, no way that Arkin was telling the truth, but he knew he was.

"You're an Elven agent and I am your mission?" he asked, just to confirm. Arkin looked put out. This probably wasn't how he had planned on breaking the news to him.

"Yes Legon, I am. You want to ask a lot of questions, but not now. Right now we need to move camp for the night. I promise you will have lots of time to ask questions. You have that right, and I won't stop you."

Time was not moving all that fast right now, and Legon's brain was not working at the moment. It was done for the day and it wasn't going to take anymore. He turned and looked at Sasha. She was still covered in blood, her face pale, mouth open. She looked at him, looked him right in the eyes. Never had she looked like that. She was defeated, hurt, humiliated, and her life was turned upside down. She hated violence, and yet all she'd gotten today was that and a lot of it. There was a pleading look in her eyes, and it was this that brought clarity.

His problems could wait. He'd been in the dark his whole life, but Sasha and Keither needed to get out of this place. He and Kovos probably did too, but they would have an easer time keeping it together. After all, they had been the ones to end the situation and in a way this gave them at least some closure. He didn't want to sleep here in the blood and gore of the day, and the pressure of the situation was going to get to him eventually. He needed to move and sleep then maybe he would be fine.

"Ok, let's finish up here and get moving. Let's take their horses. We can sell them or use them for pack. I don't think it would be good to let them wander off." He let the pressure shape his thoughts, let it make the important decisions.

This was something that came naturally to him. Pressure focused him, made things clear, and presented the best and sometimes only options. Maybe that's why he was a good fighter. Most people lost their heads in a fight, like the soldiers today, but you couldn't do that, not if you wanted to win.

"I agree. We will be able to sell them easily and we can keep a couple for pack so we can move faster," Arkin said, walking over to a tent and knocking it down. He began kicking it about, breaking random things.

Kovos was still gaping at Arkin. Legon jerked his head and Keither and Sasha, which brought Kovos back. Soon the campsite was trashed and the men robbed, so he didn't think anyone could tell it was staged, maybe because they had actually robbed the men, but he wasn't thinking about that right now.

He began moving towards the horses. The ones the queen's men rode looked fine, a few with specks of blood on them but they hadn't minded the violence. Their horses weren't used to it, so they were jittery. Phantom was doing better than Murray but not by much. Both animals backed away from them. Kovos's horse Calvin was fine; in fact, Legon wasn't sure it had even known what was going on. The clanging of metal probably didn't bother blacksmith's horses, but Keither's, well Margaret's horse Pixy was freaking out. Pixy was young and Margaret hadn't worked with her too much yet. She was a good horse and he thought that she would be good for Keither. Sasha was the one in the end that got them calmed down. She loved horses. She had trained both Phantom and Murray, and both were great. Calvin wasn't too bad but she would have to help Keither with Pixy. This was probably a good thing, Legon thought - she needed something to take her mind off of what was going on.

Kovos collected the soldier's horses and was tying their "earnings" to them. For some reason this made Legon feel self conscious, like he had done something wrong, but he hadn't. The men needed to look like they were robbed, but still he couldn't help but think of himself as a thief. He turned to look at the devastated camp. Everything was still fresh, the blood still glistened off of the leaves, the ground still muddy, but that was starting to dry a bit. The sun was all but gone now. They needed to go, needed to set up a new camp, eat, and get some answers.

As he rode he looked at the arrow he'd taken back from Sasha. It still amazed him. He had loved archery for so long, and what if it was part of his ancestry… he should be mulling over what had happened, but he couldn't help but feel a little excited. His people made this, and maybe someday he could do the same… or maybe he would never do it, maybe the human side would take over, maybe he would be a butcher. This bothered him. He never thought of being anything other than a butcher, and even if he went to the Elves he might just be a butcher there.

Sasha was riding next to him, looking off in the distance, her eyes unfocused. He wondered what was going on in her head. He hoped that she was all right. The men hadn't actually raped her not all the way, but the commander came close enough, and that was reason enough for her to have issues. She'd be fine in a few days. Sasha was tougher than she looked, at least he hoped she was. Arkin pulled off into a clearing to the left of the road, going down next to the stream.

"We'll camp here for the night. Keither, find some wood for a fire. Sasha, please make something simple for us to eat. It can be bread for all I care, but we need to eat. Kovos, tend to the horses and help Legon set up the tents. I'm going to walk the perimeter of camp to make sure we're safe," Arkin said and then walked off in the woods.

There was still no talking as they set camp. When they were done Sasha went into one of the tents and changed her clothes, coming out with the bloody ones in her hands. She walked to the fire and tossed them in. No one stopped her. In fact, watching them burn seemed to make them feel better about their current situation. By the time they were burned and gone, Arkin was back and Sasha seemed to be feeling much better. They all changed and it did seem to make him feel cleaner in some way, almost like by taking off the old clothes and putting on the new ones he was cleansing himself in the process.

They sat around the fire eating bread, waiting for Arkin to start. This was his show; he had the answers, and they were willing to wait for them. Arkin looked like he was thinking hard of what to say.

"Twenty years ago, a woman I knew and was close to married an Elf. It was rare for this to happen, but what was rarer was that she got pregnant. The couple knew it was a bad idea to raise the child where they lived."

"Why?" asked Legon.

"In time you will find out, but not now."

"It's my past. Why not now?" he asked, voice getting stern.

"Because I can't tell you everything. I have taken many oaths, and no matter how much I may want to tell you everything, I can't. Please trust me on this." It was a question as well as a statement, and Legon knew that if he pushed his luck that Arkin wouldn't tell him anything.

"They decided to move by Salmont, and that's where they were going to raise you until they figured out if you were going to be Elf or human. After you were born, things were going fine. I was stationed in Salmont as protection."

There was sadness in Arkin's eyes and a helpless look. Never had Legon seen Arkin get emotional.

"It is my fault your mother was killed. If I had tried harder they would have never made it to her, they wouldn't have…" he trailed off. At first when Arkin said that it was his fault that his mother was dead, Legon felt a twinge of anger, but that left as he watched him. Arkin had never half-hearted anything in Legon's whole life, and he doubted that he had then either. In fact, he was sure that the man had been carrying this with him for years. Every time he saw Legon he had to be reminded.

"It's fine Arkin. I'm sure you did your best."

"My best was not good enough. They got to her before I could get there. I went out hunting, planning on leaving Brack and Edis to find her, but you know what happened after that…"

"Yeah, I do." He was surprised at how he felt bad. After all, he never knew his birth parents and looked at Edis, Laura and Sasha as his real family. So why feel so bad about it? They knew the risks, didn't they? Or was it because they put themselves in danger for his benefit, for his protection?

"Anyway, I got word that the Iumenta had found out what was going on when they killed your father. Apparently one of the men with him was a traitor. We never found out who. The whole party was killed, traitor and all. So after that my orders were to watch you and train you."

"Train me, and what?"

"If you looked like you were going to turn Elf then I was to take you back to the Elves. If you went human then I was to let you lead a normal life, and if you began to turn Elf but leaned to the side of the Iumenta..."

"You were to kill me." Legon finished.

Arkin flinched. "Yes. There has never been an Elven traitor, but there hasn't been anyone in your position for hundreds of years." This wasn't a shock. It made logical sense to need to protect your country from attack, but still, to think of him self being viewed as a "possible threat" bothered him.

"Ok, ok that's fine. Truth be told, if I turned out to be anything like one of the bastards we killed today I would hope you would kill me. So what now?"

Arkin looked almost proud of him and he seemed to have a more familiar look about him. "We go to Salez. You lot need to learn some new tricks." As he spoke he took the two blades off his back still in the sheaths, handing them to Legon. "These were your father's fenrra. They are yours. They have been in your house for over two thousand years." Legon took hold of the fenrra, amazed by the lightness of them. The handles were one handed and there was not much of a hilt to speak of. The sheath was a dark deep purple, almost black. The grips were wrapped with something that felt like leather. The pommel was slanted with a tree inside a triangle surrounded by a circle. The whole thing looked like it was made of gold but was untarnished and unscratched, so it couldn't have been. There was what looked like gold thread up the handles and the hilt was also gold with intricate leaves on it.

He stood and pulled on the handle of the one of the fenrra. It came out without a sound, revealing a blade that looked like a mirror, the edge of which was visible and went up about a quarter of an inch along the forward edge and about a fourth of the way up along the back edge. He felt power gush through him. He held it up in the fire light, seeing himself more clearly than he ever had. The handle felt perfect in his hand, like it was made for him. He ran his finger on the edge. It was sharper than anything he'd ever seen. He handed the other one to Kovos, who pulled it out marveling. Both men turned the fenrra over in their hands, feeling the balance and comfort. They just felt good, almost like an extension of his own body.

"They will almost never dull. Those have been sharpened only twice, once when they were made and then again about seven hundred years ago. They will also never break, or if you do manage to break them, you will be one of only a few who's managed it. That edge is sharper than anything you've seen and armor means little to them. Elves and Iumenta only wear light armor, more for humans and lesser objects. You see the thicker part of the blade?" Arkin said, pointing at the last half of the fenrra.

"Yes."

"That part there is used to deflect arrows and anything else sent your way. You won't be able to do it now, but if you turn into an Elf you'll be fast enough."

This should have floored him, but nothing was a surprise any more.

Kovos handed him the other blade and he stood amazed. They felt so natural. He didn't want to let them go. It made him feel like nothing could hurt him, like they somehow had abilities of their own.

"Now we need to sleep. Don't worry about sleeping in tomorrow. We have all had a hard day. I know it's early, but you need to rest," Arkin said.

There was a part of Legon that wanted to stay up, the same part that made him fight with his parents when he was growing up and they wanted him to go to bed, but Arkin was right and they did have a long way to go. Sleeping now was good. He replaced the fenrra in their sheaths. "That sounds good. I am assuming you want Kovos and Keither to share a tent, and you and I to take one?"

Sasha spoke for the first time in a while. "Please. I don't want to be alone tonight; can I stay with you, Legon? I promise I won't bother you."

Of course she would want to stay with him. She was terrified. How could he make her be alone?

"Of course you can. I'm sorry, I should have said that. I'll move your bed roll and bag to my tent."

"Stay with Legon as long as you like, Sasha," Arkin added.

* * * * * * *

Kovos couldn't believe this. How did Arkin get those swords and how was he able to hide in town for so long? Did anyone know? Keither was looking better and he thought that the boy would be fine by the morning. In truth he was a little proud of how well Keither had done. He hadn't complained and it looked like he was toughing it out. This was a good thing, and it would be helpful for their current situation. He suspected that there was going to be a lot of toughing it out to come, and if Keither could keep it together he may turn into a real person. *It is going to feel good to lie down and sleep,* Kovos thought as he parted the folds to the tent and entered. There was his bed roll waiting for him. He thought about stripping down to his undergarments, but decided against it. You never know when you might get attacked.

He couldn't get the day off his mind, especially the fenrra. Now that was metalwork at its best. Sharpened twice in two thousand years, and they were so *sharp*. He didn't even know metal could get that sharp. Maybe if he played his cards right he could learn how to do that.

He was also bothered by the fact that he wasn't upset about killing people. He should be, he should feel bad… but nothing,

nothing at all. He got mad when he thought about Keither and Sasha getting hurt, but doing the hurting… it didn't bother him. In fact it felt… good. That bothered him. If killing felt good, then that meant that he was capable of doing awful things, things like what those men had done, and then what would Emma think of him? Emma. Why did he think of her now! It was dark in the tent and Keither had fallen asleep as soon as he was lying down, and Kovos would have too, but now he was thinking about her. *I wonder what she's doing* he thought. *No, don't think about it.* But how could he not? What if it had been her on the ground having some sub-human on her?

He understood then why he didn't feel bad for killing the men. He didn't feel bad because it was justifiable to kill them in his mind. *But is it ok to kill people even if they deserve it?* came a voice in his head. Who was he to judge others, who was he to decide who lived and died? But at the same time he knew these men killed and raped, and who knew what else, so maybe it was ok. Either way it didn't matter. It was done and it wouldn't do to dwell on it. They did what they had to do and that was that. At the same time he was surprised at how protective of Sasha he was. Sure he'd beaten people up for giving her a hard time, but that was for his friend. Today he wasn't killing entirely for protection. He wanted to punish them for what they were going to do to her and what they had done to probably many women. Sasha was a good person, and when he thought about it, how could demons posses her? Could a demon live in someone like that? Great, now he was never going to sleep. His mind was starting to run. Maybe he could get some air, that might help.

He got up and went outside. Arkin was at the fire poking it with a stick. He turned to look at him. "Is everything ok?" he said in a soft voice.

"Yeah I think so. I just can't sleep, you?"

"I'm fine. I can stay up all night and be good to go tomorrow. You did well today. I mean that."

"Thanks. You did well yourself. So what happens now? What do we become?"

Arkin gave a deep sigh. "That will be up to you, I think. Let's not talk about that now. Let's talk about something that will put you to sleep," he said with a smile.

Kovos laughed. "Ok, why don't you tell me about some table or something you're making."

"Low blow from someone that hits things with a hammer for a living," Arkin retorted. He always enjoyed picking on the carpenter for his craft. He knew Arkin was good at what he did, but Arkin worked with wood and Kovos with metal, so there was a bit of a rivalry. They both liked to talk about what it was like making something with your hands, something that people could use for generation, like those swords. They talked for about an hour before Kovos got tired and went to bed.

* * * * * * *

Sasha woke up next to Legon, her head resting on his bedroll. She was amazed at how well she slept. She thought that she wouldn't sleep deeply because she was scared, but Legon was with her and he wouldn't let anything happen. The air felt warm, so it must have been mid morning. She crawled out of the tent to have her suspicions confirmed. The sun was high in the sky, the morning dew long since gone.

Arkin was up, or at least she thought that he was. He was sitting on his heels with his back to her. It looked like his hands were on his thighs. She didn't want to disturb him from whatever he was doing and began to go back in the tent.

"Good morning, Sasha," he said in a deep relaxed voice.

"Oh, good morning Arkin. Did you sleep well?" She wanted to know what he was doing, but she had to be polite. She did owe him her life, or at least that's how she saw it. He chuckled.

"I am meditating."

"Oh ok. I didn't want to be rude or disturb you."

"You're not. Did you sleep well? I know Kovos and Keither did. I think the whole forest knows that," he said, turning his head and giving her a slight smile.

She laughed. "Yes, I think they did."

A snort from inside the tent told her that Legon was getting up as well. He popped his head out. "Morning," he said and then looked at the sky. "Oh, sorry. I don't think I've slept this late in years."

Arkin got up and moved to his tent, returning with a sheathed blade.

"Sasha, this is for you. It's also Elven. It belonged to Legon's mother. It's the faloon. Elven women carry them."

She took it. "A what?"

"Faloon. A thin, short sword that can be worn under most skirts. The handle can be easily hidden with a bow or anything else around your waist."

"Oh, ok. Legon, do you…"

"Good idea, Arkin. I should have taught her how to defend herself a long time ago. It was dumb of me. I just always assumed that I could defend her… sorry Sash."

She was a little taken aback. He was feeling guilty about what had happened yesterday, as if it was some how his fault those bastards had tried to hurt her. She knew that he would have done anything to stop it. She saw the marks on his wrists where the rope cut into him. She could almost feel them. There was nothing that he could have done to stop it.

"It's not your fault, Legon. There is nothing you could have done. Even if I knew how to fight, do you really think that I could have stood a chance against them?"

"That's not the point. The point is that you have always been in a danger and I haven't taken the time to give you the basic skills you may need to just get out of a situation. I don't expect you to be able to fight someone, but I could have taught you how to hurt them enough so you could get away."

Arkin broke in. "The truth is, it's my fault as well. I trained your brother and yet I did nothing for you. Forgive me, Sasha, but going forward you will learn. In fact I have training for both of you while we're on our journey. We are going into situations that neither of you have faced and you need to learn what to do, and Legon, you need to learn how to use the fenrra and a few other techniques."

"Like what?" Sasha asked.

"I will start to teach you the art of the Jezeer."

"The what?" started Legon.

"Jezeer. In short, you will learn how to fully use your muscles, how to read people, inflect your voice and body language to gain favor with people and get them to do what you want. Sasha, you know a lot of the people skills because I have taught you them from the time you were little. Legon, you I have taught many of the physical, but you both need to learn both and to learn more than either of you currently knows."

She'd been being what? She knew that Arkin was training them, but to have him say it was a little unsettling, and in a way violating. Her thoughts were interrupted by Arkin.

"And you will learn the Mahann, which will train your mind to use logic, not emotion. Both of these we can learn in the saddle, but at night in camp we'll go over physical training. Legon, I will work with you and in turn we will switch training Keither and Sasha. Ok?" This wasn't much of a question but Sasha didn't fight it. She was willing to go along if for no other reason than curiosity.

Shortly after that Kovos and Keither woke up and they broke down camp and started off. They were hoping to make it to within a half day's ride from the end of the road, where it split three ways. From there they would go southwest along the mountains towards Salez. This wasn't the most direct route, but it had the least amount of towns and villages, so it was ideal for them. As the day pressed on Arkin was teaching them different exercises to train their minds and quizzing them on hypothetical situations. It made Sasha's head hurt, but at the same time it was nice. Kovos and Keither listened in and occasionally Keither would make a remark or answer a question. He always got the questions right, and Sasha began to wonder just how smart he was. Also he'd been so nice to her. She knew that it must have taken a lot for him to say what he had, and she was thankful for that. He was a good guy if you could get him to talk.

* * * * * * * *

They were riding next to the river, which made the air cool. Legon always loved the sound of a stream or river. They seemed to give him energy and yet make him relax at the same time. All the same he would have liked it more if Arkin wasn't drilling them. He and Sasha always seemed to just get half way there but rarely all the way. It was like they had been given information but only part of it. This didn't seem to bother Arkin one bit. He was rushing along, hitting them with question after question. Then he would correct something that seemed to be insignificant and move on.

He was looking forward to training tonight. He knew how to use a sword and he could use two, but the fenrra were a little shorter than regular swords, so he would have to get used to that. He was glad that Sasha was going to be learning how to fight. That way if anything ever happened to him she might be all right. The faloon looked like it could be handy too. It had a little cord that went around her waist and as it hung it moved with her legs and skirt so no one could see it. There was just the end of the handle that came up, and that could be hidden with cloth.

He could see the she was a little uncomfortable with it. Sasha had never been in a fight and never carried a weapon on her, much less one that had belonged to her adopted brother's dead mother. He, on the other hand, liked that she had the blade. It seemed to fit. As the sun fell they set up camp next to a large rock that rose thirty or forty feet above them. They were able to set up camp beneath an overhang. They placed the tents close to the rock, giving them more cover from the elements and making the smoke from the fire track its way up the rock and fan out under the overhang. As soon as dinner was done, Arkin walked into camp with a bag that looked like it contained a spare tent. He started to pull out wooden staves which were finished and polished, the same kind that Legon and Kovos had learned to fight with.

He tossed two to Legon, who noticed that they were shorter than most swords but the same length as the fenrra, and handed one to Sasha and Kovos. Sasha looked a little confused, but the two men got up, understanding it was training time.

Arkin looked down at Keither. "I imagine that your ribs are bruised at the very least, so we won't start training you for a little while. As for the rest of you," he addressed the others, "Sasha, you will be working with Kovos, who is going to start teaching you how to fight with a sword. He's a very good fighter and you will learn a lot from him. Legon, you're with me. I need to start getting you used to fighting with the fenrra. We will use the wooded staves for a few nights until you get used to the length and fighting style. After that we will put guards on the real blades. Ok?" Everyone agreed, but Sasha was looking a little nervous.

* * * * * * *

Sasha walked to one end of camp with Kovos. She was feeling a little trepidation. Kovos was nice enough, but she'd never been in a fight before and she was hoping she would never need to.

This must have shown on her face because Kovos smiled warmly. "Don't worry. We're just going to go over the basics tonight. I think that Arkin just wants you to have a general understanding, and then he will have to teach you to use that fa… feloon?"

"Faloon," she corrected.

"Yeah, that thing. It looks like a good weapon and a great idea, but basic broadsword technique will be good for you to know. Don't worry, you're not going to be good at it for a long time, so if you're not a master by the end of the week, don't lose sleep over it."

"Ok, I won't worry too much then."

Kovos nodded and placed the stave on the ground and drew his real sword, holding it in the palm of his hand and presenting her with the handle. She wasn't expecting the weight. Somehow when he'd been using it with so much speed and accuracy, she though it must have been very light, but it wasn't.

"Ok, you need to learn what everything is so that way when were working you'll know what the hell I'm talking about, ok?"

"Isn't this the blade, the handle and the pommel?" she said, pointing at different parts of the sword.

"No, that's not what it all is. You got parts right, but that's not just a blade," he said, a little exasperated.

"It's a long piece of metal that cuts things. How is that not just a blade? Don't get me wrong, it's very pretty . . ." she said, a little confused. Kovos looked scandalized.

"Just a blade?" He stood looking at her, mouth gaping. How was she supposed to know what everything was called? It cut stuff, right? That was a blade to her.

"Sorry, I didn't know there was more to it than that."

"And pretty?" he said.

Legon broke in, "But Kovos, it is pretty. I like the flames a lot."

Arkin joined in. "You put flames on your sword?" He was starting to smile. Sasha knew the carpenter-spy or whatever was about to lose his composure. "Like the ones you put on the staves as a kid?" Arkin started to laugh and laugh hard at that.

"Oh yeah, laugh it up, real funny. I'm a trend setter, just you wait. In a few years everyone will have swords with flames on them, and I will be rich and famous." Arkin was on the ground, having a hard time breathing, and it was this more than anything else that made her start to laugh. It felt good. She put her hands on her knees and could feel her eyes water. She could see Legon pointing and laughing at Kovos, who was now starting to join in. The scene must have been too much for Keither, who gave a small chuckle and then put his hand on his side with a grunt. This elicited more laughter from all of them.

"Stop making me laugh! Ouch! It hurts! It's not funny you guys," Keither said.

It wasn't that funny but the stress of the last few days was finally breaking, and Sasha could feel her anxiety leave as the fit stopped. Kovos was shaking his head, telling everyone just how much he hated them all, and that they would regret making fun of the flames and went back to teaching her.

"Oh my. Ok Sash, here's what everything is named. Just try and remember, ok? On the blade there are a few parts. This first is the tip here, it's called the Foible. Next is the mid-blade, then the forte is the part closest to the handle. Got that?"

"Foible, mid-blade, and forte. Got it."

He pointed to the edges. "This edge, the one your knuckles are on, is the leading edge of the blade, and the other side is the false edge. The parts on either side are the flats."

"Ok."

"Now this cross part here is the cross guard, then the grip and the pommel. This whole part is the handle of the blade. Got it?"

"Yes, I think so."

"Ok good. Now we will go over how to hold the sword."

"Ok." For the next hour she learned how to hold the sword and the basic names of moves.

After that Arkin brought a stop to it. She was getting into it. For some reason this stuff was interesting to her, and now she was beginning to understand a lot of the conversations she had with Legon growing up. He was always talking about "parry" this and "thrust" that, but she never really had known what he was talking about. She just smiled and nodded to be nice. She didn't even remember hearing Arkin and Legon, who both were covered in sweat.

* * * * * * * *

Arkin stood across from Legon. He was going to start learning better deflections so he could use his opponent's momentum against him. The staves were perfect for this kind of training. They couldn't take full blows with out cracking, so this would force him to deflect with one sword and then strike with the other. Arkin came at him again and again, doing the same move until Legon would deflect it correctly and then he would move on to a new one. He'd used to two-handed fighting before, but was never totally comfortable with it. You didn't have as much power with just one hand, so someone could get an advantage with just pure strength, but he also knew that people who did know how to fight well with two swords usually won, so he would put in the time.

Arkin held one stave, and it was the same size of a standard hand and a half broad sword. He swung at his side, splitting the air with the sound of smacking wood, sending a vibration up the stave to his hand. Legon turned, catching the stave with one of his own and turning his back to it, using his body to help it make its way up and over him. This exposed Arkin's side. As he did this he stabbed with the other hand, catching Arkin in the side. It felt awkward but was still effective.

"Good job, Legon. Now again, but less sloppy. Make it a more fluid movement."

"Ok. Hey watch me do it on my own and tell me where I'm sticking."

They continued until he was getting very good with the two handed technique. He was good with one sword combat, and in truth you didn't use both hands a lot of the time, as you were constantly switching hands to help with endurance and to get your opponent off guard. All you needed to do was add in a sword on the other hand and for the most part you didn't need to learn that many new moves, so it didn't take him long to get the hang of it.

After they were done Arkin took Sasha and him aside and began to teach them the Jezeer, which was basically learning how to master each muscle in your body. The hard part was isolating just one muscle. It seemed that you couldn't move just one with out all the others joining in. This training would be hard. The way they learned was with different poses, contorting their bodies to stretch and isolate different groups of muscles. By the end Legon knew that he wouldn't be sore from fighting, but from the Jezeer. He also realized that he wasn't as flexible as maybe he once was. Sasha was better at this part of this than him, but he still heard the occasional groan from her straining herself.

"That's good. Tomorrow we will do more, and you will start to work with Sasha on basic hand-to-hand combat. Nothing major, just enough to get her out of trouble, wristlocks and things like that."

The next day they made their final descent out of the mountains and to the split in the road. They went south heading for the town of Salkay were they could sell the horses they didn't need and buy supplies. The land they were in was all rolling hills with large fields and patches of trees. Closer to the mountains the forest got thick, but otherwise they were in open spaces. Within a two day's ride they would reach the Kayloose River and the town of Salkay. Spring had taken a much firmer hold on the lowlands than it had in Salmont. The road was clear, but right off to the side the grass in the field grew up to the horses' bellies, and there was the soft sound of birds singing and the occasional bug going by their heads. The scent of wildflowers dominated everything. They tried to figure what each cloud looked like and were having a good time. Everyone was in high spirits by lunch. They sat in the shade of a tree to eat and let the horses graze on their own. Keither seemed to be out of his element. He was terrified of bees and other insects. It was obvious that he didn't spend much time outside.

* * * * * * *

Keither knew the others were crazy. How could they possibly be enjoying themselves? *There are bugs everywhere, and the bees . . .* he thought to himself. There was a reason he stayed in the house all day, and this was it. What if one stung him? Could he die from it? He didn't know but he heard one time that someone had died from a bee sting. They stopped breathing and everything. Did these morons not know that? He kept his head down all day and he didn't answer too many of the question that Arkin would ask Legon and Sasha, not that it mattered anyway. He spent most of his time telling them to clear their heads and stuff like that. When there was a question he almost always got it right, even if he didn't answer. They were easy really, all hypothetical questions, not unlike the stuff he thought about on his own all the time. He was amazed they didn't know how to solve them. Didn't everyone think about this stuff? Not everything was bad though. Sasha was an amazing cook. Even when she didn't do anything to the food it was better than home.

He reared back and swatted at a black flying thing. *Whoa that was close,* he though. His ribs hurt and he wondered how long it would take them to feel better. His face hurt too, but that was already starting to do better. He was still going to look horrible in Salkay, not that it mattered. He looked bad anyway. He was fat and pale. People were always asking him if he was sick. When he said no they asked if he was hurt, and that's why he was so large. *Jerks,* he thought. *Just because I don't spend my day pounding on metal or wood....* He liked to think of himself as the first scholar in Salmont, but now that Arkin was revealing this other side, he thought he may be number two. What was up with Arkin anyway? He sure played his part well, but it didn't make sense to not take Legon back to the Elves where he belonged. No, there was more to this story, and the others should be asking question but they weren't. They trusted the man to the hilt.

They were riding again. Well the rest of them were, but Pixie was still eating. "Come on, let's go!" He clucked his tongue. This worked for Sasha, why not for him? He tried to kick Pixie's side. She snorted.

Sasha was calling back to him. "Come on, Keither. You're in charge, not her. Kick her sides and she'll go."

No, she wouldn't go. They had been going through this exercise all day - he kicked, Pixie ate. And that name! What were people going to think of him when they found out his horses name was Pixie? Sasha was heading over now. She looked calm and he knew she was patient, but he still knew this must be driving her nuts.

She got off Murray. "Here Keither, ride Murray the rest of the day. Pixie just needs to be trained, that's all."

He got off and remounted Murray, who seemed to be much larger. Once again the horse didn't seem to want to respond to him. Sasha got on Pixie and to his amazement she turned Pixie and started toward the others, clucking just like he had done but this time the horse responded. He grabbed on hard to the saddle as Murray started after Sasha. Clearly Pixie was not the one in need of training.

Chapter Eleven
Salkay

"It always amazes me that people believe only that which they want to, no matter how absurd. Of course, that being said, people tend to be easy to lead for the same reason, and provided their leader is just, even the truly wicked amongst us can be made into good people."
- Memoirs of the Ruler of the first dynasty

They made camp right outside of the town of Salkay. Kovos couldn't see it, but it was there just over the hill. He could hear the sound of the Kayloose River, one of the largest rivers in the area and the basis for Sakay's rapid growth. Most towns and villages were built near a body of water, be it a river, stream, or lake. This was the case for Salkay. From what he understood there were mills in Salkay, and mills meant money.

It was cool this morning and he could see his breath when he got out of the tent. He appeared to be the only one up except for Arkin at the edge of camp, looking not towards the town but back up the road where they'd come, sitting on his heels and not moving a muscle. This must have been the Jeesie or Jezeer or what ever it was called. Kovos didn't know and frankly he didn't care. All that stuff was fine for Arkin but not for him.

He began to build a fire. He loved the mornings when he was camping, or at least he loved them when he was sitting at a fire eating. He felt a hand on his shoulder. It was small and soft. His heart skipped a beat. Emma? No, not Emma. Sasha.

"Good morning. How are you today?" she said, yawning.

He spoke more to the ground than to her. "I'm fine."

"Just fine?"

"Yeah I'm fine, really I am." She was giving him a knowing look.

"You thought I was Emma, didn't you?" she asked softly.

"I'm sorry Sasha. How did you sleep?" And moreover how did she know what he was thinking?

She smiled at him. "Why are you sorry? I'm sure she misses you too."

"Do you think so? I mean, she said that she loved me, but I don't know. Now I'm gone and I bet she's has her eye on others. I don't know." He chuckled a bit. "Listen to me, I sound like a moron. You don't want to hear my sob story."

She laughed, and this caught him off guard. "You don't know anything about women, do you?"

Now it was his turn to laugh. "Well no, I guess not."

"I don't think you're a moron, I'm happy for you. It's cute the..."

"Oh no, don't start that 'cute' stuff. Emma says that crap all the time when I get all soft," he said pointing a finger at her in a playful way.

"It is cute, and I'm sure she misses you a lot. She even talked to me about you, so there's a sign."

That was definitely a sign. Emma didn't talk to Sasha; none of the girls in town did. They talked about her for sure, but it wasn't kind.

"She did? What did she say? What did you tell her?" She had his attention now; he didn't want Sasha to think he was soft, but this was too good. She sat down opposite him and held her hands out over the growing fire. They didn't even notice Arkin looking at them.

"Well, she came up to me in town and offered to buy me tea. I knew something was up because her parents don't want her to talk to me. We went to the tavern and she started asking all these questions about you. She thought that you and Legon talked about your relationships all the time."

"I want to make one thing clear: We *never* . . ." Kovos started.

"Yes, I know your men. Gods forbid you show emotion. Anyway, after a bit she was trying to get me to tell Legon to tell you to propose to her, so I would say she likes you, even loves you. When you go back home she'll say yes. And then her dad will probably kill you," she finished with a smile.

She wanted to marry him. This was great! But something didn't make sense.

"Sasha, I'm confused."

"I'm sure, you're a man."

"Ha ha. If she loves me, why didn't she say it or have you tell me to marry her? Why Legon?"

There was a sympathetic look on her face, the same his mother gave him whenever he did or said something stupid but tried to do the right thing. "She dropped lots of hints."

"Like what? She never dropped a hint. I'd have noticed."

"She asked you to come pick out linens and table cloths," Sasha said with a hint of exasperation.

"Yeah, so what?"

"For your new home together." She was spoon feeding him something but still it didn't click.

"No, it was for her aunt, not our house."

"Oh my goodness Kovos, are you really that thick?"

It clicked.

"What!? That's stupid! Why did she do that? If that's what she wanted why didn't she just say it?"

Sasha rolled her eyes at him. "We don't say, it we hint, and apparently you guys don't get it."

"If you guys want something and don't tell us, then it's not our fault, it's yours."

Sasha chuckled in a bit of a menacing way. "Ha! It's our fault you aren't bright enough to figure it out?" Kovos was about to talk but was cut off by Arkin.

"Kovos, she likes you and that's what matters. Sasha, men are dumb."

"Thank you," she said.

"And so are women," Arkin finished, walking to his tent before Sasha could retort.

* * * * * * * *

Keither thought he heard a debate heating up outside, no doubt Sasha and Kovos talking about relationships. That never ended well. It was a good time to keep quiet. Not that he talked much anyway. The conversation cooled down after breakfast, and Kovos seemed to be in a good mood about Emma liking him.

Keither was happy for him in a way. Except for once, Keither hadn't ever really liked anybody. That one didn't matter though; he hadn't had the balls to talk to her, and the queen's men had taken her earlier in the year. She had been nice, though. She was one of Sasha's friends. Come to think of it, her only friend. It's too bad people were terrified of what they didn't understand.

Keither left his tent and tried to help break camp, but his side was killing him and Legon told him not to do anything.

"I can help," he insisted.

"I know you can, Keither, but your ribs need to heal, and the fastest way for that to happen is for you not to do much for the next few days. Don't worry. Once you can help, you will," he said with a smile.

"Trust him on this one. He knows what he's talking about," Kovos added.

Odd. His brother was being nicer to him than before. Maybe he felt bad about what had happened. It didn't matter; the change was welcome. He knew that Kovos cared about him and only wanted him to be safe and happy, so he didn't really hold it against him when he was mean. Still, this new way was easier to take. When they were ready to leave Sasha walked Murray over to him. "I want you to ride Murray for a few days while I work with Pixie, and then it will be your turn to be trained, ok?"

"Ok. Sorry I'm not good at this stuff. Thank you for your help."

"Don't be sorry. We all have to learn, and you've never had a reason to."

She was so nice to people. Why on earth was she like that? It didn't make any sense. These thoughts left him as they rode. They were coming over the hill now and that meant Salkay would be in view. He was excited; one of the traveling merchants that came to town said that Salkay was growing due to the new mills they had built over the last few years. Mills. Now that was where it was at. He had never seen one, so this was going to be good. Most people didn't appreciate what mills could do.

As they came over the hill Salkay came into view. It was larger than Salmont, but not by much. There was a big wall surrounding the town and a road leading to the river, which was wide here. The road split in two, each path leading to the river where it then became a fortified mill bridge. The bridge closest to them had five large wheels underneath. On the left on the bridge and closest to the town were two buildings, both with tall roofs and no smoke. Downriver a bit were a larger bridge with seven wheels and two more buildings, both with huge amounts of smoke coming from them.

"Are those mills with fortified bridges?" asked Kovos.

"Yes they are," responded Arkin.

"What's with the one with the dome thing by it?" asked Sasha.

The dome thing; Keither hadn't noticed that. He looked harder. "No way."

"'No way' what, Keither?" Sasha asked.

"Arkin, is that a sanitizer?" he asked excitedly.

"Very good, Keither. Why don't you tell the others about the mills and the bridges?"

Why had he spoken? Now he was going to have to try to explain this and they were going to think he was a moron. "Come on," prompted Arkin.

"Well ok, bear with me. I will explain each in turn." He paused, gathering his thoughts.

"You see that fist bridge, the one with five wheels?" They all nodded. "The bridge is fortified because those wheels are the most valuable part of the town. Without them the town will bust, so they need to be protected." He held up his hand, forestalling questions.

"Let me finish and then you can ask away. Ok, here's how it works: those wheels are turned by the river's current and in turn they lead to a gear building. From there the building turns shafts that lead to the structures on either side for various works. Ok?" They nodded, and a proud look crossed Arkin's face. So far this was going well.

He pointed to the mills closest to them. "Neither of those building have smoke stacks, so that probably means that one is a grain mill and the other a saw mill. Like Arkin's shop, an open flame is an issue in both those buildings, more so for the grain mill. There is enough dust in there to actually make the building explode if ignited." This time there were a few "wows" from the others.

"There's probably a loom on the lower level of the bridge too, it looks tall enough. Now the big one downstream that has a lot of smoke is a foundry. The wheels drive billows and hammers, helping them to make a lot of stuff faster."

Kovos broke in. "Yeah, I've heard of those. They're used to make large scale stuff and to refine ore into ingots that other smiths can use, but what is the dome for?"

"That a good question. I don't know much about them, but I do know they are made by the Iumenta, and that most large cities have them. Arkin, can you help me out?"

Arkin smiled warmly at him. "Well done, Keither, and yes, I can help you out. Legon, can you tell me what happens to towns with dirty water?"

"People get sick, and I mean really sick, diphtheria and other disease; that's why towns put their dung heaps a good distance away from town or in a river to sweep it away."

"There. You hit it right on the head: put in the river and swept down for another town to deal with. This is one of the only times you will hear me say that the Iumenta did something good, even though they only did it to keep their work force in better condition." Arkin really did hate the Iumenta, but Keither wasn't sure why. They had done some good things, hadn't they?

"If you look closely at that bridge you'll see intakes where water is going into the far building. In that building are augers that are powered by the river. They carry water up to a main well in town. As soon as the well reaches a certain level it encounters another pipe that diverts water to another well, and so on and so forth." He paused, waiting for questions.

"Ok, so it's easier to get water," Legon said.

"Yes, and when the well reaches another level the water is diverted to a pit where people dump waste, be it food, dung or otherwise."

"So then the waste is flushed to the river, I got it."

"Not yet. The waste is flushed to that dome, which is called a condenser. Under it is a pit that's around thirty feet deep and at the bottom a huge steel plate. Inside the main building and under the steel plate is a furnace. Bellows are run from the mill, keeping the furnace hot. All of the waste wood and grain from the other mills go there and to the foundry, too. The leftovers from the other mills are small and burn hot and fast. Also, the belongings of sick people can be burned here as well, and in some cases the corpses of the sick."

"So whatever it is doesn't spread, right?" asked Sasha. With her background, Keither figured she would show an interest in anything that kept illness from spreading.

"Right. The furnace makes the steel plate hot and boils off the water in the pit. There is another auger that is pumping water inside that dome, which is made of ceramics. Iumenta use a lot of ceramics; it's one of their specialties. That water keeps the dome cold, so as steam hits is it, the steam condenses into water and is caught in a little ridge with holes that circles the rim of the dome, and then it goes into the river clean."

"So the waste doesn't infect another town," said Legon.

"Correct. At the end of the day there is a stop in the pipe leading to the pit and people go in there and collect all of the remaining waste to be burnt in the furnace the next day. There are some other details from there, but you get how it works now," he finished.

"Seems like a lot of time and money just to keep a work force alive," Keither added. He wasn't sure just how bad the empire could be. After all, most people lived in relative comfort, and wasn't it the good of the many that mattered? Moreover, he was feeling confident. None of the others could figure out the stuff he had, so why would Arkin be any different?

"It keeps your work force healthy, yes. From my understanding this was a big fight with the Elves. Humans resisted placing measures like this in towns and cities because of the cost," Arkin responded.

"So where the Elves failed the Iumenta have succeeded. Isn't it possible that the Iumenta are not as bad as some people think, and that they think of the good of the many versus the cost?"

"You'd better not say the Iumenta are misunderstood, Keither," Sasha said. He was taken aback by the tone in her voice. "Do you think the Royal Guard that killed a woman in front of your eyes was misunderstood? Or was that for the good of the many as well?" There was a defiant bite to her tone now. She did have a point, but the actions of an isolated group of human soldiers didn't tarnish the entire Iumenta race. He began to open his mouth to retort but was cut off by Arkin.

"We are near town now. This talk can wait for later, and yes Keither, it is a talk we will have. You don't have to take my word. The Iumenta are not our friends. I'm sure you will be given more evidence than you have already."

"But why not now? The…"

"Because we are fugitives and I don't want attention, that's why." Arkin sounded irritated, like Keither had said something ignorant or childish. Was it wrong to want to continue the conversation?

* * * * * * *

Sasha felt anger seething in her. She couldn't believe what Keither was saying. Didn't he understand, didn't he see how the queen was? This was all "academic" for him; he wasn't in any near danger of being made a slave, he wasn't there when they took Sara. She gripped the horn on her saddle harder, hearing the leather creak. It was rare for her to feel anger this strong, but when she did it was usually justified. It wasn't that Keither didn't have good points, the good of the many and such, but he was justifying the end result. There was a lot more to justice and good than most of the people having a comfortable lifestyle.

Or was there? She wasn't sure. She knew the queen was evil, but why? That's what mattered. Keither's logic was sound but still she knew it was wrong. She thought hard, not noticing Salkay come closer and closer. Arkin had taught them one of the principles of the Mahann: "Black and white is all there is. Grey is just misunderstanding." What did that mean?

Her eye caught a glimmer of something silver. They were at the gate of Salkay, and the glimmer was the end of guard's spear. The owner was leaning against the wall of the town talking to another guard on the other side of the entrance. The man was tall and wearing leather armor with a wooden chest plate. There was about a week's worth of black stubble on his face that matched his hair. The man looked very friendly, like the guy everyone knew and liked, ideal for a guard.

* * * * * * *

Legon wasn't nervous about the guards. They probably wouldn't bother them.

"Hey there, can I help you find something here?" said the guard.

These men were paid by the town to keep order and deter robbers, but also to act as guides. They were nothing like the guards from children's stories that always harassed people who came by and were always ready for a fight. If there was no threat there was no need. It didn't make sense for the empire to place soldiers in every town; if you did that then your fighting force was too spread out, so each town paid people to do the job. These people would fight, but they also helped the town thrive. They knew every shop and resident, so if you needed something when you came to a town you weren't familiar with, the guards could guide you. This was also a great way to protect a town; happy and cheery guards got people talking, and people that might be trouble often gave themselves away.

"We need to get some supplies and I need to sell some horses," Arkin said to the guard as they approached.

"Then you'll want to see Bear. Go to your left and you can't miss him, and if it's traveling supplies you're in need of, there's Peg's shop next door that can help you out."

"Thank you. Bear?" Arkin asked.

"That's a nickname. The guy is fat and hairy and looks like, well, a bear."

"Does he like that name?"

The man laughed heartily. "Nope, not at all, but he'll tell you he loves it just to save face."

"Thank you for your assistance," Arkin said graciously.

They entered the town and started to Bear's shop. As they went Legon noticed that unlike Salmont, Salkay was a planned city. That meant that if you wanted to build in the town you first needed to submit plans to the regent, and the building needed to meet certain guidelines. This was for several reasons. First of all, Salkay had a wall and a defensive plan, so if your building hurt that plan or affected it you may not get approved. Also, things like sanitation were taken into account.

They made their way through narrow streets. Most of the shops along this way were travel related and there weren't a lot of dwellings. Soon they came to a one-story building with a large fenced in area off to the right side with horses, donkeys and mules walking around. Attached to the building were stables.

They all dismounted and followed Arkin through a large door that horses could go through as well. The room was a hall that had stalls going up either side. At the end of the hall there was sunlight to the right, indicating the exit to the fenced in area. A short round man with black hair and beard came out of a stall to their left, and sure enough he looked like a black bear.

The image was made stronger by his soot covered clothing that indicated he made his own horseshoes. Arkin diverted his eyes, trying not to chuckle at the accuracy of Bear's nickname. Bear approached them with a large "I'm going to take your money" smile on his face.

"Well hello there. What can I do for you today?" His voice was energetic and happy. The perfect salesman.

"I am assuming you're Bear," Arkin said, extending his hand. The man flinched for just a moment.

"Yes that's me. They call me Bear because, well not to sound like I have a big head, but I'm strong like a bear." He laughed in an exaggerated fashion. "Silly, really. I tell people not to call me that, but you know how people are."

"Yes I do. We are traveling and in need a few things. Can you help us?"

"Well I'm sure I can. By the looks of it you have more than enough horses. I take it you need tack and things of that nature?"

"Yes, and we would like to sell seven of these horses as well."

A look of incredulity crossed Bear's wide face. "You want to sell seven?"

"Yes. Can you buy them, or would you like us to try someone else?"

"No, no, I can take them. Let me have a look. I hope you're not expecting a lot for them, I mean," Bear said, walking up to Calvin and Phantom.

"Not those ones. The ones that have stuff tied to them. You can have whichever seven you want, it doesn't matter to me." Bear inspected the horses that a few days ago had belonged the queen. Legon wondered if Bear would figure it out.

"These are exceptional horses. You can tell just looking at them. I wouldn't be surprised if they were military grade. Say, how did you get them?" There was a suspicious look on

Bear's face. He was going to figure it out. They must look guilty bringing in this many horses to sell.

Arkin didn't lose his cool and said in a calm voice, "We killed ten royal guard and these were their horses."

Legon looked at Arkin in disbelief. He wanted to say something but his voice wasn't working. Bear looked a little uncomfortable; he looked them over, eyes lingering on Sasha and Keither, and then gave a loud bark of laugher.

"Ok, ok, I get your point. I won't go sticking my nose into your business. Killed ten royal guards, eh? I like you, buddy. Ok, so here's what my thoughts are: there are five of you and you are going to have eight horses, so my guess is that three of them will be for pack. Now I don't have the money to pay you for all seven, but," he said raising a finger,

"I will do this instead: I will take the seven and will trade out the riding saddles for the three you keep with pack saddles. Then I will shoe all your horses and make any repairs to your current equipment." Bear smiled widely, like he was going out of his way. Arkin took a moment to answer.

"We'll take that deal, plus four hundred shells." Legon did another double take. That was a good chunk of change, and they didn't need the money. What was Arkin doing?

Bear frowned. "Three hundred and I get help with the shoes."

Arkin looked at Kovos. "It's your call - you're the smith."

"Oh, you're a smith?" Bear asked.

"Yeah, ok, deal," Kovos said. "But one question: Why don't you go to the forge? Why do you need my help?"

"Ah, the forge. Well, that's government owned and you can buy ingots from it, but as far as production it only does government work."

"Like what?" asked Keither.

Bear looked at the boy and smirked. "Looks like you had a riding accident. If you like I would be happy to give you some lessons while you're here."

"Thank you, but I'm not interested," Keither replied. "What does the forge make?"

"Oh, the forge. Well, anything for the government really, armor, weapons, wheels, you name it."

"So nothing for the town?"

"No it doesn't, that's why we need a smith, and…"

"We don't want to take any more of your time. We need to get a few other things while we're here. How long with this take you?" Arkin asked.

"You can leave sometime tomorrow afternoon, provided your companion here knows what he's doing."

"I'll have the shoes done tonight. If you can get the tack and other stuff we can leave by morning. You guys go run your errands, I'll hook up with you later," Kovos said, starting to rummage through his bags. Bear gave them directions to a local inn and shops they needed to go to. By nightfall they were done with their shopping and were in Arkin's room at the inn.

"Why did you tell Bear that we killed those men?" Keither asked. Arkin looked at him with a wry smile.

"Because no one would admit that, and it's hard to believe. Sometimes the best way to hide something is to put it in the open. No doubt your next question will be about why I asked for such a steep price for the horses when we have money. Well that's also easy - if we look like we're rich then we draw attention, but if we look like we're just bargaining then we won't."

Kovos came in the room filthy. "Ok they're all done. We can leave in the morning, and believe me, that will not be soon enough. Bear is driving me crazy!"

Legon chuckled. "Why is that?"

"He will not shut up, and he keeps trying to sell me stuff. He tried to get me to buy this old nag that looked like it was ready to die. Told me it was a great 'pre-owned horse'. Honestly!" Kovos sat hard on the bed next to him and placed his hands on his knees.

"Well he's a used horse salesman, what do you expect?" Sasha said.

They continued to talk for a bit and then decided to head off to bed. Arkin had his own room and Legon and Sasha were sharing one. The place was nice, a lot like their home, but it felt odd not to have his own room. Not that Sasha was a bother, but the man at the front desk had asked about them being married and that had made his skin crawl a bit. At the same time he wasn't keen to leave her side. He was in protection mode right now and he probably wouldn't sleep unless he knew she was fine.

It was nice sliding under the sheets and putting his head on a somewhat soft pillow, almost like this was just any other trip. Soon the ceiling he was looking at faded away as sleep took over.

The ceiling was replaced by clouds. In his dream he rolled on the ground. *Great, another one of these* he thought. He was on the field tonight, but to his left he saw dirt and gravel, so he was somewhere in between the two... two... whatever these were. To his left in the mist was the outline of the black dragon, to his right just mist. This was such and odd dream. He never saw the other dragon, just the one that he associated with evil and bad things. He wondered... if he only saw the black dragon, did that mean that he was a bad person? There was an overwhelming feeling of confirmation, which somehow he knew was coming from the black dragon. He was a bad person, but why was he moving towards the field where perhaps the white dragon was?

The feeling came again, this time saying he couldn't make it. But there was a new feeling now, one that came somewhere else, one that felt good and hopeful. There was a grumble from the black dragon; he needed to be paying more attention to it. *No I don't. Maybe I need to concentrate on the other feeling*, he thought, or did he say it? Could you think to yourself in a dream? What did all this mean anyway? Did it mean anything? He wasn't sure.

He thought about this for awhile and then looked down, noticing that he had gotten closer to the black dragon. Fear came. He didn't want to be closer to that one. Still on lying on the ground, he started to inch the other way but somehow he kept getting closer to the dragon. He rolled around on his belly, facing the field away from the dragon, crawling, straining to remember the feeling of hope that he had felt. The more he thought about it the more he moved away from the dragon. He wanted to turn back and look but something made him keep his eyes ahead of him.

The mist was getting thick now and he couldn't see the ground, even on his belly. There was a thunderous THUD… THUD. The second was softer and coming from behind him. The dragon was leaving. THUD. He pawed the ground, wanting to keep moving away but it was so hard to figure what way to go. THUD. His fingers closed around a vine that was on the ground. He pulled himself along, holding to the vine, hoping it led away from danger, THUD. Soft now. Deep breathing from high above him. There was the fear again. What if this was not the white dragon? What if this was just another Iumenta? He looked up into a bright flash of violent blue.

Chapter Twelve
Empathy

"It has been said that love is the strongest power for good in this world, and that if more people loved there would be far less suffering. I would disagree with that theory; it is not love itself, but what and how we love, for surely the tyrant loves the suffering he causes just as much as the mother loves her child."
- Teachings of the Restored Queen

Legon's eyes blinked open. He felt cold sweat covering him and his breath was ragged. He stared up at the canvas ceiling of the tent; he couldn't hear Sasha's breathing. He sat up trying to wave off the grogginess.

Where is she? he thought.

The dreams were always a bit better when she was close, but she wasn't in the tent. Then it came to him

"The Jezeer," he said.

Tonight Sasha was learning the Art of the Waking Sleep, a form of meditation that allowed you to stay up for hours with no sleep at all. You could put yourself in a state that was almost as beneficial as sleep, only it took a tenth of the time. Tonight was her night to learn. He had to admit she was doing well with the training, but it still seemed as if they were missing something.

In the two weeks following their departure from Salkay, both of them had learned a lot but felt as though they hadn't. It was aggravating in many ways. That wasn't going to matter for long, though, since they were almost to Salez and then maybe Legon would get some answers. Or maybe not, it was hard to say. He wasn't sure of who to talk to or what to do, and Arkin wasn't talking about what he needed to do there.

He lay back down, still exhausted. The dreams had been going full tilt now, yet it was odd that they changed every night. Some nights he was close to the black dragon and other nights to that blue light. No matter what he did, he couldn't figure out what that light was supposed to be. Arkin had said that dreams symbolize what was going on in the mind, but there was no answer for these dreams. What was he supposed to be figuring out? The way he felt when he went to bed seemed to have an effect on what the dreams were like. If he was happy with himself and his day, usually he was closer to the blue light, but if he was unhappy he felt closer to the black dragon.

Legon realized it was going to be morning soon. He needed to sleep. They had a big day tomorrow. They would be entering Salez, and he was going to need his wits about him. As soon as he closed his eyes, though, a noise outside made him start and shoot straight up. *What was that sound?* It sounded like a voice. It could be that he was just hearing things, but better be sure. He stuck his head out of the tent and saw Sasha sitting next to the fire, eyes closed, trying to master the Waking Sleep. Arkin looked at him with an eyebrow raised.

"Nothing," said Legon. "Never mind. Thought I heard something." He flopped back down; he hadn't heard anything. It was just in his head.

* * * * * * *

Sasha was vaguely aware of Legon saying something as she was deep in concentration, trying to figure out the Waking Sleep. In theory, once in the right state she would have waking dreams but still hear her surroundings. It wasn't going well. Her mind was reaching a different state for sure. However, that state was sleep. She kept drifting off and Arkin would catch her before she slumped into the fire. She thought she had come close once, but it turned out to be nothing.

Then it happened. She heard everything around her just like Arkin had taught them. She was aware of what everything was, and she could feel her mind and body filling with energy. Strange dreams suddenly filled her mind's eye. Dreams she wasn't in control of but could still see, hear, and feel. Time seemed not to exist either, but somehow she knew how long she was out. She brought herself out of the waking sleep and looked at Arkin, who was smiling in the light of the sunrise. She slumped down.

"Why was I out for so long? I thought I should sense time, right?"

"You should. I was ready to tell you to go to bed and get some sleep the old fashioned way, but just then you achieved the Waking Sleep, but only for about five minutes. Then you fell asleep for five hours." There was a placating look on his face.

"Why didn't you wake me up?"

"You were fine where you were, and I figured if you woke up on your own you could have another try."

Arkin stood and walked off without another comment. She was a little put out. She had been sitting there all night long sleeping and he had just watched her? Or did he go to bed himself? If she had been doing what she was supposed to she would have known that, but still, what if she had taken a header into the fire? She stood, feeling stiff, and started on breakfast.

"Morning, Sash," Legon said, coming out of the tent.

"Good morning. How did you sleep?"

"Meh. Had another one. I don't know why they affect me more when your not there."

"I have a soothing personality." She turned and gave him a warm but fake smile.

He laughed. "Yeah that's it."

As the day wore on they drew closer to Salez. Soon they could see a dark haze over the next hill, indicating that the city would be just on the other side. Arkin's training had filled the last few weeks, but some of the most important training was how to protect their minds. Magic users and Dragons could read thoughts, but if you knew what you were doing you could block them out.

"Remember, there are going to be many people at the gate, so if they do have someone checking thoughts they'll only be looking for obvious things like aggression. In light of that, keep your thoughts focused on the mundane, understand?" Arkin warned.

"But what if one tries to go deeper?" Kovos asked with a little nervousness in his voice.

"You won't know if they do, but if it looks like someone is paying a little too much attention to you, clear your head. If that doesn't work then try to hurt yourself."

"Do what?" Kovos asked.

"Fall off your horse or something like that. Anything that will agitate the people around you and more importantly, your mind"

"Don't worry. I'm sure I'll fall off my horse anyway, so I wouldn't be too worried about it," Keither said with a chuckle.

They headed east and came over the top of the hill. When they crested the top, Legon felt his stomach drop. In front of them was the largest city he had ever seen. Salez was beyond huge. The smoke from thousands of chimneys formed a dark haze floating above the city. The harsh smoke made him want to sneeze. The city was built on two hills that were separated by the Kayloose running between them. Farms surrounded the city which was encircled by a towering stone wall. From the hilltop vantage Legon could see that the wall even spanned the river, which passed though grates built in along the bottom. Towers were spaced evenly along the massive wall. Behind them was slate roof after slate roof.

Further up, he could see other walls with towers indicating where the city had once ended. He counted five of these inner walls, but only the largest outer wall connected both hills. The city rose from the horizon like two mountains, each topped with a fortress. The fortress on the north hill was large but nothing compared to the fortress topping the south. The building had tiers, giving each new level the ability to shoot over the first. He could see nine towers along the first wall just from where he was sitting. It looked like the city walls and fortresses were made of whitewashed granite, making the city bright, but also giving it a striped appearance because of the slate roofs. Legon saw splashes of red, blue, green, and orange everywhere, but from a distance the granite and slate dominated.

"Arkin, how many people do you think live there?" Legon asked.

"Oh I don't know, around two hundred and fifty thousand. But keep in mind, Salez is not the largest city."

"You mean there's ones bigger than this?" Sasha asked amazed.

"Much larger, yes. Now when we get into town, I will go talk to my contact here and find out if he knows anything. You lot will go to the Claw Foot Inn and wait for me. If it looks like we've been compromised we need to leave fast, got it?"

Legon wasn't happy about this part of the plan. After all, he was the one in need of answers, but at the same time the order to arrest him came from the Queen in the capital. Salez seemed like a good place to find those answers. Still, he needed to take Arkin's lead on this. After all, the man had been living in the middle of the empire as a spy for years.

"Ok, we'll take your lead," replied Legon. As he spoke, they saw a large orange creature fly from the north fortress. Far reaching bat-like wings pushed its long body through the air effortlessly. It flew northeast away from them. A chill ran down Legon's spine as he noticed that the dragon seemed to leach light from the sky, although not nearly as much as the one in his dreams.

"That was an Iumenta Dragon, wasn't it?" Keither asked. There was fear in his voice but also interest.

"Yes it was. Now let's go." Arkin started forward to Salez, seemingly unfazed by the monster.

* * * * * * * *

Keither marveled at the dragon that was now just a small dot in the sky. There wasn't a lot of information available on Dragons, mostly because the Iumenta controlled what information was available to the public. Keither did know that they were a key part in the Queen's takeover and subsequent reign.

Salez was beautiful, with its whitewashed walls and the way the main city was contained within the barrier. That was real security. As they drew closer, Keither could see that they were easily forty feet high. As they joined the large group of people entering the main gate, he saw that it was roughly as thick as it was tall. That seemed odd.

"Arkin, why is the wall so thick? Isn't that way too much stone?"

"It's not solid stone. Most if it is earth and timber. It makes the wall extremely strong. Men can patrol the top and keep ballista and catapults up there with their supplies."

There was something else that was odd about Salez as well. As they entered they were not greeted by beggars. There should have been lots of them in a city this big, but there was no one out asking for offerings. Sasha noticed this as well. "Where are the people begging for food and money?" she asked.

"They're in the Queen's care. There are no beggars in the empire, or at least not in any city big enough to be called a city," said a man that was next to them leading a donkey laden with parcels. "There hasn't been in about five years now. If you lose your home you are taken into the Queen's care".

How could the Iumenta be bad if they got rid of homelessness? Keither thought. Arkin was off base; he needed to figure out what was wrong with the man.

"For how long does one stay in the care of the Queen?" Kovos asked.

"For the rest of your life, of course. If they left her care they would be back to clogging the streets in a week," the man said with derision.

Well maybe it wasn't so good. If the Iumenta took care of the poor until they could function on their own, that would be one thing, but for the rest of their lives?

"Ok, you go find the Inn. It should be up that road a bit," Arkin said, pointing up a street to the right. "I will meet you there in a few hours. Don't worry about getting us rooms, we may not be staying."

* * * * * * *

Legon wasn't all that thrilled about going off in a big city without Arkin, but he would have to get over it. Thankfully, it turned out the inn wasn't that hard to find. When they entered, they were greeted by a wave of musty smoke and sound. The inn had a tavern on the lower level and people were coming in from all around for lunch. The group moved toward the last table and sat around it. Legon sat with his back to the window, watching the people and waiting impatiently for Arkin. A tall woman with long red hair and a green dress came by and asked if they wanted anything to drink.

"What's good here?" Kovos asked.

She smiled warmly. "Everything."

"Ok, what do you like the most?" Kovos was flirting with the waitress. He loved Emma, but Legon knew that he just couldn't help himself. That was just how Kovos was. The woman placed her hand on his shoulder and turned herself just a little, subtly indicating that she was talking only to him. Her low cut blouse and the way she tilted herself just a bit to Kovos wasn't lost on any of them. This woman was a pro, and Kovos her sucker for today. This was going to cost them.

"Well, I like the ginger tea." She was playing with his shirt. This always happened. This lady was going to get Kovos to buy the most expensive thing on the menu and then he was going to leave her a huge tip. Sasha was rolling her eyes, looking disgusted.

"Yeah, we'll all have a cup." Kovos handed her way more money than any tea was worth and the woman walked off. It was a good thing they had stiffed Bear on the horses. The waitress wasn't even that good looking.

Kovos turned back to them with a stupid look on his face. "What are you all looking at me like that for?"

"Give me the money," Sasha said, holding out her hand.

"What? Why?"

"Because you are a moron, that's why. Ginger tea? Are you for real?"

"She said she liked it."

"She liked your money," spat Sasha. Then added harshly, "Our money."

"Like you would know. I bet it's great."

"And if its not?"

"Fine, you can have the bag, but if the tea is good, I get it back," Kovos said as he held out his hand with the money bag. Sasha promptly took it.

The tea came out and was terrible. Legon liked ginger but not like this. Sasha was forcing down a sip when she stood up and clapped her hands to her mouth.

"Oh it's not that bad. I kind of like it…" Kovos started, but she was out the door.

Legon turned to see her running out in the street and letting a blonde woman inside. As she entered he took a look at the newcomer. Her hair was long blonde and she was thin with green eyes and a . . .

"SARA!" he said, getting up and crossing the room. He wrapped his arms around her. "I can't believe you're here. Come sit down with us, how are you?"

"Um, well, I…," she began, looking totally dazed and shocked.

"Sit down, sit down. Oh, I am so happy to see you," Sasha said, planting Sara next to Legon. Sara took a moment to rearrange the red dress, hiking up its low-cut neck line, then checked to make sure she hadn't lost any jewelry. He was surprised by all of the makeup and jewelry. When he had known her she wasn't a flashy person at all and was a little on the chubby side. Now she was thin and looked good, but there was something off about her.

"I thought you were in the Queen's care?" Keither asked. Sara's face darkened and she looked down.

"Yes, I am."

"Well you look like you're doing great. Looks like the Queen's care isn't so bad after all." Keither looked at them all smugly.

"No, it's…" Legon could see tears in her eyes now. The low cut dress. The makeup. The jewelry. It all suddenly clicked. She was a slave and slaves didn't have that stuff.

She looked like she couldn't talk, as if she was ashamed. Like she wanted to go and hide under a rock. With her eyes diverted away from them she said, "Keither, I'm a slave and was sold to an Iumenta that owns a brothel."

Her voice was etched with the same shame and sadness that adorned her face. Legon was surprised that pain and sadness, not anger, boiled up in him. There was a warm sensation in the back of his head. He tried to ignore it and shifted away from the window, closer to Sara and out of the warm sun. Keither looked dumbstruck and embarrassed. Sasha and Kovos were looking down as an uncomfortable silence grew.

"Can you get away?" Legon asked

"No, they mark us with magic. Here, look," she said, turning to them and lifting her hair. It felt like ice water was being poured down his whole body. On the back of her neck was a black tattoo with two circles inside each other. At the center was a six pointed star. The symbol itself was not the part that unnerved him, but more how it was put there.

"If I leave town and anyone see this tattoo, I will be taken back to my owner, and then…"

* * * * * * *

Arkin turned the corner into an alley in between two large buildings, looking for the man he was supposed to meet. This part of town wasn't where you would expect to find an informant. Most of the time you had to go to the bad part of town, the part where the snitches were. Not Monson, though. He wasn't what you would expect, either.

A figure walked out from behind a carton and waved to Arkin. As he approached, Arkin saw the young man, really a boy around fourteen. His father had been the original informant, but not anymore. Monson's family was from one of the old human houses, one that had been in charge before the Iumenta swine took over, the House of Grey to be precise. The family was an example of how the queen was able to destroy human nobility. The imposed taxes and penalties that were imposed made it impossible for a family like theirs to exist. Subsequently, all of the noble lines had dissolved, and humanity lost more and more sway in the government. The person in front of him was the last of a line. A line that the Iumenta were keen to destroy.

"What are you doing here?" Monson asked.

"Not happy to see me?"

"It's not that, but from what I've heard, your charge is a wanted man."

"He is. We took out ten royal guards and are on the run headed south. What can you tell me? How did they find out?"

"Ten royal guard? They really are pathetic, aren't they?"

Arkin smiled. This is why he liked Monson. He was his dad from his mannerisms down to his attitude. Long black hair obscured much of Monson's scarred face, a permanent reminder of the fire six years ago. The same fire had killed his father. It was amazing the young boy still lived. Arkin didn't know much about what had happened, but from all accounts there had been foul play. Monson's mother had taken it hard and dedicated herself to fighting the Iumenta. As soon as he was old enough, her son joined her. Monson was great at gathering information; because he was so young, people didn't suspect him.

Monson continued on. "Well, from what I can tell this is being kept quiet. The Queen's Senashow is in charge. It looks like he just sent out a wide sweep for his first attempt at locating you. But that doesn't mean that he was planning on his pawns bringing your boy in."

"What do you mean? And the boy's name is Legon."

"Well, here's the way I see it: They have to know that your charge has some sort of protection, and the royal guard is great at beating things out."

Arkin gave Monson a wry smile. "I thought you said they were pathetic."

"Ha! I did and they are, but the Senashow is not. Look at what his planning accomplished. You were flushed right out into the open and now you're scampering around the Cona Empire without a plan."

He was probably right. They would need to move fast. By now the empire would have figured out that they were missing soldiers. He kicked himself. It had been dumb to come to Salez, but he needed to figure out how much the Iumenta knew.

"Ok, what else do you know?"

"Nothing. Do you think you're the first to ask? The Iumenta seem to actually care this time. You need to get south, but be careful. The army has been shipping supplies down that way for a while now."

"What do you mean? They can't have everything blocked off."

"No, but I don't know what they're up to. It's platoons of the main army, so it's not the Senashow's doing. But if you're on a wanted list you'd still better avoid the area."

Monson turned at a sound down the dark ally. He looked at the end where light was making an attempt to penetrate the dark space. Monson turned back to him. "We need to leave. Just get your people out. Take the long way back to avoid large cities and rivers. If I find out more I will send word."

And with that Monson Grey walked to the other side of the alley and disappeared Arkin hurried back to the inn and found his four companions sitting in the tavern with . . . Sara?

Empathy

* * * * * * *

Arkin walked to the table, surprise on his face. Legon noticed that the surprise was part hesitation as well.

"Arkin? What are you doing here? In fact, what are all of you doing here?" Sara asked.

There was silence as they all sat, waiting for someone to talk. He reached up and scratched at the back of his head, which was now tingling. Sasha gave him a stern look.

"Where do you live?" Sasha asked Sara, trying to change the subject.

"In my owner's business. We work at night, mostly, but it's really whenever a customer comes in or when we're shipped off to the army for a week or two."

"They do *what?*" Kovos said, all signs of sympathy replaced with anger.

"We go to the barracks sometimes when business is slow, or when we first get here as part of our orientation."

"Orientation?" Legon said with his head now positively buzzing.

"When we get here, if we aren't willing to work then we get *oriented* to our new life."

"What is involved in this orientation?" Keither asked, looking scared.

"A lot of stuff. Usually we are beaten and then given to a large group of people. They're told to show us the ropes for a few weeks, but not to do any permanent damage to us physically. Even after they break us we stay in orientation until new girls arrive." Her face was now very pale. "Mine was three weeks," she said in a whisper.

There was a pit in Legon's stomach. He felt for this girl. She had gone through a lot in the last few months and he could see that she was hurting. He wished there were some way to make it better, to take away her pain. He reached out to place his hand sympathetically on her forearm, but as his hand touched her, the feeling in his head shot down his arm. Images, scents, sounds, and feelings flashed in front of his eyes. He was a terrified girl being dragged along. Now he was being whipped. He could feel each lash as it burned across his back, splitting the skin. He gasped as he saw the lash marks heal without a scar. He realized that the whip was enchanted.

The fear was so strong now. He was in a room filled with men, all smiling and calling out. They were on her now, ripping off clothes, hitting and kicking. Then the violation, the humiliation tore through him. The memories of the day he broke, letting them do what they wanted, doing to them what they wanted. Then images of client after client ran through his mind. Every time he felt all the emotions, all the pain, everything. It was too much.

He pulled his hand off her arm, breathing hard. Sara yelped and clapped her hand to her neck. Sasha was up in a heartbeat, scrambling around Sara and lifting her hand from her neck.

"It's gone," she said with a gasp.

"What's gone?" Legon asked.

"The tattoo." Sasha looked at him. There was an awed and frightened look on her face.

Sara looked at him with new tears in her eyes, but this time they were tears of gratitude. "I felt all of my pain leave me. I felt your compassion and love and now my tattoo is gone." She looked at him intently, looked into his eyes.

"You're a Venefica."

"A wha…" he started.

"Silence," snapped Arkin. "Sara, don't say another word, not here. You know what could happen. You lot clear your minds."

"But . . ." Kovos said.

"Do it now," Arkin barked as people from around the tavern looked at them.

"Sara, you cannot go back to your owner. You know as well as I do that they will find out what happened. And we all need to leave now. Sasha, give Sara some clothes so she will look normal walking out of the city, and the rest of you get ready. We're leaving. Now."

"Arkin, what about getting…" Keither started.

"We have answers, now go."

They all stood, but Sara looked apprehensive. She was obviously torn between the possibility of newfound freedom and the fear of her owner. Legon had taken her pain into himself for just a moment, but in that moment he had gained an understanding that would have taken years to learn, if not a life time. To feel what someone else was dealing with, how they thought and felt during a situation…. He wondered what kind of person he would be if he had this knowledge his whole life.

The sensation in his head was gone now. He should have felt scared about what he'd just done, but he didn't. After all, he did what he had wanted to do. He wanted to set Sara free and to take away her pain. Was it magic? It had to be, there was no other way to explain it.

Sara moved along slowly with the others and Arkin showed them out the door and down the street. The streets were clogged with people and the going was slow, but Legon wasn't paying attention to that. He kept rolling the thought of magic around in his head. What had Sara called him? *Venefica*, he thought. What did that mean, and how did she know about it? He also wondered what Arkin had learned that made him want to rush out of town so fast. They reached the stables next to the entrance of Salez.

"Sara, do you have a horse?" Arkin asked. He noticed Sara was now in one of Sasha's dresses. It fit well, but when did that happen? He needed to get his head in the game.

"Ah, no, I don't."

"We'll buy one, then."

* * * * * * *

Sasha walked close to her friend. She couldn't believe that Sara was here, but at the same time Sasha felt sad to see her. When Sara had been taken into the queen's care Sasha had always just hoped that she would be made a common servant of some sort, but that obviously hadn't happened. Sara looked like she was shell shocked and very obviously scared about what could happen to her.

Arkin left to buy Sara a new horse. Legon and Kovos took to walking around the group in wide, meandering circles. Over the last few days Arkin had started to teach them defensive techniques that they now were employing.

"You guys have been through a lot, haven't you?" Sara asked. Sasha started a bit.

"You could say that. I will tell you more on the road, but yes, we've had a hard run so far. Are you ok?"

"I'm fine, just nervous is all."

"I can see that. Are you worried about getting caught?"

"Yes. If the mark on my neck is gone I should be ok, but still."

Arkin came back shortly with a new horse in tow. He was also accompanied by a group of children leading the other horses along. He handed the reins of the new one to Sara. She took them and they all began to exit the city. Two soldiers stood guard at the city gate. One was young looking with shaggy, sandy hair and a long nose. It appeared that he was new because he was eyeing every passerby with interest. The other was older looking with a short, scruffy beard and a look of extreme boredom on his face. As they passed, the younger guard stopped them.

"Hold up. You know you can't leave," he said, directing his voice at Sara.

"And why can't she leave?" asked Arkin in a challenging voice.

"Because she belongs to the brothel up the way, that's why."

Chapter Thirteen
Imperia

"In all my research I have yet to truly understand the depth of the journey that the Everser Vald made, but I think that if we narrow our focus we can find individual events within that journey and learn from them. Maybe if we understand we can recreate greatness, but perhaps not."
- Atavus Imperata House Evindass, Secunum Renovatie

Kovos knew that they needed to act fast before the situation got out of hand. He walked up to the man.

"What do you mean the brothel?" He tried to put as much menace in his tone as he could.

"She's a whore. I have her at least once a week. Isn't that right, sweetheart?" The man smiled at Sara, who was looking terrified.

Kovos wasn't sure if it was a good idea, but it was worth a shot. He dropped his horse's reins and lunged forward, hitting the man hard in the mouth and sending him sprawling back. His companion leaped up and stood between them, sword drawn and leveled at Kovos. People were walking away quickly, not wanting to be a part of whatever was going to happen.

"What do you think you're doing? That's a…," the older soldier started.

"I'll have a go at anyone that calls my fiancée a whore!" Kovos roared at the men.

The soldier on the ground was getting up and spluttering. "She's a whore, I know she is!" the younger one said.

Arkin turned Sara around and lifted the back of her hair, showing her unblemished neck. "Are you sure?" he said.

The older man stretched his neck to look and then turned to his companion and hit him in the gut.

"You imbecile! She's not marked! And to think I was going to defend your worthless hide." He turned back to Kovos and Sara. "I'm sorry, he's new. I would still warn you, however, not to hit a soldier, but in this case I understand. I would have done the same. Just move along." He eyed his downed companion with distaste.

Kovos walked up to Sara and placed his hand gently on hers. "Come on, dear. I'm sorry about this." There was no way that had worked. He thought for sure the men would figure it out. He and Sara hadn't even been standing close to each other. They mounted their horses and started south away from Salez.

After they had some distance behind them, Arkin rode in close to him. "That was some fast thinking on your part."

"Is that a good thing? I took a big risk."

"Perhaps, but shocking the men was about the only way to get out of that, I'm afraid."

It was good Arkin agreed. The guy knew what he was doing, so if he said it was a good job then that's what it was. And what the hell had Legon done to Sara back at the tavern? It kind of gave Kovos the creeps. Not that what Legon had done was bad; it was good that Sara was free now. Still, the thought of his friend being able to use magic was odd. How did he do it?

Salez was moving farther away and they would set up camp in the next hour or so. Then maybe he would find out what was going on.

* * * * * * *

Legon looked down at his hands, still trying to figure out what he had done back at the tavern. The scariest thing was that he hadn't really done anything. He had just wanted it to happen and it did. He was having a hard time looking over at Sara. In a way he felt like he'd violated her by taking on memories that weren't his. At the same time he felt for her and cared for her in way he never had before. He was also confused because she didn't seem to be mad at him for delving into her mind. Maybe it was because he had freed her and now she felt obligated. At any rate he needed to apologize for what he had done. He steered Phantom up next to her.

"Sara?"

She looked over at him.

"I'm sor- sorry for going into your head like that. I shouldn't have."

"Why are you sorry?" she asked, looking perplexed.

"Aren't you mad at me? That was private stuff I saw and felt."

Sara reached out and placed her hand gently, almost lovingly, on his arm and looked him in the eyes. "You took my pain from me. You gave me relief from my suffering. You should never feel sorry for doing that for someone."

"I guess I don't understand."

She paused, gathering her thoughts. "Ok, when you saw all those things that happened to me, you felt it, right?"

"Yes, everything. It was horrible."

"Yes it was, but when you were in my head suffering those things, I couldn't feel it anymore. I only felt the compassion that you had for me. Now you are truly the only person on earth that can completely understand that part of my life and who I am."

"Ok, but don't you still have the pain? And aren't you upset with me for invading your feelings?"

"Not at all. I can remember the pain, but I can also remember the compassion that you have for me. And if I ever want to talk about it I know I can go to you and you'll understand perfectly. Have you ever truly felt love from someone? Actually felt what they were feeling?"

"Well, no, I guess not."

She smiled. "Exactly. I have now, and I will always remember that. I can say that I truly know that someone does care about me and that I'm not alone. Do you realize what a gift that is?"

She gave his arm a squeeze, trying to emphasize her point. He felt himself begin to smile. He hadn't thought about it like that. When she put it that way he realized that perhaps he had done something kind for her. There was something noble about taking on another's burden. He was willing to do it again, too. In fact he was willing to do anything for Sara's well being. He would pay whatever price he needed to.

"I guess it hadn't occurred to me to look at it that way. Thanks." Legon paused. "Oh, I almost forgot. What was that word you called me back at the shop?"

"I called you a Venefica."

"What does that mean?"

Arkin spoke from behind him. "It means 'user'."

"'User'?" Legon asked.

"Of magic," Sara clarified.

"Good. Sara, I take it living in a city close to Iumenta has taught you a thing or two?" Arkin said.

"That's one way of putting it," she said with a bit of a grimace.

Arkin's voice took on the teacher's tone that was becoming the norm. "What you did today was magic obviously, and people who use magic are called Venefica. They practice the art of Imperia."

The word was foreign to Legon. "Imperia?"

"Yes. That is what it is called when you use magic. The word is Elfish. All magic is done in that language."

Trepidation started to creep into Legon's mind. "Arkin, do you know magic?"

Arkin paused for a while. He then held up his hand and clicked his fingers saying, "Flamma."

From his fingers a jet of green flame shot up about six inches.

Legon reared back. "What kind of…"

"The color is different for every Venefica, but the more magic is infused in the flame, the stronger the color will appear. We'll talk more after we set up camp somewhere." Arkin didn't seem surprised by this development in the least bit. If anything, it seemed to be what he'd expected.

The sun was still relatively high in the sky. They had a few hours before dark, plenty of time to move away from Salez, which was good. Sooner or later Sara's former owner would realize that he was a person short. There was a lot to worry about, but nothing that Legon could do at the moment so there was no point dwelling on it. In his mind Legon recited a script that Arkin taught him.

Fear is the blinder. I am the light and master of sight. I will master my fear and never again see night.

As he repeated the script, he took deep breaths through his nose, each time letting tension out of his body. As he calmed, more things brought themselves to his attention. He focused on his sense of smell. With each breath he inhaled the scent of grass and trees. Next his ears, the sound of the horses and Sasha and Sara talking, the creak of leather and the buzz of a fly. Now he concentrated on touch, feeling the soft breeze as it cooled, telling him the sun was on its way down. The northern breeze was moist and dense. It would rain tonight. He had better take extra care setting up his tent.

* * * * * * *

What the hell was going on? Legon could do magic? Keither wondered what he had gotten himself into. He shifted himself in Murray's Saddle. Kovos slowed his horse and fell back in step with him.

"What do you think?" Kovos asked.

"I don't know. We're in over our heads, I'll tell you that much," replied Keither.

"Why is that? What do you know about magic?"

The others couldn't hear him, but he still kept quiet. People who used magic were rare, and magic itself was treated with respect and care. People were also scared of it because, frankly, not that much was known about it, at least not by the common person.

"I don't know much about it, but it may explain why Arkin was able to hide in Salmont without detection," Keither answered.

"Do we need to worry about getting taken over or something?"

This was an odd turn of the tables. Kovos was coming to him asking for advice. He never did that. Kovos had always treated him like a helpless little boy, but not now.

"Well, if Arkin wanted to hurt us he could have done it a long time ago. And I don't think that magic users can take you over, but I'm not sure."

"Ok, thanks."

Kovos righted himself in his saddle and resumed a normal pace. Keither should probably be worrying about magic right now, but that wasn't what was on his mind. Sara was on his mind, and also what he thought of the empire and the queen which, just hours before, he had thought weren't that bad.

In general the whole of society was well taken care of, but at what cost? What Sara had gone through was appalling, but sounded like it wasn't uncommon. Sara was a prostitute, sure, but not everyone had to be that, most were probably labor of some short. A chill ran down his back. How many luxuries did he have due to slavery?

Arkin was right. The queen was evil. That was the only word for it. How much of what Arkin told them was true? Also, how much of the propaganda about the resistance was true? There were a lot of questions running through his mind, and a lot of his previous views were changing rapidly. If Kovos had asked him a week ago about magic users, he would have said that they were bad news unless controlled by the government, but after what Legon did…. *Maybe having people who know magic free of the government's control is a good thing,* he thought.

Then it dawned on him. This whole thing was about magic and controlling it. What Legon had done was proof that if enough people in the empire knew about magic then the government could be held in check. Or could it? People still knew magic and yet they still allowed horrible things to happen.

It felt good to be thinking. It was his element, his weapon. He leaned back in the saddle, finally comfortable on the horse. He tilted his head from side to side feeling his neck pop. Up ahead Sara was doing the same as she talked to Legon and Sasha. It was good to see her again.

* * * * * * *

Legon felt that sensation in his head again and stopped hitting the tent spike he was driving into the ground.

"What is it?" Sasha asked concernedly.

"I think I'm going to use magic again." He shouldn't be scared but he was. What if he couldn't control this stuff? What if someone got hurt? Arkin spoke from across the camp.

"Is there something you really want done?"

"No not particularly. Actually, I could go for not feeling, well, whatever this is."

Arkin laughed. "Come here. I think we can put that to use."

Legon walked carefully over to the fire pit where Arkin was standing. He knew he looked like a moron, walking slowly as if he were holding a pail of water, but what if his control slipped?

"Don't worry, you can walk normal," said Arkin.

"I don't know. Are you sure?" replied Legon. "I mean, how much do you know about this stuff?"

"Obviously a lot, Legon, if he hid in town for as long as he did," Keither said.

"You don't know that."

"He's right Legon." Arkin bent over the wood in the fire pit and uttered, "Flamma."

As he spoke, an emerald plume of flame erupted in the pit and then turned into a normal orange fire. There was a collective gasp and Kovos jumped as if someone had thrown a snake at his feet. Legon stopped, mouth open. How was Keither able to figure it out?

"How did you do that?" Legon asked.

"It's easy. You try." Arkin waved his hand over the fire and it died. "Come close to the pit and place your hand over it."

Legon knelt next to the blackened wood and placed his right hand tentatively over the still warm pit.

"Good. Now concentrate on that feeling in your head. Let it fill you."

"Fill me?"

"When you breathe in, imagine a flower blooming in your head, like when you feel energy move though you doing the Jezeer."

"Ok." Legon breathed deeply and concentrated. He felt the energy grow.

"Ok good. Now I want you to think of starting a fire, ok? Picture flames in this pit in your head."

"Ok, got it."

"Good. Now, concentrating on that image, say the word *Flamma* and let the energy run down your arm and out your hand."

"*Flamma*." The sensation shot down his arm like before. He jerked his hand up and with a yell from everyone, a jet of violet flame burst from his hand and into the air. Sasha and Sara screamed, but the flame only lasted a second and then died. He noticed that he was on his feet and franticly shaking his hand.

"You're ok Legon. Your hand is not on fire, relax," Arkin said.

"What the hell!" He slowly shook his hand, waiting for it to burn again. The flame didn't hurt; in fact it just felt kind of warm and good. Still, that was fire. Kovos looked amazed and excited.

"Do it again!" he shouted.

"Wha-?"

"Do it again. That was amazing. You shot fire out of your hand."

"I know, I was there. Why are you happy about it?"

"I thought I made it clear - you shot fire from your hand! Do it again, here, at Keither this time." Kovos reached over and grabbed Keither's arms, holding him in front of Legon.

"Kovos!" Sasha said angrily.

"What, Sasha? He'll be fine, come on."

"I'm not shooting fire at your brother. That's messed up," Legon said.

There was the sound of suppressed laughter. He turned to see Arkin and Sara both doubled over, shaking with laughter. Sasha gave them a stern look that was fading into a smile.

"Sara, you're laughing too?" she said.

"Yes, I can't help it. Kovos, come on, that's sick," she choked out through tears.

"Let go of me," Keither said, slapping Kovos away.

"Oh what? You would have been fine. The fire was fast. It would only take off your eyebrows and some hair. Not a big deal."

"Kovos, only a smith would think that wasn't a big deal," Arkin said warmly. They settled down a bit and Arkin decided that it might be a good idea for Legon to learn more about magic before trying it again. They all sat around the fire pit and waited for Arkin to start for yet another night.

"Ok, Legon, I'm sorry. Truth be told I didn't think you would even produce a spark for your first time trying to use magic."

"Well, is that bad then? And I did it by accident in Salez. I mean, is there something wrong?"

"There's nothing wrong with you, but you must be a powerful Venefica," Sara said. "I would think at least a class four... but wait, you're human." Sara turned to Arkin, looking concerned.

"A class what?" Sasha asked.

"Arkin is he part-"

"Elf? Yes, I am." Legon filled in the gaps. Sara's forehead knitted together and then a look of incredulity and joy crossed her face.

"You mean the Everser Vald?" Her voice was almost a whisper. The start of a tear formed in her eye.

"What di-" Legon began.

"Nothing. She said nothing," Arkin started hurriedly. "I will explain classes to you."

"He doesn't know?" Sara said with hurt and anger in her voice.

"Don't know what?" Legon asked.

"Wh-" Sara began.

"Nothing, Sara." Arkin went from impatient to angry. Sara opened her mouth but fell silent at a murderous glance from Arkin.

"Arkin don't you stop her, what was she saying to me?" Anger was flooding Legon as he turned to the carpenter. What was he not being told? "Tell me I want to know?"

"You aren't ready to know, and even if you were I cannot permit it!"

"What you can do is tell me what you're hiding!" Legon stood and started towards Arkin slowly. He noticed Kovos by his side. Sasha reached up and grabbed his shoulder. He tried to shake it off but couldn't.

"Legon, no. This is not the answer."

It wasn't the words that stopped him, but the emotions. He turned to look straight into Sasha's glassy blue eyes. He could feel her overwhelming desire for no more violence. His anger left almost as fast as had come, and then the connection to Sasha stopped. He turned slowly to Arkin, who no longer looked angry, but rather sad.

"Arkin what is happening?" There was fear in Legon's voice; more than he knew he was feeling.

"I want to tell you, but I don't. It's a great and terrible thing. Please, I have made many vows to keep this secret. Don't break them for me, not yet, not now."

"We won't." It was Sasha who spoke. "But please tell us what you can."

"Sit down and I will relight the fire."

They sat in a circle around the pit and Arkin placed a trembling hand over the pit and muttered, "Flamma." A merry fire instantly began to crackle in the pit.

"Magic is an amazing thing. With it you can control the elements, make things grow, heal wounds and so much more." He paused. "You see, magic is like a muscle. You can train it and make it stronger, but like a muscle it can become worn out. You can cast a spell and feel no tiring effect on your body, but if that spell is too strong for you then energy is pulled from your body."

"So can you die from a spell then?" Legon asked.

Arkin looked relieved to hear the question. "No, you can't. You can pass out but you can't die. Once your mind loses consciousness it can't sustain the spell. However, it can take some time to recover. Once again, think of this as a muscle. Now, there are what are called 'classes' to Venefica, Sara, do you know them?"

"Yes, my owner is Iumenta and a Venefica, so I learned a lot just being around him. There are eight classes. A class refers to the amount of power a Venefica has, regardless of skill."

"Meaning what?" Keither asked.

"Meaning your class has nothing to do with your ability. You can be a class five and not know what magic is," continued Sara. "Classes one and two humans can attain, usually just one. Next, Iumenta and Elves can reach up to class five, and I know dragons are higher, but that's it."

Arkin looked pleased "Very good. To 'Ascend' is to become a dragon. Only a class five can do this, and even then only a rare few. When someone 'Ascends' they will be classes six through eight. Now, the difference in each class is large. There is a gap between them as far as power goes. Meaning that if you are a strong class two you are still relatively weak to a class three. The same is more so for Ascending. The difference between classes five and six is like comparing a mountain lion to a kitten. Class sevens are extremely strong and class sixes are closer to them relatively speaking, but class eight…" Arkin shook his head.

"What?" Kovos said.

"It's like there should be a class or two in between seven and eight, but there's no eights left from my understanding," Arkin answered.

"Why not?" Sara asked.

"That is another lesson," Arkin answered with a warm smile. This was starting to get on Legon's nerves. There was one secret after another. What possible threat could he be? Hadn't they proved that they were no friend of the empire? Also, what was going on with this new ability to sense emotions?

"What class are you?" he asked.

"I'm a class two." He was a two? Well, maybe if Legon was a three or four he could overpower Arkin if need be. He was out-classed in skill so he still might lose, but still this was a small comfort.

"Ok, so what all can magic do?" Legon asked.

"A lot of things, and there is still more and more being learned about it. Basically, magic is the lynch pin in the war between the queen and the free lands."

"You mean the resistance?" Keither asked.

"They're hardly that."

"What do you mean? They fight the Queen, don't they?" asked Keither.

Arkin responded. "Just because they fight the Queen doesn't mean that they are a group of rebels. In fact they're the opposite. The Elves are their own nation, and for that matter the humans are too. You see, when the Queen took over she just took control of an existing nation."

"Yeah, but there was a war with the Elves and free humans, right?" Keither asked.

"Yes, the Elves defended their territory and the humans fought for independence, and that's what they got, for the most part. The war has never really ended," Arkin responded.

"Ok, but what about magic?" Legon said, not wanting them to go off on a tangent.

"Sorry. Yes, magic. Well, like I said, it works much like a muscle, but it can do things that your muscles never could. For example, you can use magic to alter the physical attributes of those around you."

"Like how?" Legon asked.

"Here, I will show you. Kovos, will you be so kind as to show us the progress you've made teaching Sasha to fight?"

Kovos looked confused. "I thought you were going to show us how magic affected stuff?"

"I am."

Now Sasha looked confused but, to his surprise, she stood and walked to her tent for her stave.

"No, not with the sticks. You will use real swords tonight. Sasha, you will use mine," Arkin instructed.

They both paused and Sasha began to fidget with her hands. Legon knew what she was thinking. Sasha was learning how to fight, but it wasn't her thing. She could shoot a bow, but she was having issues with the blade. She walked to Arkin, who stood and presented his blade out of the sheath. He placed a guard on it. Kovos pulled his blade out and they stood apart from each other. Sara had an amused look on her face. What did she think was funny? She and Sasha were friends. Did she want to see her lose?

Kovos nodded his head at Sasha. "Remember what I've taught you."

With that he lunged forward, swinging at her side. Sasha barley parried the blow as she stepped back. As she blocked hit after hit, Legon noticed that with every blow her blade moved closer to her body; she didn't have the strength to stop it. In fact, the only thing keeping her from getting hit with her own weapon was that Kovos was not hitting full force. She tried a thrust, but Kovos flicked the blade away almost lazily. Arkin started to talk.

"You see how this is going? It's not just that Kovos knows what he's doing, but that he is faster and stronger then Sasha. Now let's see what can happen with magic."

Kovos again slashed at her side, and to everyone's surprise Sasha's blade flashed up to block his in the blink of an eye. Kovos's sword stopped dead on hers and both looked open mouthed at the point where they touched.

"Woo! Yeah, Sasha! Kick his butt!" Sara yelled with a wide, knowing smile.

"Yeah, that's not going to happen," Kovos said. He brought his sword above his head and down. This time Sasha side-stepped in a flash and swung. There was a loud clang of metal on metal as Kovos blocked her blow. He stumbled back a bit.

"How on earth…?"

Sasha smiled. "I'm winning, Legon. Do you see this? I'm winning."

Kovos gave a loud laugh. "Oh, heck no!"

No one took sides but everyone cheered them on as the fight progressed. Sasha was still a sloppy fighter, but she was moving so fast and with so much power that Kovos was having a hard time getting to her. Even though she was going to walk away with more than a few welts, she was still doing great. Arkin looked pleased, and Legon noticed a bead of sweat forming at his brow. "Are you all right?"

"Ok, that will do," Arkin said.

Kovos and Sasha separated and both sat back down around the fire. Sara put her arm around Sasha. "I knew you could do it."

"Yeah but how did she do that? I've never had anyone fight like that." Kovos asked

"That is because I used magic to make Sasha faster and stronger. This is one of the many applications for magic in combat."

After that Arkin spent the next few hours talking about how magic could be used to make things better. It was late by the time they were ready for bed.

"Sash what tent is ours again?" Legon asked.

"Oh, it's the one over there, but I was going to stay with Sara if that's ok?"

"Sure, you're fine, so long as you feel ok."

She looked at him for a moment. "You know what? I think I will be." She hugged him and followed Sara.

Legon turned to Arkin. "Well, looks like you get to sleep with me, Arkin. How do you feel about that?"

"Ha! Don't get your hopes up. That's going to take more than ginger tea." Arkin walked to the tent, leaving Legon alone.

"What was that supposed to mean?"

* * * * * * *

Sasha closed the flaps to their tent and began to get ready for bed. It had been a long day, but she wasn't feeling all that tired. It was so good to have Sara with them. She looked like she'd been through a lot. She had lost a lot of weight since they had last spoken back home, but she was happy now that she was free. As they both lay down, Sasha looked at the flickering firelight coming through a small crack in the tent flaps.

"I know you have questions, Sash. Are you going to ask them?"

"I want to, but at the same time you seem so happy. I don't want to bring you down."

"You always did put others ahead of yourself. I'm glad to be with you and Legon again."

"We're happy that you're here too. Can I ask about today?"

Sara chuckled. "Yes."

"What happened?"

Sara took a deep breath. "Legon took my pain."

"He what?"

"When he touched my arm and got rid of my mark, he also pulled my pain and suffering into himself. I actually felt the pain leave me, and it was replaced by his caring."

"So does he still have it then?" she said with a little concern. "The pain?"

"No, it came back as soon as he let go, but I remember what he did, and that's why I'm so happy."

"I guess I don't understand."

"Sorry." Sara rolled onto her side and Sasha could see the energy in her eyes. "Have you ever felt someone's emotions before?"

"No, how could I?"

"That's my point. To feel that someone cares for you, to actually feel what they feel and then to feel your pain and memories leave you for a short time, that is the greatest gift of all."

"Because that person truly understands what you're dealing with?" Sasha asked.

"Yes, and knowing that there is someone who cares and understands you makes the pain so much easier to take. For once I'm not alone."

Sasha looked up, letting this new information roll around in her head. She had felt someone's emotions before now that she thought about it. Quite often, in fact, but it had always been on a smaller level than what Sara had experienced. She changed the subject and after a bit they fell asleep.

The next morning Sara helped her with making breakfast, and Keither was finally able to help them take down camp. Sasha would start working with him today, but as she started to get on Murray, Arkin stopped her.

"Legon, come here."

"What's up?" Legon asked.

"I want you two to ride together today."

"Um, why? We have the horses . . ."

"It's for training, you'll see. Now let's go."

Legon mounted Phantom and then helped Sasha on behind him. What was Arkin up to? Why did they need to be on the same horse?

"Legon, last night you wanted to hurt me, right?" Arkin asked. Sasha felt her brother tense just a bit.

"Yeah, sorry for the loss of control." Legon replied.

"Don't be. I was hoping you would be upset."

"You wanted me to be upset? Why?"

"Why didn't you do anything?" Arkin continued.

Come to think of it, why had he stopped? Sasha was sure that he was going to try and hurt Arkin, but as soon as she had touched him, he…

"I stopped him," Sasha blurted out.

Legon smiled. "Sash no offense, but…."

Arkin nodded his head. "She did stop you. You felt her restraint, didn't you?"

Legon was silent for a moment. His eyes widened. "How on earth…?"

"Magic users can communicate with their minds. Lay people can do this too, but it's very hard to learn. The key is making the first connection. After that it will get easier."

"So are you saying I can read minds, like Elves and Iumenta?" Legon asked.

"Yes. And Venefica can nudge people's thoughts and emotions to an extent as well, but more on that later. You and Sasha are extremely close, so you already have this connection. Sasha's episodes have always been better when you are around. This is an example of that."

"You know what? That does seem right. Think about it Sash. When I'm with you they're not as bad. You don't get as hurt, and you've said before that you can feel me there."

"Yes, I can sometimes, but you haven't been able to use magic so…"

"Yes he has," Arkin corrected her, "But he hasn't had the need of it, so it hasn't presented itself. Ok, enough talk. I want you two to try and open your minds to each other."

It was worth a shot. She tried to remember last night and pushed with her mind, or at least she thought she was pushing. After several minutes finally she thought she felt something graze her thoughts. Frustration, and then alarm, and then it was gone.

"Did you feel that?" she asked.

"Yes, I did," Legon replied. "Wow. Arkin we did it!"

Arkin nodded his head. "Good. Now do it again."

* * * * * * * *

Arkin turned back to the road, satisfied. They were getting it fast. It was going to take about three months to get to the border towns on the route the army's movement was forcing them to take. He felt drained. They were searching and searching hard. How long could he keep them hidden? Legon wouldn't be ready to learn how to mask their presence any time soon, but if he learned fast he could be a source of energy. Right now he needed to help their connection grow stronger. But it had worked. They were linked, and soon their minds would be working together, and years of half-training for both of them would come together in a few short weeks.

Chapter Fourteen
Reprieve

"The adversities in life are there to teach us, but it is the space between them where we grasp at the meanings of the lessons."
- Tales of the Traveler

The last two and half months had been some of the most intense and wonderful in Legon's life. He was growing stronger with magic. Now he could heal small wounds, light fires without shooting flames everywhere, and with a myriad of other things. Also, the connection between him and Sasha was stronger. They could communicate with their minds fully and had access to each other's knowledge. To their amazement and Keither's disappointment, they were able to handle all of Arkin's questions now. When they asked why they could suddenly handle all his questions, Arkin explained to them that he'd been training them their whole lives with only half the pieces, and now that they were able to combine their knowledge, the training was made complete. Arkin called it mental networking, explaining that it was how most parts of the Elven and Iumenta governments were run, by literally putting their heads together.

Arkin would talk to them now in their minds, so their learning was progressing faster and faster. It was amazing what you learned when you saw exactly what the teacher was trying to tell you. With their increasing knowledge of the Mahann and Jezeer, Legon was able to use the Jezeer to target and affect his and other's muscles or other biological things. Sasha's development was similar. Legon and Sasha had gotten to the point where their minds never truly left each other. They may not have been able to see exactly what the other was thinking. but they were always aware of the other. This came in handy with Sasha's episodes.

Legon and Sasha also found that not only could magic enhance the people and animals around them, but hinder them as well. When Sasha would slip into an episode Legon was able to keep her body from hurting itself. The energy involved was great and he couldn't stop all of her convulsions, but she no longer sustained injuries and didn't need hours to recover after them. She still lost visible consciousness, but she was awake and active in his mind. That was, unfortunately, the bad part. Now Sasha was aware of each episode and, more important, the pain of them. Before she hadn't been awake and had no recollection, but now she was keenly aware of her body fighting itself, and Legon felt all of it.

He dipped a rag in the stream next to their camp. The water was cool and refreshing as it ran over his fingers. They were still heading south in a meandering path. Summer was in full force and this part of the empire was hot and, to his distaste, humid. The wet heat was oppressing, the air seemed to weigh down their lungs and they were always covered in sweat. The land was flat now, but they were in a dense forest and the scent of moss and earth became more apparent.

There weren't a lot of major waterways in this area, so towns and villages were sparse. On occasion there would be large clearings or they would approach a co-op farming community.

The co-ops usually had no town center and the people in the area tried to support one another. They were seldom bothered by bands of robbers because the people really only had the food they grew and tried to sell. Because of their meager belongings, these people fought hard for their property. At any rate, many robbers at some point in time, usually when they hit bottom, had worked for one of these people. All in all Legon liked most of the people in the co-ops. They were usually kind and they banded together.

It was also rare for people to go into the Queen's care from these communities. The empire was in control of these areas, but just barely. The openness of everything gave people places to hide anything, like family members. In addition, the cost of harassing the people in remote places like this was too high, thus they were left alone for the most part.

Legon pulled the rag out and wiped down his face, neck, and upper body. He felt a week's worth of trail debris and filth rub from him. They had been passing creeks for the last week, but none of them were clean so they weren't able to bathe at all. This was one of the major discomforts of the road. Back home, working with his father as a butcher, and Sasha working with his mother as a healer, there had been strict laws about cleanliness. Breaking those laws was expensive, so every day they cleaned everything, from their workspaces to themselves. He normally did this at the end of the day as a means of washing off the death of his job, but still he washed his hands before work and after lunch. On the other hand, as healers Sasha and Laura washed after every patient. Kovos also had grown into the habit of regular bathing, not due to any laws but rather the desire to not look like he was constantly rolling around in soot. Keither, on the other hand, hated it, and Arkin had to force him to do it. It was as if the boy thought that by getting rid of the grime from the road he was somehow more susceptible to the elements.

Keither slipped on some moss and landed on his side. Legon looked up at him. "Are you ok?" he asked.

"I cut my elbow! Dang it! I look like a moron," Keither said, exasperated.

He understood what Keither meant; it hadn't taken a genius to notice that Keither harbored feelings for Sara. This was actually good. He wanted to prove himself and so he tried harder with everything to impress her.

"Here, let me look at it." Legon said.

"Oh, you don't have to. I mean, it's not that bad."

Legon chuckled. "I know you're tough, but Arkin wants me to fix everything with magic so I get better."

* * * * * * * *

Across camp, Sasha paused for a moment as she felt Legon accessing information in her mind. This wasn't uncommon for either of them to do. Arkin wanted Legon to use magic to check every injury and then heal it. While he had a detailed knowledge of anatomy, he didn't have knowledge of the healing arts like Sasha did. Legon's memory was prefect like her own, but there still was no reason keeping all the information the other knew. Sure, they would retain memories from each other that were basic and common, but if they weren't then why waste the space?

She went back to preparing some eggs in a cast-iron skillet. Sara was humming to her left. Sasha smiled at her. The last couple of months had been the best in her life. She knew that it was odd to think that; they were on the run, living in tents, and not talking to the rest of the world, but it was true. She missed her parents and the valley, but other than that she missed...well, nothing. People in Salmont had treated her like an outcast and wished her harm, but not here, not these people. She was with her best friend, who was now free and happy, her brother, Arkin, who she was thought was amazing, and Kovos and Keither. Even Kovos treated her differently than before. He was always nice, but the other day he came up to her and apologized for thinking less of her for so many years. It took her off guard. She knew that he was always a little nervous around her, but not anymore.

Legon was inspecting an elbow. She broadened the connection, but not to the point of seeing out of his eyes. She had done that once and only once. It was last week when Legon and Kovos had been bathing. Legon had been discreet about it and didn't tell anyone, but it still was a little awkward for her for the next few days whenever Kovos touched her. *Still, Emma is a lucky woman,* she thought. Her face flushed at the memory. Sara looked at her and smiled.

"See anything good?" Sara winked. Of course she had told Sara.

"No, I'm not looking."

"Ah remembering, I see."

"Oh shut it. Keither hurt himself and I was just wondering."

Sara tried to take an unconcerned tone. "Oh, what happened?"

"Nothing, really. Legon thinks it's just a laceration. The humerus looks good and so does the subcutaneous…"

"English please."

"Oh, sorry. He cut himself."

"See, that was not hard at all, was it?"

Sasha stuck her tongue out and went back to the eggs.

"We need to get you a man, Sash."

"Yeah, because there's a lot of great ones out here," she said, gesturing with her hands around them. "But you, on the other hand…there's Keither, or Legon."

Sara laughed. "Your not going to try and hook me up with your bother again, are you?"

"Why not? He's got a good trade, he's part elf, and I may be biased, but he's good looking too."

"Yes, he is all those things, but no; I've had my fill for a while. But you... let's see, who is there?" Sara smiled. "Kovos is taken, but... Arkin? Come on, the older man."

"Yuck, Sara! He's cute for his age I guess, but he's like my dad. So is this the part where you tell me that men age like fine wine?"

Sara walked by her to get something out of the tent. "Well, not everything ages well." She winked at her.

"Oh that's nice, Sara." Sasha paused again feeling an odd amused feeling. She stomped on the ground.

Sara looked concerned. "What is it?"

"Dang it dang it dang it!"

Sara was alarmed in a flash. "What Sasha, what is it?"

"I'm a moron. I didn't close my connection with Legon at all." She was so mad at herself. She always did stuff like this.

Sara paused for a moment. "He's been listening?"

Oh course he was. How could he not? If she wasn't being a dunderhead she would have noticed the men talking as well. She huffed. "How could he not?"

Sara considered this for a moment and then she asked, "He still there?"

"Yes."

Sara raised her voice. "Bring back firewood." She smiled. "Nice Sash, very nice."

* * * * * * * *

Sara busied herself with breakfast. When the men returned, she placed the new firewood in the pit. She looked over at Keither, who looked away quickly. He obviously had a thing for her. The thought of trusting a man was odd to her now. She knew how to say what they wanted to hear and how to make them think they were in love with her, but she had done that with lies. She hadn't cared about a single client that she had. In fact she hated each and every one. They knew she was a slave, and for some reason they liked it. They treated her horribly. Like that prick in Salez who had tried to stop her from leaving. Oh, she remembered him. He was cruel and got a discount because he was one of the Queen's. The thing that disgusted her about him was that he too was in the care, but had shown aptitude at fighting so was placed in a special regiment. He would get his someday. Those were the front-line men; most did not make it long. Sara had needed to be good at what she did. If she made the owner good money then she didn't go to the barracks, to the soldiers in the care and the others. She shivered on the inside remembering them. Avoiding the barracks was worth talking a man out of a week's pay any day of the week.

She looked at Keither. There was nothing that was physically appealing about him; and he was young with no social skills, and also in need of a diet. At the same time he wasn't like most men. Kovos and Legon weren't either, but they were strong and looked it. Keither was just a mind, and that was it. He was harmless. He was also the type that would probably follow a woman with puppy-like devotion, not because he was a romantic, but rather because he suffered from low self-esteem. He would be simple to manipulate, but due to his lack of status, money, or appearance it was unlikely that anybody with a malignant disposition would fall for him. But, that knowledge aside, there was a part of her that wanted to protect him, safeguard the innocent. It wasn't attraction she felt, but compassion. Could that change to something more? She didn't think so. She didn't want to have to take care of a man for the rest of her life, and unless Keither changed, that's what she would have to do.

Still, the thought of what Sasha said about her and Legon… the Everser Vald. *Don't think that name,* she said to herself. Arkin would be angry if he knew she was dwelling on it. She looked at Legon. What would it be like being with an Elf? He was going to turn, that much was obvious. This wasn't something she knew much about, but Arkin had filled in some gaps. She pushed the thought from her mind. It would be a horrible existence when she thought about it. One would grow old, weak, and die while the other would be left behind, young forever. At the same time, she was more connected to him than anyone else in the world. He knew and understood her, and in a sense she did him as well.

He wasn't hard on the eyes, either. She had a crush on him as a kid. Well, if she was being honest, she still did, but it wasn't worth her friendship with Sasha. Plus, what would the Everser Vald think of her? She knew that he loved her. She couldn't ever deny that and she could trust him to care and protect her… *Stop, Sara its not going to happen,* she thought.

She was so thankful for all of them in their little party. Every night she prayed to the White Dragon to protect them. She wondered if they believed in him. Or did they think that he was merely mythical? Sasha knew; she had to. But Legon?

She handed a plate of eggs and cheese to Kovos.

"Thanks, Sara."

"You're welcome."

Kovos was changing as well. He was more tempered now. He was going to make a great husband for Emma. Now that he was sharing thoughts with Sasha, she was changing them all, making them better.

* * * * * * * *

Kovos followed Legon and Arkin back to camp with Keither close behind. Legon gave Sasha a funny look when he passed her and she flushed a bit. Kovos figured she was still feeling awkward from the day he had said that he was sorry for the way he had thought of her his whole life.

As they rode he became lost in thought. He was questioning a lot about himself lately, and he wondered what kind of man he was going to turn into. Legon and Sasha were up front with Arkin learning who knew what. That stuff made him uneasy. Lately Legon had taken to joining the minds of all those around him for training. The idea was simple. If they got into trouble, Legon and Arkin would use magic to fortify themselves and those around them. When his mind was connected with Legon's he was privy to the other minds he was connected to as well. Sasha was an excellent shot with a bow, so if a fight ensued she would stay back with Sara and Keither firing arrows into the fray. With all their minds "networked" as Arkin put it, she knew where everyone was going to step and they knew where she was shooting. She was scary accurate. In a small farming co-op, Arkin bought Sasha a hundred pound bow that she could shoot when Legon used magic. It was an odd sensation having an arrow streak past your ear and not be worried about it at all. Also, with all their perspectives being taken into account, the group became hyper-aware of their surroundings. In a way, they gained the experience and perspective of those in the network. It made everyone a better fighter when they would practice three on three. Knowing each others fighting styles in detail helped as well.

Legon, Sasha and Arkin could use pure logic, too. Sometimes, when Legon would use magic, he would tap into Sasha's mind to figure out wind speed and trajectory, and she in turn would do that to others when shooting. When this happened, it didn't have that much of an effect on him. It was like background noise. But at any rate, it was changing his view of the world drastically.

Arkin appeared to be done with teaching for the time being, and Sasha went to work with Keither on the horse, Legon went to talk to Sara. Arkin came up to Kovos and smiled. "What's on your mind?"

Kovos ran a checklist in his head. "Oh crap, do I have my mind open?"

Arkin smiled again. "No, but your body is, and I can see that you are thinking. I won't cross into your mind without permission unless necessary. Besides, you would be able to feel it now."

"That's good to know."

Kovos was happy that he was to the point where he could feel another mind and, if necessary, reach out to someone. It was also a comfort that his consciousness couldn't be breached without him knowing.

"Now, what's on your mind?" Arkin asked

He thought about lying to Arkin but, mind protected or not, Arkin knew him too well. "This stuff is kind of freaking me out a bit."

"Why is that?"

"I don't know. It's just odd seeing Sasha and Legon sitting silent next to each other and then laughing. Or feeling other people in my head."

"Ok." Arkin sat silent, waiting patiently for Kovos to say what was really bothering him.

They were moving along a clearing in the trees, probably close to a co-op. As they went he could see a line in the landscape. On one side of the road were dense trees and forest. On the other were open fields. To the right of him where the fields began was a waist-high stone wall marking the edge of someone's property. On the other side of that wall was a wheat field. It looked as if there had once been a forest where the field was, and it made him wonder at the dedication of these people. They would have had to clear cut the land and then pull all the stumps. Not to mention removing all the stones that would break a plow. And that was probably where the stones from the wall had come from. The wheat was high now, and as he looked out at the field he noticed a breeze playing in it. The wheat looked like a sea of giant gold waves rippling away from them. The contrast between the forest and the field seemed to be a good analogy for what was happening to him.

"Do that elves do this a lot, the mental networking? I mean, I see true benefit in it and all but… I don't know what I'm saying." He really didn't know what he was saying. He was having a hard time keeping track of his thoughts these days. Too much stress, too much home sickness. Well, more Emma sickness if he was being truthful.

"Isn't it nice to know what the other person is thinking?" Arkin asked

"Yes it is, but I don't know… I think that maybe I've been messing up in life and if I knew what others were thinking…." He breathed out. "I can't stop thinking about how much different my life would be if I knew what, well…"

Arkin helped him. "What Emma was thinking?"

"Yeah, is it bad to want to know that?"

"No, not at all. You know what the dot on Legon's Tattoo means, don't you?" Arkin asked.

"Yes, it's for when he gets married."

"Exactly. I haven't told you about Elven society as much as I have Legon and Sasha. I should have included you in that. I'm sorry."

"Don't be, why does it matter?"

"When elves get married they stay connected mentally, and after years of having a perfect insight into their partners they almost become one mind," Arkin explained.

"Ok, so that's why they're able to stay married forever. If you understood the other person, really understood them, it would be hard to split up."

"Yes, but there is more. They rely on each other to the point where they are completely dependent on the other person. That means that when one dies, the other is always quick to follow."

"What do you mean?"

"Their bodies do not become frail like ours, but losing that connection kills their mind and their will to live. Once that happens, the body follows."

Kovos sat pondering this new information. It was amazing to think about people so close to one another that one dies when the other does. Amazing, but also sad and beautiful.

"I want that," he said with a surprisingly high amount of conviction.

"Good. You can have it. You have the ability to connect with someone if you try. Now remember, you are your thoughts."

"So I'd better start being the man I want to be with the kind of mind that Emma will want to live in," he said, smiling.

Arkin patted his shoulder. It felt like a great weight had been taken off him, and he decided that from that point on, he was going to work his hardest on himself. He was going back to Salmont to get Emma, just as soon as they got Legon and Sasha to the border.

* * * * * * *

Arkin, rode separate from the others for a while trying not to let his fatigue, suddenly felt Legon's presence.

"Are you ok?" Legon's voice said in his mind. It was followed by energy that coursed through his veins. Arkin told Legon about the Iumenta searching for them, and almost at once Legon offered his strength to him. It was rare that Arkin felt the pull of other magic users on his spells this hard. He pushed it from his mind knowing the drain wouldn't last long. Legon inquired about what kind of spells he could use for protecting. Silently, Arkin explained that wards were passive forms of magical protection. You could have a ward active and feel no drain until it was needed. Legon was months away from using the complex magic needed for masking them, but

Arkin could use Legon's considerable magical power to do it himself.

Suddenly Arkin felt a huge drain on his wards. There was thick forest on all sides of the road now. Legon rounded up the others, bringing them in close to him. It was easier to protect things that were close to him as magic was affected by space. Arkin felt his heart race as another huge hit on his wards drained energy from his magical reserves and his body.

"Dragon," he said in a hoarse voice.

They all moved off the road and Legon came up next to Arkin, placing his hand on his shoulder. He felt Legon open the connection between their minds all the way. The power was amazing. He felt a deep well of magic in him, but still it was nothing to the dragon that was coming. They may be able to resist the seeking spell if the dragon wasn't looking that hard, but if it noticed the drain on its own power it was sure to investigate.

* * * * * * *

Legon felt the pull on his magic and now his body. He rushed to connect his mind with the others and the horses. As he made the connection, he began to siphon off energy. There was a dull thud in the far distance. Sweat was forming on Kovos' brow from the drain, but he kept his mind open. The thudding was closer now, much closer. He needed more power. He tapped Sasha, Sara, and Keither, and saw all of them place their hands on their chests from the sudden taxation.

THUD... THUD.

More. Where was there more? There were blue dots popping in his eyes and he saw Arkin slump in his saddle. The horses. He could use more from the horses.

THUD.

Phantom was starting to shake. Still there was more needed. He rummaged in the minds of the others, spiking hormones and endorphins, causing their hearts to race. They were producing a lot of energy, but not enough. Arkin was almost unconscious now. They needed more, and the beating of the dragon's wings was like thunder. He reached into Keither's mind and body, forcing the fat cells to give up their contents, forcing as much energy out as he could. He looked up through a gap in the trees to see a pale green sky. No, not the sky. Wings and a long, snake-like body with four black-clawed feet. The dragon seemed to be leaching light from the sky as it passed over head. The trees blew from the torrent of downward air but it didn't look down. Finally, the sound of wings died down and Legon released the magic.

* * * * * * *

Sasha took an inventory of herself. She felt like her whole body was buzzing now that Legon was no longer draining it. Her heart was pounding and she closed her eyes, breathing deep, repeating a calming script. The sound of wings was gone, and she thought that the dragon either hadn't seen them or didn't care. The thing that amazed her was just how strong it was. When it passed overhead it hadn't even looked down, so it must not have been concentrating on whatever spell it was using to find them.

Murray was covered in sweat, along with all the other horses. Sasha felt like she needed to sleep, but there was something that seemed off to her. There was something missing in her mind... Arkin! She got off Murray and rushed over the carpenter, who was lying across Phaedra's neck, passed out in his saddle.

"Arkin, Arkin, are you awake?" she said, shaking him but trying to not to be loud.

"Yes, Sasha, I'm fine. It's passed now. We will sleep here tonight."

She looked around. This was not a great place to camp for the night. They were off the road, which was good, but they were in thick trees. Still, the brush could be good in case anything else flew over head. Kovos still had his head cocked up to the sky, looking, waiting for the dragon to come swooping down on them. Legon looked fine, though; he wasn't breathing hard and he looked calm, his eyes closed and body still. She poked him with her mind. His voice came reverberating back into hers.

"I'm fine. I'm trying to see if the coast is clear."

As he said this to her she became aware of the minds of other animals. There was a deer that was about fifty yards away sniffing the air and looking for whatever had caused the trees to move. Further was an eagle that was surveying the forest with shrewd eyes. This was new to her; she had never thought of using the animals in an area to do reconnaissance, but it was smart. Legon was taking advantage off all of their senses and using his mind to gently nudge them to look and go where he wanted. Mostly he wasn't doing much; he was letting the animals' survival instincts do most of the work. Also smart. He opened his eyes.

"Are you all ok?" he said. Sasha sensed that he knew exactly how much energy he had taken from all of them, but this was the polite thing to do.

"Legon, I've seen that one before," Sara said, sounding terrified. "He's from Salez. We need to get to the border soon."

Arkin spoke. "He was looking for us. There's no denying that, but we have about two weeks until we reach the border towns and safety. Now we need to rest."

"Arkin, are you going to be alright?" Sara asked.

"I'm fine, just very tired, as are all of you and the horses. That was a lot of energy we needed to use." He looked up at Legon with look a new-found respect.

"Using the fat in our bodies along with hormones and endorphins was very wise of you. I am impressed."

"Thank you," Legon said

Legon was thinking hard; Sasha could feel it. She felt him tapping into the logical part of her mind. He was using the information from the animals to figure out the best place to rest for a day or so, and the best ways into the hiding spots and out of them.

"There is a good place about one hundred yards over there," he said, pointing into some dense brush.

"But that's thick wood," Kovos said, looking cynical.

"Only for a little way, then it opens. The forest canopy is high there," Sasha said.

"And how do you know this?" Keither asked.

"The minds of the animals in this area. They have been hiding from threats for years. Now let's move," she said with a bit more force than she was planning on. Arkin looked at Legon again and smiled.

They worked their way through the thick underbrush, and sure enough it cleared to a perfectly secluded place. The ground was bare except for some twigs and leaves. It was round with more than enough room for all of them and the horses. Twenty feet above them the trees became so dense that there was barley light to see. Not even the dragon could see them from overhead now. Legon instructed everyone to place their bedrolls on the ground; there wasn't room for a tent or a fire. Everyone agreed. They might need to leave in a hurry, and the tents would slow things down anyway, and a fire could attract attention.

It was mid-day when they made camp, but within a few hours the clearing was already dark. They laid on their bedrolls in a circle with their heads to the center, trying to rest.

"How are we going to see?" Keither asked. He always forgot about magic.

"Lumanaighty," Legon said. And with that, a violet orb of light bloomed in his palm. It floated about four feet off the ground to the center of the circle, hovering. The light was sufficient for their immediate area but ended within ten feet, the way only magical light could. The light was taking almost no energy from Legon, so Sasha wasn't concerned. Everyone looked odd in the violet glow, their faces washed of color. It made the colored parts of their eyes look like dark gray stone. Sara and Arkin's fair hair glowed in the light, making them both look otherworldly. There was blackness where the light ended. The thick woods did not allow any sound or light to penetrate them. They were a dot of light in a sea of nothingness.

Arkin stirred. "I have protections still in place, but what are you doing Legon?"

"I have a weak connection with animals in the area; I used the information from an eagle to find a nice place for deer to lie down for the night near by. Also, there is an owl in the area. If they see anything out of the ordinary, or if they get frightened, I will feel it and broaden my connection with them."

Arkin smiled widely at him and looked much better. "Passive surveillance. Very good, Legon. With the waking sleep you will never lose contact with them, but with a weak connection other magic users won't be able to stumble on to it."

"They can do that?" Kovos said worried.

"To an extent. They will be feeling the emotions of the creatures around them, and if something seems off they will investigate. But with a weak connection Legon will not be influencing anything, so they won't look."

After that, no one looked like they wanted to ask anymore, but contented themselves with resting. Legon and Sasha began the waking sleep.

Chapter Fifteen
Fate

"Our enemies always beat us in the way we least expect it, and therein lies the problem. We toil our days away trying to find that weak spot in our armor when we shouldn't have been fighting to begin with."
- The Great Defeat, Secunum Renovatie

Keither opened his eyes, blinking at the ever-present lavender glow. He wasn't too sure just how long they'd been in their hiding spot. It appeared the dragon had found something. Maybe it was them, maybe not. But there were people in the area. Legon was having a harder time sensing their surroundings as the group of soldiers searching the area had scared off all the larger animals. He was now forced to tap into the minds of rodents and squirrels. The thing that was odd was that Arkin's spells hadn't been tested at all. Kovos suggested that they try and check the minds of the men, but the idea was snubbed when Sasha pointed out that they may have a Venefica with them. It would be unwise to take on a large group and a magic user. Keither laid his head back down. It would almost be worth getting caught just to see light and a color other than purple. Legon breathed out a long breath.

"What is it?" Sara asked. It was good to hear a voice again. They'd been quiet for several days.

"They are leaving. They weren't looking for us."

"They weren't?" she said.

"No. I was in the head of a rat when a scout approached and said that they caught the deserter."

"This was about a deserter?" Sasha asked incredulously.

"They are close to the border. He could have been a spy. We should have known when they didn't use magic to find anything," Arkin said with relief. He was looking better now; all of them felt better. Maybe the few days of down time had been good for them. "We will wait for them to leave the area. Legon, let us know."

Legon nodded at Arkin and closed his eyes. After a few hours passed, Arkin brought the horses out of the deep sleep he had placed them in so they would not make noise. They packed their belongings and began to make their way out through the thick brush. The light from Legon's magic was just bright enough to dim any light that could have made its way in to their hideout, so Keither wasn't sure what time of day it was. As they moved out of the thicker parts of the trees and back on the road, he was blinded by dazzling light. He held his arm up, blocking the sun from eyes that did not seem to want to adjust.

* * * * * * *

Legon leaned back in Phantom's saddle feeling the warmth of the sun. He had seen the sun through the eyes of the animals but hadn't opened the connection enough to feel it. The only feeling that he had allowed himself once was that of a bird flying in the trees, popping in and out of the canopy. The animal seemed to like his presence and enjoyed showing its abilities to the world. The feeling of freedom was amazing. The wind in his, well, feathers, the exhilaration of a dive. Before, the thought of flying had been frightening; he was terrified of heights. But he thought he was over that now. It was all about perspective when it came down to it.

The road was growing narrower as they went and they were using a number of switchbacks. At one point in time the road became only a game trail, so it wasn't strait but it was long. They would be continuing on the road for about one and half weeks, at which time they would need to go off the main road and across wild country to avoid towns and the army. There were just a few towns on this road, and that was a problem. They were unavoidable, but they didn't have to stop at them. The hope was that the towns were still being guarded by their own appointed people and that the military would be expecting them to handle security.

Over the next few days he felt the group's apprehension building. They kept mental connections nearly all the time and had forgone the usual nightly training to cover more ground. They didn't see many people, thankfully, and those they did chose not to talk to them. His connection with birds of prey primarily helped them avoid road blocks and check points, but these detours took time and that normally meant not sleeping much at night. Kovos rode up next to him.

"How are you doing, buddy?" Legon asked.

"Been better. I won't lie to you on that. How do you think I'm going to make it back up to Salmont without being discovered?"

"I honestly don't know." Legon paused. "You don't have to go with us if you don't want. You said that you would come with us to the southern towns and you have. I don't want you and Keither to -"

"Don't be dense. I'm not turning back." Kovos said

"Are you sure?"

"Yes, I am."

* * * * * * *

Kovos looked at his friend; he didn't need a mental network to figure it out. Legon thought that they were going to run into trouble, and he agreed. But that didn't mean that he was turning back.

It seemed that even nature knew something bad was coming. The closer they got to the boarder there were less of the normal signs of life everywhere.

The trees parted suddenly up head, giving way to fields and stone walls. They were about three days from the next town, so this must be a co-op. They decided to stop at a farm and see if they could buy fresh food. They made their way down a thin path that led to a small cottage with a thatched roof. They dismounted and walked to the door. Nothing was there to greet them. No dogs, no kids... nothing.

"Maybe they're in the fields," Keither said.

"No, they're not," Legon said slowly.

"What do-"

"Shhh, Keither," Arkin said drawing his sword. Kovos followed. Sasha attempted to string her bow. There was no magic to help her.

"Legon, can I get some help here?" she asked.

His eyes were closed. "There's nothing in my range. Just rats, birds, and other small animals."

"Can you tell what is going on? I don't like the feeling here," Sasha said

"No, I can't."

"Let's move on to the next house," Arkin suggested.

They mounted the horses and rode slowly to the next house. Empty again, and then another, and another. Finally, they reached what must have been the co-op's center. There were signs of violence here. There were five buildings; most looked like they were once storage, but not anymore. Their roofs were gone and blood was in the street and on the walls. A chill crept up Kovos's spine. Where were the people?

"Do you think that the army…" he began.

A woman crawled out from under some rubble. She was covered in gore, from head to toe. Her clothes were ripped and there was a large cut down the right side of her face. She stood and walked to them slowly. Sasha swung off Murray and started to her, but was stopped by Arkin.

"Get on your horse!" he barked.

"But Arkin…." She stopped, and even Kovos felt fear course from Arkin's mind to hers. She leaped back on the horse, which also sensed that all was not well here.

"What happened here?" Arkin asked.

The woman responded. "I'll tell you what happened here: they happened."

"Who are 'they'?" Arkin asked

"Dragons." She looked around. There were no tears. Kovos figured she was in shock.

"Were there others?" Sasha asked

"Yes. If we tried to leave town then their archers got to practice on us. But mostly it was the dragons."

"What did they do?" Sasha asked, terror in her voice.

Sara spoke coldly "Iumenta dragons prefer fresh meat."

"So they…," Kovos started.

The woman broke in, tripping on her words. "The army needed the livestock for their human and Iumenta soldiers, now didn't they? But what of the dragons? They needed meat too. And that meat was…."At this she seemed to snap. "They ate them. They ate them! They'll get you too!" she screamed. She ran away as Kovos heard in the far distance a soft but distinctive THUD. He was moving even before Arkin began yelling for them to run.

* * * * * * *

Keither clung on to Pixy for dear life. Up until this point, he thought that she had been doing rather well. Presently that belief was being challenged. Pixy was young and smaller than all the other horses, not to mention that she was carrying the greatest weight, but her will to live was apparently far greater than the others as she was pulling ahead of all of them. He wasn't sure if he was still holding the reins or not, but even if he was it didn't matter. He chanced a glance to his side. They were passing Sara, who was riding the mare they bought her in Salez. She was white, so Sara had named her Ghost, and she was fast, real fast. Sara yelled at him.

"Keither, are you ok? You looked like you were going to fall."

That's because I am *going to fall, Sara,* he thought. The question wasn't *if* gravity was going to win, but rather *when*. If they made it to the forest and he fell, that may not be that bad. If he went before, there was no way the others would be able to stop their terrified animals before he got eaten.

He looked down desperately, trying not to get thrown off. They were coming up on the forest. Thank goodness the co-ops were small. He couldn't hear the dragon over the sound of hooves and his own heart, but he knew it was there. He must have been holding the reins because they suddenly slipped out of his hands. Then he heard it. Heard a roar from behind him. It was a sound like nothing he'd ever heard before, piercing him to his core. They were just about to enter the forest when he looked back, morbid fear getting the best of him. Was it on them? No, it was hovering over the former center of town, presumably angry that there wasn't more than one lowly person to eat. It brought large gray bat-like wings down, raising itself further from the ground. He knew it was too far away but he swore he saw blood on its mouth. Had the woman from town met her end? The dragon reared its head back and opened a giant mouth to show black teeth. *Look away,* a voice in his head said. But he didn't.

Fire erupted from its mouth like a wild river of flame and destruction. The fire covered the ground in an instant, swallowing two of the buildings. Then as the dragon drove its wings down the force of the wind carried the flames over the rest of the center, curling up to meet the sky. Never in all his life had Keither even dreamed of anything like this. The dragon busied itself burning the center with a continuous stream of fire that must have lasted thirty seconds. Then it looked in their direction, following the cloud of dust from their frantic retreat. Two grey eyes with yellow where the whites should have been met his. As the first tree of the forest passed by him, Keither knew a new kind of terror, one that he knew would haunt his dreams for the rest of his life. Of course the rest of his life was a very relative term right now. Chances were there weren't going to be any dreams now that he had locked eyes with an Iumenta dragon.

He looked forward, panicking. Now they were in the forest, but it was like a dream to him. Nothing was real. Just terror; that's all that existed. Maybe he could use a script from the Jezeer. He thought, but he couldn't remember them. Sound was gone, but then he heard that roar again and jerked in his saddle. Pixy was delirious with fear, not unlike her rider but still running. She was trying to throw him off. It worked. The last thing he saw was the trunk of a tree.

* * * * * * *

Arkin reached out with his mind, trying to make contact with the resistance. The dragon didn't pursue them, which had its pros and cons. The pro was that they were alive. The con was that it had surely sent people to come find them. He stretched again, hoping to feel someone, but nothing was there. They were holed up in yet another clearing that Legon found with animals, but this one wasn't as ideal and they needed to move as soon as Keither woke up.

The boy had hit that tree hard and Arkin was sure that he was going to have a concussion. But that was better than death. For the first time in many years, Arkin felt a very real fear. So much work had gone into this whole thing and the people he was guarding were innocents. Any of them dying would forever stain his hands with blood. He repeated the fear script in his mind.

Fear is the blinder; I am the light and master of sight, I will master my fear and never again see night.

He repeated it again, controlling his breathing, changing his heart rate.

"Wh… what happened?" Keither asked as he started to wake up. Maybe he wouldn't remember the dragon at all. Wouldn't that be a wonderful thing?

"You fell and hit a tree," Kovos said, hovering over him. He hadn't gone more than a foot away ever since they had arrived at their hiding spot. Seeing his brother awake, a look of relief washed over his face.

"Do you remember anything?" Sasha said as she checked his pulse and looked at his eyes.

"I don't think so. The last thing I remember was a tree and that I was scared… because we were running from…"

Keither tried to get up but Kovos held him down. "It's ok," he said.

"No it's not, no it's not! I looked into its eyes! We are not ok!"

So much for hoping Keither wouldn't remember.

"It's going to be fine," Kovos said soothingly.

"No it's not, Kovos. I'm going to die out here and it's your fault. Your fault I came with you to warn Legon, your fault we left Salmont."

"Keither, I'm-"

"You're what? Sorry? You're sorry for me getting beaten, sorry for me watching someone die, sorry for all this?"

"I don't know what to say other than-"

"There is no 'other than'! This is your fault that I am out here! If you want to go get yourself killed for Legon and Sasha that's fine, but you didn't need to bring me into it!" Presumably Keither was only kept from yelling from a massive headache.

Kovos looked hurt. "Look, I can't change what has happened, and I told you that I was warning Legon about danger."

"Then why did you drag me along? Couldn't you tell that I didn't want to be there? Or did you want proof for Emma that you weren't a horrible person and that you cared about people other than yourself?"

Kovos's face flushed and he gritted his teeth. "No, I didn't drag you along so I could make my girlfriend like me, Keither. You wanted to come and then changed your mind. I wasn't going to let you go walking around in town with royal guard around."

"Oh yeah, and why is that?"

"Because you are helpless, that's why. You don't think before you act, you don't worry about consequences. How many times have I had to pull you out of a sticky situation that you put yourself in, huh? How many?"

"You only care about yourself. Don't blame me."

Kovos laughed coldly. "Only care for myself huh? Is that what you think? What have you ever done for someone else, Keither? Tell me, when have you helped at home? When have you ever tried to pull your weight? This has been the most I've seen you work in your life, and even then it's what, taking down a tent? Oh, never mind, you gave up some fat to help Legon keep your ungrateful hide alive."

* * * * * * *

Kovos felt anger seething in his body. He wanted to hit Keither, wanted to smack him in the mouth. After all the sacrifices he'd made for his younger brother…. But still, it was his fault that Keither was out here, and he hadn't been a good person. He felt himself deflating. Kovos knew he was hard on the boy, and it was obvious that Keither hated him. His own brother hated him. It was etched in his face. But how could he change that now? How could he show him that he did care and that he loved him? Legon brought him back to reality.

"Shut up you two," he hissed.

"But…" Keither was cut off by a hand to his mouth.

"We have company."

Kovos heard the sound of many feet coming their way. From the trees in front of them, men in full armor spilled into their little clearing. They were found. Their training took over. Arkin and Legon took their places up front while Sara frantically readied arrows for Sasha. As they approached, he felt Legon's magic making his muscles tighten with extra strength. Light glinted off his sword as it was unsheathed and he saw out of the corner of his eyes the shine of the fenrra.

An arrow hissed by him and buried itself deep in a soldier's shoulder. He felt the animal inside him coming to life, the one that obliterated thought and feeling. The one that felt no pain. The berserker. Before he let it take him one thought bubbled in his mind.

You will never see Emma again.

With that, the rage took over and he lunged forward with a yell and brought the blade across his front with incredible speed and force. It sliced the man in front of him across the belly, spilling his intestines on the forest floor. The world was in slow motion with the enhancements being made by the two Venefica flanking him. He pushed the falling man aside an closed in on another.

* * * * * * *

Keither stumbled over to the horses and retrieved Legon's giant cleaver. His job was simple: keep enemies away from Sasha and Sara. He came lumbering back up, still feeling dizzy from hitting the tree. Sara was handing arrows to Sasha at break-neck speed, and Sasha in turn was shooting them at the on comers. Keither noticed that she wasn't shooting to kill, but rather to injure and incapacitate. He started as flashes of emerald and purple illuminated the clearing. Legon and Arkin were fighting with magic. He looked to see Arkin snap a man's neck with a bolt of green magic. Legon followed suit by firing a blast of amethyst light, obliterating half of a man's pelvis.

Keither was having a hard time following the magic battle. Arkin, Kovos, and Legon were like blurs and they easily felled ten men, but more came. One made it by Legon and ran at Sasha. She didn't see him coming. Keither needed to hit him with the cleaver, but he couldn't. He was too afraid. He dropped the cleaver and fell back away from the oncoming soldier. Sasha turned to see the man raise his battle axe. It started forward. Keither couldn't look and covered his face. Then the sound of someone hitting the ground…was she dead? He looked to see the man lying on the ground, Kovos's hunting knife protruding from the side of his neck. A voice came.

"Keither!" It was Sara. He looked at her very red and angry face. "Time to be a man. Do your job, got it?"

He stood and took the cleaver in his hands.

* * * * * * *

Sasha was aware that she had nearly been killed, but thankfully she was almost in a full Mahann state and wasn't feeling emotion right now. She was taking full advantage of the Mahann and the magic making her stronger. She was acting as the center of the mental network with everyone connected through her. She could sense the changes Legon and Arkin were making to spells, and who Kovos was going to decapitate next. Sara was keeping her busy with a steady amount of arrows which were quickly running out. Keither, however, was not connected. He was too scared; his mind was closed. Not that Sasha would have let him in with his current level of fear. She couldn't have an unstable emotion clogging her network.

Sasha was aiming for major joints like shoulders and hips. They were debilitating injuries and made the men scream bloody murder. Hopefully there were a lot of conscripts in this group and the screams of their comrades would take the fight out of them. However, the strategy didn't seem to be working, and a steady stream of new soldiers was filling the clearing.

She told Kovos to move over a foot. As he did, she let an arrow go. It flew past the man he was fighting but hit another square in the shoulder, embedding itself in the joint. She continued to fire but paused as she saw a new figure entering the clearing. Not even the Mahann could stop the emotion this time.

A tall man in all black jumped into the clearing. His long silver hair, thin face, grey skin, and yellow eyes struck fear deep into her. The Iumenta had two fenrra in his hands and looked at her. He was about fifty yards away, well within range. He came forward, covering ten yards in a few steps. She began to rapid fire the arrows at him, not caring about hitting joints, just going for a hit. He flicked the arrows away lazily with the fenrra as he came. Kovos moved in his path, swinging his sword hard. The Iumenta parried the blow and lashed out at Kovos.

* * * * * * *

Legon was aware that for the second time in his life he was slicking the surrounding trees and landscape with other people's blood. This came to him after cutting a man's throat with the tip of the fenrra in his left hand. They now shined crimson with their new coating. He moved forward coming, down close to the ground in between two men. He pivoted on his right foot, swinging a fenrra at a man's leg, chopping the femur in half and severing the femoral artery. More blood sprayed everywhere. As the leg came free of its howling owner, Legon turned and with the other blade stabbed the other man. He turned the tip of the fenrra so it effortlessly passed through the man's ribs, slicing lung and heart.

The soldier's armor seemed to have little to no effect on Arkin, Kovos, and himself. With the magical enhancements to their bodies, they even cut through chainmail without issue. Still, he was feeling a definite drain on his magic. In the beginning he had been sure that there would only be a few of them, but they didn't seem to stop. Arkin was using his magic to fortify their bodies from injury, so if a major vein was cut, the bleeding would stop instantly. Sasha was managing the whole thing from a distance, tapping into their minds and using logic to decide the best amount of energy to be used and where.

Suddenly, on the other side of the clearing an Iumenta stepped into view, and Legon felt his body go cold. Even with magic helping them he wasn't sure they could stop and

Iumenta. What if it was a Venefica? He felt Arkin's emotions boil up in the connection.

Sasha was shooting as fast as she could. He felt more emotions, but this time from Kovos. They were ones of finality and sorrow. His best friend stepped in the path of the Iumenta, slashing hard at him. He was no match, but Legon and Arkin both started dumping copious amounts of magic into Kovos, who was fighting as hard as he could. He was starting to acquire minor nicks and cuts but didn't seem to care. The Iumenta was backing away. Kovos was winning!

Still more and more men entered the area. Their camp must be somewhere nearby. Legon could only see one way out. It was going to knock him out, but it was their only hope. He felt magic building in him and also sensed Sasha's apprehension. The spell was simple, really; it was just going to shred twenty or so men in the area. In the pause Arkin could help Kovos and kill the Iumenta. If they were lucky, when others arrived to see so many of their own dead and a slain Iumenta they wouldn't pursue.

He felt the magic hit a point that it hadn't ever reached before, even more than the other day when blocking the dragon. He released the spell, pointing the palm of his hand at the rushing soldiers. Time stopped in that instant. He saw an orb of lavender magic form in his hand and start to leave. It was size of his head and tear shaped. The tear was a translucent purple with bright veins of lilac glowing around it. The smaller end stayed connected to his palm. He'd never seen magic like this before. It always had moved so fast; this was beautiful. It continued to stretch, the tiny bit connected to him. Then, moving like water, it snapped back to him, covering his hand and moving up his arm.

He tried to scream as he felt his skin tear and bone shatter. His eyes were on fire. All he could see was magenta light. He felt all of his spells failing as Sasha franticly attempted to disconnect his mind from the others. The pain was unimaginable. He wanted to die. He tried to cry out, but time was going too slow and he couldn't open his mouth. He opened his scorched eyes to see the smoke that must be his own body burning from the magic. He begged for mercy in his mind and felt something tugging at his consciousness. A deep voice told him that he was worthless, but that he would be made better. He remembered his dreams then, and felt for hope, felt for Sasha and her love. The smoke in front of his eyes cleared to reveal a massive wall of glittering diamonds. They where white and radiated light. A horizontal seam in the wall opened to reveal a violet blue eye the size of a shield.

Chapter Sixteen
Distance

"When people look at my sister, they often don't see the pain of those early days, the days without comfort or solace; but I do, and I love her for them. Had she not had the strength to endure then, where would we be now?"
- Excerpts from the Diary of the Adopted Sister

Sasha frantically worked to disconnect Legon from the others. The moment the spell reverberated back on him she felt raw magic course down the connection and with it, pain. All of Legon's spells failed simultaneously. She needed to disconnect him so that Arkin could adjust for being one Venefica less than before. She severed Sara's connection, seeing her friend fall to the ground. Lastly she cut her own. She looked at where Legon was supposed to be, but all she saw was blinding lavender light. She covered her face with her arm and fell back. She hit the ground, causing the back of her head to buzz.

The light faded, and in front of her stood a figure that resembled her brother, but it couldn't be. He was the same size as Legon with the same clothes and hair, but his skin seemed to have a slight glow to it. Or maybe it was the light. She looked to his ears, which were rounded before but now were tapered at the tops, and from the side his eyes looked slightly larger and more almond shaped. More . . . Elven.

She marveled at the Elf Legon standing in front of her. Perhaps it was the sound of men screaming 'Elf!' that made her look, she didn't know. She turned to look at Kovos and the Iumenta, who both stood stalk still, mouths gaping. Then at the same time, they seemed to realize that there was no longer magic protecting Kovos. He slashed out at the Iumenta, who caught the blade with a flick. She saw Kovos's muscles twitch with magic as Legon reestablished the connection with him, but too late. She could only watch in horror as the Iumenta's other fenrra came across Kovos at his neck. Time ceased as Kovos's head separated from his body as he fell to the ground.

* * * * * * *

Keither watched in horror as his brother's body fell to the earth. Pain erupted from his knees as he hit the ground himself. Legon cut a man in half and was now on the Iumenta, but the outcome of their fight did not matter.

The Elf and Iumenta were flitting around the clearing at amazing speeds, the fenrra just a shiny blur. A steady spattering of blood was coming from the fenrra, not from fresh wounds, but from the blood of the slain now being flung off by the tremendous speed at which they were being swung.

His brother was dead. He saw the head roll away from his body which still held that ridiculous sword in a limp hand. He felt hot tears rolling down his cheeks and he was aware that his throat hurt. He was screaming himself hoarse, but he didn't hear the sound. Sara and Sasha were clinging to him, trying to drag him back to the horses. Arkin was attempting to clear a path as the two non-humans fought, pushing themselves to kill the other. Keither hoped they did it, hoped that Legon would kill the bastard.

A knife flew by him, nicking Sara's arm causing her to yelp. He heard that sound. He looked at Sara's arm now with blood running down it. He looked at his brother, the one who had protected him his whole life, who had tried to make him a man. The one that would never let bad things happen to good people. He had proved that with Sasha.

Rage filled Keither. Rage at what he had been through, what Sara had been made into, and what the Iumenta had taken from all of them. His hand was still on the cleaver and he gripped it with white knuckles. Now the scream was not that of loss but of a terrible drive to stop those that had hurt the people he loved. To kill all of those that murdered in the name of the Queen.

Sara let go of his arm, and Keither ran forward, raising the cleaver. One of the morons looked at him coming and smiled, thinking he was going to get an easy kill off of this fat kid. Well fat he may have been, but under that fat was the muscle that carried it all. The man attempted to block with a flimsy metal shield. The cleaver dented it and the man's arm gave way. Again and again the cleaver came down. The shield was a wreck of what it once was. Again the cleaver came down, removing the pathetic hunk of metal from its owner. Now the look of amusement was replaced with one of terror. The cleaver came down again, hitting at the base of the man's neck, crunching and slurping as it came out.

Another man was at his side raising his own weapon. Keither jerked the blade out of one and hit the other in the ribs, dropping the screaming man to the ground. This time the blade was stuck, but no matter. He was next to his brother's body. He reached down and grabbed the sword with the ridiculous flames on it, but they weren't ridiculous to him anymore. Now he understood, now he saw them for that they were. Arms grabbed around him and he saw Arkin pulling him to the horses.

The bastard is using magic! he thought. Arkin pushed and pulled him to the horses, but he resisted. Finally, the look on Sara's face made him reluctantly get on.

* * * * * * *

Legon was now very aware that he was no longer human. He saw his soundings in sharp clarity. Colors were more vibrant, minute details in the world were now clear. He would have continued his appraisal of the world if it weren't for his current situation. He was also aware that his spells had stopped when he had changed. His magical power should have been drained, but it was far from tapped out. He could feel it in every fiber of himself. He saw Kovos and an Iumenta, and with that sight clarity was restored. He tried to fortify Kovos...too late. He saw the tip of the blade passing along the back of Kovos's neck as the rest of it removed his head. As Kovos fell, Legon's eyes met with yellow ones and an ancient bloodlust filled him. He went to move to the Iumenta, and a soldier stepped in front of him.

Legon slashed hard with the fenrra, cutting the man in half at the waist, the blade passing through like butter. He sidestepped the organs splattering on the ground and moved to the Iumenta, who in turn was coming at him. The Iumenta seemed to move slower to him now. He realized instantly that Elves were faster. Both lashed out at each other. The Iumenta parried with his left fenrra, as did Legon. The sound of the metal clanging was incredible, but his ears were stronger now; the clanging didn't not bother him. They began to stab and spin, leaping from side to side, sometimes jumping to low branches and then over their opponent. He never knew that he could move like this, but even so his new physical abilities did not give him an edge.

The Iumenta was a match to him in everything but strength. Legon was stronger, but he was larger too, so no surprise there. Legon poured magic into himself, trying to give him an edge. Still, no matter how fast or strong he was, the thing in front of him had hundreds of years of experience on him. He was losing ground and fast. He was aware of Arkin in his head telling him it was time to go, but the Iumenta was not going to let him go without a fight. An idea came to him then, one that he should have had a while ago. He shot a bolt of magic at the Iumenta's feet, making a stone explode. His opponent flinched and backed away, and Legon slashed across his chest. The tip on the fenrra grazed him but nothing more. The Iumenta backed away further, ordering his men to rush forward. Legon crossed the clearing in a few steps. He couldn't help but think how handy being an elf could be. He jumped on to Phantom and turned away from the clearing.

"Where is Kovos's body?" he asked, not having time to feel emotion.

"There isn't time," Arkin said.

There was time. They weren't going to leave him here to be eaten or who knew what.

"No. We are not leaving without him."

"We have to Legon, there's no choice," Sara begged.

Sasha tugged at his mind, and he looked at her. Her face was spattered with blood. Kovos had saved all of them. He gave his life so they could all live and have a chance. Legon wasn't about to waste that sacrifice. He turned with them and they started to ride.

* * * * * * *

It wasn't more than a few moments before Sasha heard the sound of pursuing horses. Maybe they should have stayed and died in the clearing with Kovos. No, that was stupid, but she was still unsure about how they were going to get away. Even if they somehow managed to put distance between them and their followers, what then? They had too much land to cover. She felt Legon entering her mind, accessing the logic portions of it. What was he doing? There wasn't enough information to properly use the Mahann, was there? She became aware of all of their minds, even Keither's and the horses. She needed to have Legon check her out when and if they stopped. Her head was still buzzing. Then she felt it, felt the magic. Something she had felt before, but not like this, not even when she had been connected with Legon. She couldn't feel the magic but she did now. Legon widened the connection and she felt a mind that was Legon's, but now alien and vast. The power of the magic, it was so strong. She felt a deep well of it in him, and then the spell that stuck her and the rest of the group to their saddles, locking them in place.

Now he was fidgeting in all their heads, tapping every mental resource they had. She felt logic and spatial reasoning centers being activated. The sensory organs of the horses were being boosted and glands in their brains being manipulated to dump huge amounts of endorphins and adrenalin into their bodies. They could now run themselves to death and not feel it with the chemicals coursing though their veins. Now the magic was reinforcing their hooves and bones, making them stronger and more resistant to heat. What was he doing? She felt compelled to look ahead; he was using her to figure out speed.

The horses were going close to thirty five miles an hour. That was dangerous on this kind of road. Then she remembered that they were altered by magic. Now he was shutting down organs saving energy. Even her own body was changing. The muscles in her hands clinched around the reins. The wind was building as the shouts of the men behind them were growing fainter.

Then the burst of energy came. Massive amounts of magical and physical energy ripped out of Legon and into the horses. They were starting to accelerate, and she felt herself being pulled back but being held by the sticking spell. The wind was strong at forty miles an hour. More and more energy poured from him. Now fifty, then sixty. The trees were starting to blur as they hit seventy miles an hour. A town was fast coming up, the Queen's banner flying at the edge. But at seventy five miles an hour, the town flew by them, the guards never having time to figure out what was going on.

Now eighty, and the acceleration finally leveled off. The sound from the hooves was just one continuous noise. After a bit they slowed back down to sixty, but still they kept going. The horses were tiring fast and so was Legon, but still he put more and more into them. Finally she sensed him losing consciousness and worry crept into her mind. If Legon passed out then the spells helping the horses would fail and the animals would be left running at sixty miles an hour. They would fall for sure.

They slowed gradually at first and soon they were close to what they could do on their own. As they slowed to fifteen miles an hour, Legon passed out and Sasha unstuck from her saddle. The horses were not completely spent, and she knew that there were still plenty of chemicals in their blood to keep them going for a few more hours.

"Arkin, should we keep going?" she asked, knowing the answer.

"Yes." He didn't say any more and she was no longer able to connect with his mind. This worried her too. Kovos's death was sad. She knew that it would hit her soon and then she would lose it, but Arkin took their safety as a matter of personal responsibility.

They trotted along the road with no one talking. She glanced at Keither, who was looking at the back of Pixy's head and not making a sound. He had been like his brother today, fighting the way he did. She was proud of him. As she thought this, her eyes began to burn and she tried to focus on logic. There would be time to mourn later.

* * * * * * *

Keither knew that he should be crying, but he wasn't. He just didn't have it in him. And Kovos wouldn't have wanted it that way. He wouldn't want people sulking over his death. He tried to calm his cluttered mind but couldn't. The last thing he said to his brother was that he was selfish, which was something Keither knew to be untrue. He knew what his brother had done from him over the years, kept him from getting hit with arrows, saved him from being trampled by animals...it was too hard to think of the number of times Kovos had saved him from harm if not death.

But what had he done for Kovos? What had he done for anyone? There wasn't much that was for sure. He always had great intentions of helping, but when it came time to do it he wasn't there. It should have been him that had been killed by the Iumenta, should have been him that had made the ultimate sacrifice for the group. All of the others put in effort, but he was just along for the ride.

Wasn't that the way that he lived his entire life? He never thought about a trade, never cared to learn his father's, never tried to do well at anything. About a week into their journey he had turned fifteen. They would have celebrated, but that was right after their run with the Royal Guard and by the time he thought of it he didn't care. Still, fifteen years and nothing to show for it. Yes he was young, but that was no excuse.

By this age most of men in Salmont had picked a trade and were actively engaged in it. What was he going to make of his life?

* * * * * * * *

Arkin rode ahead of the others, trying to fight back emotion as he went. Yet again he had failed as a protector, first with Legon's mother and now Kovos. He knew that the effect of his death would carry farther than anyone could ever understand. Most didn't see the connections that all men have. Not only was Kovos's life ended, but his brother, parents, and an innocent girl back in Salmont had been hurt as well.

No, our actions are far reaching he said to himself. He kicked himself. He couldn't afford to wallow in self-pity at the moment. There would be time for that later. Now he needed to get them all to safety and to the resistance. Legon had brought them to within a few days of the border. Never had he heard of someone using magic to that extent. Well, at least not a person. A dragon yes, but not a person. Still, a small part of him was happy. It must be true now that he was an Elf, wasn't it?

The land that they were in now was far more barren than they had yet seen. Thankfully, the area was hilly so they could rest for the night. The sun was almost to the horizon when Arkin found an area for them to camp. Legon was still out cold on Phantom and Arkin instructed them to leave him in case they needed to leave in a hurry. Their camp was surrounded by trees but he still didn't feel comfortable starting a fire or using magic to make light. It would be easy for scouts to see and infinitely worse, dragons.

No one was hungry or talking. Arkin walked to the edge of camp and knelt, projecting his consciousness out. After hours he finally felt something on the other end. It was a new person that he didn't know, but he had the right passwords so he passed on his report. He didn't leave anything out, but most important he told of Legon's transfiguration. That one got their attention. The person on the other end was shocked; Arkin figure the man wasn't high enough ranking to be in the loop on Legon. He was instructed to head straight south and to move fast. They would try to send help if they could, but it was doubtful. Arkin made it clear that he understood and broke the connection.

Something was nudging at his mind. It was Sasha. She was trying to reestablish the network. He allowed the connection, and the first thing she wanted was a damage report.

He returned to them. With Legon out it was going to be up to him to heal any wounds. He'd enhanced their bodies during the conflict only enough to stop major injuries, so only Sasha and Sara were spared from minor cuts and bruises. The cuts he would heal to prevent them from infection, but he couldn't waste energy on the bruises in case there was another attack.

* * * * * * * *

Sara was cleaning up Keither. He hadn't been hurt all that bad in the fight, but the tree had left a nice cut on his head. Even with Legon healing it there was blood caked in his hair and on his face.

"Sara, I can do this you know," Keither protested

"I know that, but you don't have a mirror and you don't want to miss any."

She wasn't just doing it to make him look more presentable for the horses, but more because she was worried about him. His brother just died, and Keither had killed for the first time as well, but there was no emotion in his eyes. Shouldn't he be wailing or something? She would have been if it were her brother. Or was he in shock? That was more likely. She was having a hard time looking at him the way she did before. He was always a harmless boy, but now he wasn't. He was like his brother in some ways, especially in the way that enabled him to go out of his mind with rage and kill. That trait was one that she didn't like. Or did he kill indiscriminately? He didn't hurt them when they had pulled him back to leave. Phantom snorted off to her right and she chanced a glace at the Everser Vald. As she looked, she felt warmth bloom in her chest.

* * * * * * *

Sasha looked intently at her friend. She was staring at Legon in an odd sort of way. Not in a bad way, but almost lovingly.

"Sara," she said.

Sara looked at her and she saw longing in her vibrant green eyes. "We should get Legon down and clean him up, and look for injuries," Sara said in a timid voice.

That timidity was odd for her. Sasha studied Sara carefully, looking at her in the ways of the Jezeer, trying to place her sudden change.

"I suppose so, but I don't think that he is hurt," Arkin said.

How would he know? Legon and the Iumenta had moved so fast that they wouldn't have noticed him getting cut or something. Yes Sara was right. She started towards Legon When Keither passed her walking to Phantom, the horse shied away from him. The constant mental contact affected the horses, and she wouldn't say that they were smarter but they knew a thing or two about their riders. This was made apparent in towns and co-ops. Their horses responded to people as their riders generally felt, even if they didn't show it. Ghost, for example, had no reason to fear men; she never acted oddly around them until they started networking their minds. Arkin told them that making a connection with your horse was a good thing to do so that they would understand each other better. It wasn't possible for them to communicate the way people did to each other or even the way they did to one another, but emotions could cross the rift. Arkin facilitated most of the links so that the horses could come to know their riders. After about of month of this, Ghost had become increasingly apprehensive of large men. Not necessarily fat ones but ones with big muscles. Sasha hadn't figured out why until she felt Sara's emotions one day in a town. It wasn't that Ghost was frightened of the men, but rather that Sara was, and Ghost picked up on it.

Now Phantom was shying away from Keither because Legon thought of the boy as clumsy. Sasha tended to agree, but this wasn't the time to ostracize him. She sent calming thoughts to Phantom, who stopped moving. Keither came up to his side and patted him lightly.

"It's ok, Phantom. I wouldn't drop him. Remember, there is muscle under this fat. How do you think I walk around?"

He worked himself under Legon and began to hoist. Sasha looked at Arkin, who should have at least offered to help. What was wrong with him?

"So, you need help?" she asked now giving Arkin a stern look. Keither answered with surprise.

"No I don't. He can't weigh more than either of you," he said, and then corrected, "Not that you're heavy. You're not at all. Legon should be close to two hundred pounds but he can't weigh more the one ten. Arkin, are you doing anything to me?"

"No I'm not. He is an Elf now, and they are made of different stuff then the rest of us." He paused but forestalled questions. "We will wait until he is awake before I explain. Forgive me, but I don't want to repeat myself."

Keither had Legon off the horse and was carrying him over his shoulder to the center of camp. He placed him down on the ground. He still resembled his old self but was clearly different. Even with his eyes closed, Sasha could see that they were larger and almond shaped. His face looked more slanted with higher cheek bones. It almost resembled a sculpture, as if someone had taken a masterpiece and then superimposed Legon's characteristics on it. The result was wondrous. He still had the same short brown hair but now his ears tapered at the top. His skin seamed to almost glow, but she knew it wasn't; it was just healthy and without blemish, like a baby's. His figure was the exact same as it was before. He was still large with plenty of muscle, far more than the Iumenta had. She wondered if he would thin out over time. Overall, she had to admit she had never seen anything so…beautiful in her life. Though she would be sure to tell Legon that he was handsome and leave out the beautiful part.

She knelt down and inspected his body for injury. There was none. She knew he had been hurt before he had changed, but the injuries were gone now. All that was left was dirt and blood from the battle. His clothes were torn in a few spots. If she hadn't been able to see his chest move she would have thought he wasn't breathing.

"Arkin, is it common for Elves to have low breathing like this?"

"Yes very. They are much quieter than we are."

"Why is that?" Keither asked. Sasha was happy to see him getting his mind off the day and back to thinking.

"They can hear your heartbeat across a room. Now that being said, loud sounds don't hurt them as much as they do for us. But when you can hear a pin drop you tend to notice just how noisy we all are and walk a little softer."

It made sense to her, so she didn't worry about the breathing. In fact he probably wouldn't snore anymore. That would have been nice when they were sharing a tent. She pushed this trivial thought from her mind to focus on her unconscious brother. Sara had knelt down on the other side of him. She brought a rag to her mouth, wetting it and beginning to wipe the dirt off his perfect face.

Sasha watched. Never had she seen Sara clean someone with such care and love. She would occasionally wet the rag and keep going, like a mother would a child or a sick loved one.

"Sara?" she said.

Sara looked up at her. "We can't have him all dirty now can we?"

Sara went back to her cleaning and tears began rolling down her cheeks. They fell off her chin onto Legon. Sara noticed this and it seemed to make them come faster, but she didn't look sad. She was starting to hum gently, a tune Sasha had never heard. Arkin was standing over them now. She heard him pick up the tune and saw tears in his eyes as well, once again not tears of sorrow but of happiness. Sasha looked at Keither, who looked just as confused as she was. She scratched the back of her head to get rid of an itch.

Sara was smiling warmly at Legon and started to talk bellow her breath. "My whole life around you and I didn't know. I am so ungrateful. This whole time I have been upset with my lot and yet here I was the first."

"You where the first what?" Sasha was concerned.

"You will find out, Sasha, when he wakes. Won't they, Arkin?" She looked up at him and he nodded without question.

The buzzing in Sasha's head was driving her nuts. Her breath caught and she excused herself. Walking away from the group still intently looking at Legon, she walked out of their clearing and past the trees that blocked them from view. She stood alone looking at the blank hilly landscape. Trembling, with her head still buzzing, she held her hand out palm up. She looked at it, never having done this before, not wanting to do it, but she had to…

"Flamma."

As she spoke a plume of ruby flame blossomed in her hand. She closed it, stopping the flame in an instant. She looked out at the field not truly seeing it, shaking and covered in a cold sweat.

Chapter Seventeen
Everser Vald

"A fulfilled fate is a great and terrible thing. Great in that the thing we hoped for has come to pass and all of the things that come with it, but terrible in that the thing we hoped for has come to pass and we must see our own faults because of it."
-Teachings of the Restored Queen

S ara looked down at Legon, numb to anything in the world other than who she was kneeling by. Sasha came up to her, tugging on her sleeve. Sara looked at her. Sasha looked worried and excited all at the same time.

"What is it?" she asked, not really wanting to be interrupted from her reverie.

"Come with me." Sasha was not asking; she was telling her to come. She pulled at her arm again.

"Ok, ok."

Arkin gave them an inquisitive look. "Is everything all right?"

"Fine. Don't worry Arkin," Sasha said, smiling dismissively at him.

Sasha led Sara outside of camp and to the other side of the trees, turning to face her.

"What is it?" Sara asked, a little worried at the sudden change in her friend's behavior.

"Wh- when we were connected, or when I tried to break the connection with Legon, did you feel anything?"

Sara paused. "I don't know, like what?"

"From the connection," Sasha asked frantically.

"I don't know, I guess," she said. "Yeah, it was kind of a tingly feeling in the back of my head. Was I not supposed to feel that?" Great, what had happened now? Had something in her head broken?

"No, you weren't. Do you feel it now?"

Now that Sasha was talking about it, she did feel something in her head, but that was no surprise. That always happened. If someone asked you if you were tired, you'd yawn. This was probably no different.

"Yes, I guess so. What's the problem, Sasha? What's gotten into you?"

"You've felt it when Legon has used magic, right?"

"Yeah, of course. Arkin wanted us to feel it so we would know what was going on in a fight, but I don't see how that…"

"Try it," Sasha said

"What?"

"Try it… magic, try to do it."

"But Sasha…"

As she spoke Sasha held out her hand. "Flamma."

Sara stepped back, gasping. "You…"

"I think you can too. Try."

She thought about it, but the idea was ludicrous to her. Sasha had lived around Legon her whole life, so maybe this was part of their connection.

"Sasha, I can't."

"Neither could I until he turned," Sasha responded. "Now do it."

"Fine, give me a sec ok?"

Sasha nodded and stepped back. Sara concentrated just like Legon did, but he had done it so fast. She raised her hand. "Flamma."

The feeling shot down her arm to her hand, but nothing happened. Sasha looked disappointed but undeterred.

"Try again. I'll help you."

Sara felt Sasha's mind join hers and again she tried.

"Flamma." A spark! This time Sasha didn't help. "Flamma!" A flicker of silver flame popped in her hand and then went out. Again and again she tried until a small silver fire burned in her hand. She was a Venefica, a real Venefica. Never had she dreamed of being one. Sasha looked relieved and dismayed all at once.

They heard Keither's voice through the trees. "Hey, I think he's waking up." They rushed back to the camp.

* * * * * * *

Legon lay with his eyes closed. His head was pounding and he felt something digging into his back. Had he fallen off the horse? He decided to find out and opened his eyes. At first there was just a blur of color and he blinked to bring the world back into focus. Sasha, Sara, Keither, and Arkin were all huddled over him looking terrified, sad, and happy. He noticed how big the pores on Arkin's nose were. What an odd thing to notice. His head was swimming. He knew he'd been on a horse but wasn't sure about the rest. He did remember a horrible dream though. Kovos had been killed by an Iumenta and then he had turned into an Elf.

I wonder what Arkin will read into that, he thought. But at the same time, where was Kovos? Sasha's lips were moving. She was close he could see little specs of brown and hazel in her eyes. Everyone had little flecks of color in their eyes he knew, but you needed to be really close to see them. She needed to back off. The sound coming from her lips was just murmuring. He tried to read them. He thought she was asking if he could hear her. Arkin's lips moved, saying something to the effect of "His brain is coming back up one piece at a time. Give it a moment." What did he mean his brain was coming back up?

What was that smell? It was Sara. She smelled like blood, sweat, and dirt, but there was a hint of something sweet, too. What was it? He smelled the others too; maybe this was a dream. You can't smell people like that, could you? Then, finally, sound clicked back in. A lot of sound. Not only could he hear those around him, but also birds, flies, and a bunch of little things he was sure were in the ground.

"Are you back? Can you hear me?" Sasha asked, placing her hand on him. He could feel her pulse through her hand even with his shirt on. It wasn't a dream. He was an elf. He sat bolt upright.

"Kovos?"

He looked around from face to face, trying to hear, see, or smell. That couldn't have happened. He wasn't dead. He was.... He knew. He remembered everything. He brought his knees up to his chest. There were tears in the other's eyes now, no one excluded.

"He's gone, Legon," Keither said, choking.

All this pain was for him. It was his doing. If he hadn't let them come.... There was only one thing for it. Remembering back to when he met Sara in Salez, he reached out to the others. Not to their conscious minds, but to a deeper part, accessing them in a way that could not easily be blocked. He found pain there. He pulled at the last day's worth, absorbing it in himself. He felt the loss of a brother, of a friend, and an overwhelming fear that connected it all together. All these emotions and more flooded in. All of them were near the point of insanity, if even just for a short time. The mind had its limits, and they were near theirs. At first they resisted him, but it was so easy to let go of pain when another was willing to take it from you. Eventually they stopped trying. It was immense but some how bearable, as if this was something he was born to do.

Arkin had said that Venefica had specialties that showed themselves when they hit a class four or five. One was that of healing. Being able to take another's pain was a gift of the healer. The magic allowed them to take on pain and suffering without destroying themselves. Still, taking this on and still shielding his sanity strained his magic. Eventually the pain would crush the Venefica and they would let go.

Legon didn't want to be protected by the magic. He wanted to feel it, wanted to know the damage caused. He let the walls down, letting it flood over him. He felt scared. It was too much. This was stupid. Why did this have to happen? Why did there have to be so much suffering in this life? Was that all life was?

His body was shaking with sobs of fear and pain of all kinds. He had opened the link with the others too far. He'd been warned of this; he could lose his mind.

Darkness shrouded him as all light turned to dark and the litany rang in his head, for it was a litany he realized; it was more than a script that one recited. It was truth and hope.

Fear is the blinder. I am the light and master of sight. I will master my fear and never again see night. I will become the dark and the light, my fear will pass through me, and I will stand alone in the light.

He repeated it again and again in his mind. It was fear that he faced. He saw that now, but to face fear he must leave the light. He let the darkness of pain and thought flow through him, let it saturate his mind and body. Leaving the others behind, going on a journey that no one else could take with or for him, he was the darkness. He wanted to die but the litany brought him back. He saw a pinprick of light. It expanded and he felt heat from it. Soon the dark was light. The fear was gone but the pain remained as it should, as a reminder. No longer would he be afraid of it. Pain was part of life. Without it there could be no happiness. With this realization he found peace. He would not feel pain and sorrow to the point of no return; it could only destroy him if he permitted it.

* * * * * * * *

Sara felt her body relax as her burdens of the last day left her. This time the void they left was not replaced with love and kindness like before. She would have to fill the void on her own. The pain in her arm left her and she had a feeling of euphoria. It was difficult to feel distressed because when she did, it left her and went to Legon. She did not want to increase his suffering, so she focused instead on the present and the break that she was receiving from her pain. She was grateful for what she had been given. She had experienced many trials, but she'd been given a lot too.

She didn't notice time go by as she knelt next to her Everser Vald. She looked at her situation with a new perspective, one that was not filled with doubt and hopelessness. Gradually the pain in her arm returned, along with all of the rest of it. But now from her reprieve she knew what she was to replace the suffering with. She still felt stress and anxiety, but now she tried to see the two perspectives separately. Adding them together, she came up with a new one, one that was her choice, one that didn't discount the bad but pushed her to the good.

Legon sat quietly with his eyes closed. He was breathing deeply. She and the others waited patiently.

Soon he opened his eyes. They were different. She saw them in incredible detail, etching the image in her memory forever. She locked eyes with him, and she attempted to look into his soul to unravel the mysteries of the Everser Vald, but the answers didn't come. Still, the eyes were different, not just in physical appearance but in substance. There was… more behind them now. Was that from being an Elf, or from what he had done?

She looked away. She wasn't worthy of holding his gaze, not after all that he had done for her and what he would do for them all. It wasn't that he was deity or a prophet. No, it was rather what he was destined to do that made her feel a sense of awe. She also now knew his lineage, but Arkin wouldn't reveal that, nor would she. That was the Elves' place.

Legon looked around the circle and Sara followed his gaze. Arkin was looking down, but not at him or anything else, judging by the look in his eyes. Keither was looking at him, not believing what he was seeing. Here was one that looked at the world through logic, Sara thought, but magic was still beyond him. Sasha had great tears running down her cheeks now. Sara knew that they sprung from happiness. Her brother was free of growing old and dying. She wouldn't have to know the pain of losing him. She would have to look at Sasha differently as well. Legon spoke to her then.

She was caught off guard by a finger under her chin, guiding her face. No more was this the rough hand of a butcher, but the soft tender hand of the healer. He looked her in the eyes, not letting her look away.

"What are you thinking Sara?"

What an odd question, but this whole scene was odd. There was a reverence to it that wasn't appropriate for the mourning of a friend and loved one.

Her throat caught as she spoke.

"Un Prosa," she said, using what she knew of the old tongue. Her head jerked from his hand as she looked down. She could just see his face. He paused, looking curiously at her.

"Why do you look away from me?" He was hurt, but that wasn't the intent. Arkin answered for her.

"She means no disrespect. In fact, she respects you very deeply, but I am afraid that she knows more about you than you do."

"Is it time to break your oaths Arkin?" Sasha asked politely.

"Yes, I think it is."

* * * * * * *

Keither knew that something far greater than himself was happening here and tried to clear his mind. It was close to daybreak, but the moon would not set for some time to come. It was that part of the year when the sun would be rising and the moon would stubbornly hang in the western sky, refusing to bow to its more powerful brother. He sat on his overly large behind. All of them were sitting now. Sasha gave Legon a piece of bread to chew on. He would be hungry after all, wouldn't he?

Arkin took a sip from his water skin, collecting his thoughts. "It won't do to get right to the part where you two come into this story, so I will start further back." When he said, 'you two' he inclined his head to Sasha as well as Legon. How was she involved in this?

"As you know, there was a war when the Queen took over this section of Airmelia. And in that war, human, Elf, and Iumenta fought. All sides took casualties, obviously; one of these was a dragon. His wife was killed. Now it doesn't matter what killed her, only that she was killed and his grief was great. All of you remember what I have said about what happens when an Elf's spouse dies, don't you?"

They did. Keither wondered how a dying Elf had anything to do with their current state, but he listened on.

"Before this great dragon expired, he used magic and the Mahann to ascertain the future, for he wanted to know how long it would be until the rest of his house fell to the Iumenta."

Legon spoke, preempting Arkin. "But he didn't see their end."

Arkin looked surprised at Legon's intuitiveness. "No, he didn't. He saw in the future one man that would either choose to belong to the Elves or the Iumenta. He would be an Elf, but the choice would be his to make. Now this man would do many great and terrible things if he chose, but in the end he would restore order."

When Keither first started to hear about a 'prophecy' he scoffed at the idea, but this was not so much a prophecy but rather a probability. The Mahann used logic to figure things out, and this dragon used the Mahann to tell of these things, so there was logic here. It had to be a probability, but he didn't see it yet.

"That 'hero', as he was called, would be known as the Everser Vald, meaning, in the Elven tongue, 'the destroyer of great power'. This meant that if he chose the Iumenta side the Elves would fall, but if he choose the Elven side..."

"The Iumenta would lose control of the land," Sara said, beaming at Legon.

Legon interrupted them all. "Wait, wait. That doesn't mean that it's me. You said that there had been others in my situation before. There have to be signs or something to say who it is."

"Yes Legon, there have been others. But let me finish. The prophecy spoke of signs that would appear, of course and I will get to those, but there is more. This hero, this Everser Vald, would be greatly influenced by another."

Sara said incredulously, "An influencer? I have never heard of an influencer in this story."

"No you haven't. Only a select few have heard the prophecy in its entirety. This was done as a protection, not only to the possible hero, but to that influencer as well. This person would be the deciding factor in what side the Everser Vald would choose, and that meant that we had to step lightly when a potential person fit the signs."

"But I haven't had an influencer," Legon blurted. But he had. Keither saw it, saw her for the first time. Pieces fell into place now. It never made any sense at all to keep one like Legon so deep in the empire but now it fit, she fit! Who else could have had an impact on someone as headstrong as Legon? The same person who had impacted all of them over the past few months. The name came out with our thinking. "Sasha."

Sasha looked at him, what color left in her face draining away. But it was her. She had taught him empathy with her episodes, made him a better person. She was his drive for doing everything; he would attack the Queen herself if it would save Sasha from suffering. Truly Keither had never seen anyone love another person the way Legon loved Sasha. And it fit. How could he not choose the right side?

"So this whole thing was a setup?" Keither said.

"How do you mean?" Sara said, sounding agitated.

"Sasha is the influencer, so he was put with her to make him the Everser Vald, wasn't he? And moreover, you said that Legon has been using magic with Sasha during her episodes his entire life. If he wasn't around her then he may not have turned, correct?"

Arkin looked uncomfortable. Keither knew that he was right and that angered him. All of them had been through hell for this and it was just a setup.

"No Keither, this is not what you think. Edis and Laura didn't know anything about what Legon was or who he would become. But yes, he was allowed to stay with them on account of Sasha. Even at a young age it was apparent that she was an unusually good person. If he was taken back to the resistance we don't know what would have happened. Even being raised on our side wouldn't guarantee that he was going to turn Elf or-"

"That I wouldn't become a tool for the Iumenta. I don't fault you for what you did. I don't want to think of life without Sasha. Please, tell me of my father," Legon interjected.

Part of Keither's mind told him what Legon had said was probably right, and though this made his life harder, perhaps it was better for the world as a whole.

* * * * * * *

Legon wasn't affected by the news that Arkin just shared. Somehow he knew it all. He wasn't sure when he had figured it out but he thought it was when he had been transfigured. The White Dragon had shared a message with him, but he couldn't remember it. He wanted to know about his father and his mother, but it wasn't their character that he was worried about. After all, he still viewed his adopted parents as his own. As he asked the question he saw a look of confusion on Sara and Keither's faces. Sasha was firmly connected with him and she knew what he was looking for.

She was feeling uncomfortable at the moment, having just found out her place in all of this. She had disconnected the weak network she had established with all but him. He sent soothing thoughts to her, reached over and held her hand gently. She in turn gripped his hand harder and he was aware of just how soft her skin was. He felt all of the muscles in her hand contracting and relaxing as she adjusted her grip. There was a steady pulse coming from her. He had never felt someone's pulse from their hand before, but he did now. He also felt the moisture building from their hands being together, all odd sensations to be having for the first time.

He remembered what Arkin had said about Elf senses and he concentrated on background noise seeing just how diverse it was. He focused on his immediate area, breathing in Sasha's and his scent. Hers was soft and almost sweet; his was that of the dirt and the horses. He listened to their hearts beating. Arkin was bringing them up to speed about how rare Elf-human children were. He knew this but he waited so the others would understand.

"Now Legon, you wanted to know more about your father. He was an Elf, obviously, and he held a high place in society. He was a good man."

This wasn't what Legon was looking for. He put the question to Arkin, knowing the response that it would cause. "Was he ascended?"

Arkin spluttered for a moment. "Why would you ask?"

"If I am to be the destroyer of power, I must have come from good stock, right?"

"You are more than what you were born with."

"I am aware of that, but there are things that we *are* born with. So tell me, was he ascended?"

"Yes."

There was a collective gasp that ran through them. Legon felt oddly saddened by this news. Up to this point he hadn't been sure what he thought of this prophecy. It seemed to him that if his dad was just a regular Venefica then maybe that's all he would be after all. But his father was ascended, and that might mean someday Legon would be as well.

No. His mother was human, and surely that would prevent him from that change. Sasha gently ran her thumb over the top of his hand as she held it. She didn't need the connection to feel his reaction to this news, no matter how expected it was. The others were silent, waiting for Legon to talk. The sun was peeking over the horizon, softening the air. The sky was turning to warm oranges and reds.

"And what class was he?" Legon asked

"Seven," Arkin responded.

"And how was he killed?" Legon asked in a calm voice.

Arkin shifted as he sat. Legon knew that, as he had earlier, Arkin was attempting to draw strength from the litany.

"His party was ambushed by two dragons and a small ground force. He was in his Elven form when it happened, and even though he transformed it was too late." Arkin hung his head low, looking at the ground. Sasha and Legon both had the realization at the same time.

Legon asked another question "You were one of his, weren't you?"

"Yes."

"And that is why you have taken this matter to heart, isn't it?"

"Yes, Un Prosa. I am fulfilling my orders that I was left with, but also those of my heart."

Arkin was much more than a carpenter after all. They were sad for him. He had dedicated his life to a master that was long dead and he had served with such faith and diligence. What was the carpenter going to do now?

Legon wanted to know more. "And when we reach safety and your duties fulfilled, what will become of you?"

Arkin looked up at him with determination in his face and a fanatic fervor that, in their combined memories, they had never seen before.

"Your father was my Lord. And as I belonged to him, so too shall I belong to you. I am under orders for now, but once those are fulfilled and you are recognized, I will be under your command."

"You are willing to continue giving your life for us?" Legon asked, for he was giving his life. It was easy to die for a cause or a leader. It only took a moment of time. But to give your life was truly hard because it required a constant sacrifice that few could make.

"Until you have no need for me or I die, yes, I will give," Arkin said.

Chapter Eighteen
The Choice

Most of our lives we feel as if the weight of the world is on our shoulders,
though we know it is not. Sometimes, however, it is;
o choose wisely."
- Diary of the Perfectos Compatioa

The gravity of Arkin's pronouncement would have to be considered later. Right now Legon knew that Arkin was in command and he didn't care to challenge it, though clarity of his situation was coming as a result of finding out that he was the one spoken of in the prophecy. The Queen was going to try and secure herself a new kind of slave, despite his thought that it was unlikely that the Iumenta would believe in prophecies. The Queen was intelligent and would see the threat of having the people who resisted her, not to mention her subjects, thinking that their time of deliverance was at hand. But this principle could work in her favor. If she managed to produce the real Everser Vald then it would solidify her control in the empire and weaken the resolve and credibility of the resistance.

Both sides had played a dangerous game. However, the Queen was right to try and capture or kill him. As for the Elves, their play was to see what direction he was going in, then, if need be, take out the threat. With that in mind, he wasn't sure if Arkin would have been able to do it.

This was a call to arms. He needed to make a choice of what he was to be, but the choice had already been made for him. If he abandoned them to go off on his own, the Queen would gain at least a small victory in that the resistance would have placed hope in a false icon. Still, the resistance would make mistakes, and in so doing would cause suffering and injustice. By standing with them he would not only be marked with that blood and the blood of those that died in his cause.

There was a pit in his stomach. No matter what choice he made, people would die and there would be suffering. This wasn't just his decision, he realized. It was Sasha's as well, and whether he liked it or not she was now just as much a part of this future as he was.

They were getting ready to leave camp. Sasha was busy but he still brushed against her consciousness, looking for her counsel. As they conversed, they agreed that he would make the logical decision and that she would validate its ethics. She hated to do this, but he knew that Arkin wasn't lying when he said that Sasha was the most pure person he'd met. It wasn't going to be a choice of whether to join the Iumenta or the Elves, but rather to join the Elves or hide for the rest of their lives. She saw the problems in both, but said that the right thing to do for the many was to join the Elves. Logic said that they would die if they hid and that many would die if they joined the Elves, but it also said that the Queen would continue to enslave and kill her own subjects, as well as try and conquer the resistance. It wasn't a question of the short term effects; either way had bloody results in the fairly near future. The decision needed to be made for the far distant generations. What choice was best for the unborn? What choice would secure the lives of those who would not live for hundreds of years to come? And would it be a world they would want to live in?

Sasha's voice rang in his head. "This war will happen with or with out us, and even if we are picking the losing side, this is the right call. It is better for us to have our hands stained with blood trying to do the right thing than have them stained with cowardice."

He agreed with her and finished preparing to leave. He had no doubt that the empire would be sending more people to find them; it was just a question of when and who. If it were men then they might be ok; they only had two days to go. If it were Iumenta, they were dead, and if it was a Dragon… well, there was always the hope that he would at least cause the foul creature to get a stomach ache.

Humor aside, he did feel like they would make it. He could always make the horses run fast again, but was hesitant because even with magic they could only take so much. But now was the time to act; of that there was no question. This was bigger than both of them and he wasn't going to let those he cared about down. He had been kneeling over a bag and stood up much faster then he'd intended, so fast it would have just been a blur to the others. Arkin held out a hand.

"Sorry, I'm still getting used to this new me. It's an odd sensation feeling out of place in your own body." Legon said.

This wasn't a lie. Before, physical things weren't hard for him. He was strong, but now if he wanted to do something it just seemed to happen of its own accord. He had to be careful when he walked so as not to look like he was running around the camp. From the minds of the others he was aware that he was…well, for lack of a better term, graceful. With the new and better sense of balance and the ability to feel everything, he just moved easily. Apparently it looked graceful to the others.

There were other differences, too. He could hear all of their hearts beating, and feel the heat off their bodies. He even swore he felt energy coming from them when they moved. He noticed every detail now even to the point of seeing skin flush and perspiration increase. He had seen some of that before, but not like this; now he saw it all.

Sara was the oddest. He knew she found him attractive; with the mental network there weren't a lot of secrets and Sasha had a big mouth when she thought she could set someone up. But that being said, when he locked eyes with Sara he heard her heart speed up and saw blood rush to her face. Did that always happen to girls? Maybe it did and he could just see it now, but it was uncomfortable. Her thoughts about him were…well she hid them well, but apparently she was happy with the new him.

He felt his own skin getting warm and focused back on Arkin. Arkin chuckled a bit, which he was glad to hear. "I imagine it is uncomfortable getting used to a new body."

Legon decided to change the subject. "Ok, well I think we best get a move on. We will have company soon I'm sure. Arkin, lead the way."

"With pleasure."

And with that Arkin began issuing commands, telling them what to bring and how to pack it. Soon they were loaded up and ready to go. Arkin then took a few moments to teach Legon a few blocking wards. They were complex and they used a lot of magic when tested, but they held off most attacks, leaving Arkin to deal with the more detailed wards. Sasha stepped up to them timidly. Arkin looked concernedly at her.

"What is it, Sasha?" he said, not unkindly.

"I have, well, Sara and I have something to show you."

Keither stopped what he was doing to look at the two girls.

"What is that?" Arkin asked

She held out her hand and produced a strong ruby flame, and then in turn Sara conjured a weaker silver one. They stood waiting for Arkin's response.

The ability to see stuff was handy. Legon's mind flew now and while the others didn't see it, he saw three emotions cross Arkin's face in a heart beat. First there was shock; understandable. Then concern, and finally confusion. The carpenter had no clue what was going on, but he recovered fast.

Arkin spoke. "Amazing. When Legon turned you must have been given the ability to use magic through the mental network."

"But what does it mean?" Sasha asked.

"I have no clue. This is way beyond my understanding. Sasha, you are obviously more powerful, so you will take an offensive approach with Legon if needed. Sara, you will as well, but pick your shots with care."

Legon separated Sasha from the group and gave her a huge hug. She retuned it. He tightened his grip the way their father used to whenever he gave them bear hugs as kids.

"What was that for?" Sasha asked him

"I'm just happy that you're all right. I want to thank you for being my 'influencer'. You're going to make a great Venefica, I just know it. Think of how many sick people you'll help."

Legon knew how much she enjoyed being a healer. It was something that she had always wanted to do. Laura had to almost restrain her from helping sick people in town. He let go of her. She smiled warmly at him and walked to Murray.

* * * * * * *

Arkin mounted Phaedra. He was feeling much better now that everything was out in the open. Sasha was reestablishing the mental network in preparation for leaving. They were now four Venefica and one non-user which, provided there wasn't an Iumenta Dragon sent, put them in a very good position. Yet more benefits of the network made themselves known to him. Even though Sasha and Sara had no magical training, they felt Legon use spells and, more importantly, had both his and Legon's knowledge if needed. Both of them could fight and Arkin wouldn't even need to teach them.

Arkin saw a flicker of purple surround them all, indicating that Legon had activated his wards; this was followed by green from his own. Before he had been using more passive concealment spells, but the ones in place now were meant for combat. With the network in place, most would be hard pressed to get passed all of them.

He waited for Legon to check that the coast was clear. He marveled at just how adept Legon was with accessing the minds of hawks and eagles. They were clear and started to move out. Legon kept a firm connection with the birds in the area. This would be a tell-tale sign to other Venefica, but it gave them more time to run. They had about two days to go, and if they played their cards right, the army would be unwilling to follow them after about a day. By that point they would be too close to the border. The border itself didn't hold some unseen power over the enemy, but rather the human and Elven forces that were just beyond it. The Dragon patrols didn't hurt either.

They moved quickly from grove to grove. He laid down a spell to help reduce the dust from the horses. It would have been nice to do this in the dark, but time wasn't on their side right now.

Besides, we can't see in the dark he told himself. Then he thought about it some more. *Well, most of us can't.*

Legon would be able to see clearly in all but the darkest nights, his night vision even surpassing that of the horses. Arkin felt Phaedra's excitement. There was a bond between them and she always matched how he was feeling.

Soon the sun was high in the sky and he felt his forehead burn. These southern lands were hot and after his nineteen year exile he wasn't used to them. They would push on until ten or so tonight and then they would rest for a while and start back up. With this pace they would be in the clear by tomorrow night.

* * * * * * *

Setting up camp that night consisted of rolling out bed rolls, Legon killing some rabbits with magic, and Sasha and Sara doing their best to cook them in a way that was appetizing. All in all, Keither thought sarcastically, this was shaping up to be a night of luxury and enjoyment. This whole trip had been that. He lay back on his bed roll, not going inside his tent. It was too hot out, but at least clouds were starting to fill the sky. They might just get a break tomorrow.

The others fell asleep quickly. The only ones still awake were Legon and himself. Legon was scanning the area for danger, but this land was barren, which would make playing look-out easy if there were owls or any other wildlife in the area.

Keither rested his hands on his belly, noticing that despite his perceived hardships, he was the only person not to lose weight. Thoughts about what his brother had said right before he died came to mind. He really was worthless when he thought about it. But still, that's who he was; why try to change? He was uncomfortable and sat up, turning his torso and causing his back to crack and pop soothingly. Legon glanced over at him.

"Why aren't you asleep Keither?"

He was sure Legon would take the big brother role to heart.

"One could ask the same of you," he said, trying to sound insightful.

"True, but then who would be keeping a lookout, you?"

He felt uneasy. That had been a dumb thing to say. "Point taken. But aren't you tired of doing this every night? I mean, you just changed. You have to be worn out."

He thought he heard a small chuckle come from Legon. He answered in a calm voice. "I am very tired, yes. But I don't see what that has to do with anything."

"What doesn't it have to do with? Don't you want to quit or stop or anything?"

"Of course I do, Keither, but it's not that simple now is it?" There was a firmness in his voice that told Keither to step lightly.

"Well, I guess I don't see your point. If you're tired, rest."

"And if danger comes, should we just wait to find out when they get here? Or would you tell them to take a load off for awhile, too?" Legon looked away. There was a point here; Keither was sure. Some lesson he was to learn.

"When you put it that way I see your point. I didn't think about that."

"You rarely think very far down the road, Keither," Legon said.

Ah, the point was here, but for once he was going to listen to it. In a way, Legon was like his brother, Kovos. He had tried to drive home something to Keither, too, but he never got it.

"I know, I'm lazy and I don't think ahead, yeah I get it." Well, he thought he understood it but didn't get it. He was starting to see now there was a difference between the two.

Legon turned to him. "Do you get it? If so, why not change your behavior? You're not dumb Keither. Surely you see that if it was you that we followed the whole lot of us would be long since dead by now."

That was a stinging remark. Legon had always been nice to him, and even now he wasn't talking unkindly. But he was being very frank.

He felt himself tense for an argument. "So, you're right and I'm wrong?" Keither spat.

Legon's response was genial. "Only if you perceive being alive as the desired outcome of this little adventure."

"What kind of dumb thing is that to say? Why would I want to die?"

Legon brought a finger to his lips, telling him not to wake the others. "If you do care about living, why don't you act like it?"

Keither was at a loss for this. Legon was using logic against him, and winning by the looks of it.

"Why do you do nothing with your life Keither?"

There was real interest and concern in his tone. Legon was trying to understand, trying to figure out why someone would choose the life Keither did.

"Well I, I want to, but it's not…well…"

"It's not as easy? Don't you want things in this life?"

"Well, yes." Keither said, of course he did

Legon pressed "Like what?"

He stopped at this. What did he want out of life? He thought for a moment, taking in his surroundings, stopping just a moment longer on Sara. A normal person wouldn't have seen the pause, but someone trained in the Jezeer would, and so would an Elf. Both sat before him in one person. "If you want her, you will need to try a bit harder, don't you think?" Legon asked.

"What did Kovos think of me?" Keither blurted without thinking.

He saw the outline of Legon's head tilt to the side. "Do you really want to know?"

Did he? Was this something that he could handle right after his brother's death? Within hours really, was he ready for the good or the bad?

"Yes."

"What if it is unpleasant? Once said there is no taking it back."

Obviously there was no taking things back. Was talking about the effect that it might have on him? Well, this news would have an effect on him, that was for sure.

"Yes, tell me please." As he spoke, he tried to send the message with his mind as well, showing the emotions that showed his desire.

"Very well. He loved you very deeply, and wanted only the best for you. He thought that you were more intelligent than him and that you had more natural talent as well."

Keither was at a loss for words "He did? Wow. I always thought that he loved me as a brother but didn't like me all that much."

Legon leaned forward. "You are more intelligent than him and more talented, I agree. But I didn't say that he liked you. He loved you, and there is a difference. You don't have to like someone that you love."

"Oh. Well, thank you for telling me."

"I'm not done Keither. He thought you were lazy and stubborn beyond reason. He didn't like you because you are throwing your life away, a life that he would have liked to have. You make no attempt to hone your skills, barring trying to prove people wrong. You also refuse to grow as a person."

There was a lump in Keither's throat at this. He wasn't ready for this news. Keither knew this was hurting Legon to say. The man had taken his pain for a short time; there was no way causing more would feel good.

"Is there more?" Keither asked

Legon started again. "Yes. He was convinced that you hated him. That was what he thought at the end, but he was willing to do what it took to give you a shot. Keither, I'm sorry, I know this was not what you wanted to hear, but remember he and I both think that you are capable of great things if you try."

Legon gestured with his head at where Sara slept. "And she does as well."

Legon was telling the truth, and that's what stung the most. Keither's brother was a hero, but he was... *A lump of lard,* he thought.

Legon spoke, not needing to read his mind. "But it is a choice, know that. You choose what you are. Make sure it's a choice that you will not regret on your death bed."

"Ok, I will," was the only response he had.

"Now," Legon said flatly.

"What? Why now? Can't I think about what I want to be?"

"I'm not talking about a trade or where to live. Decide who you are to be now so when presented with obstacles in life you have already chosen what to do. Not choosing is a choice. You have thought long enough. I will support you in whatever choice you make."

Keither knew that was a true statement. Legon would take the mantle of older brother, but unlike Kovos, he would not make decisions for him. Keither looked down, thinking. He wasn't unhappy with his life; he was content. He looked over at Sara. To him she was the embodiment of a different future whether she chose him or not. That path would have lots of pain in it, and sorrow; his current path would not.

"My current path is easier and will mean less suffering in this life..."

"But it will also mean less happiness as well. Life is a balance. Your capacity to do good is only as strong as your ability to do evil, remember that."

He had a point. Keither was content with life but that was it. He wasn't all that happy or sad. This little adventure of theirs made him feel more alive than he ever had. Still, he didn't want the suffering. He looked at the sleeping form of Sara almost as if it would tell him what to do, and in a way it did. This was going to be wonderfully horrible, he thought. It was his choice of what he did with this life. He may have the potential to do bad things, but he didn't have to choose them. He could still choose the good. A shiver ran down his spine as the thought of what might be his true potential and, more important, the road that it would take him down.

"I will be a real person I will be what I was meant to be." It sounded odd for him to say, it sounded pompous and arrogant, but at least he was trying.

* * * * * * *

Legon was looking intently at the boy, wondering if he would choose to be a man or remain a boy. It tore at him to hurt Keither, but he was to take Kovos's place, a job he took very seriously. It was cruel of him to tell Keither the truth of Kovos's and his thoughts; you were supposed to say that someone loved and cared for you and that they were proud, yet this was a lie. But if Keither chose to be something then this night would be a reminder for him in dark times, a defining moment. Conversely, if he chose not to move then this would haunt him for life and there might be no chance at convincing him again.

Was this his place? He purpose was to restore, right? But what was he to restore Keither to? A voice in his mind said he was also to destroy, but was destruction all bad? He would have to destroy the Iumenta to restore order, wouldn't he? This was just another function of the Everser Vald. This was the risk that was taken; it would be up to Keither to decide the outcome. Either way, Legon would live with it and do his best for the boy or man, depending on what he decided.

Keither was now looking at Sara, and he could almost see the wheels turning in his head. He was standing on a path now, but which one was it? When Keither turned his attention back to Legon there was a look that could have been hate or determination, Legon wasn't sure. With Keither they often came together. After his pronouncement, though, he knew it was the latter, and he smiled inwardly.

"Good, Keither, now sleep. Tomorrow we will reach the precipice, if there is trouble you will be the lead rider so the rest of us may fight with magic."

"What's the precipice? Sorry I wasn't listening to Arkin earlier"

"It is the outpost for the Elves and Humans in this part of the land. It is said to be the only one for the humans. The rest of their lands are blocked by the Cornis mountain range to the northwest and then Elven lands to the east."

"Is there no way by the sea? We're close to that now, aren't we?"

"Yes, I think we are, and the city that feeds and takes care of the precipice is called Manton and it is a coastal city, but the Iumenta won't do anything via the sea."

"Why do you think that is?"

Legon thought this might be a good time to let Keither do what he was good at. Making a new life didn't mean that he wasn't to think any more. "Well, why would you avoid attacking by sea if you were the Queen?"

He saw Keither thinking it over. "Well, the Queen has more resources, but…"

He would get it, Legon told himself, just give it time. "But the humans have Elves for allies."

"And why would that help?" Legon asked, knowing the answer.

"The Elven navy is unrivaled. It would be expensive and extremely difficult to do. You could harass them a bit, but a full on attack would mean going head to head with an undefeated navy."

This was true. Legon didn't know much about his people's military, but he did know the tales about their Navy. It was unsurpassed and to attack it was suicide. The Iumenta came from landlocked areas, whereas the Elves had an obsession with the sea, according to stories. Keither was right; it would be a bad idea to try and take Manton by sea, and by land you had to hit the precipice. He wasn't sure what advantage taking the city would hold anyway. It was at the edge of their territory and therefore not a hub for trade. He guessed that must be why it had never been attacked. There is a certain security in being in unimportant city, he thought; this was the case for Salmont as well.

"Very good, Keither."

"Thanks, I really apprec-"

Legon held up his hand, stopping Keither.

"It's time for you to lead, get up!"

He started rousing the others. The intruders were coming fast; they would be there within the hour. Everyone was moving slowly, not wanting to get up.

"We have company! We need to move now!"

With this they woke up and frantically began to gather their things. Within ten minutes they were on their way. Sasha had the network up and running and Legon was giving the horses just a little help. As the sun rose they saw a plume of dirt rising in the distance behind them. Their pursuers were gaining fast, too fast in fact. Then it hit him.

"Venefica! They're helping the horses! Arkin, we need help."

"I'll see what I can do," Arkin responded.

Arkin needed to separate from the network to make his connection. One of the rules for connecting to the precipice was to not have anyone else who wasn't known and trusted with them. Legon looked back at the incoming force; there was no using the animals now. They were gaining fast, but he was hesitant to do too much with their horses. They could drop if more chemicals entered their blood stream, and he couldn't work for them for long. As they closed in he saw around thirty or so men on horses. It was time to raise their defenses. Arkin activated the wards. As he did he saw flickers of purple and green around them. On the enemy's horses he saw orange, yellow, and blue flickers. There were at least three Venefica with them.

As the gap between the two racing groups closed Legon sent Keither a message to lead the group. All he had to do was keep them going in their current direction. Off in the distance the peaks of the Cornis mountains were coming into view, their best hope for safety. The gap between the forces was closing rapidly and soon their pursuers would be in range. Legon faded back, placing him self at the rear of the group. Undoubtedly they knew more magic than him, but he was stronger and he had the assistance of Arkin, Sasha, and Sara, so not all was lost. Just mostly lost.

Arkin had instructed them in the basics of magical combat, so it was no surprise when Legon saw a bolt of blue fly from the horsemen. It was a large ball of energy. It hit a wall of purple about five feet away from him with a deafening crack. This spell was not attacking them directly; it was designed to hit wards and weaken them.

Legon felt a small tug on his energy at this, and countered with a spell of his own. He only knew of a few breaking spells, as they were called, but he sent one their way. It smacked into a wall of yellow, causing a crack like thunder to rent the air, and at once a flash of orange came at him, this time hitting him directly. He felt his fire ward activate, stopping the flame curse. He knew what they were doing now. The Venefica with the yellow magic was protecting the group as a whole. There would be wards by the others as well, but this person would take the brunt of the attack, then the blue would try and take out their shield and the orange would take shots at holes in their armor. As if to enforce this point he saw another bolt of blue collide with his wards, and this time he felt the mind and energy behind it. The first had been a test. Now the Venefica was attempting to break the wards. He pushed with magic and his mind, reinforcing the shield. Legon felt it begin to buckle and he poured more into it, but he couldn't hold them too long. He wasn't good with wards yet and, powerful or not, it didn't matter.

He sent commands to Sasha and Sara, telling them to attack only when he ordered. He wasn't about to have them waste what little energy they had. He sent another breaking spell their way, and this time when it made contact he held it, changing it, working it around as if he were trying to extract a splinter. He felt a hole open in their shield and sent the command to Sara and Sasha.

They sent simple spells at the enemy. Red and silver bolts shot by, hitting their intended targets, one hitting blue the other orange. He told them to focus on the blue, and again he hit the yellow ward and again they sent spells at one of the men covered by the blue Venefica. The man looked terrified, and as the two spells hit, the ward around him failed and his head wrenched back, breaking his neck.

There was now magic flying back in forth between the groups at an incredible speed, but they were winning, Legon was too strong, and even when the blue Venefica broke his initial wards the orange spells were stopped by Arkin's and his others.

"Help is on the way," Arkin said across the network.

"Good, you take command."

Arkin acknowledged this with commands. "Legon, attack with everything you have. Don't worry about their wards, simply overpower them. Sasha, go for random people but don't use much power. Sara, use yours sparingly and only target those whose wards flicker and fade. Legon, when I tell you, hit their lead horse's brain."

Legon started to send spell after spell at them. With every hit one or two men went down; his attacks were too strong for the other Venefica to counter. He sent a fire spell at a rider in the lead, causing the man's head to burst into flames. The rider immediately rolled on his horse, disrupting the others. Sasha took advantage of the situation by sending a burst of pure light at them; it wouldn't hurt anyone but it continued to sow mayhem, causing two more men to fall off their horses.

Then suddenly the message from Arkin came and he sent his spell at the lead horse, ceasing its brain activity. The animal dropped. The other horses running close behind tripped, sending riders and horses all over the place and a gap began to open between them.

That's when he heard it. He looked up to the gray sky and heard it again, a soft *thud*. No. Not another Dragon, they couldn't take the twenty or so men left and a Dragon. THUD. It was overhead now, almost as if it were going to drop on them. THUD. Or behind them?

In the distance a figure dropped from the clouds and his heart skipped as the long body fell, a thin line in the sky with its wings folded close to its body. He squinted ahead, trying to ascertain the appearance of their foe. He knew that Dragons came in every shade and color but he was having a hard time believing his eyes. He felt Sasha's confusion and then her question.

"Is that Dragon pink?"

It was a vivid shade of pink, but there was more to it than that; its horns were white and its scales glittered in the sun, but there was no direct light hitting it. The Dragon was seemed to be producing the light and he felt his heart leap again; it was an Elf! The pink Dragon's wings snapped open just before the ground and it rushed at them. The men pursuing them scrambled to get out of the way, but too late. It was on them all now.

Legon saw the flicker of pink indicating wards that the other Venefica would not be able to break. He wondered what type of magic it was going to use. He did feel a little apprehension when he saw the huge mouth opening to revel white teeth, then he closed his eyes right before a torrent of pink flames erupted from the mouth.

The fire swept around them; any amusement or doubt caused by the Dragon's bright color disappeared at the sound of screaming from behind, but he only felt a warm tickling sensation. He opened his eyes, to see a world of total pink. He couldn't see anything in front of him; he was in the fire, but his wards were not being tested. Why not? Then he remembered what Arkin had said about magical fire: the brighter the color, the more magic is in it. This Dragon was using pure magic, so the flame would burn only what it wanted.

* * * * * * *

Keither looked frantically at the pink flame that surrounded him, trying to figure how long it would be until he was burned to death, but then it passed and he heard a great *whoosh* from above and looked up to see a giant pink Dragon. He didn't feel the regular fear he would with other Dragons. This was in part due to the whoops and yells coming from the others, but also when it passed overhead he saw white claws, not black. This Dragon was producing light around itself as well. The Iumenta dragons seemed to leach light out of the sky and their scales refused to sparkle in the sun. This was not the case for this Dragon; there was a slight glow around it and its scales twinkled even with no direct light.

As it passed the Dragon turned its head, and for the second time in a few days Keither locked eyes with one of these creatures. The Iumenta Dragon's eyes were the same color as their scales, with yellow instead of white surrounding the colored part of the eye. With this Elven Dragon the eye was pink but the sounding area was white as snow. It blinked at him… or was it a wink? He felt a rush of air as the Dragon's large powerful wings swept it away and off into the distance.

He chanced a look behind him to see the look of awe on all but Arkin's face, which had a wide smile on it. He waved to him, which was an odd sort of thing to do, but he waved back. They weren't being pursued any more, or rather there weren't people on the horses behind them, who looked to be relevantly unharmed. There were, however, blackened and charred corpses on the horses, burned to the bone. He shuttered at the sight. It had been a display of power when the Iumenta Dragon had burned a town in a breath, and that display would stay with him forever. So would this one. They had all been covered in fire, but only their pursuers had been killed, not their animals, not those they pursued, and not even the grass of the field. It was a targeted attack, executed with terrifying surgical precision.

Ahead, the large rocky peaks of the Cornis Mountains were fast approaching. They were incredibly intimidating mountains, barren except for scrub brush and goats. Because the main road was two days away, they were taking the hard way into the precipice, a narrow goat trail bordered by large cliffs and canyons. No force would be able to go through it as it was a single track most of the time. Keither hated heights, but he hated getting beat-up and attacked by the militia more, so the treacherous land it was.

* * * * * * * *

Arkin rode, smiling at the land of his birth. He had been raised in this area and was looking forward to seeing people and places he knew again. There was a tug at his mind. She was leaving, and he just saw her as a dot on the horizon. Why did they send her? *She probably asked for it,* he thought. He was happy it was her in a way, the same part of him that was happy about not being dead or hurt by a misplaced spell, burning them to ashes and not the enemy. He was going to get it when they arrived, there was no doubt about it, and he could already hear the taunts about having to bail him out of baby sitting duty. She respected him greatly, but even as kids she had given him a hard time. He smiled. Legon would like her, and he thought that she would like him as well.

He could feel Sasha in all their minds, checking pain centers for injury. He smiled again. For sure she would like Sasha.

Chapter Nineteen
The Precipice

"History repeats itself, or so I've been told. One could then ask the question,
'If I have a perfect understanding of the past, can I see what lies ahead?' I
would be inclined to say yes, yet after all this time the
future never fails to surprise me."
-Conversations in the Garden

Sasha looked disquietedly at the looming mountains before them. There was a reason the Cornis Mountains had held back the Empire for years. They were known to be very dangerous and easy to get lost in. At their base was brown grass and sage dotted with large rocks and yucca plants. The mountains rose steeply then, forced upwards by millennia of pressure. The land looked tortured as it gave way to the razor-like gray stone peaks. It would have been fitting to see vultures and ravens in the air, but there were none. There were, however, white figures dotting the side of the mountains. She stretched her neck to get a better view. Legon flashed the image from his eyes to her mind and she saw mountain goats as if they were no more than the fifty yards away. They spoke to each other in their heads.

"That's incredible," she remarked.

"I know it is. Here, you can look around if you want."

She felt and odd sensation as her mind not only joined his but took over much of the control of his body. Conversely, he was controlling hers. She felt what he was doing in her body but it was a separated feeling, almost like when you touch your arm after it falls asleep. The feeling of remoteness soon dissipated as she took in her surroundings through Legon's eyes.

She could see the world in much more detail than she normally could. She saw the peaks in a new light. They were gray rock yes, but they were also covered in lichen and there were birds flying high above them. She heard the goats too, jumping from rock to rock in the far distance. She was inundated with smells and feelings as well. His mind spoke to hers.

"Look, if I concentrate on an area my eyes will zoom closer to it, like a seeing glass."

As he spoke he focused on the goats and her view rushed forward until she was viewing them as if like they were no more than a few feet away. Before, his field of vision had been much like hers, albeit more clear and detailed. Now she understood the true depth of his sight. He could focus on something and bring it closer. Perhaps this was something that she could do as well. She asked him to do it a few more times, paying close attention to what he was doing. He was using his mind to magnify the image, so in theory she could do the same.

She realized that she had done it before, as had all of them. Whenever you worked on something small, you got tunnel vision and the object took up your entire field of view. But could she do it consciously? She tried returning to her body. She focused on an area just ahead of them where the hill rose and the single path began. She focused her mind on it like Legon did, but it was natural for him. Her vision became a blur and he tried to help her. He took control and after a moment her sight narrowed but was still unfocused. He tried something closer and it worked.

"I wonder why it didn't work as well in my head," Sasha said

Legon replied, "I don't know. Let's see if Arkin knows anything about it."

They broadened their connection to the rest of the group and told them of their attempts.

"Wow, you can do that?" Keither said aloud.

"I knew Iumenta and Elves could see well, but this is amazing," Sara said after seeing the view from Legon's eyes.

None of the rest of them could connect as deeply as Legon and Sasha could to each other, so they were not able to take control of his body, but they could still view the world through him.

"Arkin, you have incredible aim with the bow. Do you do anything?" Keither asked.

"Yes I do, but I am using magic most of the time to make my eyes better. However, I do know what you are talking about. When you focus on something that's close to you, your eyes are already taking in all of the detail that you see through Legon's eyes. Your mind just discards stuff as it takes in the information."

"So we see the same as Elves," Sara said, looking unconvinced.

"No, not at all. Their eyes are much, much stronger than ours and are able to take the extra detail. It's not that they are smarter than us, but that their sensory centers are far more advanced. Now Legon can see far away because he is getting more of the image. When you do it Sasha, your eyes can't see as much, so the image is blurry."

That made sense to her but she still had questions. "Arkin, can you augment this with magic to get a better result?"

"I don't know. I suppose so, but I'm not an Elf."

She laughed. "Come on, you know everything."

Now it was his turn to laugh. "Ok I know that up to this point I have been a teacher and mentor to you all and I hope to always be that. But please understand that I have taught the basics. All of Legon and Sasha's training up to this point was in fact directed by the Elves and I had to constantly contact them for help."

Legon interrupted. "Wait a moment. You have been able to talk to the Elves from Salmont? That's too far."

"For one man yes, but I checked in at the same time every week, and when I did I would connect to someone who was in range and then they with another and so on. In this fashion you can span any distance and talk in someone's mind like we do."

The implications were astounding to Sasha. Up to this point she was amazed by their apparently limited abilities. But to communicate across that much space was unimaginable.

Arkin went on. "I had to be precise about my time, but you get the idea. Anyway, they told me everything that I needed to do with you, and as time went on I needed less and less help. But still the core of my training is in combat and concealment. Magic is a vast subject, but I'm sure you can ask another Venefica that specializes in this topic."

Sasha made a mental note to do so and continued to experiment in her mind. She knew that Arkin was limited, as were all people, and in a way it was a comfort to have finally found some of those limits. In another way she was saddened. Arkin had always been a hero to her. Nothing could stop or stump him, but this was unfair to expect of anyone. She began to admire him more for his ability to recognize when he was lacking and go to another for help. That was the true mark of a wise man, and a hero.

* * * * * * *

Arkin sat forward in the saddle as Phaedra started up the steep goat path. They rode in a line with him in the lead and then alternating pack mules and riders, with Sasha brining up the tail. She was by far the best with the horses and if there were problems he wanted an experienced rider at the back to help the others along.

Soon the rocky hill to their left gave way to a space in the rock. A deep fissure that not even a goat could jump ran next to the path. They wound along, climbing all the time. It was slower than Arkin remembered and there was moisture in the normally parched air.

After three hours they could no longer see the great rolling hills of the Empire. They were deep in the mountains, which were unforgiving. There was a certain amount of fear coming from all but Legon, whose superior senses would be a comfort in these lands. For Arkin he felt no fear. He had grown up in Manton, which was surrounded by these peaks. He had played in them as a boy, hunted rams with his father here. No, these mountains were not his enemies, but his friends. He felt a drop of rain on his brow and contemplated stopping for the night. The rocks became slick in the rain and mudslides were commonplace.

After a while the rain came harder. Arkin searched his memory for a resting place; one was close if he wasn't mistaken. The path was leveling onto a rock ledge, and against the wall of the mountain was an opening. To the untrained eye it looked to be a small alcove, but he saw the sanctuary within.

"We will rest here tonight," Arkin said over his shoulder to the others.

"Why? The rain isn't that bad," Sara protested.

"Not yet, but I promise it will be, and the lightning will be as well. Come. This may not look it, but it's a large cave."

There were caves all throughout the Cornis Mountains. These were once the only true strongholds of humanity. He dismounted and walked Phaedra through the low entrance. As he was shrouded with darkness he produced a light showing the high ceiling and long cavern that he'd known was here. He heard the intake of air as each entered.

"How big is this?" Keither asked.

"It's large. There will be chambers where the horses can stay and others where we can."

He looked to the entrance. The rock was shaped in a way that didn't allow the rain to enter the cave but that allowed the smoke to float out. This refuge of man dawned back to the time when dragons came to be. This particular cave had thousands of years of history.

Humans had been the first to separate themselves from the other races. He didn't know for what reason their ancestors had done, this but he knew they had. Man lived in the desolate lands long before the Iumenta. When the Elves and Iumenta had split they were already much more advanced than man, but still they didn't attempt to inhabit this land. After the Great War men still lived here and as they adopted Iumenta and Elven technology these caves had changed in form and function.

He walked to the wall and ran his fingers along it, feeling the history. If they went deep into the cave there would be paintings on the walls from primitive man. Up here at the opening there were signs of more modern times, when these caves had been communities and guard posts. He became aware of the others' silence. They were listening to his thoughts, at first waiting for instruction and now taking in their heritage.

"Even you have a place here, Legon. You are the only Elf alive that can claim these mountains as home," Arkin explained

The rain was roaring outside. A great curtain of water covered the entrance as sheets of lightning ran across the sky. If one listened they could hear the rocks shifting as dirt turned to slippery mud. Arkin exhaled, relaxing. The rain would cover their tracks and no one would enter this area. They were safe, perhaps safer then they would be in the Elven capital.

The rain was making things cold, and Arkin could soon see his own breath. Farther into the cave was a world in itself; it refused the control of the outside, and while it was cool here, the inner chambers would be warmer than the cold rain and wind that now drove at them.

He was aware of the group's collective interest in this place and those like it, but he was tired and pushed the feelings from his mind. He walked to a chamber. There were enough chambers here for each traveler to have their own, but he knew that the others would probably sleep together at the cave entrance. He didn't blame them. The cave was just another vulnerable hiding spot to them, and perhaps their concerns were right. But never mind that now. He sat, leaning against the cold hard stone wall, and extinguished his emerald ball of light.

* * * * * * *

Sara sat on her bedroll at the entrance to the cave, her knees under her chin. This was a cold place to her, yet it felt like home somehow. The rain was loud outside, but after traveling the first few feet into the cave the sound became muffled and distant.

Legon searched in their packs and procured a small loaf of bread, passing it to her. "Give Sasha my portion."

Their supplies were light and this was the last bit of bread they had. Now it would be up to Legon and Arkin to kill animals for food. They were close to the Precipice, Sara knew, but with this weather and their luck, there was no guarantee that they would be in friendly company soon.

"Legon," Sara said.

"I am stronger than you. I do not need it."

Sara nodded. She knew he was stronger than she was. She broke the bread into three pieces. Arkin had retired for the night, and after last night's meal said the he would rather eat the dirt of the field than more stale bread. She knew there was another reason for his distaste for eating this bread, though. They had found it with some other food on a table in one of the huts from the now burned co-op. It was she who said to take it. She knew that there was death in that place, so why save food for the dead?

Sasha was off exploring the cave, but Sara would save her portion. It was just her and Keither now. She handed a piece to him.

"I'm fine, thank you."

She looked at him sternly. "Just because Legon didn't…"

"I am not trying to emulate him, but while he is strong with character and has the body of an Elf, I have the fat for three. Doing without is just as much good for me as eating my ration is for you."

He smiled at her then, and she saw that it wasn't a bad attitude that precipitated this but rather a genuine concern for her. She ate the stale bread. She undid her water skin to drink. *Dang it,* she thought.

"Keither may I borrow some water from you? I'm out."

"Sure, let me get my water skin for you."

He walked off and then returned. "It's empty."

"Well, that won't do now will it."

An idea came to her and she took both skins to the entrance.

"It will take you all night to fill those, you know," Keither said warmly.

That wasn't her plan. She concentrated on the magic in her mind, seeing the water coming down in sheets outside. She held one of the skins in the deluge and released the spell.

"Auga." She used just the name for water and let her intent do the work. The water formed together, falling as a stream about three inches wide. It took almost no energy but she felt her spell slipping as her mind did. She held the skins, filling them. When they were full she walked back to Keither.

"Nice," he said smiling at her.

* * * * * * *

Sasha rested in a chamber deep enough in the cave that all sound from the outside world was blocked off. The room was and oval about ten feet across and fifteen feet wide. The chamber wasn't tall, only going up six feet or so, and she saw signs of tool marks on the ceiling and walls. This place was not part of the original cave. The floor was flat. She knelt, planning on taking advantage of their rest for some training. She accessed Arkin's memory, thumbing through it like a book, looking for the desired subject. He didn't resist and had encouraged them to do this. Anything that he didn't want them to know was blocked off. She soon found what she wanted. Arkin didn't have much in the way of training on it, but she still took in what he had.

The principle was called the Pronos. She reviewed what he knew of it and began. The Jezeer was vast, and even with the training they had been given, she knew that it was a subject that they hadn't even begun to tap into. The Jezeer was about the body, mind, and voice, about ways of thinking, acting, even moving, but the principle or practice she wanted now was that of perspective. She was able to change her sight today and that had to be part of the Jezeer. She looked at the Pronos. In essence it was changing the world around you, if only in your mind. You could project your mind's eye onto your surroundings. The mind still saw the real world and noted it, keeping you aware of your environment, but your eyes and senses saw what you wanted. This room was a good place to try this out. It was isolated and when she stopped the light spell the darkness was almost palpable. She disconnected from the network, calming herself.

This first attempt was to be simplistic. She was going to keep her eyes open and select a color, then see the color in her surroundings. After that she would attempt to make other images with her open eyes.

* * * * * * *

Legon felt Sasha leaving the network in pursuit of the Pronos. It was a worthy endeavor and he knew why she did it. Life was perspective. If you changed that you changed reality. He had been walking the cave and rejoined Sara and Keither. He wondered if Keither gave up his ration. He sat next to them, leaning on the wall. Both were asleep but still sitting up. He reached with his mind, out looking for anything intelligent to link with and found it in the form of goats in the area. He settled back into the waking sleep. It was going to be good to get to the Precipice. Maybe there he could get a real night's sleep.

The sun was peeking over the mountains when Sasha's presence roused him from the waking sleep. The rain had stopped in the night and the air smelled clean and fresh. From a rams perspective he could see the sky was relatively clear. Sasha looked tired and somewhat disappointed.

"Were you at it all night?" Legon asked

"Yes, and I didn't get far. I'm afraid this part of my training will require patience. How did you sleep?"

He chuckled. "I didn't really. Come sit with me, you are tired."

She plopped down next to him and he placed his arm around her, bringing her close. They would leave soon but she had a little time to sleep. This was to be a big day; she had been foolish to pursue the Pronos last night. But could he blame her?

She was already asleep and he accessed her unconscious mind. Since she was not opposed to this when awake her unconscious mind didn't resist. He transfused energy into her body. She would have protested, but she was asleep and needed it. When Arkin eventually came to wake them she looked up, blinking rapidly.

"Are you alright?" he asked.

"Yeah I feel good. Wow, you always said that power naps were good but I guess I didn't believe you."

She got up and they prepared to leave. It was only going to take two or three hours today to make it out of the highlands, and there was excitement in the group as they loaded up. As they left their cave and hideout, the excitement soon faded with the hot sun and treacherous terrain that seemed to bother even the mules. By midday, however, the path started down a steep hill and soon a valley was in the distance. The land was improving as well; there was now short trees and grass around.

Legon heard the sound of running water. The path met up with a stream, which they followed down into a surprisingly green valley. The turf was short here but still green despite the heat. He saw irrigation canals, telling him that the greenery was not native to this area. They met up with what must have been the main road into the valley, and he realized that this was not where the Precipice was. This valley was more like an antechamber for its larger brother.

They approached a corner of the valley with large cliffs on either side that left only room for the road and stream to pass. Warmth blossomed in his chest as they entered the main valley. It was vast, and at the far end was a set of buildings, most looking like they were made of wood. To the right of the buildings was a stone fortress with four towers and to the left was a large dome-shaped hill. It was covered in green turf and looked out of place. It was a perfect half circle on the horizon, almost as if it was man-made, and Legon wondered how it came to be that way. The road they were on meandered around the valley, which seemed to be barren of farms and houses. He asked Arkin why this was.

"There is base housing for those whose families are here but they're to the rear of the valley so those families can safely leave to Manton in case of emergency."

"Shouldn't there be guards or something?" Sara asked.

"Our arrival is expected, and from what I hear exercises are going on today. But there were guard posts in the canyon that you didn't see. I'm sure we will be joined soon. Also, keep in mind that this is a large valley and most activity takes place on the other end."

As if in response to this, Legon heard the sound of horses trotting along in the distance. Three men wearing wooden armor approached them. They didn't look unkind in the least bit, and after their past experiences Legon was expecting a bit more of a hostile welcome.

"Are you Arkin's party?" the leader asked.

"Yes we are, we seek asylum fo-"

"We know. You have no need for formality. We've been expecting you. I assume you got caught in the rain?" the man asked.

"Yes, we did," was Arkin's reply.

"Well I'm glad you lot are all right. Shall we go? The boss wants to meet up with you before you go talk to the Elves."

Arkin gestured with his hand and they followed the men. They skirted along the hill and gradually they saw more and more people. While there were no farms here, Legon saw people herding sheep and cattle. Indeed, it had appeared to be an empty place until they reached the hill; now it was just as busy as any town. They saw a large wooden building that Legon figured was the barracks. Behind the hill were neat rows of cottages with little yards and fences.

The men leading them seemed to enjoy giving them a tour on their way in, explaining that the cottages were for soldiers with families. Instead of staying in the barracks, the wives and children could live on base with them. This was also good because it provided a civilian staff to help run the base, from cooking and cleaning to tending the livestock. All of this was done by civilians.

There was a small town center that they rode by, closing in on the four-towered building. Somehow it seemed too small to Legon, but he wasn't sure why. It just didn't look like it could fit all of the men that must live in the Precipice.

They approached the gates and dismounted. There were two men standing at either entrance of the building. They didn't seem to notice them walk by. Instead of being led into a courtyard like he expected the entrance led to a staircase and halls. This was more like a business center than a fortress, he thought. Sasha shared his disquiet, wondering at the capability of the human resistance.

The ceiling was high and above them was a chandelier made of ram horns. The interior was dark wood with a scratchy looking rug on the floor that the soldiers wiped their feet on. Arkin sent a mental message saying that this was an entrance rug and that you were to wipe your feet on it to avoid dirtying the rest of the building. They drug their feet obediently, losing any filth from the road.

As they reached the top of the staircase they entered another small hall, at the end of which were two large double doors with three men standing guard. Up to this point he had only seen wooden armor, but these men had the expensive chainmail and plate armor.

The guards opened the doors and their escorts gestured for them to go inside. The room was large and dark, lit only by a granite fireplace on the right side of the room. On either side of it were two bronze fish whose tails wound towards the fire, reflecting the light across their bodies. Above the fireplace was a green banner. In the center of it was the powder blue outline of a triangle. On the triangle was a fish in the same color, its head and tail curving up. This banner was not Iumenta or Elf; this was for one of the few great human houses that were left. There were rumored to be only five outside of the Queen's control.

Legon looked to his left, glancing over a desk and noticing two figures stooped over a table with a map on it. One had shoulder length brown hair; the other's hair was long and silver. The one with the brown hair had an average build; he held up a hand telling them to wait. The other with the silver was thinner, and Legon suspected he was an Elf.

They turned to look at the visitors. Legon's suspicions were confirmed as the silver haired man looked at them. Legon was surprised at just how young the Elf looked, not appearing to be more than twenty five. His face was thin with a good jaw line, a small nose, and almond shaped eyes that matched the silvery gray of his hair. He looked like an artist's masterpiece. Legon fought to keep from smiling as he became aware of the mental chattering going on between Sasha and Sara. Legon heard the girls' hearts race. He knew the other Elf could hear this as well, and that Sara and Sasha would be mortified if they knew Elves could hear that well. He decided not to tell them now.

The human spoke. "Welcome. My name is Enrich, representative of house Posein. This is Mantic. He is our Elven liaison."

Mantic bowed his head and focused his view on Legon, just the hint of a smile at his lips. Up to this point Legon hadn't been worried about the Elves. They were the good guys, after all. But still, he hadn't met one before and he wasn't sure what to do or how to act. He knew almost nothing about their culture, his culture now.

Mantic spoke. "Legon, you will have many questions, I'm sure. We have only a few things to attend to here and then you will be taken to see the Elves and be given quarters there. In fact, we would like to offer our hospitality to your whole party."

Legon felt a nudge from Arkin's mind telling him that he was supposed to answer.

"Thank you very much. I'm looking forward to meeting others of my kind." That felt awkward.

Mantic gave a deep sigh and smiled at him. "You remind me of your father…and mother. I am sorry that you have been away from us. House Evindass still morns his loss."

"House Evindass?" Legon asked, feeling dumb.

Mantic looked surprised but then recovered. "You haven't been told?"

"Oh, I know I'm supposed to be the Everser Vald if that's what you mean." He knew it wasn't, but better to look uninformed then just ignorant.

Arkin spoke. "No, he doesn't. It was not my place to tell him."

Mantic nodded. "Thank you for you discretion, Arkin. Legon, I am sure that you are aware that there were once great houses that ruled over the humans?"

"Yes."

"Well, that same system still applies to the Elves. House Evindass is one of our great houses, one of the twelve ruling houses. And you are the heir to that house."

Sasha showed her amazement and disbelief. "Legon's noble?"

Mantic turned his gaze to her. "I am assuming you are Sasha, and yes he is. As his sister, you are as well."

"But he was adopted, and I'm human." Sasha said

"And you share a connection stronger than family, and in adopting him he did the same for you. Our people will treat you accordingly."

Mantic paused for a moment to look the group over. This wasn't how they had planned on doing this, and it was obvious. From the lines under Enrich's eyes Legon figured they had waited through the night, hoping for the storm to lift and their guests to arrive.

He decided to break the tension by changing the subject. "This is a very nice, ah, base that you have here."

Enrich smiled. "Thank you. We like it. We are sorry, this was not supposed to…well, we sent your welcoming party home to get some rest about an hour before you arrived."

Sara laughed, cutting the mood. "Well it's good to see the world is still working the way it's supposed to."

* * * * * * *

Keither just wasn't surprised by this information. Legon had to be something special. He had turned into an Elf for crying out loud, so why not be noble as well? There wasn't anything all that amazing about the Elf either, though Keither was a little perturbed by how taken Sara was with him. He had a weak connection with the others so he didn't think she knew what he was thinking. They were exchanging small talk now, waiting just long enough to leave without being impolite. He couldn't help himself.

"Excuse me, but is that a map?"

Enrich looked at him, puzzled. "Yes, why?" Then he corrected. "You haven't seen a full one before, have you?"

"No, just of the empire. The Queen doesn't allow anything else," Keither said

"Hoelaria is no Queen. She is just a regent as she well knows."

There was defiant anger in Enrich's voice and Keither thought he heard him mutter something about a usurping whore as well. Talk like that got you executed back home, but now…

"Sorry, yes. The usurping whore won't let us see maps," Keither said

Enrich laughed heartily. Keither wasn't trying to be funny; he just wanted to see the map.

"I like you. Ah, let's see, you must be Keither, right?" Enrich asked.

"How did you know my name?"

"Arkin's reports. Yes, you can see the map if you like."

Keither stepped up to the table and pried at the map. It wasn't a map of all Airmelia like he thought but only of the immediate area. Manton was just southwest of them at the end of a fjord. To the northeast was a line indicating where the border was and the main road that led here. From Manton there were roads leading all over the place, some moving to the Elves lands and others just south leading off the map.

Mantic spoke. "Keither, Arkin says that you have a good mind. May we get a demonstration?"

This was a bit of a shock. An Elf wanted to test him? Keither would understand if Mantic wanting to see what Legon could do, but him? What benefit would that be?

"Ah, ok. Sure," Keither agreed

Mantic walked to the map and lifted it, revealing another one underneath. This one was a broader view of the land

and he saw more cities, many running along the border to the Elves.

"What do you see?" Mantic asked

"Well, I see a lot of cities and towns along the border with the Elves, and I see that all of those roads lead back to Manton and other cities. All of the other cities are in the usual spots; rivers, lakes, big bodies of water. But the ones on the border are situated with Elven dots on the map."

"And what does this tell you?" Mantic pressed

"That the human resistance relies on a lot of supplies from the Elves. No surprise. This land must be hard to farm, mine, and defend." Did he say too much with the last part?

Mantic looked at Arkin. "You are right about this one. Who is in charge of him?"

Who was in charge of him? Were they asking who was going to take responsibility for him? Had he screwed up? To his horror, Legon spoke

"I am, and he is a good man."

"We see that. Do not worry, we would like his opinion. Keither, if you were Hoelaria, or more important her chief warlord Parkas, what would you do with a large part of your military on the border?" Mantic asked

Surely they knew the answer. This was another test. He looked at the map.

"I would hit the Precipice, and hit it hard."

"And why is that?" Enrich asked

"Well, look at it. From here you could go south and sever the connection the humans have with the Elves. Then you could slowly kill of the human resistance in this part and weaken the Elves by making them protect another border."

Arkin smiled at him and Enrich spoke. "That's what we think they're going to do, but we don't know when. We have been bringing forces north in preparation but it's been a nightmare taking care of them. Keither, when we have more time we will talk about your possible futures here if you want them. Thank you."

With that, the conversation ended as fast as it had begun. Mantic looked at them. "We will go to the Elves now and you can eat, rest, and have healers look at you. Someone will also show you around."

Mantic gestured out of the room. Keither didn't feel himself begin to walk as Enrich's words repeated in his head: "Your possible futures here."

Chapter Twenty
The Hill

"Nothing is impossible. You just haven't figured out how to do it yet."
- Memoirs of the Rule of the First Dynasty

Mantic led them out of the building and towards the large dome-shaped hill. Legon was confused as soon as they left the main town area and walked to the base of the hill. Were the Elves just on the other side of it? As they approached the hill he realized just how large it was. Its base had to be close to the size of Salmont and it was easily two hundred feet high. They started to walk up its perfectly shaped side. He wondered if the people had built up the land like this, or if it was once a natural hill that they had shaped. Keither's mind suggested that it was left over from mining silver and gold. Mines often had large piles of ocher dirt outside of them, and this place may have been formed with that. Sasha was unsure of what the purpose could be. She tried to ask Arkin but his mind was closed.

"Perhaps there's a military advantage to giving them high ground," Legon suggested.

The turf on the hill was short with small flowers blooming all over. There were also leafy plants that covered the ground as well. He looked over his shoulder and saw that the town was now below them. They were about half-way to the top. If he remembered right when they saw it from a distance, the top looked like it was cut off, like a plateau. Then it hit him: this was a raised area and the Elves lived on top of it! He walked with surety now knowing what to expect at the top.

As they reached the top, however, that surety left him. The hill had an indentation at its top that went down ten feet or so. At the center of this indentation was a gaping hole that was easily one hundred and fifty yards across. As Legon stared he heard the tell-tale sound of a dragon. He instinctively looked behind him to see a blue Elven dragon gliding down to where they were, passing overhead and into the hole in the hill. But it wasn't a hill; it was a massive structure.

Mantic turned, smiling at their awestruck faces. "Welcome to our Dragon Dome."

"The what?" Sasha asked in confusion.

Arkin answered. "Dragon Dome. This is the Elven base."

"This thing is our base?" Legon heard himself say, though he wasn't aware he had told his mouth to speak.

"Yes it is. Both Elves and Iumenta use dragon domes. They were invented towards the end of the War of Generations," Mantic said.

"The Great War between the Elves and Iumenta," Arkin clarified.

They all nodded in understanding. Mantic led them down the lip and then along the small patch of land between them and the opening. "All entrances to a dome will be at the top."

He stopped at an alcove, walked into it and turned to his left, opening a door. This entrance would be perfectly blocked from any enemy attack. Legon marveled at the thought behind it. As they entered he was met by the smell of the forest in spring, an odd smell to encounter at the end of the summer. The hall ceiling arched. The walls, floor, and ceiling seemed to be made of one solid piece of wood. Occasionally they would reach ribs in the hall that were a darker wood, but his Elven eyes saw no line where the different woods began and ended.

Along the walls there were little silver fixtures that were mirrored. In the fixtures were little shining sticks that stuck up from them. On the end of the sticks were bright balls of white light, presumably magic, that reflected off the shiny surfaces lighting the hall.

"Mantic, this workmanship is amazing. It looks as though this is one solid piece of wood," Sasha said, running her hand along the wall.

Mantic looked over his shoulder with warm gray eyes. "That is because it is. In fact this entire place is one piece of wood, and it's alive."

"This thing is a tree?" Keither said, incredulity etching his voice. He'd stopped.

Mantic looked appraisingly at him. "Not a tree but an organism, a plant. Yes, Elves can make plants grow as I'm sure you know. So, if you are aware of what you are doing you can make a plant grow however you want. We grow everything. That's how we mine, how we get our food, clean our water… everything."

Mantic walked on, stopping any questions. This was fine. Legon was sure that none of them would have a shortage of questions any time soon, but he didn't think they would be able to comprehend much right now anyway.

The hall led out to a balcony. To their right was a vast room that would give most people vertigo, though it didn't really seem like a room. The opening in the top of the dome was about two thirds the size of the floor below them. They could see a large area where people and, more importantly, dragons could maneuver. The room was circular with large alcoves around it,

Legon guessed twelve in all judging by their size. The alcoves were lined up next to each other with only ten feet of wall separating one from another at the bottom and openings that arched to a point at the top, which was about fifty feet tall. Some had large cloth looking doors that closed in the center, showing the Dragon's crest on it. Some were open and Legon saw the blue dragon walking into one. The hangars, as Mantic called them, were large in themselves but still not big enough to take up the whole dome.

"Are there other things like this here?" Legon asked.

"Yes. The dragon hangars are only in the center but there are apartments, dining areas, an infirmary, and even a swimming area in this complex," Mantic answered

"Swimming area?" Sasha asked, confused. Back home they had learned how to swim and Legon enjoyed swimming in the pond, but he had never heard of a swimming area. He too was confused.

"It's easier to show you," Mantic said with a smile.

There were halls that connected to the walkway and he saw them going deep into the dome. It was much larger than he had originally thought, and he was sure that it went deep into the ground as well. Mantic turned into an opening that led down a winding staircase that seemed to go on forever, with exits every fifteen feet to a new level.

When they got to the bottom they walked out onto the floor of the main room, but it wasn't the bottom. The dome had to be over two hundred feet high and this room, while large, couldn't have been more than eighty feet tall.

Legon looked up above the hangars to see large rectangular pieces of wood that stuck out from the wall. They were about half as wide as the hangar's base and they were about twenty feet long.

"Mantic, what are those?" Legon said, pointing to the blocks.

Mantic smiled. "Those are the protective sheaths, if you will, for the defensive crystals this dome uses."

"I don't get it," Sara said.

Mantic explained that magic could be stored in other objects like gemstones, which Arkin had already told them about. He then went on to say that during the War of Generations both the Elves and the Iumenta were engaged in a magical arms race. It was impractical to find gems big enough to store any significant amount of power, and they were finicky and hard to enchant.

During that time of the War, dragon domes were not in existence. The Elves grew hangers that were just curved buildings that the dragons stayed in. They grew fortresses out of trees and other plants too. They could place spells on these structures, allowing the energy of the plant to power spells, and the domes today still used that principle. The structure was alive, and its energy went into everything.

However, these forts put the Iumenta at an extreme disadvantage; they could not make plants grow at will, so it was they that had discovered crystalline technology, discovering what made gems so good at holding magic and then finding a way to grow crystals with those specifications. From there magic evolved rapidly and both sides began working on crystals, though even to this day, Mantic explained, Iumenta crystalline technology was far more advanced than Elven.

He went on to explain that there were crystals littering this dome that controlled everything from the dome's growth to its lighting. They also powered spells that allowed the dome to see far away, sensing enemies and even weather patterns. More importantly, these crystals powered protective wards that were extremely powerful, so strong, in fact, that no Elven or Iumenta dragon dome had ever been defeated.

Legon felt his head buzzing with the information. Mantic looked sympathetically at them. "This is a lot to take in. It will take you years to learn all that this place holds and does. Don't worry about it for now, just understand that it works."

They nodded. He waved for them to follow. They walked next to hangars, most empty or closed with different crests on the door. As they approached, a woman walked out. Legon's stomach gave a slight leap at the sight of her. She was an elf, slender like all the Elves were, but her figure was incredible. He felt Keither's brain function stop as well, and he understood why Sasha and Sara had reacted they way they did to Mantic.

She was wearing a pink dress that looked to be made of silk or some other rare and expensive cloth. It was like no other he'd seen. It was as if a piece of fabric was wrapped or inexplicably flowed around her body, simple and elegant. His eyes moved up her body. Her face was warm with thin red lips and a small nose. It was her eyes that seemed to make time stop, though. They were a deep blue green, rich with color and character, with metallic looking specs in her irises that reflected pink. They were amazing. What were they? Then it hit him as Mantic reached forward to introduce the woman.

"You're a dragon!" Legon blurted without thinking.

It was the flecks of pink that gave it away. Arkin had told them that magic affected the look of one's eyes once they are strong enough to ascend. The more flecks in the eyes, the more magic. He hadn't understood what Arkin meant by "flecks" until now. She smiled widely, showing perfect white teeth.

"Guilty. My name is Iselin." She gave a slight bow to them.

She turned to Arkin and her voice become playfully condescending.

"Babysitting didn't wear you down to much did it? Do you need any more help?"

"Ha ha. I missed you too, Ise. Thank you for saving our collective behinds," Arkin said

"Anytime."

"You were the dragon that saved us?" Keither said incredulously.

Legon and Keither felt the slight horror of knowing that their new true love had burned twenty people to a crisp not to long ago.

She laughed. "Why, do I look like a fire breathing beast to you?"

"Ah no, no…that's not what I'm saying," Keither stammered. "You're very attractive. Not that I was looking…"

Sara spoke. "He's fun to mess with."

"I can see that," Iselin said, smiling.

Keither chose silence. Legon thought that was a good idea. They stood quiet for a moment. He focused on Sasha's mind. She was thinking. What was she going…?

"So Iselin, I'm sorry we've been rude. I'm Sasha, this is Sara, Keither, Arkin you seem to know, and this is my brother Legon." As she finished she nudged him slightly forward. Reason and logic dictated that Sasha avoid doing anything embarrassing, something she usually succeed at except for in one particular situation: Sasha's favorite pastime was trying to set him up with people. To her credit she was good at it, but he needed to find a way out of this. Too late.

"You are a very beautiful woman Iselin. Your husband is lucky," Sasha said.

Iselin looked a little uncomfortable. "Oh, I'm single…"

Sasha didn't really try and conceal her happiness at the news "Really? Well are you going to be the one that shows us around?"

"Ah, I don't know. I can if you would like…"

It was clear Sasha had taken Iselin off guard, and Legon wasn't sure that it was a good idea, considering she was in fact a fire-breathing monster, albeit a very attractive one.

"It's just, well, you seem so nice, and you know Arkin, and Legon is new to this Elf thing so…" Sasha trailed off.

The lights visibly went on in Iselin's eyes as she turned her prefect gaze on Legon. He knew she was on to Sasha. She looked him over. He felt blood rushing to his face. Oddly, he found himself reciting the fear litany in his head. This was all the more embarrassing because Iselin, like Mantic and probably every other Elf in the room, could hear his heart speed up and see his face flush, even if the humans couldn't. And worse, Mantic and Iselin most certainly felt the heat off him. This was great. Maybe he should go back to bothering the empire.

He spoke. "That's ok Sash, I'm sure that..."

"No, I think it's a good idea. Mantic, I will take them from here. Sasha, Sara, I like you two. We're going to be friends, I can already tell."

Mantic looked like he had been taken off guard. Clearly this was not part of the plan, and clearly Iselin had no authority to do this, but he turned and walked off anyway.

* * * * * * *

Sasha knew that she probably shouldn't be trying to set Legon up with the first elf she saw, but Iselin seemed to have a good sense of humor and probably wasn't the type to be bothered by this behavior. Arkin was standing behind her and she could hear him trying not to laugh. Iselin made a jab at him and it appeared to be in good fun. She wondered about their history.

"Well, I will show you to your quarters first and you can rest and refresh yourselves. Then we can eat and I'll show you around. Oh, and Legon, Mantic is in the process of contacting your house so they and the other great houses can ratify you."

"Ratify me?"

"Yes. They need to certify that they believe you are who you are. It's a formality, not to worry. They'll have answered by this evening."

Iselin whistled and Sasha gasped as she saw a large cat come walking up to her. It wasn't a cat, though. It was made of pink fire and was in the likeness of a cat, slightly transparent with glowing eyes and a grapefruit sized ball of bright pink magic in its chest. The cat walked forward to inspect them, stopping first at Arkin rubbing against his legs like any other cat would do. He petted it. Iselin looked inquisitively at them, and then seemed to realize something.

"So Arkin, what exactly did you teach them about magic?"

Arkin looked up, his countenance showing much irritation. "Oh, I'm sorry my lessons weren't up to your standards. Forgive me for keeping them alive."

Iselin laughed. "Touchy aren't we. Come, cat."

"You still haven't named her yet?" Arkin asked flatly

"No. Why should I? Cat is so perfect. She is a cat, after all."

"She's a familiar, not a cat," Arkin asserted.

"She's in a cat form right now, so…"

"I'm sorry, but I'm confused," Sasha said.

Iselin answered. "Oh, sorry. Cat is a familiar. She's made of magic, as you can see. This light in the center is where the crystal that powers her is. Familiars are very handy but take a class five to make and they're hard to do. You will learn more about them. If you see cat and need my assistance, you can ask her and if she is in range she will contact me."

"Thank you," Sasha said

"You're welcome. Now let's go."

* * * * * * * *

Iselin turned and started to walk off, her cat close behind. Sasha liked Iselin so far, but she was also overwhelmed by this place. Everything about it was alien to her. They walked through passage after passage passing other Elves, all just as gorgeous as Mantic, or "delicious", as Sara was thinking, but no humans. Finally Iselin spoke to Arkin.

"Will you be a dear and show Legon and Keither to their rooms and give them the tour? I will tend to Sasha and Sara."

Arkin must have known where they were going because he nodded and turned down a hall with Legon and Keither. Sasha and Sara continued to follow Iselin, but something was bothering Sasha.

"Dang it!" she said.

"What is it?" Iselin asked.

"I forgot our things. I'm sorry, Iselin can you tell me how to get back in here and I can go get our stuff?"

Iselin smiled. "You don't think that we have things for you?"

"Well I don't…"

"When Mantic said that you were being offered our hospitality it didn't just mean a room. He did offer, didn't he?"

"Well yes, but…"

"We will have someone bring your things in, don't worry about that. But all of your clothes are for colder areas; you must be hot," Iselin said.

"We are," Sasha replied

"Good, then you will like the clothes we give you. They're much lighter. I and another Ascended picked them out for you."

"Oh you did? Thank you. And Iselin?"

"Yes?"

"What's an Ascended?" Sasha asked.

"Sorry, a dragon. You can use either term, but with the Elves you will mostly hear Ascended, as it's the correct term."

Sasha nodded and wondered: had Arkin given their measurements in his reports as well? She decided not to ask. They stopped at a plain looking door.

"This is your apartment while here. I will show you around," Iselin said.

Iselin opened the door and Cat darted in like all cats do when doors are opened. So far she had been impressed by the dragon dome, but her quarters topped it all. There was a large living space with two white couches and a divan. The room was all wood with dark beam-like ribs running up the walls, meeting in the middle of the ceiling which was about ten feet high with a large dome shaped light at the top. She noticed that the beams had intricate leaves carved, or rather grown, in them. The floor was the same dark color as the beams. To her right was a small sink that had a funny looking pipe coming out its back, to her left a closet. On the floor was large rug. Separating the couches was a table not more than two feet from the ground. She walked to the couches, examining the intricate woodwork. Sara sat on down on one.

"Even when I was sent to a rich man's house I never saw luxury such as this."

Iselin started apologetically "I am sorry for the meager apartment. As a lady of one of the great houses you should have more, but unfortunately space does not permit."

"This is normal?" Sasha asked.

"Of course. You must remember we come from different worlds. To Elves this is average at best. When you go home you will see real luxury. Now come, I will show you how everything here works and where your chambers are."

Iselin took them on a tour of the apartment, starting first with the sink and the funny pipe, which was called a faucet. It was astounding. Next she walked them into a bedroom. They were met by a bed the likes of which Sasha had never seen. It was much larger than she had ever slept in. She pressed down on the soft silky sheets. It was squishy. Iselin smiled at them and showed them the bathroom, as it was called.

Their amazement didn't seem to end. There was a round thing you sat on and did your business like an outhouse, and Iselin said that the waste was taken by the dome. Then there was the 'shower', which consisted of a space you stood in naked and an odd looking set of hollow tubes close together coming from the top of the wall sprayed water on you. Against the wall was a ridge that you moved your hand along until the water was temperature that you liked. There was a sponge and a liquid soap for your body and another for your hair.

"You two look a little overwhelmed," Iselin said

"That's a good way to say it," Sara said.

"Well, I'll tell you what: Sasha, you can stay in this room, and Sara, you can stay in the one across the living space. It's set up the same. Take a nice long hot shower. Trust me, you will feel better and I wi…"

Sasha didn't hear anything else. The episode came on fast and unexpected.

* * * * * * *

Sara waited next to Sasha for her to wake up. She would only be out for a few minutes. Iselin had moved quickly when Sasha fell. She didn't even make if half way to the ground before Iselin swept her up with surprising speed and strength. She took her effortlessly to the bed and laid her down. Sara needed to remember that despite looking beautiful and fragile, Elves were far from it, and dragons doubly so.

"Does this happen often?" Iselin asked.

"A few times a week, but they're better when Legon is around."

Iselin was sitting on the bed next to Sasha, holding her hand. She saw that the elf was bothered by this and she wondered why.

"Back home people said that she was possessed with devils. Legon and his friends got in a lot of fights defending her. That's why she came with him. It wasn't safe for her in Salmont with him gone."

"I see," Iselin said.

"Is everything all right Iselin? I promise Sasha will wake up and she isn't possessed with anything. She's the best person I know. Nothing evil could live in her."

Iselin looked at her. "I know she's not possessed. I was allowing a healer to look through my eyes to figure out what Sasha has."

"Do you think you might know what it is?" Sara asked.

"Yes, and the Iumenta would have known as well. Sasha would have had a very different life if people knew what was wrong with her physically and not treated her so horribly." Iselin gave a deep sigh.

Sasha began to stir. She looked up. "Wha...?"

"You had an episode," Sara supplied.

"No, you had a seizure," Iselin said.

"What's that?" Sara asked for Sasha.

"It's what you've been having your whole life. I have sent your information to the head of our medical staff. He says that you have something called epilepsy. It's a medical problem. You're not possessed."

Sara looked intently at Iselin. "Did Arkin know about it?"

Iselin looked at Sara. "No, he didn't. He's been trying to figure it out for years but he has had limited contact with us, and truth be told his handlers cared a lot more about their schooling than medical problems. We needed more information. She needed to be around a very learned healer or someone that could send the healer information while it was happening."

Iselin placed her hand on Sasha's chest right below her neck and Sara saw a pink glow from under the hand. Sasha gasped sharply and her eyes widened. Iselin took her hand away. "Better?"

"Yes, thank you. It should take me a few hours to recover from that. Are you sure it hasn't...?"

Iselin laughed. "You two need to remember that I'm a dragon. I have more than enough strength. Now take your showers, and trust me, you will feel wonderful afterwards. I will bring you clothes to wear. I am leaving Cat here if you need anything else while I'm gone."

* * * * * * *

Arkin walked down the hall to the approaching Iselin. She looked concerned. "What is it?" he asked

"Sasha had a seizure. We think its epilepsy. I can explain later. How are Legon and Keither settling in?"

"They're fine. Both are still shell shocked with this place. I'm getting them something to wear now. The girls?"

"They're fine. I like them both. You did good."

"A complement?"

She was alongside him now. They turned down a corridor. She placed her arm around his shoulder. "Tell anyone and I'll eat you."

He laughed. She had been this way since they were young. They continued along until they came to a shop that was inside the dome that sold men's and women's apparel. They both got what they needed, Iselin picking up four of five dresses for both girls, as well as shoes and everything else needed.

After that they went back to Iselin's apartment to get Legon's ring and Sasha's necklace. They were important figures now, so certain precautions needed to be taken. For Legon it was a ring with a large amethyst crystal on it. For Sasha, a necklace that was made of platinum, in the center a large tear-shaped crystal that looked like ruby. A smaller ring and necklace for Keither and Sara were there as well. These were for protection. Yes, they looked nice too, but they were laden with magic. Once on they could only be taken off by the owner. They had wards that protected from many things that an assassin might use, including most poisons. Arkin figured Iselin had made them herself. She was incredibly skilled with magic. She had only been an Ascended for about ten years now, but she had grown in notoriety. Her charisma and prodigy-like skills helping her outstrip all of her peers.

After Legon got dressed, Arkin explained what the ring did and how it worked. Legon didn't seem to mind the ring at all, and all he wanted to know is if Sasha and the others were getting protection as well. Arkin informed him that that they were, but that he and Sasha were to get the most.

"We are going to go to the girls' room now and then to get dinner. I suspect that they will test your magic when we get there," Arkin said.

"And how do they do that?" Legon asked.

"There is a crystal you hold; it has a spell to tell them what class you are. Be thankful - it used to be you had to demonstrate your power. Now you simply hold a rock."

* * * * * * *

Keither knew that he was now out of place with the others. They were all Venefica, even Kovos would have been if he still lived, but Keither wasn't connected when it happened. So he was still just a regular human.

The clothes they were wearing were comfortable. They felt soft and smooth and they breathed much better than their other clothes. Arkin shooed them out of the door and down the hall. This place was like a maze, and though he knew its size, the lack of windows or other natural light made it seem small to him.

Arkin led them to a room that was presumably the girls'. When they entered they saw that it was an exact replica of the one they were in. Building with consistency and precision was rare, but apparently the Elves mastered it. The only difference in the room was that the girls had white furniture; the men had red.

Iselin walked into the room from the bedroom to their left, followed by Sara and Sasha. Both looked completely different. Their dresses were similar to Iselin's; Sara's was silver with a silver necklace that looked like a diamond but that he knew was a crystal. His heart raced a bit as she smiled at him, but Sasha, who had always been the prettiest girl in town, looked amazing. Her dress was red, and he realized that both dresses matched the color of the magic of their owners. There was a giant tear-shaped ruby of a crystal hanging on her neck and she wore shinny red lipstick. Sara's lips were red too. They seemed a little unsure of their steps.

Sara caught his eye and mouthed "Fancy shoes." He knew what she meant. Women in the large cities would sometimes wear shoes that elevated in the back. It was supposed to look better, but this was his first time seeing anyone wear them. Salmont had dirt streets, so shoes were purely functional, but large cities and apparently dragon domes had hard floors that were even, so fancy shoes it was.

Legon spoke. "Wow, you guys look amazing."

"Thanks. I feel out of place," Sasha said, looking down at herself.

"We're hot, what are you talking about out of place?" Sara said jovially.

Iselin laughed. "So I did well, then?"

"Very," Keither said. But wait, he didn't actually say it, did he?

"Thanks, Keither. So does this mean your going to ask me on a date?" Sara poked.

"Sara!" Sasha scowled at her friend. "Thank you, Keither. That was a very sweet thing to say."

Keither felt all of the blood from his body rushing to his face. Legon mercifully saved him.

"Iselin, I hear there is some test I am to take?"

"Yes. All of you in fact. Even Keither and Arkin."

"Why me? We know I'm a two," Arkin protested.

"But we don't. If Sasha and Sara can now use magic, Legon's transformation may have affected you as well, and Keither. Even if it hasn't presented yet."

"So what do we need to do?" Keither asked.

"Just hold this." Iselin said

She handed Keither a clear crystal. It was cold and that was it.

"Ok. You're not a Venefica. No surprise. Arkin." Iselin moved on.

Arkin took it and the crystal lit up. He was still a class two. Sara took it; a class one. Sasha took it and it lit up.

"Class two..." Iselin looked at the crystal again. "That's not right. We need a new one; this is broken."

She knelt down to a bag and took another one out and gave it to Sasha, and again it looked the same.

"What is it?" Legon asked.

"Let's test you first; then I will try and explain." Iselin looked confused and worried. Legon took it and it lit up bright. She smiled and looked close at it.

"Class five biologic or healing as most humans say, with the potential to ascend. Once again no surprise, though the biologic is rare."

"What? I'm going to be a dragon?" Legon said.

"No, I said 'the potential to ascend'. The whole dragon thing is up to life. It's like when you changed into an Elf - it may or may not happen depending on how good you get with magic and how strong of spells you use." She turned back to Sasha. "But you, dear, you're the confusing one."

"Why am I confusing? It lit up like Arkin. Doesn't that mean I'm a two?" Sasha asked.

Iselin answered, "You're a two, but the thing is that no one under a class four has a minor, as they are called. No one in *history* under a four has had one. They don't have a natural tendency to any of the forms of magic, be it Elemental, Biological or Energent. Legon here is a biological, which isn't a shock considering what he has done with all of you, and I am an energent."

Chapter Twenty One
Discovery

"We plot and scheme, putting all our energy into a task, doing our best to ensure our foe's demise. However, in the end we always create our greatest adversary. What is it that makes us do such a thing? We never do it intentionally; perhaps this is what keeps the world in balance..."
- The Exiled Captain (Author Unknown)

"I don't get it," Sasha said.

Iselin paused and spoke as if she didn't entirely believe what she was saying. "You are a class two elemental. You have a minor."

Legon woke up wrapped in silky sheets that felt incredible. He thought back on their first night here two weeks ago. After they had met up with the girls and Sasha found out that she was "special", as Iselin had put it, they went to the dining hall where he was introduced to more people than he had ever met at one time, all Elves just as attractive as Iselin and Mantic. Well, maybe not as attractive as Iselin.

The food had been incredible as well, and he was amazed to find out that the Elves had figured out how to get plants to grow meat-like fruit. When he heard this he was hesitant to try it; he was a butcher, after all. He knew meat. Still, he wasn't able to find anything wrong with it. Not the chicken, beef, pork, or any of the other "meats" that he tried. The others had contented themselves with one portion of food, but apparently his enlarged appetite had nothing to do with being Elven. They ate the same amounts as humans did. Iselin said that the human men in the area would sometimes have eating contests, and that he could be the first Elf to join. He said that he might just do that. Looking back on it now, he wasn't sure if she had meant it as a complement.

During dinner Mantic had come in and said that he had been ratified and was now the head of a great Elven house, a thought that made even his hunger go away. Iselin showed them many of the dome's marvels, including an area where you could swim indoors, and a small pool of heated water that you just sat in, soaking. It felt wonderful.

They hadn't been able to figure out why Sasha had a minor, but to him magic was still new enough that it didn't affect him. Iselin got along great with all of them despite Sasha's constant attempts to set them up together. They had also met the dragon that was in charge of the military here. His name was Sydin. He was also loyal to house Evindass, making Legon his commander. Still, he wouldn't be questioning Sydin any time soon.

All of the Elven dragons that they'd seen were bright vibrant colors, most assigned here in part because of that. The Elves wanted humanity to see a brighter, nicer side to the dragon, but Sydin was here because house Evindass was currently in charge of this dome.

Dragons and warriors from all over the Elven Empire were here, but the great houses took turns being in charge of a dome. The Elven government worked as a cohesive unit and Legon wasn't sure what was meant by being in charge.

His thoughts drifted back to Sydin, who was not brightly colored but was soot black, though soot didn't glitter and have slight glow about it. Sydin was also a class seven and over six thousand years old, but Legon didn't see him that way. He was friendly and fiercely loyal to his house and respected the fact that Legon needed to be raised outside of the Elven Empire. He had insisted on hearing about his and Sasha's lives in detail. He was proud of Legon and insisted that if he had known the extent of Sasha's hardship he would have flown on Salmont and burned it to the ground. This had taken them both off guard. Elves were normally reserved and didn't just make hasty and unwise decisions, but they could tell there was more to this declaration than what they could see. Neither could figure out why Sydin would have been willing to risk his life to save Sasha from being ostracized.

Legon pushed these thoughts from his mind. Today was going to be... different. Today their old friend Barnin would be returning to the Precipice. He hadn't seen Barnin in close to a year and a half, and he wondered what kind of greeting he would get. Would Barnin be mad at Legon for getting Kovos killed?

He got up and walked in to the shower. This was his favorite of the Elven inventions. He ran his hand along the ridge, turning the water on, and then placed his hand in the spot that made the water right below scalding. He breathed in deeply. When he was done he got dressed and walked into the living space. Keither was sitting on one of the couches reading a book. Dragon domes didn't have too much in the way of libraries but they still had one bigger than in Salmont, so Keither had taken to reading everything that he could get his hands on.

"Morning. What are you reading?" Legon asked.

"Hey. It's a history of the Mahann," Keither responded.

"That sounds fascinating at this time of the morning."

"Oh, it is! I'm reading about..."

Legon stopped him. "I was being sarcastic."

"Fine, suit yourself." Keither put down the book at looked at Legon. "I'm nervous about seeing Barnin again. Why do you think that is?"

"There's a lot that we have to explain, both him and us. But I feel apprehensive too. We're walking into the unknown on this one."

Legon opened the constant connection that Sasha and he had, asking if she and Sara were ready for them to come by. "The girls are ready. Let's get breakfast and see what happens."

Barnin was a close friend, and surely he had been filled in on what Legon meant to the Elves and the resistance. The question was going to be how he would receive the news that Legon had let Kovos die. Sydin told them that Barnin had moved up quickly in the ranks, mostly due to Arkin's training, and now he commanded a unit for the cavalry. He was stationed right on the border with the Empire, but Legon wasn't thinking of it as the Empire so much anymore, but as the Iumenta occupied territory. Barnin was brining a two communications from Parkas, Hoelaria's chief warlord, one for the humans in the area and another for the Elves. This was commonplace Legon was told, as the humans and Elves were two different countries.

There was a lot of tradition between the two powers, the Elves and Iumenta. Many of these originated before the time of the War of Generations but some came about after. It was a fine line both sides walked to avoid open war. It appeared that statecraft was a game of wit, not might. Both sides had been plotting for millennia after the war that had claimed seventy percent of the life in Airmelia.

Iselin joined them for breakfast but Arkin didn't. He was no longer in charge of them, and as a result was being given different tasks to do, most of these assigned by Sydin. Iselin could see that they were all tense.

"You have nothing to fear. Barnin is your friend and supports house Evindass. He knows who you are, Legon. How could he not?"

"What house do you give your loyalty to?" Sara asked.

Iselin paused at the question. "Not every Elf claims allegiance to a great house. Many may support a Great House or a Lesser House, but many are independent in a sense."

"Are you independent?" Sara pressed; she was genuinely curious.

"Sydin and I are loyal to House Evindass. That is why I am your guide while you are here. If I weren't loyal to Evindass then Sydin would be your guide."

"How many of my house are here?" Legon asked.

"Two dragons, Sydin and myself, and then 500 units. The other ten dragons are from several houses and a few independents. The same goes for the other 3,500 troops here."

"There are 4,000 in this dome?" Keither said with amazement.

"Yes there are," Iselin said.

There wasn't much talking after that, and Legon contented himself with his eggs.

* * * * * * *

Barnin rode up to the Precipice with the two communications in his bag. This wasn't the first time that Parkas had sent something, but it was never good. Tradition dictated that they send a message to Elves and humans before a major invasion. In that message there would be terms for surrender and so on. He was feeling uneasy for another reason as well. Rumor held that the Everser Vald, who he knew to be Legon, had reached the dragon dome. When Arkin had helped him leave Salmont and the Iumenta occupied territory, he had told Barnin what Legon might be. Arkin had given him a message for the resistance as well.

What would his friends think of him now that he was an accomplished warrior and had moved quickly up the ranks? He reached down, stroking the neck of his black mare Poison. The dome was in sight now and he felt better. It was going to be good to catch up with Legon and Kovos. He wanted to talk to Sasha as well. When he left he had found himself feeling concerned for her. At first he thought it was from years of protecting her, but he knew better now. Magic affected people's minds. A Venefica could nudge you in one direction or another; this was how the Iumenta stayed in control. Dragons infected areas with little notions and beliefs, and even if you didn't buy in at first, over generations people were slowly swayed to one form of thinking. This was used in battle as well. Dragons helped those who were under them keep their morale high and, more important, helped how you felt after a battle.

The Iumenta disliked people like Sasha. They influenced people to avoid those with handicaps, thus keeping these people from having kids and tainting their workforce. It was disgusting, but many had to leave the Cona Empire to avoid going into the care. The city of Manton was an excellent example; it had the most people who had fled persecution.

Manton had been an eye opening experience. He had heard of blind and deaf people before but he had never seen one. Those people couldn't find work in the Empire, so they were homeless and often taken into the care, never to be seen again. The thing that got him the most was all the kids in Manton. Families that had kids with problems were forced to leave. The Iumenta had been sowing beliefs that people with mental problems were evil for decades. He'd felt these feelings. They were subtle, but they were definitely there. He had felt them about Sasha when he lived back home. Even though she was kind, he knew she was possessed. Those feelings had assaulted him his whole life like fiery little darts, but not any more.

He handed the message for the humans to the man next to him, telling him to make sure it got to Enrich. Then he started to ride up the side of the dome. When he got to the top, Legon, Sasha, Keither, Arkin, and two Elves were there, as well as Sara. But where was Kovos? Had he been injured? He got off Poison and approached them. How did Sara end up with them?

"Hey," Legon said, giving him an awkward half hug and half hand shake.

"How was your trip?" Barnin asked.

"Hard. How have you been?" Legon asked.

"I'm fine. Where is Kovos?"

Legon and the others looked down.

"He didn't make it," Keither said.

Barnin felt a pit in his gut. 'He didn't make it.' He had lost friends in war before; this wasn't new to him. But this was unexpected. Keither launched into how it happened. It sounded like it wasn't really Keither talking, just the form of Keither relaying a message. As Keither went on he felt himself feeling proud of all of his friends. All had shown incredible bravery and fortitude.

"And that's how it happened," Keither ended.

"It was a good death. He died a hero. For that we should not sulk. Please, I want to hear the rest of your story," Barnin said, trying not to sound upset.

"You don't blame us?" Sasha asked.

Did he blame them? He felt anger rise from inside him. "No, how could I? The filth drove you from Salmont. It was they who pursued you. It is they who are to blame. They will pay, don't you worry about that." His fists where clenched. They would pay, and not just for Kovos but for everyone they enslaved and killed.

"Yes, they will," Legon said, looking at him. Barnin believed him. Legon told the rest of their story, leaving nothing out. His fist tightened again when he heard about what they were planning on doing to Sasha and what had been done to Sara. The Elves would be irate. They viewed Sasha as one of their own, the lady of a great house. And the Iumenta were stupid to try and kill the heir of house Evindass. There would be blood for sure. He abruptly remembered what he was there to do. They could catch up later.

"We need to go over this message. It's from Parkas. My guess is he's telling you that he is going to invade."

An Elf with black specks in his eyes that he knew to be called Sydin spoke. "We will go inside to discuss this. Barnin, thank you for your diligence. If you would follow us, please."

Barnin followed them into the dome, not talking much. They went into a small room with a table and five other Elves already waiting. Sara and Keither were told to wait outside, along with himself. Sydin took the message and Legon and Sasha followed him inside.

"Why can't we go in?" Keither asked as soon as the door was closed.

"Because that was a message for the Elves, not us," Barnin said.

"But Legon and Sasha…," Keither started.

Barnin cut him off. "Legon and Sasha are heads of a great house. They are nobility, regardless of how we know them."

* * * * * * *

Legon entered the room close behind Sydin and Iselin. There were five other Elves there that he had met already. They nodded to him and Sasha. Sydin opened the message and read it aloud.

Discovery

Greetings to the great and Noble Pawdin Empire. We write you this epistle to inform you that we will be invading the renegade province of the Cornis Mountains. Our forces will not be attacking any members of the Pawdin Empire. We apologize for any causalities that we may unintentionally inflict upon you. We ask that in order to avoid this undesirable outcome you evacuate your forces to within the Pawdin Empire's borders. If you choose to uphold your alliance with the human faction in this section of the land, your people will be treated as hostile.

"So what was that for? They're letting us know that they're going to attack?" Sasha asked. Legon shared her confusion. Why would you tell your enemy that you were coming?

Iselin responded. "There are a lot of formalities between our two countries. But also, in this way the Iumenta can say that they warned us to leave, and therefore our government can't get angry when they kill us."

Sydin placed the message on the table. "They have six human legions along the border. We are outnumbered. Defeat is inevitable unless we are able to match their strength. Let us connect." Legon knew that Elves and Iumenta ran their governments through metal networking, but it was still an odd feeling to join the minds of those that were thousands of years old.

After examining the situation, it appeared that virtually every angle was blocked to them, except one possible route. Normally the commanding officer would return the message, saying that the Elves were going to uphold their alliance with the humans. But if Legon stated that he and House Evindass were in full support of humanity, then...

He broke the connection. "I don't get it. I am more than willing to tell the Iumenta that I plan to fight them, but how will that affect this fight?"

Sydin spoke. "Because you are the head of a great house and you are coming out in opposition to Hoelaria and her

control of the Cona Empire for the first time. If they hit with
their full forces and you die, then the rest of the great houses
may declare open war with the Cona Empire and the Iumenta
country, the Impa Empire."

"But isn't that what all of us want?" Sasha asked.

"They want it, but on their terms. If they send in a small
force then the great houses won't be as apt to go to war," Sydin
stated.

Legon thought about it and decided it was worth a shot.
They prepared a reply and at the end he signed it, adding that
the House Evindass supported humanity. They gave it to
Barnin.

"What do you think will happen?" Legon asked Iselin.

She smiled. "I suspect that they will not attack us with their
full army, but I don't know."

Legon smiled in return. "So I guess we get to wait."

She placed her hand on his shoulder and smiled again.

* * * * * * *

Barnin rode toward the Iumenta envoy. He glanced up at
the gray sky. It was rainy this time of year, leaving the sky was in
a state of perpetual gray. Oftentimes it would rain or drizzle all
day, but today was just cloudy. That meant that there could be
someone of importance waiting for him. He squinted, looking
into the distance at six figures on horseback.

Iumenta he thought. He was thankful that even the Iumenta
adhered to the "don't–kill-the-messenger" code of conduct,
but he still didn't want to talk to them. He didn't see the army.
They would be kept far back from the border so as to not
interfere with negotiations. That wouldn't stop them from
slaughtering innocents with small bands of soldiers, though.
But hey, who's counting? he thought.

A chill ran down his spine as he reached the Iumenta. The One with long silver hair was Parkas, Hoelaria's chief warlord. Not a good sign. Next to him was a man with black hair. His clothes had Hoelaria's crest on it. Barnin wasn't positive, but he was pretty sure that this was her Senashow, also bad. He raised his mental shields; you never knew what they might do.

He was the most nervous about the Senashow. A boy and his brother, former servants of the queen, had joined the resistance not to long ago. The boy had delivered the queen's dinner late, and the Senashow was there at the time. The boy had dropped the plate and was missing a tooth as a result. After that the Senashow had blinded his brother as punishment. The boy had been there when he did it, laughing the whole time and calling them apes.

Focus Barnin, he thought.

"I come bearing a message from the Pawdin Empire," Barnin said.

"They send a dog to deliver the message?" the Senashow said coldly. Legon had given him permission to speak his mind. Indeed, the Iumenta would make a lot of assumptions about Legon from this encounter. He needed to be rude. They needed to think House Evindass unstable and reckless. He was good at being rude, but he didn't care to get killed. Still, you don't kill the messenger, right?

"Did you think of that all on your own? Here is the message. Should I read it for you, or do you think you can handle it?" Barnin taunted.

Iumenta didn't flush, but if they did he was sure they would have now. "What did you say to me you worthless little ape?" the Senashow asked.

"I thought I was a dog? Ok, I'll read it to you. It's ok." He unrolled a scroll that had the message. He didn't want to look at them anymore. He could feel the Senashow's anger.

Parkas spoke. "Do not get angry, old friend. He is a messenger, and one that is terrified. No doubt he was told to be rude. Give me the message, I can read it."

He got off Poison and walked to Parkas, handing him the message. He tried not to walk back to his horse too quickly. When he got back on he saw Parkas looking concerned.

"House Evindass has no head."

"Yes, it does. His name is Legon," Barnin said with pride.

"There is no heir to Evindass. He was killed in Salmont," the Senashow responded.

"No, he wasn't. And he wasn't killed by any of your men over the last few months either. Now which one of you was that?" he said, looking the two over and pointing a finger.

Parkas glared at the Senashow. Barnin pointed at him. Now was the time to deliver his real message.

"It was you? Tsk, that won't go over well. Could have taken out the Everser Vald before he was an Elf. That's rough. Oh well, do you have a response?"

The Senashow started to talk but Parkas held up a hand. He could tell that Parkas was now just as mad as the Senashow, but not at Barnin.

Chapter Twenty Two
Preparations

"There are two halves to every coin, and together they make one whole that is capable of doing something. If you were to find a way to separate that coin, to take the two halves and set them on their own, you would destroy the worth of both. It is this that I need, but it is also what I fear."
- Confessions of Love, The First Wife

"We will continue our campaign. Tell Legon that I look forward to discussing his surrender in the gardens of Manton, if he lives that long," Parkas said.

With that they turned and rode off. It had worked, he knew it. Parkas would not send his full force without finding out more about Legon. He relaxed and started back to the Precipice. He had just insulted two of the most powerful people in Airmelia. He didn't drink, but he might start tonight.

Sasha followed Legon and Iselin into a room deep inside the dome that was called the preparation room. Along its walls was an assortment of weapons. There were several doorways leading from this room into practice areas, including an indoor archery range.

"Legon, now that you are an Elf, you need a new bow. Your old combat one will not do," Iselin said.

She handed him a bow that appeared to be plain oak with a simple clear coat. No intricate leaf work ran along its length.

It was a simple and uncomplicated design; indeed, it was its simplicity that made it a beautiful weapon. It oozed a refined power. Legon balanced it lightly in his hand.

They walked into the adjoining archery range. The room was a hall that didn't seem to end, with targets placed at different distances. Each archer stood at a marker indicating the range he or she was shooting at. Sasha saw Elves firing rounds at speeds she never before thought possible. She didn't even see the arrows fly down the range. In one instant an Elf was drawing the bow and in the next the arrow was somewhere far down range, sticking out of a target.

Legon was standing in front of a sign that read "One hundred yards". He nocked an arrow and drew back, then hesitated and spoke.

"Iselin, is this the right bow? I can shoot a 200 pounder, I promise."

She chuckled. "I would hope so. Remember, you're stronger now and I've been doing research on humans that translates into Elves."

"What have you found out?" Sasha asked. She was curious; there were only a few documented cases in history of humans becoming Elves.

"Well there's not a lot, but one thing that I have figured out is that your translation continues for a few weeks," Iselin said.

"What do you mean?" Legon asked, dropping the bow to his side.

"Well when you first changed, Keither said he picked you up and you were around 110 pounds, which is average for Elves. We just don't need the muscle mass humans do."

"Ok…"

"But here's the thing: you are much, much larger than most, if not all, Elves," Iselin went on.

"I don't know. I seem to be pretty average," Legon said.

"Your height is average, but not your muscle mass. You see, the only documented people who have changed said that they kept all their muscle mass but they weighed less. This doesn't make any sense."

Sasha thought she knew where this was going.

"These people reported that they continued to gain weight after they changed until they were closer to their old weight," Iselin explained.

"But Arkin said that you Elves were made of different stuff than humans," Sasha remarked.

"We are, and it is more lightweight, but Legon was very large before and it's safe to assume that his weight will go up to 160 or 170 before long, and his strength should follow close behind."

"160 isn't that heavy for me," Legon said.

"But it is for an Elf. You will be able to overpower any Elves and Iumenta you fight. They may be faster, but you will always be stronger, which is a big help in magic."

"How big?" Legon asked.

"Big enough that you may never test your strength enough to ascend," Iselin said.

Legon shook his head. "Ok, I don't want to think about this now. Can I get a real bow please?"

Sasha started when she heard Sydin start to talk. She hadn't even noticed him enter the room. He sounded amused. "Legon, she's saying you're stronger now. That bow is close to seven hundred pounds. It just doesn't feel that way. You don't know your strength yet."

"It's what?" Legon said

"Here, give it to Sasha. If it's a hunting bow then she will be able to fire it without issue," Sydin said.

Legon gave her the bow. If Legon said it was a hunting bow then that's what it was. It was light. There was no way it was 700 pounds. She nocked an arrow and tried to pull back.

The string didn't move. She pulled harder. Nothing. It *was* 700 pounds. She felt her jaw drop.

"So, Sasha?" Iselin asked, smiling.

Sasha handed Legon the bow. "It's 700 pounds."

Sydin spoke to Legon. "Come, Um Prosa. I wish to test you myself. Iselin if you will, Sasha."

"Of course. Sasha, come with me; we will need to change before we begin," Iselin said, gesturing her to follow.

Sasha felt trepidation at this but followed Iselin anyway. They changed into pants and regular shoes. Iselin took her to a large room which she had requested be stocked with weapons. Iselin asked Sasha if she remembered to bring her Faloon.

"No, I'm sorry. I didn't know I needed it," Sasha said.

"That's fine, we have others." Iselin walked to a bench and picked up two swords, handing one to Sasha.

"Ise, there's no way I can beat you. I'm terrible at this." Sasha felt embarrassed. She saw Iselin as a friend and she didn't want to look like a fool in front of her. She saw how fast Legon was, and even with magic she was no match.

Iselin spoke gently. "Sash, I'm not trying to embarrass you. This is just to see where you are at. Don't try and use magic; it won't help you."

* * * * * * *

Iselin took in Sasha's stance, studying her and feeling bad. This one was so kind and gentle; the last few months must have been horrible for her.

"Don't we need guards on the blades?" Sasha asked timidly.

"No. I don't plan on hurting you, nor do I plan on you hurting me, but if you like I will guard the blades with magic."

There was the telltale flicker of pink. Sasha had fought before; she had to when Kovos was killed. But she was using the Mahann then and she had to fight. Now that Sasha was among friends, Iselin could see that Sasha was not really able to handle it. No, it was Legon that had gotten her through the violence. Just as Sasha affected him, he gave her strength; he had a strong connection with her at all times.

Sasha was holding the Faloon in a ready position. A human wouldn't have seen the slight tremble, but Iselin did.

"Are you connected with your brother?" Iselin asked.

"Well no, not really. Why, should I be?"

"Yes, open the connection just a bit." The trembling stopped. Iselin breathed in deeply, fighting back anger.

"Iselin, I'm sorry. What did I do wrong?"

"You didn't do anything wrong. Let's begin."

* * * * * * *

Legon stood across from Sydin, covered in sweat. They had been going at it with the fenrra for close to an hour, and he was finally starting to get tired. To his great pleasure, so was Sydin. He bested Sydin about half the time, which also made him happy. Sydin was six thousand years old and had a lot more experience.

"I can't believe I've beaten you as much as I have."

Sydin laughed. "Don't be too proud, Um Prosa. I've been ascended for thousands of years, and we dragons don't use swords as much as you might think." He winked at him.

"Thank you for the motivational talk. That makes me feel all warm on the inside."

"That's why I'm here. Now, I have something new to show you."

Legon walked over to Sydin, who was picking up a blade in a sheath. The definition of broadsword was like its name: broad. There were small ones for close combat. These only needed one hand and were short. The most common in Airmelia was the hand and a half like Kovos, and now Keither, used, but there were still more. Some were six or seven feet long and used like an axe. Sydin was holding a sheathed blade that looked to be along the same lines as the fenrra, but it wasn't.

"Take it out and have a look."

The sheath showed that the blade, whatever it was called, was just slightly longer than a hand and a half, but it was significantly wider. Legon gripped the overly long handle and pulled. Like the fenrra, the sword slid out silently. He held it vertically in front of his face, examining it. It was a match to the fenrra in all but the width, which was close to six inches. He instantly felt the balance. Like the fenrra, the handle was a counter weight, but why so wide? It was also very light for a weapon this size.

"Is it hollow?" Legon asked, stunned.

"Very astute of you. In a way, it is. This is a fenna, or a Venefica Battle Sword, as some like to call them," Sydin explained.

"A what?" Legon asked.

"You see crystals break; they're brittle, so you can't make the core of a sword out of them. But there are some metals that hold magic, and those can form the core of a sword. Although the metals lose power much faster than crystals, you can still see the potential."

"So you can use these to do magic. But I still don't see what makes that so special. Can you kill with them easier or something?" Legon asked.

"Well, yes and no. They give you a certain edge. What most do is imbue the blade with wards that affect only the blade. Then if, say, a ball of fire is shot at you, then you can deflect it with the blade and not tax your own wards. They are impractical for offensive magic."

"Why is that?" Legon asked

"You know that magic is affected by space, so a ward only has to protect the surface of the blade, which is very close. Never does it have to affect anything that's not itself. If it does it takes much more energy."

"But you could still do it?" Legon asked.

"Yes, you could. You may try and kill a dragon, for example. They have wards that help against swords and claws, so you could use the energy to get past those wards and more importantly the wards that help the dragon heal after getting hurt. But I make this warning to you now, Um Prosa: if you used the fenna in that way it will take all of the blade's energy, and then you are stuck with an oversize fenrra against a dragon. So pick your attack well or don't try it at all," Sydin said.

"I'll keep that in mind."

"Now, did Arkin teach you how to fill objects with magic?" Sydin asked.

"Yes, he did."

"Good. Fill the sword as much as you can over the next few hours as we have lunch."

After that they went and ate lunch with Iselin and Sasha. Iselin seemed to be irritated about something, but she wasn't letting on. Sasha told him about her test with Iselin. She went on to say just how fast and graceful Iselin was and how powerful she was when using magic.

"You fought with magic?" Legon asked.

"Yes, and your sister did very well," Iselin said.

Ise wrapped her arm around Sasha and squeezed.

"Did her minor help her at all?" Legon wondered.

"Yes, it did. She is very good with elements like metal, fire, and water. I want to start working with her on crystals as soon as we can. I think that she will show promise in that area."

Sasha beamed at Legon. He was happy to see her doing well. No one other than family had ever told Sasha she was good at something or doing well, or at least they didn't to her face. He knew just how much Iselin's praise meant to her.

"That's good. We need as many people as we can working with them," Sydin said.

After lunch Legon was to have his test with the fenna and magic. Sydin said that because Iselin saw him fight with magic once before, they would go straight to working with the blade and magic together. Sasha and Iselin were to join them for this. Sydin explained how to activate spells in the fenna.

Legon gripped the handle. There were four gold bars that moved down it and into the blade, providing a faster connection. It felt odd in his hand. Once charged it moved differently. It was connected with him, and as such it felt like a small extension of his arm, but an extension that almost seemed to think for itself.

Sydin pulled out one a fenna of his own and stood opposite Legon. Iselin had been giving Legon new spells to learn, ones more advanced than what he had learned on their journey.

"Legon, you need to put a stop-all ward on me, and I will put one on you. Think of this as a guard," Sydin said.

"But if we get through each other's wards, won't it hurt the attacker and the defender?" Legon was talking about draining his own ward if he made it through Sydin's.

"No. If you ward me, you can produce the most powerful spell in history and it will stop harmlessly against your own wards, no matter how weak. That's why you can have fire in your hand and it won't hurt you. Now stop stalling," Sydin said with a smile.

Legon raised his wards, seeing little flickers of light, and then on the other side he saw black flickers indicating Sydin's wards. Last, he placed a stop all around Sydin. These were crude wards and could be broken by amateurs, but apparently not by oneself.

He saw the flicker of black around himself. Sydin's eyes seemed to glitter more than usual and they walked in a circle. Who would attack first? Legon noted the flickers of color around Sasha and Iselin; no doubt Iselin was protecting them from any stray spells. Sydin nodded and they added their own.

Sydin thrust his hand forward and a great flash of gray-black magic shot from his hand. Sydin was an elemental like Sasha; this would be an element of sorts.

The Jezeer had taught Legon to use his muscles like he were playing a fine instrument, and play he did, pivoting out of the way as the dark blur shot past him. Legon sent a cutting curse flying at Sydin, but the first attack had been a feint. Before the curse left Legon's hand, Sydin's flame curse hit him hard. He felt a jolt of energy leave him. There was another curse right behind it. This time he swung the blade, deflecting the magic without effort. He understood now.

The fight progressed quickly. Soon Legon was jumping off walls and benches, sending magic in all directions. Sydin followed suit, but Legon was much too strong for him. Legon came in close, slashing with the blade and forcing Sydin to stop and fight hand to hand. He did this a few times until he learned the more powerful Venefica's style. Sydin broke the encounter by coating the floor with ice at Legon's feet. Legon came in close again, and this time when an ice spell came at him he deflected it down in front of them. At the same time he feinted back, tricking Sydin into moving forward without thinking.

It worked. Sydin slipped on the ice and landed hard on his back, at the same moment flicking up his blade to block Legon. Soon Legon was anticipating Sydin's moves and he changing his style frequently to keep his opponent off balance. Finally, Sydin called a stop, which was a good thing. Legon could feel that the sword was almost spent and then he would have definitely been in trouble. His own magical reserves were all but gone as well, but Sydin looked as though he hadn't done anything.

"Good Legon. You are good at changing style and learning your opponent. Even very old and experienced class fives will have a challenge with you in one-on-one combat," Sydin remarked.

"Are you sure? You don't look tires at all," Legon said.

Iselin laughed. He started. He had forgotten she and Sasha were there. "Legon, when are you going to learn that we are not like you two? We are Ascended. I'm a class six and Sydin a seven. Our skills are far beyond your own."

"I'm sorry, you're right. That was…" Legon said.

"Look, I'm not mad. You're new to this. It will take you a while to overcome this perception. But hear this: if you see a Venefica with flecks in their eyes, you run and run fast, you got me? I'm not going to your funeral," Iselin said firmly.

"Yes we do Iselin. Thank you," Sasha said.

"What about in combat? Haven't people ever attacked a Dragon, I mean an Ascended, before?" Legon asked.

"That is a good question. Yes, if you are in combat and there are two dragons fighting on the ground you may assist, but likely the Iumenta will be doing the same. In that case it would be wisest to attack the Iumenta. But be careful. You may be strong, but you can still be crushed," Sydin said.

The point was made. Abruptly Sydin's eyes slid out of focus. He was receiving a message.

"What was it?" Legon asked.

"Our trick worked. The Iumenta are only coming with three legions of humans and half a Legion of Iumenta," Sydin said.

"How many ascended?" Iselin asked.

"Twenty-four."

"Twenty-four? That's twice as much as-" Legon started.

"No, there are others in the mountains. They're in case the Iumenta tried guerilla tactics," Sydin assured them.

"So we need to get moving then, I take it?" Legon said.

"Yes. You will have to make do with what training you have. We will teach you more on the go. Now we need to get you armor, and Sasha, we need to get you a store," Sydin said.

"A what?" Sasha asked.

"It's a large crystal you wear on your back. During the battle you will be connected with Legon, giving him a broad perspective of the fight. You will wear the crystal so that he may get more energy for magic. You will see. Now let's go," Iselin explained.

* * * * * * *

Barnin let the kid finish buckling his armor. The empire was making its move, so they would be heading out as soon as possible. Unfortunately, most of their troops had to be sent back to Manton due to the difficulties of keeping an army fed. They would be too far away to help, but initial intelligence said that the Cona forces were comparable to their own.

Barnin moved his arms around, feeling the confinement of the armor. It would loosen up in a little while. The cavalry was considered to be a specialty unit, so they got better equipment than the other units. Even so, most of his men didn't have plate armor and chainmail. Legon had fixed that problem. House Evindass made a donation to his unit, and now all twenty men and horses were fully armed. Barnin looked them over. They looked more confident now that they shone like mirrors and the horses looked better too. They would be an intimidating force.

"I am truly sorry, my old friend." He heard Legon's voice coming from the entrance. All of the faces in the room turned to see Legon and Sasha walking in.

"For what?" Barnin asked.

Legon walked up to him, inspecting his new armor. "Even with all of this, you can't fix ugly, but I promise we are working on a way to fix your ailment."

"Blow me," Barnin said.

"But seriously, how is it working for you guys?" Legon asked.

"It's great. Everything fits nicely and we're a lot more protected. Don't worry, we'll earn it," Barnin said.

"We know you will," Sasha said with a grim smile.

"Sash, you're not sticking around, are you?" Barnin asked.

"Yes, of course I am. I have to - I'm a Venefica," she responded.

Barnin turned curiously to Legon. "You're going to let her go into combat? Are..."

"She's not going into combat, but she will be there connected with me and helping me out. It's common enough, and she will be safe," Legon said.

Barnin didn't want to push the subject. If Legon said that Sasha was safe then she was.

Legon was in armor as well, but his was extremely lightweight like all Elven armor. With their speed and the use of fenrra, heavy armor was impractical and ineffective, so they went for the light, fast-moving type. This armor was just for stray arrows, and as such it did almost nothing for the fenrra. Barnin noticed a large shield-looking plate on Legon's left shoulder. He nodded to it, not wanting to move and disturb the kid finishing up with his armor.

"It's heavy armor. When we charge we lean into opponents with it to try and, well, we ram people with it," Legon said.

"Ok, got ya. There's Keither and Sara," Barnin said.

Keither and Sara were walking to them in a hurry. They looked like they had something big to tell them.

"What's going on?" Sasha asked.

Sara went first. "I'm a medic. I can do minor healing so I will be working with the medical staff at the battle, all behind the front lines of course."

Then Keither broke in. "And I've been put on the strategy committee. Well, I'm assisting the committee on this battle, but I made it on."

Barnin broke in. "They put you on that? Wow, Keither, I'm impressed."

The strategy committee was what commanded a battle. They used the Mahann and mental networking to figure out what the enemy was going to do and how to respond. It was a big deal and that meant that if Keither tried, for once in his life he could be in command of entire armies.

Keither was looking at Legon's armor, confused. Barnin helped out.

"Elves don't have a cavalry. They're too fast on their own and most can outrun a horse that's laden with armor. That plate on his shoulder is for ramming his opponents and Iumenta. An Elf and Iumenta running at full speed into each other create a lot of force."

"Why did you ask what it was then?" Legon asked, confused.

"I didn't. I nodded and you took it that way. I just wanted you to have that one time in your life when you felt like you knew something I didn't, that's all." He gave him a toothy smile.

Legon shook his head at him and Barnin saw him place his hand on the handle of a large sword. There was a purple glow. He knew those swords. They were called fenna, and he must be charging the blade. Legon was going to the front line. This was sobering; his best friend, the last of his childhood, was going to the front line.

"Are you a forward then?" Barnin asked.

"Yes, I'm a class five," Legon responded.

"My unit will be with you then."

"What? But you–"

"I get to choose what unit I back up, and it will be yours. You guys will take the Iumenta and we will take the human cavalry that's with them."

* * * * * * *

Sasha saw what Barnin was doing. He wasn't going to have another friend die. She felt a twinge of sympathy for him. Was he thinking that he was somehow to blame?

A tall man walked up behind Barnin. He looked to be in his early twenties and was about six foot seven. He was thin with sandy hair, pale blue eyes, and a friendly face.

He spoke. "My lord, you have given us this armor. We owe you. Also, if you are going to have a cavalry unit with you, it may as well be the best."

Confident and respectful. Those were a good traits. He knew where the line in the sand was.

Barnin smiled. "Meet Ankle. He's my second."

Sasha paused. "Ankle?"

"He's never had a major injury in combat, and believe me he puts himself out there enough. But get him back home and try and play a game and crack, he sprains his ankle every time."

She wanted to ask more but she sensed Iselin's mind requesting that they go back to the dome and to her hangar. They left at once, Keither and Sara in tow. It didn't take long to get to the hanger where she saw Iselin waiting. Against the walls were piles of metal that looked like armor, but way too big to be any normal armor. There were five other Elves there as well.

"Good. I'm glad you are here. I thought you might like to see a dragon getting fitted for battle."

"What could you guys get fitted with for battle?" Sara asked.

"Watch. That's why you're here," Iselin said warmly.

Sasha felt Cat winding her way around her legs. She reached down and picked her up. Iselin walked to the center of the hangar and turned to them. Sasha's heart stopped as she saw her. Iselin's head jutted forward and up misshaping itself. Her hands stretched to the ground and wings came from her back. She grew huge, and scales glittered along her body. The tail was there now snaking out behind her, and then in just a moment there stood a giant pink dragon in front of them. She looked down at them all and winked.

"Pretty neat, isn't it?" she said into their minds. They chose to speak aloud.

"Very," Legon said.

"Good. Now help out if you can."

Iselin spread her wings, keeping them level with the ground. Her tail was outstretched and her neck was level. At once the Elves started moving around the metal and Sasha realized that it really *was* armor. The Elves directed them to help and Iselin explained in their minds what everything was.

As they wrapped her neck and back with chainmail and plate armor, she informed them that it was mostly for show. The chainmail was nothing to dragons; only a few pieces actually did anything.

Sasha figured those out on her own. They were obviously different. They were made of the same material as the fenrra, but they were thicker. There were pieces that went along her spine, at least four inches thick, and then long ones that ran along the leading edge of her wings. These were eight inches thick. All of her joints got the real armor too, and then a helmet. There was no bottom, leaving her jaw free to move, but there was a large piece that covered her head. On the nose were three blade-like spikes. They reminded Sasha of a drawing that Arkin had shown her once, something he had called a "rhino".

Next they put long, curved extensions on her claws. Heavy plates also went on the bottom of her feet. They had to be a foot thick and they restricted her movement. Iselin told them that these were used to block blows from other dragons. They also lifted a set of large plates on to her chest. In the center of them was a dark blue dot. In that dot were a purple triangle and a green tree, the crest for house Evindass. Sasha felt a bloom of gratitude upon seeing how loyal Iselin was to their house.

The final piece was the most terrifying. On her tail they placed spikes and an elongated blade. The whole thing looked like it was from a nightmare. When she walked it sounded like she was on over-sized tap shoes. Sasha was a little confused about how thick all the armor was. If it was as strong as the metal that the fenrra was made of then it should be unbreakable. She asked Iselin about it and she heard a voice from behind.

"I told you that you would be hard pressed to break it, but for a dragon, well, they're just a little bit stronger."

Sasha turned around. "Arkin! How have you been?"

"Well. That plating on her feet is for blocking the tail blades of other dragons. The rest is just for show. It's not even up to human standards and will be shredded within the first few minutes of battle."

Iselin folded her wings and Cat turned into a ball of light that flew under Iselin's right horn and out of sight. Iselin flew out of the dome.

On the other side Sasha saw Sydin, his mirror-like armor and snow-white horns and claws contrasting with his black wings and scales. All of the dragons were starting to leave. Each and every one looked ominous and terrifying to her, but Sydin by far was the most intimidating.

Mantic was walking up to them with a bright yellow familiar in cat form in tow.

Preparations

"Um Prosa, I would be honored if you would allow Feena here to act as your familiar during the battle. I will be in the back helping command and will not have a use for him as you will."

Chapter Twenty Three
Crimson Sky

"I look at life as a bridge with a toll on it. Depending on what part of the river you are crossing, you must decide if the toll is too high and how badly you need to cross the river. If the toll is too high then you move downriver to the next bridge. In my experience, I have never found a bridge whose toll is too low. Find the toll you are willing to pay and pay it. Once paid, cross the bridge and move forward."

- The Great Defeat, Secunum Renovatie

Feena looked cute, but Sasha didn't think that cute did much in a fight. Apparently Legon didn't either.

"Thank you, but won't he get-"

"He won't get hurt, trust me. But he may save your life. You will see."

She felt Legon's apprehension through their connection, but in the end he agreed. Feena walked over to both of them and rubbed appreciatively against their legs. She reached down and picked him up. He nuzzled against her neck. These things were so odd, but she had to admit she wanted one. After that they started in the direction of the horses, soon to make the journey to the Sentinels, two large hills that marked the road into the Precipice, where the empire waited.

Legon walked next to Sasha as he took in his surroundings. They were nearing the lip of a hill. On the other side of it was a large flat area of rock where the battle would take place. This hill was rock as well. There was a slight breeze and his nostrils caught the scent of something foul. He thought back, wondering where he'd smelled it before. He had, when he had fought the Iumenta who killed Kovos in the clearing. Maybe he could find him in the battle. Right behind them was his guard, a group of Elves that were loyal to house Evindass. They would be his guard during the fight, allowing him to fight with magic without too much hand-to-hand interference. They wore the same armor as he, House Evindass' crest emblazoned on their chest plates. They all tensed with distaste as they smelled the vermin in the distance.

As they crested the hill they were immersed in the ranks of humans and Elves. They walked in between catapults and ballista. In this battle there would be no time for trebuchets. Nervous, Sasha closed the space between them. This was not her element and she would have to wait until just before battle to go into the Mahann state needed for the fight. He extended his arm and held her hand, interlacing their fingers. He felt that her pulse was high, but it slowed as he ran his thumb along the side of her hand.

"Sorry I'm not brave like you and Iselin," she said with the hint of shame.

"You shouldn't have to be," Legon replied.

He tugged on her hand, making her shoulder gently bump against his. Her pulse slowed down some more. He saw the guard closing ranks around them and felt Sasha's apprehension through the mental network that he was running. As they closed ranks she calmed more as she felt their concern and, surprisingly, love for her.

Taking his attention from Sasha, Legon looked at the sky. It was dark gray and no doubt it would rain soon. He brought his eyes downward and out over the sea of people on the other side of the battlefield. They were like waves with sparkling armor, blades, and banners. Along the back row were the dragons, armor dull looking as they leached light. It was not difficult to see their colors. They had the same armor as the Elves, their leathery wings uncovered except for the leading edge.

They were approaching Iselin, with Feena trotting right in front of them. Iselin was standing stone still, and he felt a drop of rain on his cheek as he reached her side.

"Will we fight in the rain?" he asked.

She answered in their minds, as all dragons did. "No, we won't fly in rain, nor will the Iumenta. It will be a big storm. We will wait it out."

"Sash, give me the store. I will hold it," Legon said.

"It's not too heavy. I'm ok."

"I know you are, but it feels like a small rock to me."

She took off the pack that held the store crystal and handed it to him. He slung one of the straps over his shoulder. The rain was starting to come down much harder now and he too saw that this was going to be a bad storm.

This land was hot and muggy, making the rain warm and not refreshing in the least. He was on the verge of placing a spell over Sasha to keep her dry when Iselin extended her wing out over them. The rain sounded like it was hitting canvas as it struck the pink membrane. She craned her neck down and winked at them.

"This won't wear out your wing, will it?" Legon asked.

Legon heard a deep growl, but Iselin's mind felt playful. "I am fine. This is like standing around for me."

He looked behind him to see water flowing from the back of her wing like little waterfalls. He noticed that all the Elven dragons were doing the same. He saw this on the other side as well. But whereas the Elves let anyone who was near by stand out of the rain, he noticed there were only Iumenta under their dragons.

The downpour helped clear his mind. The sound of rain on Iselin's wing acted as white noise that quieted all of his worries and apprehension. Sasha was now sitting next to

Iselin's front leg resting against it. Water was running under the massive armor and streaming out over Iselin's pearl claws and gemstone scales. When he thought about it he never really had seen anything so beautiful in his life as Iselin. Maybe Sasha was right to try and set them up.

No, don't think about that now, he thought.

Still, the thought of either of them getting hurt bothered him profoundly. It felt like only a few moments had passes, but it must have been longer. The rain was now starting to slow, and as he looked out over the landscape he saw large burlap sheets over both sides protecting them from the rain, and a steady stream running in the middle of the soon to be battle field.

* * * * * * *

A sound woke Sasha from a shallow sleep. There were chills running along her spine. Her eyes were still closed, but what was that sound? She opened them and listened to the eerie sound more intently. It sounded like animals, all small ones, all angry. She was still batting the mental fog away when she noticed the loudest one. It was a cat yowling. She looked to see Feena with his fire fur raised, teeth bared, yowls coming from his open mouth. She looked around to see other familiars in the forms of many different animals and elements, some bear cubs, some dogs, some cats, all predators. Then she realized the din was also coming from the opposition as well. All of the Iumenta familiars joined their cries, begging their masters to let them loose on the enemy.

Sydin joined her thoughts, directing her to go stand with the other spotters. These were the spouses of Elven Venefica; they too had stores slung across their backs. They would all stand along the top of the hill, looking and directing their Venefica. All of them would network their minds and in turn the command would do the same. Everyone's perspective was figured into commands.

She started to let the Mahann take her, but before she did she walked over to Legon, kissed his cheek, and hugged him. There were no parting words that she could think of, so she took her position. She saw him and his guards walk to the frontline, saw from her eyes and his. She felt scared, but then the Mahann calmed her and emotion left as she connected with the others.

The Dragons started to roar and a few took off and hovered above them. The Iumenta were doing the same. Both armies were mobile and forming into ranks. Legon connected with her and she felt the wards that he raised around his men and Barnin's unit. There were the flickers of wards over both sides, and then large ones from the dragons, designed to defend against the other dragons and siege weapons.

She was in Legon's head now, seeing the front line. They looked down out of the same eyes to Feena, who was all but screaming now. That's when she saw it. Feena screamed, but as he did it changed from a scream to a roar. As the sound changed so did the cute little yellow cat. His canines grew, extending down past his bottom jaw. His tail vanished into a stub. Huge muscles rippled under the fiery fur and his eyes glowed bright with intensity.

Feena was far from a cat. His new form was some sort of animal, but what was it? She reached in her mind. Years ago Arkin had showed her a picture what was it called. It was some kind of tiger, she thought. Now that she listened there was no longer the barking and howling of small animals. All on both sides were now full sized predators. She looked to her left and caught Mantic's eye. He winked at her; now she knew what familiars were for.

She looked to the sky above the Empire forces to see the Iumenta dragons roaring and shooting flames across the sky. She saw and felt the fire above her and she looked up to Iselin and saw a jet of fire ripping from her mouth, stretching hundreds of feet across the sky. It reflected off her armor and she felt the mental presence of many dragons pushing hope out to the ranks.

She couldn't feel much of her own emotions with the Mahann, but she felt Legon's as he stared across the field at a group of gray skinned Iumenta. The hate was so strong. His body was vibrating, begging him to rush at them. Then her eyes caught a flash of color that shot across the sky from an Iumenta dragon. The ball of magic was deflected by Sydin. She felt Legon prepare to use magic as she looked at Sydin. A gray black light ran down his tail and he flung it at the Iumenta. As he did she was blinded with the light of hundreds of Venefica sending curses across the lines.

She clapped her hands to her ears as she heard the thunder-like claps of curses hitting wards. The field was covered in flashing light in every shade and color, like some nightmare thunderstorm on the ground.

Above them it was the same. All of the dragons were sending spells at one another. Every time she closed her eyes there were new little spots of light. She felt Legon penetrating the wards of a human Venefica, saw him slash apart a few of their frontline men with a spell, and she closed the visual connection with him, not wanting to see anymore.

The armies would charge soon; she could feel it. The other spotters were directing their spouses to different parts of the Empire's frontlines and she realized that even though she wasn't aware of sending commands to Legon, the rest of the network was sending them for her. She engaged the Mahann more and more fully joined the network and soon lost herself in the vast sea of minds.

* * * * * * *

Legon felt his body wanting to rush forward. Feena's roars next to him echoed his feelings. An Iumenta Venefica stood across from him with a large blue wolf with raised fur next to him that was pacing agitatedly, growling at Feena. Then, mercifully, the order came. He heard Feena's claws digging into the ground as he charged forward. He felt the wind against his face as he flew across the open landscape.

Soon Barnin's unit was falling behind them as he knew they would. The sound of boulders crashing shook the ground, and he looked up to see an orange Iumenta Dragon and Iselin collide in the sky. Both flew through torrents of fire to crash together, letting their chest plates take the force of impact. He looked forward and saw the Iumenta closing, choosing targets; he squared off with a raven-haired one.

As the space closed he dropped close to the ground and leaned his left shoulder in. The Iumenta did the same. Pain erupted all over his upper body as he hit the Iumenta. The two shoulders plates made a horrible grinding sound when they hit.

In the moment of impact he felt the Iumenta's shoulder buckle. Like Iselin had said, he was heavy for an Elf, and his body continued forward, his momentum too much for the smaller Iumenta. His shoulder plate slid off the Iumenta's and he turned himself, bringing it against the base of his opponent's neck. There was a crack as the Iumenta's neck broke. He dropped, rolled on the ground and up, not needing to look back at the filth that was now dead.

He drew the fenrra and fell upon an Iumenta that was getting to his feet after hitting one of his guard. The Iumenta had his own fenrra out, and soon Legon was consumed by the fight. The Iumenta Venefica held back, waiting for Legon to lose strength before he engaged him at close range, but his familiar and Feena were rolling around, biting and clawing at each other.

One of Legon's guards joined him in his fight against the Iumenta. Legon's early kill gave them an advantage that they fully planned on taking. Soon the Iumenta was down, and Legon saw that his guard was winning. He turned to his left to see one of his men go down, a giant gash across his chest and through his lungs and heart. He heard Barnin's unit behind them and saw two Imperial cavalry units approaching. Barnin's men were outnumbered, but the Iumenta fell back to let the horses do their jobs.

* * * * * * *

Barnin raised his shield and felt a blade hit it. Poison was kicking and biting the other horse and he was doing his best to kill the other man, but they were outnumbered two-to-one and good armor or not, that wasn't good odds. The rider to his left slashed at him, hitting him across his back. He felt whip-like pain where the blade hit. Thank goodness Legon had given them chainmail and plate armor. The armor would keep them from getting cut by other humans for the most part, but it didn't protect against them from getting bludgeoned to death.

The Iumenta were retreating, letting the clumsy mortals hack it out for awhile, but Legon and his guard turned on the enemy cavalry. Barnin watched with detached horror as they attacked.

It was one thing watching the Elves and Iumenta fight each other. It was fast and difficult to follow, but he hadn't seen them attacking humans before. The Elves, his friend included, were jumping from horse to horse slaughtering the men, who were screaming in terror and agony. The Iumenta Venefica would be giving them strength just like Legon did for them, and he noticed that the men and horses were starting to get faster now. The Iumenta Venefica were able to dump more energy into their remaining charges, making them formidable to say the least. This meant that Barnin was now losing the fights that he was winning before. The enemy was getting faster and stronger. He wasn't sure how long it would take, but soon they would be able to cut the armor with their new power. Warm liquid splashed across his face and he turned to see Ankle removing the head of a man next to him.

"I had that one!" Barnin roared.

"Yeah, that's what it looked like, sir. Sorry for saving your…"

He didn't hear the rest of Ankle's retort as he turned his attention back in front of him. The Iumenta were back, and this time they were on the side away from the Elves, tearing their way through his men. He saw one, two, and then four men go down. He had a faint connection with Legon and he tried to communicate, but it was Sasha's voice that answered in his mind.

"He knows. I am directing them to the Iumenta." She sounded detached, the Mahann making her calm and unemotional.

Barnin saw Legon turning to them and they moved quickly through the battle. He was putting away his fenrra. Why on earth would he do that? He jolted suddenly as he felt the spell hit. There was a flick of purple around him as Legon's ward took the blow and he moved just in time to have a blue bolt of magic fly by his head. The other Venefica was joining the fight.

Barnin yelled for his men to fall back and as he did, Legon ran by him, drawing the fenna. One of the enemy's cavalry got in the way and Legon slashed up with the fenna, hitting the horse's midsection and slicing up through the animal and the rider's legs. The man screamed. Blood and organs gushed out of the horse, covering the ground as Legon hit the rear half of the horse with his shoulder plate and moved it out of the way.

Something wet hit Barnin's face and he wiped it with his fingers. It was blood. Then another drop. He looked around him. It was like rain now. What on earth? He looked up. The pink dragon and the gray Iumenta dragon were above them. They were slashing at each other, their claws dripping with gore. Their tails swung out to be caught by the armor on their opponent's feet. Their glittering armor was all but gone now. Only the real stuff remained, and he saw as they bit and scratched that they were wounding each other deeply, causing blood to pour from the cuts. It fell like scarlet rain from the gray sky in great drops. Almost at once the injuries healed. The dragons didn't seem to notice that they were bleeding all over the field. An involuntary chill ran along his spine, and he looked to see Legon start to engage the Iumenta Venefica.

* * * * * * *

Arkin felt his lungs burn as his broad sword severed a man's spine. This was not his kind of fighting. He was more used to playing hide-and-seek before he killed someone. The constant exertion was getting to him. It was getting harder to stand as well. This area was all rock, and neither army was making any headway. The ground was littered with bodies and, even worse, their entrails. It slopped on his boots and made the flat rock slippery. All his wards were also being pushed to their max. He was losing people left, right, and center. The Empire had a higher Venefica to normal soldier ratio than the resistance, and that meant casualties on a large scale. He was doing everything he could get keep his people alive, and sadly the more men he lost the easier it got.

Arkin ran up to a man in all black wooden armor with some sort of cheese cloth over his face. Arkin swung at him and the man raised his sword with surprising speed.

He must be trained in the Jezeer, he thought.

This whole unit that they were fighting was like this. They all had the cloth over their faces and each was amazingly fast, and they didn't back down. Their skill was formidable, but they weren't Iumenta. His opponent was gaining ground and Arkin had to duck so as to not lose his head. He tried to change his style and trip up the soldier. Nothing. The soldier countered him easily, almost playfully. Arkin knew the man would be protected with wards form the Iumenta, so he couldn't use magic.

Pain erupted across his chest as the enemy slashed a shallow wound across him, slicing his pectoral muscle and vein beds. He staggered back as blood rushed out of his chest. The man was coming up fast now, not wanting to waste time. He clutched his chest and tried vainly to stop the onslaught. He fell back landing on his tail bone, feeling it crack as it hit.

The man was over him now and raised his sword for the death blow. In that moment he saw the flick of light, the flick that said that the Venefica protecting the soldier was dead. Arkin shot his hand forward and sent fire spell at the man's head. It evaporated in a cloud of blood, bone, and brains that spattered his face. There was a metallic taste in his mouth; he had forgotten to close it before the spell hit. He rolled on his side and retched, seeing the blood from his chest soak the ground. He blacked out.

* * * * * * *

Keither took in the field before him. It was an epic story gone horribly wrong. His ears cringed at the sound of grinding metal from the dragons. There was no progress being made there. Then there was the sound of spotters gasping or shrieking, then falling dead as their wives or husbands were killed in battle. The river in the center of the field no longer appeared to be running with water, but he knew that it was foolish to think that it was all blood.

Both sides were taking heavy casualties. They had gotten their wish. The forces were equal and as such neither gained ground. This battle would not have a true victor. His eyes were getting used to the flash of magic, and as he looked through the seeing glass he saw Legon fighting an Iumenta Venefica. He was using that large sword and both were sending spells in rapid succession at each other, but it looked like Legon was slowly winning.

Barnin's unit was with Legon. The tall one, Ankle, was fighting a man. The soldier fell and tried to get up, but Ankle thrust down stabbing the man in the chest. Keither saw the tip of the sword exit the soldier's lower back instead of his chest. He saw another of Barnin's unit on the ground, holding his hands up futilely as he tried to keep a horse from trampling him. The horse was trained well and reared up on its back legs and drove its front hooves into his chest and abdomen again and again. Keither shook his head and looked away. He noticed Sara and the Elves' chief medical officer standing by them.

Sara was a medic, and most of those were busy at the moment, but she only knew how to fix things with magic and even then only minor wounds. She would learn more over time, but for this battle she was going to be most useful at the end when men returned with scratches and other small injuries.

He reconnected with the rest of command. The problem was dragons. They were evenly set, but with the somewhat tight air space they were being forced to fight in, only about half could engage at any given time while the others circled over their sections of the army, strengthening wards. It was rare for dragons to die in battle, but often they would get hurt and have to retreat. This wasn't a problem in this fight; all they had to do was get close to being truly hurt and then fly back away from the fight and rest.

Sara interrupted him. "The lights from the magic are something else, aren't they?"

He nodded his agreement.

* * * * * * *

Sara knew she shouldn't be bothering Keither, but she needed to get her mind off the battle. It was so gruesome and Sasha would have been no help since she was too busy helping Legon. The Elves' chief medical officer was next to her and she was feeling a little uncomfortable. She couldn't remember his name but he had remembered hers of course.

He spoke to her. "Are you ok? You look a little nauseated."

"Oh, I'm fine, thank you. It's just the flashing light from the fight, and the blood, and the flying colored things in the air. Ok, well, I guess everything."

He nodded grimly. "It has the ability to turn one's stomach. The light especially. They can make epileptics have seizures just by looking at them."

"They can? That's horrible." She was trying to remember what that was. She knew it was important. She vaguely remembered learning about it not too long ago.

She pushed it from her mind and stood for another few minutes before the thought buzzed back in her head. She decided to go and access Sasha's mind to see if she remembered. The girl was a store of information. When she connected with her Sasha was still in a Mahann state, but not like she should be. There was something else that was going on, and Sara noticed that she was having issues with her connection to Legon.

Sasha's body had a slight tremble to it and she kept closing her eyes and trying to steady herself...

"You said the light can cause seizures?" Sara asked

"Yes, why? You're not epileptic, right?. The only one I can think of here who-"

He broke off and they both bolted down to where Sasha was supposed to be stationed. He out stripped her with ease, moving faster than a horse, but she made it to Sasha faster than she thought possible.

Sasha was on her knees, violent tremors jolting her body, but she was awake.

"How is she awake?" Sara asked.

"It's the store. Its energy must be keeping her here, that's the only way." the medic said.

Sasha broke in. "Please take it off me. I can't connect to Legon. Please..."

"But what if you have an episode by taking it off?" Sara responded.

Sasha's eyes blanked out for a moment and Iselin's voice rang in their heads.

"Take the store off of her now! Legon is out of energy and is getting cut to ribbons by another Venefica. Do it now!"

Sara didn't need that voice twice. She wrenched the store off Sasha and threw it on herself noticing as she did that Sasha was now slipping into a full seizure. She found Legon's mind with ease. He was panicked about Sasha and his men. She needed to connect fully with him. For Sasha she could just partially connect and send the energy needed, but Sara wasn't advanced enough and had to force to connect all the way. As she did, she felt burning strips of pain along her left arm. She gasped and clutched it as the pain grew. His bicep was almost cut in half. It must have been a cutting spell that did it. She accessed the store and started dumping copious amount of energy across their connection. This too hurt. She couldn't handle it, but she poured more and more, feeling her body shutter under the pain.

She felt a cold hand against her skin, and then Sasha's mind joined hers. She was still weak, but determined. She altered their connection with Legon and the pain vanished in an instant. Sasha forced the connection with Sara and then accessed the store and directed Legon's healing wards, targeting the bicep and healing it in a moment. Moreover, Sara felt seething anger emanating from Sasha at her lapse in composure. Sara had never really thought about how Sasha felt about her episodes, but anger made sense; anger she understood.

* * * * * * *

Legon felt Sasha's mind firmly reconnect with his and with it came an instantaneous stream of energy from the store. His arm knitted together instantly; the Iumenta looked worried, as he should be. Legon shot forward, swinging with the fenna, changing his style every few blows. Soon the Iumenta was receiving small injuries, unable to use magic effectively under the constant assault. Legon saw fear in his yellow eyes, saw the Iumenta tasting mortality for the first time in his pitiful existence, saw the pain that it caused. He did not enjoy cruelty, so he decided put this poor animal out of its misery.

He feinted to his left, and in his fear and fatigue the Iumenta took the bait. Legon crouched and brought the sword up, hitting the Iumenta square in the leg. Most of the Iumenta's weight was on that leg and he crashed down, clutching at the gushing stump. He was screaming in pain. Legon walked to stand over him. The terrified eyes locked on him and the scarlet fenna he held in his hand. The Iumenta seemed begging for life in Elfish. Legon wasn't sure; he didn't know much of the language yet, but the look on the Iumenta's face was unmistakable. The man wanted something from him, that was obvious. Legon pulled the blade back, ready to thrust it into the thing lying on the ground, and the Iumenta closed his eyes serenely.

Legon stopped. This man wanted to die. He wanted the pain to stop. He didn't want the humiliation of having to go home disfigured, and most of all he didn't want the shame of being spared by an Elf. Legon was going to kill him anyway. It was fine that he wanted it really, but then he remembered the co-op and Sara and the boy that Barnin had told him about.

"Tell the queen hi for me," Legon said coldly. "Curatias Crurim!" he barked, holding out his palm.

A bolt of lavender shot from his hand to the Iumenta's stump, stopping the bleeding and cauterizing the wound. Then he kicked him in the head, knocking him out, and gave the order to leave him for his own medics.

Two massive thuds shook him as something hit the ground. He turned to see Iselin fighting the gray dragon. She was covered in cuts and bite marks. It only took him a second to realize that the gray dragon was far more powerful than Iselin. She was going to lose. He left his guard, sprinting toward the two dragons thrashing on the ground. Iselin's front Leg was torn up bad and so was her shoulder. She was bleeding a lot, even for a dragon. To his horror two Iumenta appeared behind her. One jumped onto Iselin's back. The Iumenta steadied itself, aiming his fenna at an open place in her armor. Legon wasn't going to make it.

He reached deep into the store, sending magic to his legs and shooting himself forward. He jumped, bringing the fenna up above his head. The Iumenta turned and faced Legon, the look of triumph melting off his face as the fenna made contact with his lower hip. The blade slid through him like butter, cutting his abdomen and ribcage and catching just a bit as it went through his shoulder blade. Legon landed on the other side of Iselin, winded from the loss of energy. She had no idea he was there. The other Iumenta was coming down at him, blade raised. He couldn't stop it.

A flash of yellow struck the Iumenta, and Legon rolled to see Feena on top of him, slashing wildly with his claws, ripping off armor and flesh. He sunk his dagger-like teeth in the left side of the Iumenta's ribcage and thrashed him around like a dog playing with a rag doll. There were muffled screams and a ripping sound as his ribs and shoulder pulled away from the rest of him. Then he stopped screaming and his body separated, one large chunk in Feena's jaws the other flung limply to the ground.

Legon heard the rocks under Iselin crunching and he leapt just in time to avoid getting crushed. She fell on her side, the gray dragon tearing viciously at her. Logic and reason told him to run, that she was lost, but he couldn't leave her. Despite his constant dismissal of Sasha trying to set them up, he did feel something for her. It was probably a crush, nothing worth dying over. The fight would be done soon and the dragon might turn its attention to him, and then not even Feena could save him. He thought of what Sydin said about making it count. He would. Iselin would be angry with him putting himself in this situation, but he would make it count.

He knelt down, as did Feena, taking his lead. It was like the dragon was a deer and he a mountain lion. He moved, not wanting to attract its attention. Feena suddenly leapt at the dragon, who moved to bite at him. When the dragon moved he turned his head to Legon's right, exposing himself. As Legon jumped at the gray dragon, he activated cutting spells and brought the blade down over his head, aiming for where the head met the neck, but the dragon was fast. It saw him and began to turn its head. The fenna hit the lower part of the dragon's jaw, stopping just short of going all the way through.

Legon hung from the bottom of a dragon's mouth, clutching the fenna tightly. He knew claws would be coming soon, but without the fenna he was done for. He twisted his body and kicked hard off the lower tip of the dragon's mouth, using his body to try and leverage the blade. There was a crack as the bone gave way and the fenna came loose, sending him plummeting to the ground. He hit hard and a congealed liquid splashed his face.

He heard the dragon roar in pain and the overwhelming thud of its wings as it took off. He opened his eyes without thinking. The sky was crimson. He wiped the dragon's marrow away, retuning the sky to gray. The dragon was above him now and he saw gray light from the broken jaw. The dragon's magic would heal it soon, and his sword was spent. Iselin jumped into the air, thrusting her wings down in a torrent of wind. She flew up and clamped her teeth on the dragon's throat at the base of its head and neck. It gurgled a roar and she twisted her body in the air like a corkscrew. There was a loud report as the dragon sized vertebrae broke, and the lifeless body stared its descent. Iselin pulled back, ripping a chunk of the Iumenta dragon's throat out and sent it sailing to Parkas' command tent, followed by a river of fire.

* * * * * * *

Sasha felt her jaw drop as she watched Iselin throw the dragon flesh at the enemy. The next moment she clapped her hands to her ears as all of the Elven dragons roared in celebration, causing a deafening din to fill the air.

Everything sped up then. There was a gray flick in the center of the Empire's lines as the dragon's spells failed. At once the resistance and Elven forces surged forward, all of the Venefica dumping energy into the forward group. They split the enemy line in a moment and the dragons all rushed forward, taking the stunned Iumenta off guard. The Iumenta dragons tried to block them, but it was too late. Rivers of fire rained down on the Empire's men, scorching them in an instant.

Sydin had said that the empire would retreat if they lost the advantage, that they weren't ready to truly try their luck, and he was right. They sounded retreat. All of their dragons pulled back and their men ran, their hopes crushed with the slain dragon. Sasha heard over the mental network that Arkin was hurt, but that he was stable. As the men continued forward to secure the Sentinels, she felt Legon walking amongst the dead and wounded. She ran down to him, almost knocking him over.

He smiled at her. "Hey."

"You're an idiot!" she said, feeling the tears fill her eyes.

He smiled weakly and she heard a groan. She looked down. There was a man at their feet, dying. He was mumbling something about his wife and son. She didn't know whose side he was on and it didn't matter. They had no strength left to heal him. Legon knelt down and held the man's head up off the stone.

"Who's going to take care of them?" he was gasping. "M- my boy is too young and it will break her heart. What if they don't-"

"They know that you love them," Legon said in a soothing voice.

She felt him in the man's mind. He was bring forward all of his happy memories, and with a gentle flick he forgot about his cares. Grateful happy tears filled the man's eyes.

"Tha- thank y- you," he said.

After a minute he passed. Then she heard the waling and the crying from the other wounded. Legon went to as many as he could. He took their pain away. He made it so they didn't have to die alone, so that someone was there, comforting. Finally, he was too weak to stand and she helped him across the field back to camp, the whole way biting back bile from what the day had cost.

Epilogue
Propositions

"Our journeys never seem to end. That is what makes life enjoyable, or at least that's what I tell myself when I'm camped out in a rain-soaked tent. If I thought of that more on the sunny days, maybe I wouldn't need to journey for happiness."
- Tales of the Traveler

Legon's feet were sore as he made it over the lip of the dome. He had his arm around Sasha, supporting her and also not wanting her to be too far away from him. After what he'd seen and done he wasn't going to let her out of his sight. As they entered the dome Iselin flew overhead, just a little closer than was strictly necessary. He knew he was in for it. Ankle nearly rolled out of the way.

"She didn't come that close, retard," Barnin said.

"Easy for you to say. You're what, five-three?" Ankle retorted.

"More like five-four," Sara said, holding her hand above Barnin like she was measuring his height.

Barnin gritted his teeth. He hated short jokes. They were making their way down the staircase to the floor of the dragon dome. As they entered the large circular room they were met by the sound of Elves working to get mangled armor off the dragons.

They were almost to Iselin's hangar when they heard a loud clanging of metal and then a crash. There were similar sounds across the floor as dragons shook off their armor into heaps onto the ground. They rounded the corner of Iselin's hangar and entered. She was still in her dragon form, but within a few seconds she was back to the beautiful blonde with blue-green eyes. His heart gave an involuntary jump. There wasn't a scratch on her. She walked over to them; no, it was more like a glide. When she was close there was no mistaking the fire in her eyes. She glared at him for a moment.

"I'm out of here," Keither said, not even coming up with an excuse. Sara called after him, saying she needed something. Cowards.

Legon wished that Iselin had stayed in her dragon form. Oddly, that was far less intimidating. He felt Ankle and Barnin standing stone-still with terror. Neither said anything, which was saying a lot for Barnin. Legon opened his mouth to speak, but Iselin hit him hard on the arm.

"Ouch!"

"You idiot!" she roared.

"What? I saved your..." Legon started.

"Don't you dare say you saved my life. I had him, and now you get partial credit for the kill!"

Now he got partial credit for the kill? She seriously wasn't mad about that, was she? She hit him again.

"Ow! Ise, you were about to get eaten! I saved your life, and *I'm* the a-" Legon started again.

"Language," Sasha said sharply.

"Yes, Legon. Language. Don't befoul the air with your vulgarity or stupidity! I was faking. You have to be used to women doing that!"

Sydin was by them now. "Iselin, that's hardly appropriate, and you were about-"

"Don't you back him up, Sydin, or so help me-"

To his amazement Sydin was backing away with his hands up in a placating gesture.

Sasha attempted to intervene. "Iselin, come on, you saved Legon's life there at the end, and if he wouldn't have done what he did you wouldn't have gotten that spectacular kill, and that was all you."

Iselin paused for a bit. Sasha went on. "And you're not actually mad at Legon for helping you with a kill, are you? It's actually kind of sweet if you think about it."

Now Iselin looked a little embarrassed. She turned to Legon. "What if you had gotten killed? Do you know what you mean to people?"

"Look Ise, I'm not saying what I did was smart, but it was better than the alternative."

"Fine. I forgive you, but you owe me."

He laughed, feeling better. "Fine, but not much, because you almost rolled on me."

She rolled her eyes at him, but he knew she was fine now. Sasha's mind was working overtime, he could feel it. She was plotting something.

"Maybe I could make it up to you over dinner?" he blurted.

Did he just do that? Sasha was smirking. Sydin and Barnin were looking away, but he thought he saw them both smile. Iselin looked dumbfounded, but not upset.

"Well, you don't know any good places to eat in our land, so it would really be me taking you out, and I don't want to go to Salmont right now…"

Ankle spoke. "Well, you'll be sailing south from Manton won't you?"

Sydin jumped in. "Yes they will, and I will be accompanying them."

"It's settled then. There is a great restaurant in Manton. You guys will love it, and it's a great first date spot," Ankle said jubilantly.

That made it final. He had asked an Elven dragon on a date. He wasn't nervous around women, but still, he had just asked an Elven dragon on a date. Iselin smiled, and he suspected that she was hoping Ankle would be saying something like that.

"Fine, but I'm getting the most expensive thing on the menu."

And with that she turned around and walked off.

As they left, Ankle sidled up alongside him and held out his fist. Legon tapped it with his own, but he wasn't sure why.

"What are you doing, Ankle?" Legon asked, perplexed.

"Good work," Ankle responded conspiratorially. "Barnin said that you were a cool guy."

"Thanks, but what was that fist thing?"

"What? Don't you do that back home?"

"No," Legon said.

"You don't? Well, it's like a high five, you know?"

"No, I don't, but thank you. So, what kind of restaurant is this?" Legon asked, changing the subject.

"It's one that his parents own," Barnin said.

"You'll love it and so will she. Just tell them I sent you, and tell them you want the table in the back corner. This is so great! Elves are going to eat at my family's restaurant!"

Barnin chuckled and murmured something about Legon needing to borrow money.

* * * * * * *

Sasha knew that there was going to be plenty of time to bother Legon about his date and for her to rub in her victory, but right now they were on their way to see Arkin. As they walked she held a little green pod to her mouth that Sydin had given her. He had given four or five to all of them.

Barnin and Ankle were biting the tips off and squeezing something that looked like sap into their mouths.

She frowned at the little pod. "What are these?" she asked.

"Power packs," Barnin answered.

"Power packs?" Sasha repeated.

It was Ankle that spoke this time. "Yeah. That's not what the Elves call them, but that's the nickname they have with the humans. They taste great and they give you energy. Lots of vitamins, nutrients, all that stuff."

She nodded and bit the tip off of one and squeezed it into her mouth. It was sweet and tasted a lot like honey. As she swallowed it her belly felt warm. She had another.

"See? They're good and they act fast, too. You'll be feeling better in just a minute," Ankle said.

It was true. By the time they made it to the hospital tent where Arkin was she had a lot more energy. When they found Arkin he was awake and looking sulky. His chest was wrapped in bandages and he looked a little pale. He gave them a weak smile and started to get up. Sasha pushed him back down.

"Sasha, I'm fine. The staff here-" Arkin started.

"Needs to change your dressings, and they're done all wrong. Let me take a look at you. Sit still," Sasha commanded.

He didn't argue with her, and she suspected that he was happy to have her there. She looked him over and then told him to sit up so she could have a look at his chest. He sat up and she unwrapped the dressings, which really did need to be changed.

"Barnin, would you be a dear and get me some hot water, a cloth, and more bandages?" Sasha asked.

Barnin looked doubtful. "They won't give them to us normally."

She looked at him. "But I'm sure they will be happy to give them to House Evindass, don't you think?"

He looked happy about being able to use the power of their name, but then she thought better.

"On second thought, just the hot water and a rag."

There was a large laceration across his chest. The wound was bleeding slightly and she knew that it went almost to his ribs. It wasn't a clean cut either. She peered closely at it. The blade that had done it was only moderately sharp, but otherwise it was straightforward. Soon Barnin was back with the requested supplies and a smile that told her he had taken advantage of being her errand runner. She took the water and rag and cleaned around the cut. When she was done she looked at it appraisingly.

"Sasha, there's no way you can fix this with magic. You don't have enough strength," Arkin said.

"But he does," she said, pointing to Legon.

"But I don't know how to fix it," Legon said.

"But I do," Sasha responded.

She smiled and accessed his mind and then his magic. She hadn't ever done this before, but she knew that dragons often used another's minor in their own spells, so it should work. Legon's reserve, while depleted, was still vast compared to her own. The power felt clumsy to her, but she concentrated on the spell and a ruby glow appeared under her hand. She moved her hand over Arkin's chest and the muscle and veins flowed together. When she was done she popped another power pack and looked at Arkin's healed chest.

He smiled broadly at her. "Thanks Sash, but I think you missed a mole. There used to be one right there."

She rolled her eyes. "You're welcome, and I didn't miss a mole. Those things are horrid. You're better off without it."

He laughed and directed his words to Legon. "So, Um Prosa, I hear you were good in the fight, and that you have a date with Ise."

They talked for a while and then Arkin decided he felt good enough to get up and leave. They went back to the dragon dome and spent the rest of the night talking about anything other than the battle.

After a few hours Sasha's vision started to blur with fatigue. She leaned back on the couch and her eyelids began to droop. The others were talking about their coming trip to the Elven lands, and she wanted to stay awake, but eventually and reluctantly she closed her eyes.

About the Author

Hi, I'm Nick Taylor. I was born and raised in Denver, Colorado, possibly the greatest place on earth. I went to Dakota Ridge High and was in band— that's right I was a band nerd and no, I don't have any cool "one time at band camp" stories, so don't ask.

That being said, you would think that I was good in English, but I am so not good at it; I suck at it. As a matter of fact, I saw one of my high school teachers at a Home and Garden show and I thought she was going to have a heart attack and die when I told her I, Nick Taylor, the kid who got a D in her class, was writing a book. So there's hope for all of you aspiring writers out there and trust me, once you start to write you're going to love it.

I didn't want to write until October of 2007. I was driving around with a friend and said, "Hey, I wonder if I can write a book." So I thought I'd try and write outline and see what happened. Well, I finished the outline and I couldn't just stop there. I needed to write chapter one and then that would be it. Do you see where this is going? Anyway, after chapter one was done I had to finish the first book. But I wanted to get input as I went in order to write a better story. As my aforementioned writing skills were not what I wanted readers to see, I decided to do a podcast of the first three chapters to see what people thought. After the first podcast, I decided that I wanted to continue to do it and more over, I wanted to get a larger listener base. Legon Awakening is my first novel.

CPSIA information can be obtained at www.ICGtesting.com
Printed in the USA
LVOW131217030313

322434LV00002B/412/P